WILLING FLESH

Adam Creed was born in Salford and read PPE at Balliol College Oxford before working for Flemings in the City. He abandoned his career to study writing at Sheffield Hallam University, following which he wrote in Andalucia then returned to England to work with writers in prison. He was Project Leader of Free To Write and is now Head of Writing at Liverpool John Moores University. He has a wife and two beautiful daughters.

Willing Flesh is the second novel in the D. I. Staffe series.

ADAM CREED

Willing Flesh

faber and faber

First published in 2010
by Faber and Faber Limited
Bloomsbury House, 74–77
Great Russell Street, London WC1B 3DA

Typeset by RefineCatch Limited, Bungay, Suffolk
Printed in England by CPI Bookmarque, Croydon, Surrey

A CIP record for this book
is available from the British Library

ISBN 978–0–571–24526–0

2 4 6 8 10 9 7 5 3 1

For Haydn and Susan

One

Elena Danya steps from the roll-top bath, her back straight and toes pointed down, as if she is doing dressage. She drips water all across her polished limestone floor. Foam sticks to her body and makes her modest. She rubs a porthole in the misted mirror and regards herself in the low, flickering candle glow. The bath, over her shoulder, looks the part and she recalls her expectations of England. When she left home, two long years ago, her mother had pinched her cheek, assured her she would make something of herself, for the family; find a prince. Elena smiles. It is coming to fruition.

What she sees now, in the mirror, is the way she likes herself: pink-skinned and with pale eyes; her hair straight in dripping tails, the palest outline of the flesh of her lips. Every last trace of her make-up is washed away. It is how God made her.

And she can be this self, again, for two whole days. She will read her novel this morning, doing a few jobs around the place between chapters, then catch the afternoon train up to the coast. It will be dark by the time she checks into the Signet Hotel and she will sit on the window seat of the bay window in her room, draw up her knees and watch the lights glimmer out at sea, then eat alone in the splendidly faded, panelled dining room – fond smiles from her fellow residents. They may think it strange that such a wholesome girl is eating alone. They may speculate at what she is running from, or towards. Some staff may recognise her, recalling her in the company of a man, or two.

Tomorrow, she will walk on the sands in a late winter dawn, way past the pier with its shiplap huts. Then Elena will take a full breakfast, and return to her seat to finish her book. She will take another, longer walk to the harbour at Warblingsea before the latest lunch she can muster because she knows that when she returns to her room and the sun sets, wintry early, she will ease herself between the sheets and she will look east across the North Sea and she will cry. Next day, on the very first train back to Liverpool Street, normal service will resume. But not for long. She is changing.

She thanks the stars that she gets such days to herself. She is lucky; other girls work seven days or seven nights and sometimes both.

Elena pads through to her bedroom and drags the sheets from the bed. Still naked, she carries the load to her kitchen and crams the linen into the washing machine and double-doses the fabric softener, sets the machine to a boil cycle.

The telephone rings, fracturing the normal, domestic ritual. She answers, sitting cross-legged on the chilled tiled floor. Rebeccah's voice is warm. She sounds like a child, can look like a child if she wishes; if somebody else wishes. Rebeccah is not so lucky as Elena. She has a different appeal.

'You're still going up there?' says Rebeccah.

'You sound upset.'

'I don't want anything to happen to you.'

'It is only the seaside,' says Elena.

'We don't *have* to do anything, you know. I've got my Frank.'

'It's arranged, Rebeccah.' She says it like Marlene Dietrich might. Re-Beck-Caah. 'We trust ourselves, yes?'

'Mitch is coming,' whispers Rebeccah, suddenly afraid.

'Is he . . .?'

But the phone cracks, dies, quick as a broken bone.

Elena takes a carton of apple juice back through to the bedroom. Apple juice is good for the stomach. She has problems with her stomach. She plumps up the bare pillows and leans back with *Mansfield Park*, draws up her knees. A part of her hates this room. The sounds and shapes she has made, right here, never quite fade to nothing.

By the end of the first paragraph on the downturned page, Elena has caught up with where she left off and she feels her mouth turn up at the edges, into a smile. Then the phone rings again. She considers ignoring it, but it might be her mother. She pictures her mother, wrapped in many coats and a thick woollen scarf around her head, in the phone box at the bottom of the block of flats, bitter winds whipping up off the snowy river.

'Hello,' says Elena.

'My love,' says the man. It is Markary. His voice is light, but guarded, suggesting someone is with him. This makes her heart heavy.

'You call to wish me a happy trip? I don't think so. You promised me two days.'

'This will be good for us. Good for everybody!' He laughs. But he is sad, really. She knows the real him. There is definitely somebody with him.

'It could be good for another girl.'

'There's only you, Lena. You know that. You're different.'

'I won't do it,' she says, holding herself tight around the knees. Something in her stomach twists and she feels her voice crack.

'Make yourself white, my love. Be gentle. He's a shy one. You're perfect for him.' He lowers his voice and sounds absolutely sincere when he says, soft as powder, 'I love you.'

Elena knows better than to tell Markary he

couldn't possibly love her; instead says, 'You should love me more.'

'It's the Thamesbank. Room 601.'

'I don't like hotels, Marky.'

'In an hour,' he says, hanging up.

She picks up *Mansfield Park* and throws it at the wall. It could tell hundreds of variations of a single tale.

Staffe knows his limit and he watches, unmoving, as the bids for the Crimean shaving stand climb higher and higher. He won't pay more than a month's take-home for any lot, ever. He could, but it would be wrong.

'Two thousand eight hundred,' says the auctioneer. He looks towards Staffe, even though he hasn't bid yet, because he knows him of old, and they talked about the stand on the phone only yesterday.

Staffe makes the faintest shake of the head, puts the catalogue behind his back and moves back through the crowd, checks his watch. He has seen an intaglio ring, from the Urals. It is of Russian gold and has an emerald, the colour of Sylvie's eyes. It is most definitely not what he came for, but, as the gavel comes down on the shaving stand, he trusts the instinct that he must have it. His watch says a quarter to twelve and he should be with

Sylvie, at the Eagle and Child, by noon. She'll understand, he assures himself; especially when she sees what kept him.

An eager brace of couples push past him from the back of the room and the bidding for the Urals ring starts at £1,200. It's worth £3,000, any day of the week, but as the battle reduces to the eager couples – at £2,000, and rising in measly fifties, Staffe raises his hand, says, loud and forceful, 'Two and a half.'

A most English gasp whispers around the medieval hall and the auctioneer can't help but smile. He pauses, for effect. 'Does anybody care for this more than Mr Wagstaffe?'

It is Staffe's one and only bid. He knows it would have crept up towards and beyond his limit, but his bid asserts that he may well go far higher. That is a lie. He closes his eyes and wishes the round thud of the gavel. He holds his breath, pictures Sylvie's face as he proffers the box.

The silence in the room deepens and Staffe can hear the hurried confidences of the two bidding couples. He opens his eyes and they each turn, look at him. The gavel thuds and Staffe goes straight to the cashier, unable to look the outbid lovers in the eye.

He drives on the limit all the way from Chipping Norton back to Oxford and shows his City of

London warrant card to the man parading the pay and display at Martyrs Memorial, gets a nod of reverence in return.

They are here because Sylvie says it's a part of him she doesn't understand. She thinks it madder than a trunkful of frogs that he shies away from his alma mater, but to be safe, he brought her this side of town, staying at the Randolph rather than near his college, Merton – the other end of Cornmarket and beyond.

Sylvie has gone from the pub, according to the American twelve-year-old managing the place, so Staffe ambles down past the Memorial, where the Protestants Cranmer, Ridley and Latimer yielded their bodies to be burned, at the behest of Mary Tudor and the Church of Rome.

Opposite the Randolph, he sees her, in the window of the dining room, laughing with a floppy-haired, chisel-jawed man her own age. He looks a million pounds in a battered tweed jacket. It must be Ollie. They were at Goldsmiths together. Staffe waits on the corner, by the Ashmolean, hoping she will see him and come out.

Even though he is hopelessly late, she isn't looking up; is too engrossed. He calls the station. Is he already missing the city's fast beat?

'You're away for the weekend, sir,' says his DS: Pulford. 'Rimmer's looking after things, sir.'

'Rimmer my . . .'

'Yes, sir?' says Pulford, with feigned curiosity.

'You just call me, right – if anything serious happens.' Rimmer isn't Staffe's idea of a detective inspector. Poor bugger. Rimmer probably isn't even Rimmer's idea of a DI. But it's in his blood.

'But I'm out on a new surveillance, sir.'

'Surveillance? Which one?'

'A couple of new labour gangs, maybe illegal. And you said I wasn't to disturb you. Under any circumstances. You said . . .'

Staffe turns off his phone, looks back up at the Randolph. He puts his hand in his pocket and takes out the intaglio ring, holds it up to the light. Tonight, he is taking Sylvie out to Great Milton, to Le Manoir for dinner, and he will play things by ear but, if all goes to plan – he will give her the ring.

Sylvie waves at him from the hotel entrance, laughing. Her hair billows in the wind and she holds it to one side as she kisses the handsome young man on the cheek; then the other. He holds her by the hips as they do it. When he walks away, he studiously avoids looking toward Staffe, as if it had been determined it would be better if he wasn't introduced.

She holds her arms open as Staffe comes toward her.

8

'What handsome friends you have,' says Staffe.

'Who, Ollie? Did you get the piece?'

He shakes his head. 'Too rich for me. I'm not made of money.'

She gives him a look, tuts. 'Liar.'

Two

Elena Danya looks up at the Thamesbank Hotel. It could have been commissioned by Stalin, with its square bulk of grey render and its uniform steel windows. They spent £60 million refurbishing it a couple of years back and crowned it with two burnished domes. Now, to stay one night, without the pleasure of Elena, commands a month of her mother's labour, back home. For an extra five hundred you could fuck lovely Elena, anywhere but the arse.

Today, in accordance with Markary's specification, she is white, and she will be supremely gentle for her shy, mystery client. Her blonde hair is freshly washed and plumped and she pulls up her oyster fur collar against the riverside chill. She truly looks like somebody's lovely sister cum sixties model. A young Saudi swaggers out of the revolving doors and stops dead, mid-step. He looks back at her, mouth open, as she goes into the lobby.

At the desk, she places her almost empty attaché case on the impeccable mahogany glaze of the counter and says, 'Papers for 601.'

'Madam,' says the concierge, looking down at

the register, where the booking has been made in pencil, paid in cash. These are charted waters.

Elena makes her way across the lobby which is the size of a tennis court. Her stilettos clip across the marble and she holds her head high, eyes upon her. A young man in a pillbox hat and high-waisted trousers leans against his luggage buggy. He looks her up and down, quite deliberately, with piercing, light eyes, almost white. Their eyes meet and she gets the impression they might know each other. His badge says 'Gary'.

The top of her leg vibrates and Elena thrusts her hand into the special inside pocket she commissioned to the lining of her fur. She lifts the phone to her ear before it rings.

'Where are you?' says the voice from the phone.

'Arra? Arra, is that you? Are you OK?'

'Don't sweat, Lena, honey. Are you there?'

Elena looks at Gary. He hasn't taken his eyes off her. She moves towards the floor-to-ceiling windows that give on to the river. She can see the South Bank, way across to her right, up river. Above, the sky is heavy with snow. In a hushed voice, she says, 'I'm at the Thamesbank.'

'You don't like hotels. Who are you meeting?'

'I don't know.'

'Is it one of his friends? You should watch yourself.'

'Why did you call, Arra?'

The line falls silent.

'Arra? Are you out of it?'

'I've got a bad feeling is all. I'm worried about Becx.'

'Rebeccah? It will be Christmas soon. Everything will be different,' says Elena, but the phone is dead. She slips it back into the special pocket of her fur, the coat's perfect form unspoiled.

She makes her way back across the lobby and Gary has beads of sweat on his temples, as if his desire has oozed. The lift doors close and something inside her dilates. She feels ready, quickly opens the attaché case and goes into her silver pillbox for a pre-taste of the finale powder. One pinch for the left nostril and one for the right, a quick dust down; doors open. She steps out, one foot in front of the other, all the time changing herself into something that she surely is not.

The door to Room 601 is ajar and Elena presses it open, ready to smile, but the room is empty. Water gushes from beyond a closed door. She steps inside and places her attaché case on the desk by the window. Across the river, she can see the Oxo Tower. Markary took her there once. He spent a fortune on the meal and they had a wonderful evening. He made her laugh and she had lobster, then a crêpe Suzette. She felt like a film star and that night she kissed him by Westminster Bridge and he took her to the place in Cloth Fair and they made love. She thinks, how much easier it would be if she could love *him* properly, if he was *enough*.

She senses someone behind her and she dilates again, unbuttoning her fur, letting it slide to the floor, leaning forward, placing her hands on the window ledge. She hears him. Close, now.

Elena tenses her buttocks and waits for the viper zzzip behind her, waits for his hands to be on her, kneading and tugging at the angel-white silk of her whore's finery. Markary said he was shy, so she doesn't turn on him, plots ahead that she will make him quick but stop him, dead! in his tracks, and then she will do what she is famous for – taking both balls in her mouth as they six and nine and he snorts a line all the way down from her navel and up again. Then she will finish him and take the money.

Right now, she thinks she must be mad for wanting to go up to Suffolk, to read a book. Sometimes, she just doesn't understand herself.

But there is so much more at stake than what she allows her willing flesh to imply.

However, this one is taking his time. She tenses her buttocks again: one; then the other; and in the window, in amongst the view of the Thames, she sees the moving watermark of her client coming towards her: lithe; or scrawny. She wonders if she should turn on him, slowly, but she waits, to feel his hands on her. She wonders if she might enjoy him. A one in twenty.

Then he takes her breath away. She feels a dull pain in her kidneys and her head whiplashes away from her, the South Bank warping, twisting out of sight as she catches her head on the corner of the radiator. She falls into the soft fur of her coat, thinks she may pass out, thinks, 'This will hurt, in the morning.' She wants to stand and fight him, but as he tugs at her, she feels all her strength seep onto the lush, white carpet. A seam of red. And with a last glance up, she sees a pale shadow over her and as the room goes dark, she sees a vision of her mother. She cannot move and the darkness deepens. She can't breathe. Her face is hard up against the soft carpet and something inside her seems to die.

Staffe lies back on the vast, plumped bed and stares out of the low window, down at gloaming St Giles. It has rained lightly, threatening to snow, and the cobbles warp the college lights' reflections.

The shower stops running and Sylvie emerges, dripping, holding a Mai Tai. He doesn't know where it came from. She bends down, kisses him, and he pulls her on top of him. She rolls away, holding her Mai Tai high. She takes a long swallow, drinking it greedily, not like a lady, but because she loves the taste and looks up at the ceiling, kind of sad. He follows suit.

'It would be nice to do nothing,' she says.

'If you like.'

'But you've booked a table.'

'I can cancel.'

'You said it was your favourite place.'

'Second favourite.' He places a hand on the pod of fat at the top of her thigh.

Sylvie leans up on her elbow, facing Staffe and hooks a leg over his. 'Sometimes, Will,' she kisses him on the temple, her wet hair dripping on him, 'you say exactly the right thing.' She takes another sip.

'Sometimes?'

'We can go to the restaurant.'

'I can compromise, you know.'

'When it suits,' she says, stroking his chest.

'Let's stay here.' He wants to know if she and Ollie ever went out, and where and when did he watch her emerge from the shower. Was he ever bad to her? Did she acquire her taste for Mai Tai from him? Why did they stop seeing each other? He sighs.

'What's wrong?' she says.

He would give her beautiful children. 'You never say you want children.'

'Will! What's brought this on?'

He looks across the room to his jacket on the back of the chair by the window. The Ural ring is in the inside pocket and he wonders if this might be the right time.

'Is this because you saw me with Ollie?'

'You were *with* him?'

Sylvie stands up, strides across the room, puts her drink down, heavy.

'People can see,' he says. 'It's dark outside and the light's on.'

'Bugger them,' she says, reaching into her bag and pulling out a fresh pair of pants. She steps into them and turns to Staffe, hands on hips. 'Maybe we should go out for dinner.'

Staffe remembers from somewhere that Mai Tai reminds Sylvie of the sun and she drinks them when she is happy, not to get happy.

'Why are you happy?' says Staffe.

'Who says I am?'

His mobile phone rings.

Sylvie looks at it and back to Staffe. 'You'd better get that.'

He shakes his head. 'I don't want to. Come here.'

She smiles and pads across the floor, wonky and creaking. She bounces on the bed and straddles him, her hands splayed on his chest. 'Babies, hey Staffe? What's come over you?'

'Most people at least discuss it.'

'You're not most people.'

'We're not most people.'

'I like things the way they are.' She leans down and kisses him.

A shrill telephone rings from the bedside table.

'Nobody knows where we are,' she says. 'That's what you said.'

Three

Arabella shivers awake. Her head aches with a low, flatlining boom as she pushes herself off the mattress and draws the sheet around her. The orange teardrop shape of the streetlight through the threadbare fabric at the window signals the day is over.

She checks her phone to see if Rebeccah has called, more from hope than expectation and, right enough, the last call registering is the one she made to Elena. 'Shit,' she says.

'What d'you say?' calls a man from the next room.

Arabella clambers off the bed and goes to the window, drawing back the fabric which is nailed up to the old pelmet. She sees her own broken and pale reflection in the cracked pane and is disappointed, but she swallows deeply and tries to convince herself that this is the better life.

'You call me?' says Darius from the doorway.

'I'm cold. Hold me.'

'I'm worried, Arra.' He is stick thin and wearing low jeans and a tracksuit top that don't match the plums to his voice. He has a mop of bible-black, curling hair and fine, delicate bones, cherub lips.

'What's to worry about?'

'I'm worried about you. Those friends of yours.'

'What about you and one of those friends of mine?'

'Don't be stupid.' He takes her into the crook of his neck and holds her tight, rubbing her back, running his hands up and down along her washboard ribs. 'You're fading away.'

Arabella pushes him away and turns back to the window. All along the street, the windows are boarded up and the builders have packed away for the day – old toilets and doors packed high in the skip. The other night, they used hammers and chains to get the squatters from next door.

'We can't stay here, Arra.'

'I know that,' she says, making herself strong. She coughs, dry as dust.

'You should call your father.'

'Don't talk to me about my father. You're as bad as each other.' She loses her balance, sits clumsily in the chair. 'I sometimes think you are on his side.'

'You're sick, Arra. You should lay off the gear for a while.' He sits on the floor, cross-legged, and jabs his fingers into his thick hair. 'There's a party up St John's Wood.' He looks up, forcing a smile.

She clouds over, fixes herself a line and a jug of sweet tea, says, 'I need forty or so.'

Darius hands her three twenties.

'You take care of me, Darry. I love that.'

'Like I said, there's a party. There's more where that came from.'

The SOC lights are brilliant and flood the beautiful woman's naked body. She seems blue as ocean in this light, her edges harsh as rocks. Her curves are long and bold. A pendant of dried blood sullies the cream carpet to the right of her head. Staffe wants to be alone with her, but the room is full of Forensics, and Josie, and Rimmer.

He can't take his eyes from the beautiful woman. She has a thin smile and, somehow, an inquisitiveness in her dead expression; a serene willingness, it seems. Staffe asks Janine, 'Is this a sexual assault?'

Janine, the City Police pathologist, crouches down beside the body and points at the confluence of Elena's buttocks and thighs with the tip of her tweezers. 'I wouldn't like to say, for sure, until I've done the autopsy, but I don't think they penetrated.'

'They left her naked,' says Rimmer, punching away at his Blackberry. He is wearing a chalkstripe suit and his shoes are brilliantly shined. You would never guess from the look of him that he hasn't got the stomach for this.

'What was the sequence of events? Can you hazard a guess?'

'I don't think it was the blow to the head. There

is skin on the corner of the radiator but no bruising. I need to check her mouth and throat, but she may well have been smothered.'

'That bastard on the desk won't tell us anything,' says Rimmer. 'He says the room hadn't even been registered, says a Finnish banker had reserved the room for tonight but he hadn't shown up.'

'Don't go upsetting the applecart,' says Staffe.

'The applecart?'

'We don't want them closing ranks. I want statements off all staff who were in the building between midday and seven.' He turns to Josie Chancellor, his young DC who was working with Rimmer whilst Staffe was up in Oxford. 'Set up booths in the main conference room. I need eight uniforms here and . . .' He looks at Rimmer, 'we'll have absolute silence. Nobody talks.' Staffe turns to Janine, 'I need a time of death.' He looks across at Josie. 'Do we have an ID on her?'

'There was only her case, sir. All that was in it was a couple of grammes of coke in a pill box.'

'Good stuff?'

'I'd say so,' says Janine.

'And the case? I need to know every shop from Stansted to Gatwick that stocks the make.'

'We're on to that, sir,' says Josie.

He runs his fingers through his hair and sighs. 'What about her clothes?'

'They left her completely naked. Must have taken the clothes.'

'Who found her?'

'A maid,' says Josie. 'She's Portuguese. Heard a phone ringing and ringing. She waited quarter of an hour.'

'Where's the phone?'

Josie holds up a tiny gold Nokia in a plastic bag. 'It was in an inside pocket of the coat.' Josie nods down at the fur, still under the naked woman.

'Have you checked to see what number was ringing?'

'Yes, sir. Someone called Markary.'

'Markary?' says Staffe.

'You know him?'

'A few years ago, if it's the same one. Check him out, and we'll need to see every byte of data in that phone.' He walks out of the room, pausing at the door. 'Call me when this room is empty, I'll be downstairs.'

Sylvie is talking to one of the waiters in the Thamesbank dining room. It is the end of service and Staffe pauses at the entrance to the grand room, a modern classic of high-glaze paint and suede upholstery. The waiter is leaning forward, hands clasped behind him, back perfectly straight, but he is making Sylvie laugh.

As Staffe approaches, the waiter sidles away. Sylvie straightens her face and pats the seat next to her, says, 'They're doing us some lemon sole and a cheese board.'

Staffe shakes his napkin loose, places it in his lap and resets his cutlery. 'You don't have to be here.'

'I understand, Will.' She squeezes his knee. 'Somebody died and this is what you do.'

He wants to say, 'That's not what you've always said,' but he knows better. He leans forward, confides, 'I think she was a prostitute.'

'Did she suffer? I mean, badly.'

He shakes his head, pours them each some sparkling water. 'I don't think so, not especially.' He sips from his glass, says, 'I could get us a room. You've got all your things in the car. I could be done in an hour or so.'

'You could come to mine.'

It is a bone of contention that Sylvie always comes to Staffe's place. There was a time, and still sometimes is, when Staffe thinks this is something sinister. He has a key to her place now, which he has never used.

'Will! I said you could come to mine.'

'Fine.'

'Look, I know you need your space. And so do I.'

'I didn't say anything about space.'

Sylvie leans back and clasps her hands together

behind her head. She blows her cheeks out, looks him in the eye and laughs. 'You're hard work, Will Wagstaffe, fuck me if you're not.'

'I'm not,' he says.

'Maybe we should stay here.' She leans down, pats her handbag. 'I've got a good book.'

'And I'll bring some cocoa.'

Staffe turns off the SOC lights in Room 601 and the dead woman seems to move. He thinks she has pulled up her knees, ever so slightly; tucked her chin, nestling down. But it is a trick of the gloom.

Janine will return for the beautiful corpse soon, to butterfly her like a delicate spatchcock and glean from the blood and tissue of her and the liquids and substances in and on her, quite how she spent the last moments of her life. She will also determine when the woman died – that he can eliminate the innocent.

Staffe leans against the wall and slides down onto his haunches. He has her in his eyeline, her cold flesh between him and the river, which is like a silver ribbon in the moonlight. This is a room designed for love or seduction, with its floor-to-ceiling windows and its opulent furnishings. It is not a place for any Tom, Dick or Harry to come a-killing.

Outside, a boat moves slowly down river, its

stern light dull in the estuary fret. He envies the skipper, making his way to sea; a whistling kettle down below and the sizzle of bacon at dawn's first; the horizon getting no closer – all day long.

He closes the door behind him and locks it, hands the key to the uniformed constable in the corridor.

'A long day, sir.'

'It'll be longer before we're through.' A new design is emerging for the night. All he has is the call from Markary and he takes the lift down, turns his thoughts to the man who was first to call this beautiful woman after she died.

Taki Markary crossed Staffe's path some years ago when a gang of Chinamen were mass-burning DVDs in a building that was leased to a company which was owned by a company which was managed by a trust whose ultimate beneficiary was a charity run by Taki Markary's wife, Sema. Markary emerged unscathed from that investigation, but during its course, Staffe became aware that the smooth Turk had made his money selling arms to Iraq in the 1990 war. That hadn't quite tallied with what Staffe had seen. Markary hadn't seemed cut out for such rough trading, seemed intent on a far finer life.

The traffic on Embankment is thin, tail lights like far-strung rubies. From the dash, his phone glows, emerald. It is Josie. 'What have you got?'

'Markary's clean as a whistle. Still living in Mayfair. His wife's got a couple of nightclubs in Istanbul. She's old money.'

'Kids?'

'No.'

'How old is she?'

'Younger than him. Forty. He's fifty, but he looks like a handsome fella. Like the one who plays cards, you know . . .'

'It's bridge. A bit more than a card game.' Staffe cuts up through Whitehall, making his way towards the frosted halls of government. 'You mean Omar Sharif.'

'That's all I've got, apart from a list of companies. He's got the Executive, off Berkeley Square.'

'That's practically a brothel.'

'But he looks legit, sir. Sorry.'

'Don't be sorry. It's supposed to be a good thing when people comply with the law.' Staffe hangs up, watches St James's clubland discharge a final few, born to rule.

The cars in this part of God's London – all Italian and German – are beginning to frost, sparkling in the soft orange street light, like candied fruits. Staffe parks his battered Peugeot on Mount Street, and looks up at the stucco building. His breath trails in the wintry air and he presses 3, waits for the response. Eventually a weary voice comes crystal clear in the silver speaker grille. Markary sounds more refined than Staffe recalls. The voice is soft; the easternness light on the edges of his vowels.

'What do you want this time of night. Who is that?'

Staffe looks up at the video camera and smiles. 'Just a word.' He holds his warrant card up to the lens. 'Inspector Wagstaffe, Leadengate CID.'

'What?'

'You phoned a girl. Something happened to her.'

'Which girl?'

'Let me in.'

'You best be quick. Second floor.' The latch whirrs. Staffe pushes the door and a light comes on automatically. Staffe sinks into the lush pile under-foot. There is a smell of the Orient and the common parts are adorned with gilded oil paintings. Pre-Raphaelite copies. The lift is silent. He can't imagine that anyone living here would ever be brought down.

When he gets to Markary's floor the door to the apartment is open and his host is on the telephone. 'They're here now. Yes. I'm not an idiot.'

'Your solicitor, Mr Markary? Odd behaviour for someone who's done nothing wrong.' Staffe fixes him, firm, in the eyes. The years have been kind. His grey-flecked black hair is cut dapper and even at this hour it is slicked back in tight waves from a matinee hairline that juts to the temples. He is no more than half a stone overweight in his polo shirt and linen trousers. 'You called her at two forty-seven.'

'Called who?'

Staffe scrutinises a painting of a woman, seemingly seated in a crowd of people but looking lost. She has fine features but her face is dirty, the clothes grubby. 'Is it true what they say about how you pay for all this?'

'Who are "they"?'

'It's what we call received wisdom.'

'We? Do you not consider me to be one of you, Inspector . . .?'

'Wagstaffe. They call me Staffe.'

'They say racism is rife in the Metropolitan Police Force.'

'I'm not with the Met. I am City. And I'm no racist. But that doesn't mean I have to give house-room to foreign criminals. We have met before.'

'I don't recall.' Markary goes to a walnut secretaire and pulls down the front, pours himself a large measure of spirit from a cut-glass decanter.

'Life continues to be kind, I take it, since your Chinamen let you down.'

Markary moves towards Staffe. 'You have an interesting karma. You are unfulfilled.'

'You're wrong.'

'Your mask slips, Inspector. But you can never see that.' He regards the painting of the woman, along-side Staffe.

'Perhaps Sickert could have shown me.'

'You know your art.' Markary squints. 'You can read her, just from this moment in time. He is a genius, to see into her this way, to commit her so.'

Staffe thinks of the beautiful, fair corpse, her face and the shape of her locked in time. 'They killed her, Taki. I'm going to find out who and why. I'd have thought you'd want the same for your girl.'

'How do you mean, *my* girl?'

'Why do you call prostitutes, Taki? Is your wife here?'

'What did she look like?' he whispers.

'I can only tell you how she looked in that last moment.' Staffe takes the glass from him, sips. It is Armagnac, of the highest quality. He holds on to it and as he takes a step back, he says, 'She looked as if she was about to enjoy what she did. She was pale as snow. Her hair had long curls and she was lying on an oyster fur.'

Markary blinks quickly, three, four times and reaches for the glass, snatches it away. 'I have nothing to tell you.' He downs the Armagnac in one and sits on the sofa, flicking through the *Estates Gazette*. Not reading it at all.

'Shame to drag your lawyer out of bed for nothing.'

'Nothing?'

'I've got what I want.' Staffe looks down on Markary and raises his voice half a notch. 'I shan't fuck about. I'll talk to your wife, if I need to, just in case she used your phone by mistake and it was actually her calling this poor murdered girl you don't give two bloody hoots for.' He feels his blood quicken and he breathes in, long.

Markary looks up, says in a tender, cracking voice. 'What did they do to her?'

Staffe looks at the painting again. 'They say Sickert knew the Ripper.'

Markary nods. 'Some say he *was* the Ripper.'

As Staffe goes into the hall, Markary's wife emerges from a bedroom. She is older than the whore, and she is beautiful.

Staffe lets himself out, murmurs, 'I'll rip *your* bloody mask off.'

Four

Janine stands back from the pale victim, livor mortis yet to manifest itself. The woman had been decomposing for approximately seven hours – until she was moved to this controlled environment. The skin will not blister or slip, for now, and she remains purest white. Janine puts the back of her hand to the woman's hip. The skin is cold as slate but the flesh yields, untethered. Janine has cut her open from collarbones to breast plate and down to the pubis. Her insides are bare to this windowless, photoflood corner of the world.

She flicks off the operating lights and an electric hum disappears into the early morning in a strange reversal of nature. But you don't get birdsong this time of year.

Janine sits in the corner, hands on her knees and back straight, drinking in the scene. Some colleagues are immune to the objects of their craft – the lives left in the wake. Janine takes counsel each month, for the loss of her subjects, and this beautiful woman with her frozen look has haunted her since she first shone a torch into her mouth and nose and elsewhere.

A knock at the opening door makes her flinch and she begins to stand, but when she sees it is Staffe, she slumps back down in her seat. He forces a smile but she can tell he is practically out on his feet. For the first few seconds, each time they meet, she can't help remembering when they were together. It was a brief affair – if you could flatter it so – and it ended quickly, amicably. She considers him a friend; fears for him, sometimes.

'You want some coffee?' She asks.

'I'll make the coffee.' He takes a jar of instant coffee and powdered milk from the cupboard beneath the high, barred window which is kerb-level. 'Talk me through it.'

'There was no sperm inside her, just a trace secretion of her own fluids in the gusset of her pants. The pants are Rigby and Peller.' Staffe turns round, raises his eyebrows and they each decide not to share a private joke. 'There is no bruising or laceration. The vagina had not been penetrated. The head and the blood on the carpet were juxtaposed. She didn't move once she hit the ground.'

'Not your typical sexual act,' he says.

'There were only six strands of fur fibre, and no carpet fibres in her nose, and none in the mouth or throat, and no trace of inhalation of the fibres from the pillowcase.'

'She was unconscious when they finished her off – with the pillow,' says Staffe. 'No struggle?'

'Look at her face; the expression.'

'I have.' The kettle boils.

'No damage to the nose or cheeks, no bruising to the lips. The skin and blood on the radiator are a perfect match. She has a bruise to her lower neck which may have been caused by a knee during a suffocation but there's a defined epicentre to the bruise. I think it was a rapid blow.'

'And the fall against the radiator an accident?'

'I don't think "accident" covers anything that happened to this girl.'

'The pillow could be part of a sexual design.'

Janine shakes her head, goes across to fix her coffee the way she likes it. Staffe has left it black, for her to finish. He remembered.

She glimpses the woman's fur, hanging in the corner. It is a vintage natural oyster mink with a wing collar. The real thing. 'Was that your girlfriend at the Thamesbank?'

'We'd been away for the weekend.'

Janine wonders why people put themselves through that. Why not fast-forward to the heart-ache and tears and save yourself the pain. 'Getting serious, hey Staffe?'

He smiles, thin-lipped. 'What happened in that hotel room?'

'Over to you, lover boy.' Janine takes off her gloves and washes down. When she is done, she catches Staffe standing over the body, staring deep into the woman's face.

'It gets worse,' she says.

'How?' he says, not looking away.

'Some might say there's another victim.'

'What?' He looks up.

Janine suddenly feels cold as he follows her look to a small table on the far side of the room. There, barely larger than a grape, is a dead foetus. 'She was pregnant, Will.'

Darius is out, scoring coke and MDMA for the party. He'll be out all night so Arabella has walked across to Becx's place on a litre bottle of super-strong cider and her last line. Becx had some crack when she last saw her and with a bit of luck, they might be able to suck on the pipe before they go out. Her feet are rubbed raw in her sharp-toed, take-me boots and she is so cold that she can't feel the metal against her finger when she presses the buzzer. Her nose is running and she stands back, hoping to see the curtains shift. They do, but it isn't Becx. The lock whirrs anyway and she pushes the door open, makes her way up the stairs.

Mitch is leaning against the frame of the door. He's wearing a porkpie hat and has tats on his neck and arms, piercings in his nose and eyebrows. He looks her up and down. He's gorgeous and knows it and exactly the type Becx always gets snarled up with, but Arabella has his measure.

'You want to . . .'

'Fuck off,' says Arabella, placing an open palm on his T-shirt chest. 'I've got Darius.'

He looks her all the way down to her heels and sneers. 'Looks like it.'

He goes into the flat and Arabella follows him in. The place is done up nice with soft lighting and ethnic knick-knacks. It is warm and a red glow comes off the electric fire pulled up to the sofa. Both bars are on.

Arra wouldn't need much to get her and Darius a place like this. It is time to have that chat with her father. Time, too, to work on her music; for Darius to go back to his art.

'Where's the guitar?' says Arabella, looking around the living room.

'In our bedroom.' Mitch smiles at her, pulling on a leather biker's jacket. 'I'm popping out.'

'When's Becx coming back?'

He pauses by the door, 'No point having a rummage.' He taps his pocket. 'It's all here. Stay out the bedroom, girl, I'm warning you.' His smile goes off like power, cut. He suddenly looks capable of the terrible. 'Slag,' he says, closing the door.

Arabella heaves off her boots and flops onto the sofa. The sheet of heat from the electric fire hits her shins straight away, works its way down to her toes and up along her long, thin thighs. She closes her eyes, the mind slowing right down, memories drifting, to that sad house across town. She misses her mother, who was Imogen and beautiful; making the men smile but sometimes crying when she drank wine, which her father didn't like. They would argue and her brother, Roddy, would run to his room, but Arabella would clutch on to Imogen's skirts, sobbing, looking up at her father and wondering how she could love such a man. After, he would hold Arabella tight and they would cry together and she loved him again.

From the bedroom, music pipes through. It is house but with a Latin flavour and the swooning trumpet loop ushers her to a deeper rest. She dreams that she cannot hear the sound of her own name in her mother's mouth.

The warmth of the fire seeps deeper into her flesh. She dreams, too, that she is standing at the gate, looking up, a small case in hand. Her father calls her a whore. 'Nothing but a whore like your mother.'

When she falters from sleep, Arabella has been crying and the music from the bedroom seems to get louder but Arabella keeps her eyes closed. She thinks, 'If I open my eyes, all the changes will begin to happen.' She hopes that Becx will come. The music goes up another notch and this puzzles Arabella. Moments later, she feels a shadow scroll across her.

A tall figure looks down at her. He is tall and fair, with a straight nose – just like her – like Imogen, too. She scrunches her eyes tight shut and rolls away onto the floor.

She waits for him to come at her, but he doesn't. He just stands there. 'What the hell are you playing at, Bella?'

'Roddy?' She sits up, peers up at him. 'What the fuck are you doing here?' She scoots back on her bottom, away from him, her back against the sofa. Even though he is her brother, whom she bullied when she was young, now she is afraid. He is one of them and a different kettle of fish when their father is not around.

'I can come see my big sis if I want.'

'I don't want. So fuck off.'

'He wants to see you, Bella.'

'Father? Is it me, or my friend he wants?'

'You have to settle this nonsense.'

'I'm not afraid of you.'

'But you can be.'

Roddy seems altered tonight, wearing twisted jeans and a white T under a combat jacket. He's put wax in his hair. 'How did you get in here?'

'He needs to know you won't do anything stupid.'

She looks her brother up and down and wishes she could feel different, says, 'Don't tell him you know I'm here.'

'Where's Darry?' says Roddy, trying hard to sound casual.

'He's providing for me.'

'He's using you, is what you mean.'

'I use him.'

'You really don't know anything.' Roddy turns his back, doesn't give her so much as a glance, says, 'You do the right thing, Bella.'

'Have a heart, Roddy. Have a fucking heart.'

He closes the door and the electricity clunks down. The place goes instantly dark. The bars on the electric fire fade from red to pink to a low, diminishing amber. Like a fast-setting sun. The elements click as they cool and Arabella says, 'God help me.'

Five

Staffe double-parks the Peugeot, puts the POLICE AWARE card on the dash and strides up to his flat, in a fine row of Georgian town houses in South Ken. The lightest dusting of snow has fallen during the night. Above, the dark sky seems set to yield more.

As soon as he puts the key to the door, he knows Pulford is in, but doesn't expect anything like the scene that is laid out before him.

He tries to school himself not to react, but he can feel his pulse accelerate away from him. His breath is short. His fingers have wound into fists.

'What in God's name . . .'

'Staffe! You said . . .' Pulford stands up, knocks a pile of poker chips to the floor and one of his friends clumsily tries to catch them. There is a thick pall of spirits in the air and bad rock thuds from a boom box. They have been smoking and pizza boxes scatter the living-room floor. '. . . You said you were away for the whole weekend.'

'You said you were knocking *this* on the head.' Staffe steps towards his sergeant – only twenty-six, but with his stubble and unkempt hair and gravelly

39

voice, seeming far older. He knows he must look as if he is going to lose it because Pulford's mates drain their glasses. One of them picks up the deck of cards and another scoops the Jack Daniels.

'See you, Dave.'

'Thanks for the game, mate.'

'Mate?' shouts Staffe. 'You're no mates. You know he's got a fucking problem. If you were mates you'd stay away, not come fleecing him!' Staffe turns to Pulford, levels him with a stare, holds it, says slowly, 'You prick.'

'I'm sorry, Staffe.'

'I take you in, and this is what you do?'

'I was winning. I . . .'

Pulford is wide-eyed and bleary and Staffe sees the cluelessness that most of his colleagues choose to focus on in the young graduate recruit. He quickly loses the heart to tear a strip off him. 'Did Chancellor call you?'

'I've been working that trafficking case.' Pulford takes a step back, shaking his head. 'On surveillance for three nights straight.'

When Staffe offered Pulford a place to stay, somewhere safe to fight his gambling demons, there had been ground rules. 'Get yourself cleaned up, and a bellyful of coffee. You're on duty as of now.'

'What's happened?'

He looks his sergeant up and down, wants to feel

sorry for him. Rimmer and the rest of the team should have been in touch with Pulford. The fact that they haven't speaks volumes. Staffe stabs a finger into the chest of the young DS. 'You are going to get some therapy.'

Pulford looks down, shamefaced. 'What's happened?'

Staffe looks out through the fog at the iced houses with their black railings and shuttered windows. 'Why didn't you answer my calls?'

'Because you said, sir, that you were away with Sylvie and if you even tried to talk about work, I had your permission to shoot you.'

Josie Chancellor puts a tray of bagged evidence on her DI's desk. 'Janine's just told me about the foetus.'

'It was eight weeks.' He rests his chin on the flat of his palm. 'Markary? How do we play this?'

'How old does it have to be – before you can run DNA on it – the baby I mean,' says Josie.

'It's old enough. Have you got that data from the victim's mobile phone?'

'Aaah,' says Josie. 'DI Rimmer is applying for a warrant, he says . . .'

'Jesus! How long will it take?'

'The papers are with DCI Pennington,' says Josie.

'And where's the phone?'

Josie opens her drawer, picks up a sealed plastic bag with the gold Nokia inside.

Staffe looks around the room and hisses to Josie, 'You keep it with you. All the time. And I mean all the time. If anybody calls, you answer it, pretending to be her. You find out who's calling and where they live.'

'You're sure, sir?'

'And here.' He tosses her a field recorder. 'Record some interference off the radio and play it when you answer.'

'What did she sound like?'

'She's foreign, is my guess. Break your English when you answer. Say as little as you can.'

Josie leaves and Staffe has the place to himself. Soon, he is lost in thoughts: this case isn't about him or Rimmer, but the beautiful girl, lying butter-flied for autopsy.

'Staffe!' DCI Pennington is standing in the doorway, immaculately suited, pencil thin. He says, through pursed lips, 'Christ, man. Looks like you've seen a ghost.'

'I was thinking, sir.'

'Well think on this, Staffe. I've heard about you barging in on Taki Markary last night.'

'How do you know that?'

'You give this man absolutely no cause for complaint. You're only just off the hook, remember.'

Staffe looks at the floor and swallows words. Pennington suckered him into the Jadus Golding conviction because the DCI extracted a 'revised' statement from a key witness, back in the summer. Staffe shouldn't have covered up for his chief. But he did. 'I remember *everything* about Golding.'

'If you go after Markary, he'd better be the right man, and you'd better have the evidence. I suggest you reappraise. Think of him as living in a castle.'

'A castle?'

'Surrounded by a moat full of eggshells.'

'I'll have the evidence, sir.' He thinks of the DNA Janine can summon from a being the size of a grape.

Pennington shoots him a warning look. 'What *exactly* have you got on Markary?'

'He called the victim.'

'After she was killed.'

'He's withholding evidence.'

Pennington gives Staffe a withering look.

'The victim was pregnant. There was a foetus.'

'You'd better hear me, Staffe.' Pennington turns on his heel, walks out, head high and back straight. 'Loud and clear.' He doesn't shut the door behind him.

'You sure we should be going to see Markary, sir?' says Pulford, sitting alongside Staffe in the Peugeot, the list of names and numbers from the gold Nokia in his lap.

'Keep reading the names, Sergeant.'

'Mobile number. Name Crystal.'

'No,' says Staffe.

'Landline, inner London. Name Bobo.'

'Mark it.' Staffe knows that, in time, all these numbers will be traced, but he's picking the men who have called the dead woman in the past week, prioritising landlines – for speed. You find your killer in seventy-two hours. After that, the tide turns against.

'Darius A'Court. Mobile number.'

'Contract?'

'I'll check.' Pulford carries on to the end of the list.

Staffe says, 'Get Josie to come up with the addresses and full names.'

He parks up four doors down, opposite Markary's place on Mount Street. It is midday, but the lights are on in the house. With such fog in Mayfair's Georgian preserve, you wouldn't blink if a horse and carriage drew up, if a gent in tails swanned out with a cane. You couldn't call Markary a gent. Not in Staffe's book, but he had clearly got into the right club. Somehow.

'Here we are, sir,' says Pulford, reading from his Blackberry.

Staffe is sad at the thought of bookies getting rich on Pulford's misery and wonders what is so lacking in the young man's life as to send him down that road. 'Go on. Let's have it.'

'Bobo is a Boris Bogdanovich, lives in the Atlee, Bethnal Green.'

'Russian? Find out how long he has been in the country.'

'Darius A'Court is pay as you go, but one of the landlines is the Colonial Bankers' Club.'

'Is that it?'

'The gold Nokia was bought in Dubai. It's pay as you go and chipped. And there's no correlation of the corpse with missing persons.'

'Colonial Bankers. How pukka can you get?' Staffe looks up at Markary's apartment. He has had it five years, since he came over from Istanbul. He paid £1.5 million for it but that's nothing compared to his house on the Bosporus and the nightclubs his wife still owns over there. She makes the Mayfair gang look nouveau riche. Some might think Markary a spiv, but his wife's family has been lording it since the Ottoman empire came home to roost.

Staffe starts the engine – the wise thing. The next time he fronts up to Markary, he'll have evidence. 'Let's visit this Bobo.'

Pulford's Blackberry beeps with another message. 'It's Janine.' He ruffles his hair and says, 'The forensic archaeologist says your woman was East European – the cranium, the eyes. And the contents of her upper intestine.'

'Lovely.'

'Beetroot and herring bones. She had one of her teeth capped. A classy piece of dentistry, apparently. But no match so far.'

'Tell Josie the victim was East European.' He sees a woman at a window on the first floor. She has full lips and olive skin, the darkest eyes which appear to have smudged their mascara.

Josie hears the vibration before the ringtone. She looks at the gold Nokia. 'The Carnival Is Over' chimes up and she wishes Staffe was here.

Bobo calling.

Trying to calm herself, Josie turns on the interference track on the field recorder and places a tissue over the mouthpiece, clicks green.

'Lena,' says a man's voice. He is foreign.

Josie says nothing.

'Lena, are you there? Hello!' The man is agitated and sounds young. He says something Josie cannot decipher, presumably Russian or Polish.

'It's me,' says Josie, softly, ironing out her vowels. He continues in a foreign tongue.

Josie says, 'In English, Bobo. You need to practice.'

'Where are you?' says Bobo.

Rimmer comes into the room and she waves him away but he paces around her. 'What are you doing?' says Rimmer. 'Is it for her?'

'You come over, Lena. You come to me. I am worried. He knows,' says Bobo.

Josie checks the prompts Staffe gave her, says, 'Who knows?'

'Tchancov. You know.'

She scribbles the name, her heart thudding. Rimmer puts the palm of a hand to his forehead.

The phone has gone quiet and Bobo says, quieter, more circumspect. 'Lena? . . . Lena, is this you?'

Staffe said to trust her instincts, and she removes the tissue, turns off the interference, says, 'Bobo? I'm sorry. This is not Lena.'

'What happens?' He immediately sounds more afraid.

'Was Lena in danger, Bobo?'

He cries out, like a baby. His breathing is heavy, irregular.

'We are police. We can help you.'

'They kill her?'

'Who is *they*?'

He begins to wail.

'Where does she live?' says Josie, but all she can hear down the phone is a low sobbing. 'Bobo? Bobo! What is her name? Her surname!' But the phone clicks dead.

47

Rimmer peers at her notes and sits down, says, 'Tchancov?'

Josie phones Staffe, says, 'Bobo Bogdanovich just called her phone, sir.'

'What did he say?'

'She's called Lena. He knew she was in some kind of danger. He mentioned someone called Tchancov. He said this Tchancov knew something.'

'Anything else?'

'He broke down, sir. Cried like a baby.'

'Did you tell him she was dead?'

'He guessed it.'

'He didn't know already?'

'I'd say not. Would he have called her if he knew that?'

Staffe says, 'A good ruse if he realised he had left her phone at the scene – with him trapped inside it.'

Six

Snow falls steadily on the city. Staffe knocks on the door of Bobo's peeling, deck-access council flat on the Atlee and stamps his feet, to keep warm, as he waits for a fragile-looking fellow, probably from Poland or Russia. Josie had said he had a 'tiny voice, like a girl's'.

The locks clatter back and the handle turns; the door swings violently open and Staffe finds himself looking into the broad-vested chest of a brute. The vest sports a gold skull on a Chelsea blue background with HEADHUNTERS writ large. Staffe casts his eyes slowly up, taking a step away as he does. The man has a neck like a 30 K dumb-bell weight; a face like a 20 K. His scalp is shiny, the nose broken and the eyes red, raw, glistening with grief.

'You police?' he says.

'Are you . . . Bobo?' says Staffe, off guard.

'She's dead? Tell me no. Tell me this not so.' He talks in fits, starts again with the sobbing, gasping his words out like a child who has fallen badly, is still in shock. 'I kill the fuck. I kill the fuck.'

'Who's dead, Bobo?' You don't often get moments

like this, when the bad guys are on the back foot, when the strong are weak, so Staffe walks up to the brute, crossing the threshold to the flat and saying, in his softest voice, raising it a pitch – as close as he can to Bobo's falsetto, 'Tell me about Tchancov, Bobo. I can help.' Staffe reaches up with his hands and puts them on Bobo's shoulders, like laying hands on weathered gritstone.

Bobo has scars all over his head: some deep and long, some fine. It is like the surface of an old and neglected windscreen. 'My Lena,' he mumbles.

'Lena who, Bobo?'

'My Elena,' he says, the words petering to nothing and Staffe sees Bobo's head come towards him. Staffe closes his eyes, raises his fists, readies himself to fracture his knuckles on this man of rock.

But Pulford shouts out, 'No! Sir, no!'

Staffe feels a great weight on him and, opening his eyes, has Bobo's face in his, the great weight of the man pushing him down.

'He's passed out, sir,' says Pulford, on his haunches, trying to hold Bobo up. 'Get hold of him, sir,' he wheezes. 'He's crushing me.'

Staffe puts his arms as far around Bobo as he can, gripping him under one arm and pulling him off Pulford. He tries to lower him gently to the ground, but Bobo crumples to the concrete, makes a sound like a side of beef slapped onto a butcher's block.

Staffe and Pulford look down at him, then at each other.

'What the hell do we do now?' says Pulford.

Staffe peers into the flat. 'You watch him.'

'You sure, sir?'

'Sometimes you've got to take sweets from the baby.'

'Some bastard baby, sir.'

The Atlee is rough, but Bobo's living-diner is painted a rich, high-glaze plum, with a long, glass dining table and high-backed chairs with pale pink silk skirted covers. The kitchen is simply one wall of black units and steel appliances. It is sleek and Bobo, for sure, keeps it spick and span. Above the stereo is a large black-and-white photograph of the beautiful woman. Elena. She is laughing and her fair hair is blowing back. She crinkles her eyes against the sun and looks beyond the photographer, as if seeing something unintended. Behind her, white horses in a high, breaking sea. At the corners of her mouth, the smile fragments.

There is a notepad on the marble counter. The top sheet says 'встреча V в'. Staffe lifts it daintily with the very tips of his thumb and forefinger, as if the sound of the paper might wake the dead. The next sheet is blank.

'V,' he whispers, to himself. As in Vassily. Vassily, as in Tchancov. 'VB?'

He glances back down the hallway where Pulford looks anxiously up from Bobo, gesturing insistently for Staffe to come, be done with his trespassing, but Staffe sees there are two more rooms to inspect.

The first is the bathroom, boasting nothing untoward in its mirrored cabinet, save two gramme bags of what he assumes to be coke. There are two bottles of prescription drugs: one an antihistamine, the other an antidepressant, Molaxin.

'V,' says Staffe, making his way into Bobo's bedroom. He closes the door and drops to his knees, lifting up the valance. Under the bed is a folded-down rowing machine and some weights. Staffe looks in the drawers by the bedside and smiles to himself. Wrapped in black silk ribbon – a stack of letters written on thick, pale lilac paper – almost parchment. Luckily for them, Bobo is a romantic. And his girlfriend, according to the second sheet, is a girl called Elena. Was a girl called Elena. Staffe sits on the edge of the bed and begins to read, but the script is foreign, written in a long and beautiful hand.

He knows that if he comes back for the letters, armed with a warrant and a translator, Bobo may well have disposed of them. So he looks at the dates and selects two, puts them in his pocket and begins to tie, but he hears a creak. The vast bulk of Bobo fills the bedroom doorway.

'What the fuck,' says Bobo, reaching towards Staffe who shuffles back on the bed, working out whether, if he can roll away from the first punch, he can get away. But Bobo, quicker than thought, flicks his fingers into Staffe's throat.

Staffe can't breathe. He clutches at his neck, dropping the stack of letters.

Bobo picks up the letters and kicks the door shut in the face of the advancing Pulford. 'You read these letters?' he sobs.

Staffe can smell Bobo's breath as he speaks. Fish and pickles and woe. 'Elena had her own place. Where is it, Bobo? I have to know. If you save me time, it will help.'

Bobo raises his hands to his head. He moans, 'Livery, she calls it.'

'Livery Buildings? On Cloth Fair?' says Staffe.

'Now you leave me.'

'Do you work for Vassily Tchancov?'

Bobo drops his hands. Despite his bulk, and the scars, Bobo's face is washed over with fear. The blood drains from his face and he looks to the floor. He mumbles, 'You go.'

'Did Elena know any bankers?'

'Go!'

'She called the Colonial Bankers' Club, the day . . . the day it happened.'

'Leave me.' His voice breaks down. Bobo looks

up, as if it takes his last drop of strength, and he reaches for the bed. He sits, lets all his weight go, and curls up like a foetus.

'Just because Bobo called Elena and let us keep a couple of letters doesn't mean he's not a suspect, sir,' says Pulford, sifting through the Companies House secure-access files on Vassily Tchancov's declared businesses.

'VB.' Staffe's finger rests in the margin of the page, next to *VodBlu*. The registered address is in Jersey. 'You saw how much he loves her. He's not our killer,' he says, typing in *VodBlu.com*.

'What if the foetus wasn't his?' says Pulford. 'Perhaps you have to love somebody enough, to be able to kill them.'

'Does this look like a crime of passion?' says Staffe, looking at the ice bar's homepage. He goes to the window and looks up towards Cloth Fair, trying to pick out Livery Buildings and Elena's flat. 'It seems that VodBlu is owned by a company registered in Jersey, run by somebody called Desai. It turns over nine million a year.'

'We should go to Elena's place,' says Pulford.

'Tchancov will soon get wind of our visit to Bobo. If we move quick, he might not know Elena's dead.'

'He'd know if he killed her.'

'Why would he kill her?'

'I don't know, sir.'

'So let's go talk to him.' Staffe tosses his car keys to Pulford and makes his way down through the building, scrolling through his phone menus to find the number of his old mucker, Smethurst – over at the Met. 'We'll keep Livery Buildings under our hat. I don't want Rimmer rummaging through Elena's life before we can.'

Making his way down Leadengate's dark corridors and winding stairwells, Staffe thinks of older times, when he was the young pup to Jessop and Smet. Pulford rushes ahead, takes the stairs two at a time and Staffe wonders whether his sergeant will ever be an old dog.

Leadengate is unsuitable for modern policing, was never intended to uphold the law; in fact, quite the reverse. It was previously the Saracen's Head, an old inn of bad repute.

They spill out into the dungeon-like reception and Jombaugh gives Staffe a sarcastic, am-dram salute, calls out, 'Take it easy, Staffe,' his head sticking up above the high counter. He is leafing through *The News* by lamplight.

'Easy?'

'I don't see Rimmer running at all that fine china.'

'You calling me a bull, Jom?'

Jombaugh smiles over his glasses. He is a tall, broad man piling on the half-stones since he became desk sergeant. At least he's still married, though. 'You just take it easy.'

Outside, the snow reflects a pale orange hue. Smet answers and Pulford starts up the Peugeot. You can see the shapes of its splutter in the chill.

'Staffe, you old bastard! What kind of trouble are you in now?' says DI Smethurst.

'It's the season of goodwill, Smet, don't you know?' Staffe presses o on his phone and pulses it three times. 'I've got to go, there's another call coming in.'

'What was it you wanted?'

'Vassily Tchancov.'

'Tchancov? He's keeping his nose clean as far as I know.'

'He just cropped up on something to do with one of Taki Markary's girls.'

'There was a coming together, a couple or three years ago.'

'Over what?'

'A gambling licence.'

'Who got it?'

'Neither. Two rabid old dogs in the manger.'

Staffe presses o again, gives it a long beep and says, 'Cheers, Smet,' clicking off.

* * *

They park up on Wardour Street, three doors down from VodBlu, which loses £600,000 a year on a turnover of £9 million. That's a lot of vodka amounting to nought, but Staffe's gut tells him that VB was never conceived for profit, but to spit out clean cash and tax credits. VB, says the sign, sculpted from ice, dyed blue. It is so cold out, today, that the sign doesn't melt at all. In summer – according to the website – they sculpt it fresh every day.

Four doors down from VodBlu, two lean, chiselled and suited men are smoking next to a blacked-out Bentley. Staffe raises a hand to them, is amused when they seem puzzled.

As they go in Pulford's words plume up from his mouth. 'Christ, sir! Is this . . .' He looks around, open-mouthed, '. . . is this all ice? Even the bar is ice.'

The girl behind the bar has black hair and powder-blue eyes. She wears a polar-white fur hat, a cropped, quilted gilet that shows her tummy, and knitted hot pants. Staffe wonders how long her shifts are. She looks happy enough and holds up a cone of black ice with a bottle embedded within. She wears white leather gloves, jiggles the bottle. 'Absolut, gents? Today's special.'

'Water,' says Staffe. 'Two, please.'

The bar is full of small groups of media types in thick vintage coats and porkpie hats or berets. One of the barmaids jokes as she goes out, cigarette at the ready, 'to get warm'.

Pulford brings the drinks and Staffe keeps an eye on a door between the end of the bar and the toilets. It is the only place that might accommodate an office, and, soon enough, a small, wiry man in a suit emerges. He has dyed-black hair with a widow's peak and electric blue eyes, like beads pressed into deep scars. He comes across to Staffe and says, 'You gentlemen have everything you need?'

'Elena sent us,' says Staffe, scrutinising the reaction.

'Elena?' says the man, convincingly deadpan.

'A friend of Vassily's?'

'Maybe you should go.' The man takes a hold of Staffe's elbow. The grip is tight as a nut and Staffe shakes his arm, can't shift it.

Pulford takes a step towards the man but Staffe says, 'This place does all right, I suppose. But you're not turning over nine million a year. No way. Maybe we'll have the DTI look at things.'

'You have a strange attitude, coming into my bar with such menaces,' says the man, in a clipped Eastern brogue. He turns to the hot-panted girl. 'Bring the gold Bison.'

'Mr Tchancov?' says Pulford.

'Vassily. Now,' he places a hand on the small of Staffe's back, 'Elena, you say?'

'She is with one of yours. Bobo Bogdanovich,' says Staffe.

The girl brings the vodka and three glasses. Tchancov tips her £10 and she strokes his arm, whispers something in his ear that makes him smile.

'Bobo does a little work for me.'

'And Elena?'

Tchancov shrugs.

'You have any dealings with Taki Markary?'

Tchancov smiles, blinks rapidly as he pours the vodka, as if his ice-cool bravado might have a thin surface. 'We're different kettles of fish, him and me.'

'You've crossed swords.'

He hands Staffe and Pulford a glass each. 'I don't believe in weapons, Inspector.'

'Bobo is very upset.'

'What has she done now?'

Staffe sips the vodka. It is ice cold and has herbal hints of the prairie. He watches Tchancov drink his in one, and notices an emerald ring on the little finger of his right hand.

'The ring. Your intaglio – it's from the Urals.'

Tchancov nods and his smile tightens. 'She was a bright girl. Ambitious.'

'Was? What *was* her name? Her surname.'

'All I can tell you is, she loves her work, Inspector.

No matter what you hear from anyone, I know this for a fact. And that's a risky business.'

Staffe mulls what he knows about Tchancov, from the couple of hours' research back at the station: that he has a house on the Bishops Avenue, a yacht in the western Med; hunting lodges in Belarus. He left Russia with a modest fortune from pyramid-selling bearer certificates in his cousin's computer business. Vassily was moved on when his uncle, Ludo, ran for governor. 'You take your share of risks, Vassily.'

Tchancov laughs, takes hold of Staffe's glass with his right hand. 'I like you.'

Pulford's phone beeps and he studies the screen. Both men look at him, frozen for a moment. 'We have to go, sir.'

Tchancov leans in, alcohol fresh on his breath. 'You were right about my ring. Very clever. But you're looking in the wrong place. Take my word for it, or find out for yourself. But don't come round my place fucking things up. I know my rights.'

'And Elena? You knew her.'

'You can go now,' says Tchancov. 'I have things to do.'

'I'll go as I please and I'll come as I please, Mr Tchancov.'

'We shall see.' Tchancov turns his back, goes back into his office; presumably, a warm place.

Seven

Flecks of snow float between the buildings on Cloth Fair. Staffe mounts the kerb outside the Hand and Shears, where Josie is waiting for them. He looks across to St Bart's church with its flint, patchwork stone and its dark, garden cloister.

Inside the Hand, the chatter is low and gentle. Josie is in the back snug, its walls panelled in dark wood. Staffe nods at Dick behind the bar: big-bellied in a Jermyn Street shirt and links.

This isn't a police pub and although the regulars know Staffe is a copper, no mention is ever made. 'Have you settled things at Livery Buildings?' says Staffe to Josie.

She nods, finishing off a tomato juice. 'I've had a chat with the caretaker, a bloke called Miles. I said I was a friend, and he said he hasn't seen her for a couple of days and nobody's been round for her.'

'We'll go over as soon as we're done with Pennington. What's agitating him?'

'He just said to get hold of you and quick. He said "fucker", actually, sir. And Rimmer was with him.' She looks at Pulford, smiles thinly.

It seems, to Staffe, that Pulford and Josie might be sharing a private joke. Not the only thing they have shared, he reckons. '"Fucker", you say.'

'What did you make of our friend Bobo?' asks Josie. 'Is he a sweetie?'

'Hardly,' says Pulford. 'But he's the boyfriend all right. I wouldn't want to cross him – especially if the baby wasn't his.'

'Sergeant Pulford reckons Bobo is our man,' says Staffe. 'Have you got those addresses from the numbers in Elena's phone?'

Josie slips him the list.

In exchange, he hands her Elena's pale lilac letters to Bobo. 'Get these translated, would you? Quick as you can, and keep them away from Rimmer. Let's meet back here at six.'

On his way out, the landlady, April, bumps into Staffe. She is a decade or so younger than her husband, Dick, with impossibly blonde hair and 'done' breasts. She craics with the locals about Staffe being 'all over her' in a moll's twang and getting a laugh from them all.

'You off, Staffe?' she says, with a lingering smile.

'I'll pop in later, when Dick slopes off for his nap.'

She shakes her head and puts a finger to her lips. 'Sshhh. He don't know nothing.'

* * *

Rimmer is sitting smug on Pennington's right. Staffe drags a straight-backed chair from the corner of his chief's office.

'I don't want a mountain out of a molehill here, Wagstaffe.'

'All we have is a body. I can't dress it up as something it's not.'

'A prostitute,' says Rimmer. 'She was a coke addict and probably a Russian.'

'She was seeing one of Vassily Tchancov's boys,' says Staffe.

'Bobo Bogdanovich,' says Pennington, as if he wishes he didn't know such things.

'She was a trick gone wrong, if you ask me,' says Rimmer.

'This wasn't done in the heat of passion, Rimmer. Did you see the look on her face? You call that a trick gone wrong?'

Rimmer smiles, for his and Pennington's benefit. He turns towards the DCI as if seeking permission to go ahead. 'The likelihood is, he is impotent. Sex crimes are often committed by men deficient in that area. Unable to *do the deed*, he becomes furious and kills her. This is what stimulates him. It's why he leaves her naked. It gives him the upper hand, a last word.'

'This wasn't a sex crime.'

'Then why was she naked?'

'Who've you been talking to?'

'They left her phone. That's not a professional job. It's a crime of passion, I tell you.'

Staffe thinks about this. He looks out of the window. 'She was killed in an instant, not during a struggle.' The snowflakes are getting thicker, heavier, falling fast to the ground now.

Pennington leans back in his chair. When he is impatient, he goes the opposite way. He talks, slowly, enunciating each syllable. 'We shan't make this case something it is not. Bear in mind what she was and where she came from. I know full well who lurks in the wings here, Staffe. You need to hold this in check.'

'This isn't a sex crime, sir,' says Staffe, making to leave. 'And I won't pretend it is.'

'She's a prostitute, man.'

'When I see a prostitute, a high-end, dead prostitute like Elena – I think about power and money. Not sex.'

Staffe thanks Miles the caretaker for letting them in to Elena's flat. Miles is modestly built, with wiry grey hair in an expensive cut, and with dandruff drifts on the shoulders of his dark suit. He hands them a master key once he has studied Staffe's warrant card, jotting down the details in a spidery hand.

Elena's place is on the New York model: exposed brickwork and high ceilings; on its surface, the flat is unstained as to the business she conducted here. You wouldn't bring just any stray tom into this place – even if Miles was in on it. The living room has two vast windows that look onto the arching wrought iron of Smithfield's meat market.

Staffe pulls on his disposable crime-scene mitts and counts the years he has been in this neck of the woods. He would come to the market with Jessop for a fry-up and a few pints of Guinness at six in the morning after a surveillance vigil or a long night of incident-room follow-up.

In the wastebasket by the sideboard there are a couple of envelopes addressed to Elena Danya, and Staffe hands them to Pulford. 'Danya,' he says. 'Elena Danya.' It is good in the mouth, this name. It rolls in the ear, makes Staffe feel sad – the tragedy a little more coloured-in. Staffe realises, with a heavy heart, that before they are done he will probably know more about poor Elena and her world than her lover and her mother and maybe even herself.

'There's one here for Markary, too, sir,' says Pulford, wiggling a letter in the air. 'It's from the management company.'

'So, he picked up the bills. Leave the place as we find it, Pulford. And tread gently.'

The bedroom smells of fabric softener. The linen is Egyptian cotton: ivory with bands of navy and powder blue. Translucent roman blinds keep Elena's bedtime world a secret. She has what seems to be a Clarice Cliff lotus jug on her painted French chest of drawers but when Staffe inspects the piece, he sees it is a modern copy. In the matching painted wardrobe, her clothes hang neatly – the kind of finery you would expect of a fancy whore. But Staffe double-checks – no mirror: not even on the wardrobes. Picking up a silver-framed photograph of Elena in a ball gown, looking into the camera with her pale eyes and her china-fine bones, it makes his heart sad to think she didn't appear to like looking at herself.

'Not your typical hooker's joint,' says Pulford.

Staffe sits on the bed and sighs, 'Not by a long chalk.' He feels something stop the mattress from taking his full weight and looks under the bed, pulls out a suitcase. It has ED inscribed on its fawn kid leather. He carefully picks his way through the contents: a pair of faded 501s, not even washed, two lumber-check shirts, a cable-knit sweater and a crocheted tea-cosy hat. Two pairs of colour-run Marks & Spencer's bikini briefs, and a copy of *Mansfield Park*. 'Poor thing,' says Staffe.

'What's that, sir?'

'This was her,' says Staffe. 'Not Markary, not Bobo. Not the bastards she slept with.'

'You heard what Tchancov said. He said she loved . . .'

'What does Tchancov know?' says Staffe, going into the kitchen.

He finds nothing out of the ordinary, sees the washing machine is full. On his knees, he goes through it: only bedding. She must have washed that day, he thinks. 'You wouldn't wash . . . It wouldn't be the last thing,' he says to himself, looking at this human remain of her final day.

'Excuse me!' Miles the caretaker stands in the doorway of the kitchen with his arms crossed. 'I'm going to have to ask you to leave.'

'A woman died, Miles,' says Staffe.

'No woman lived here.' Miles looks at Staffe, awkwardly.

Staffe takes a step towards. 'Are you changing your tune?'

Miles retreats back into the hallway. 'I shouldn't have let you in.'

Staffe wants to grab the man by the lapels of his suit and rattle the truth from him, but he tries to conjure another way. 'She was quite a beautiful girl, wouldn't you say? And popular.'

'I don't know what you're talking about.'

'You turned a blind eye. And a healthy profit, no doubt.'

'Perhaps I should call the police. You don't act like police.'

Staffe notices a stack of writing paper on the shelf of the telephone stand: pale lilac and stiff as parchment. He picks up the phone, presses *Redial* and after three rings a woman with a stern Balkan accent says, 'Signet Hotel. Can I help you?'

'You have a reservation in the name of Danya?'

The phone goes quiet and Miles says, 'I must insist!'

Staffe holds out a hand and listens to the woman say, 'You are not her.'

'Is it for tonight? I am police.'

'Last night. For two nights. She did not appear.'

Staffe hangs up and leaves. As he passes Miles, busy now into his mobile phone, he hisses, 'You wash your hands well, tonight. Get under the nails. And try not to look in the mirror.'

In the Hand and Shears, Staffe reads the translation of the first of Elena's letters to Bobo.

> *My sweet Bobo,*
> *I'm trapped here in this palace he has made for me. More like a prison and*

*sometimes I really wish I had never
come. But the life here can be so good. It
is easy to forget what it was like before. I
can't remember how cold it was, and
what we did not have. There was nothing
beautiful around us. Were the mountains
beautiful, Bobo? When I have to do
things, I close my eyes and I try to think
of the mountains. Life would be easier if
they were not beautiful.
Today, I feel low and missing you.
I love you my Bobo,
Elena.*

Staffe takes an unhealthy swallow of his Adnams. Reading Elena's thoughts, he is prompted to think of Rosa, his friend, who is bright and attractive and who will soon be too old to do what she does.

He steers himself to the next translation, but by the time he has read the first paragraph, his mind is back on Rosa. He should go round. It's been six months and he remembers full well what happened the last time – a first time.

'What do you make of it?' says Josie.

'It doesn't suggest she was being coerced, or held hostage to some habit. What did Forensics come up with at Livery Buildings?'

'Just a few of Elena Danya's prints. And Markary's,

too. According to the caretaker she was just there for a few days. Markary took pity on her, apparently. The caretaker backs it up.'

'What about the other residents?' says Staffe.

'They're saying nothing, and the CCTV is broken.'

'Are there any tapes?'

'They only keep them forty-eight hours.'

'How convenient.' Staffe feels his face soften into a smile.

'You should smile more often, sir,' says Josie, as Pulford returns with the drinks.

'There's plenty we should all do more often.'

'Word has it you're getting quite serious – with Sylvie.' She raises her eyebrows.

Staffe allows that strain of conversation to fade to nothing. As it does, a plan drifts. He swallows his Adnams, allows the plan to ferment. 'Aaah. Dick keeps his beer perfectly. They make it up in Saltburgh, Pulford. What do you make of it?'

'It's grand, sir. That's where she was going – the Signet Hotel.'

'You should get yourself up there. You want to go with him, Chancellor?' says Staffe to Josie.

'Nice of you to offer, sir. But I can see you might be better equipped to make such a sacrifice.' She laughs, as does Pulford, and Staffe revisits the second translation.

My sweet Bobo,

   I feel so low and miss not seeing you.
I am a prisoner up here and don't know
how much longer I could have done this.
Perhaps it is the winter that brings me
down. He has said I can have a few days
away and I will go to my paradise
and forget everything, I hope. I can't
remember how long it is since I saw
you . . .

Staffe finishes his pint and stands. 'You get off, Pulford. We've got a big day tomorrow. Josie, tell Bobo he'll need to account for his whereabouts between four and six o'clock on the seventh.'

As Pulford gets his coat, Staffe winks at Josie and taps his watch, holds five fingers up and mimes the turning of a steering wheel.

'Christ, sir. Is this his place?'

Kerbside, on Bishops Avenue, the dashboard dies, like someone turning off the Christmas tree lights. Opposite, though, beyond the gilded gates of number 75, Tchancov's Norwegian spruce would do the Kremlin proud.

'Oooh. What a tree.' Josie's eyes glint as a car sweeps by.

Staffe talks into the entryphone, embedded in a vast stone pillar.

'You!' responds Tchancov's voice.

'I'm going to have to ask you come down to the station, Mr Tchancov. Or we could try to handle it here.'

'And may I ask why?'

Staffe looks at Josie, letting the silence stretch. The lock clunks and a small gate to the side sweeps open.

'Wow,' says Josie, going ahead, looking up at the double-gabled, modern gothic extravagance.

'The rouble must be strong,' says Staffe, watching light glow bright in the twelve-foot porch. The front door opens and little Tchancov appears, wearing a smoking jacket and a fragile smile. Through narrow lips that barely move, he says, 'I have guests arriving. Unless you have documents, you should be quick.'

'I thought you'd want to know . . .' Staffe looks past Tchancov, sees a suited, broad-shouldered man with Mongolian eyes and no hair, dyed-black sideburns.

'Know what?' asks Tchancov, instating a broader smile.

'You're needed to identify the body of Elena Danya in the morning. Eight o'clock sharp. I'll send a car round for you.'

72

Staffe scrutinises the reception hall, decked with holly and some fine baroque furniture. On the secretaire by the curving dual staircase is a pile of post. Amidst it, a pale lilac envelope.

Vassily steps across, into Staffe's eyeline. 'I heard Bobo was tending to the identification.'

'We have a conflict. Bobo simply can't do that, Vassily.'

'Why?'

'He's been arrested – in connection with the murder of Elena Danya.'

Vassily Tchancov bats his eyes, just the once, at the news that one of his has been brought in for murder.

'What the hell's going on, sir?' asks Josie, once the car door is shut.

'I'll run you home. You're on my way.' He fires up the engine, pulls out, waving at the Mongolian, who watches them from the other side of the gilded gates.

'You've got evidence on Bobo?' says Josie.

'If we wanted him to come in and he refused to co-operate, we might have to arrest him.'

'Tchancov will soon find out if he's not.'

'Jombaugh's got two uniforms going round to get him. My guess is, he'll resist.'

Traffic is thin and the snow is falling. Going

down past the Spaniards Inn. Josie turns in her seat and says, softly, 'You just want Tchancov in front of the body. That's it, isn't it?'

'Not quite.' Staffe turns on the radio, surfs it to a classical station. Copland, he thinks, and in that orchestral prairie sweep, he lets his thoughts roam. All he has for Elena is a disputed address and a probable occupation; a surname and a boyfriend; a lover and an ex-employer. No National Insurance number or passport; no place or date of birth. An empty hotel room awaits her in Suffolk. Tchancov said she really did love what men paid her to do, but Staffe won't accept that. Nothing about Elena will be that simple, he fears.

He thinks about how long it is since he visited his parents' grave, and he fears for Elena's father and mother, feels the terrible burden of those who survive.

He calls Jombaugh, who asks who he wants to talk to.

'You, Jom. I want you to do me a favour.'

'You must be in trouble, Staffe.'

'You're my oldest friend in the Force now, Jom. You know that, don't you.'

'Big trouble!' laughs Jom.

'Your father was in the Russian army, right?'

'Only by accident. He was a Pole. They conscripted them.'

74

'I've got Vassily Tchancov coming in tomorrow. He was in the army, an officer in the first Chechen war.'

'So?'

'I'll bring in some cheesecake. Share some slices with him and chew the fat. Have a little dig around.'

'What do you want, Staffe? Exactly?'

'To find out just how bad a bastard he is.'

'That first Chechen war is a good place to start.'

Eight

Sylvie is on the chaise longue at Queen's Terrace, a nest of newspapers and sketches all around her. 'Stranger,' she says, seeing Staffe come in.

Pulford is in the armchair, a copy of *The News* and cans and a pizza box at his feet. He must see Staffe's lip curl, because he gets up and gathers the detritus. 'Sorry about this,' he says.

Staffe sits at Sylvie's feet and rubs her calves. She nestles, deeper, lifts her legs onto his lap and Staffe takes Elena's letters from his pocket – re-reading the second one as Pulford scuttles out of the room. He loosens his tie, says to Sylvie, 'What do you make of this?' He hands her a lilac letter. 'Just these lines.' He taps the paper.

'*I feel so low and miss not seeing you. I feel like a prisoner up here and don't know how much longer I could have done this . . .*'

As Sylvie reads aloud, he closes his eyes and drinks her voice, like a *digestif*. But she falters and when he opens his eyes, her face has turned sad. Her eyebrows pinch together.

'She knew an end was coming,' she says.

'Really?' Staffe knew he had missed a nuance,

76

first time round. He wonders what else might have stared him in the face, only to be missed.

Sylvie says, '. . . *could have done this* . . .'

'It might just be that she's going to have the baby?' says Staffe.

'She doesn't mention a baby,' says Sylvie, 'and this is a letter to her boyfriend, right?'

'What does that mean?'

'It means, she didn't know about the baby when she wrote the letter . . .'

'In which case she is giving up on something else.'

'. . . Or, she knew about the baby and had decided she wasn't going to have it,' says Sylvie.

Staffe sighs.

'Is it getting to you?' Sylvie runs her fingers through his hair. 'Lovely paper, though.'

Staffe recalls the lilac correspondence on Tchancov's secretaire, puts the letter away and his fingers linger on the box in his jacket pocket. If Pulford wasn't the other side of the wall, he might offer the ring up. He looks into her emerald eyes and can't remember the last time he read a book, had an early night, woke up fresh as a daisy. He stretches out, flat, between her legs, his head resting on her tummy.

Sylvie reaches for the TV remote and flicks through the channels, finally resting on *University Challenge*. Staffe can't see the screen but he surrenders to the cadence of questions and answers, the starters and bonuses. He says, in a low voice, 'You never talk about your university days. I bet you had a ball.'

'You mean boyfriends? Well you didn't go short.' She pokes him on the shoulder. 'I know that for sure.'

'You can tell me,' he says.

'I only had one, really.'

Staffe tries to remember if they have had this conversation before.

She says, 'I was a bit of a mess back then, what with my mum and everything.'

He is jealous, that she had only one. And before he can help himself, he has said it. The idiot. 'Is that where you met Ollie?'

'Ollie?'

'From the Randolph.'

'Don't be an idiot, Will.'

Rebeccah slides out of bed and feels the nip of the evening, cold as mountain water. She has slept too long, after a midnight-'til-six shift in Omega. She throws on Mitch's parka, the fur of the hood warm on her face, and she goes through his pockets. It's her money, for God's sake, but once she hands it across, it's his: 'to see the both of us right, and save you from yourself'.

But she's already planning to save herself and

tomorrow is her secret day. Her once a week. Like Elena says, it's *her* money, and she dares anticipate that one day soon she will be more like Elena. Her plans are grand, for sure.

She feeds a pound coin to the meter, and switches on the immersion, then boils a kettle for good measure. While she waits for the water to heat, Becx goes into the bathroom and pulls up the sealant strip, hooks her fingers round the bath panel and tugs it away. She reaches in for the plastic bag, having to get her head right in. The damp clags her nose.

Cross-legged on the floor, she empties the contents of the bag into her lap. She has £4,280 in the Post Office book with another hundred from Frank tomorrow and some interest to be tagged on. It's not enough. She doesn't just want a beach and a few spliffs a day; her designs are on a brand-new business and she reckons she can do it for ten grand. Clippers and brushes and a crisp white uniform with royal blue piping and a little car. And some working capital – that's what Elena said, and Arra too – 'til the pet grooming trade picks up.

She unfolds the certificate, reads that she, Rebeccah Stone, is fit to groom domestic animals. It makes her fizz with pride.

When Rebeccah told Elena what she was planning, Elena had gone all serious. Her eyes crinkled up and her lips went thin and she said, 'We'll see what we can do. There's a chance things might change for me. They could change for you too, Rebeccah.' 'Re-Beck-Caah', she called her. It made Becx sound like a movie star. It's the way her name was meant to sound, but somehow nobody saw it. Apart from Elena.

Which is why she has resisted all temptations to take a peek into the envelope Elena asked her to keep secret for her. It is marked *PRIVAT*, in Elena's long and beautiful hand. Rebeccah aches with curiosity to see what is inside the A4 manilla envelope. But she won't. Not so far.

She wonders how Elena's getting on up at her secret sea. She wouldn't tell anyone where it was, but Rebeccah begged and begged to go with her and when Elena must have tired of saying 'No', they went there together. Elena told Rebeccah about the elements. They sat on the beach holding hands, listening to the force of the moon and the water, making tides. 'Close your eyes, Rebeccah,' Elena had said. 'We are only what we see of ourselves in the dark.'

Rebeccah closes her eyes now and pictures herself the way she will be for Frank, tomorrow, in his old Bentley out in Epping Forest. Afterwards, Frank will take her to the Drunken Duck, near Shoeburyness, where nobody knows him. And he will watch her eat, say how much he loves her, but not so much that when he tips her the wink and he drops his pudding spoon, she doesn't have to shift up her dress and ease her thighs apart. His treat for the bill, he calls it. The Duck's bill, and she will laugh along with him. She wonders whether, if she closes her eyes when he slips down for his gander, it will make her feel better about herself.

The kettle begins to whistle and she runs her bath then gathers her secrets together. The Post Office book and the hand-drawn designs of her calling cards for the pet-grooming business and the name of an estate agent in Estepona. Finally, the *PRIVAT* envelope she is keeping for Elena. Rebeccah is the only person in the whole world Elena could trust with this. Even Bobo. It makes her want to sing and she returns the kept secret, just so.

The water running onto the enamel by her ears sounds like the sea in a shell. Like childhood. It'll be warm, come March, on the Costa, she thinks, returning her trove to its secret place.

Rebeccah takes her phone out and dials Elena's number, picturing her by the sea. She's got a new name to test on Elena. She likes Tender Petting, but the phone rings and rings and she is just about to hang up, wondering why it doesn't switch to message, when Elena picks up.

'Hi Lena,' says Rebeccah, upbeat and sitting on

the edge of the bath. 'What do you think about Tender Petting? Subtle, innit? And it says I'll look after them. What do you think? Really.' The phone crackles and Rebeccah looks at the screen to make sure she's got Elena. 'Lena? It's me.'

'Who's me?'

'Who's that? Lena, is that you?'

The phone goes quiet, then says, 'Rebeccah?'

Whoever it is says her name wrong. Her heart judders. Blood rushes to her head and she feels weak.

'Don't hang up, Rebeccah. Elena is gone.'

'Gone?'

The silence stretches.

'She's dead, Rebeccah. We need to speak to you. Please don't hang up. We can help . . .'

Rebeccah acts on instinct, struggling for breath, pressing red.

Josie stares at the gold handset, sees Rebeccah Call Ended. She scribbles down the number and turns off the interference track on her field recorder. If only Rebeccah had called when she had been at the station, they could have triangulated and got a fix on where the incoming call had been made. Nonetheless, the name and number tally to her data sheet. Rebeccah is an illegitimate, pay-as-you-go SIM.

Josie calls the technicians, feeds them the number, says she'll hang on while they get into the network. It is dark out and the snow glows, neon orange in the street's lights. It is a night to sit by a fire with a lover and a glass and conversations that reach for a better life. But it seems such things are sliding away.

She could go out to the Butcher's Hook and join coppers' corner, laughing and joking about the cases, flirting and winding up. But lately, it is not what she wants. Looking back into the hot summer, she thinks about the fling with Pulford and was she right to finish it. At least they are friends, still. And as for Staffe . . .

The technician comes back on the phone, says, 'Too late, Josie darling.'

'Cheers, Conor. Let's hope the next one calls when I'm at the station.'

'You going down the Butcher's?'

'Got to go.' She hangs up and calls Staffe to let him know about the call from the youngish woman called Rebeccah with her Bow Bells twang and her talk of Tender Petting. But the ether is a vacuum. Staffe's phone rings and rings and rings and when she clicks off, her flat is deathly quiet.

Darius chops out lines for them all. Six thin ones from a bag he was going to mix down and sell off, later at the Conti in Borough. But needs must.

Arabella and Rebeccah are on the sofa and thank God Mitch isn't in. The girls have been crying and talking about Elena and crying and drinking and talking about Elena, but without really talking about Elena, just trying not to be afraid.

He does his lines and calls the girls over, swigs from the Absolut and lights up a joint, sits himself down in the corner and tries to work out why he hasn't cried, reckons it must be a mechanism to protect Arra.

Arra looks up at him from doing her lines. She seems absolutely lost and he knows it is time to get her back to the fold.

'Poor Arra,' he thinks. She and Becx haven't got a prayer: the blind leading the blind and now the one-eyed queen is dead. What the hell will they do? He takes an almighty draw and wonders if he'll ever really know exactly what Elena was playing at.

'What you thinking?' asks Arra.

Darius gives her a hurtful smile. She ought to know he hates that question.

Becx says, 'I can't believe she's not going to just come in and tell me what she's been tricking. She'd have a bottle, wouldn't she, Arra? And a little something. She always had a little something.'

'A little something to get her into trouble,' says Darius.

'And what would you know?' says Arra, wrapping an arm around Becx.

'A lot less than you,' says Darius. 'Three fucking witches.' He laughs, isn't proud of himself. Something outside of his body tells him they should be making a better fist of mourning Elena.

'I've got to get away,' says Becx.

'Sshh,' says Arra. 'Don't talk like that. Not now.'

'The Great Escape,' says Darius.

Arra takes the joint off him.

'Didn't your father and Elena . . .?' says Becx, taking the joint off Arabella. She staggers back, steadies herself on the table. 'I forget how we all met.'

'Don't you have to phone in, Becx?' says Darius.

'Reb-beck-cah. That's how she said me. Loved that. She was the only one knew how to say me.'

'You should call,' says Darius.

'Leave her alone,' says Arra.

'And now they've killed her,' says Becx.

'You don't know how she died, or why,' says Darius.

'We know fuck all, that's for sure,' says Arabella. 'They won't come bothering us, will they, Darry?'

'You should go see your father.'

'I should call Vassily,' says Becx. 'Let him know. Bastard!'

Darius pulls Arabella onto his knee and she kisses

him hard, lets him put his hand up her skirt, doesn't know that all the time his mind is racing, trying to map what is best for him. And doing the same for her, hoping Becx can look out for herself.

Nine

Staffe slams the Peugeot's door and the engine ticks in the morning dark as it cools.

'Where are we?' asks Josie, bleary-eyed and sipping from her Thermos mug of coffee.

'This is the humble abode of Taki Markary.' Staffe presses Markary's videocom. Quickly, the Turk's voice emerges from the shiny grille. 'What the hell are you doing here?'

Staffe looks into the camera. 'I would like you to come with me, to identify the body of Elena Danya.'

'This is ridiculous.'

'You were her landlord.'

'You can't just turn up here.'

'And the father of her unborn child. If only . . .'

The videocom shuts down and the camera clicks off. Staffe smiles at Josie. 'I think he's coming.' Staffe rubs his hands together. Josie is pale as snow and staring into space, possibly fearing for her inspector.

Vassily Tchancov is in holding room two with Jombaugh who has been regaling the Russian with tales of his father's war, serving in the RAF having escaped a prisoner-of-war camp in Finland.

Staffe leaves Markary with Josie in holding room one and taps on room two, enters, holding a baked cheesecake. Tchancov has responded with an account of his great-uncles from the Ukraine who were saved by the English; they would have been court-martialled as deserters had they returned home to their families. Now, they toast England and Churchill. As Staffe serves up the cheesecake, Jombaugh reminds Tchancov the Ukraine was once part of the kingdom of Poland.

'But I am Russian,' Tchancov says, pushing out his sparrow chest. 'And I have served my country in the first Chechen war.'

Jombaugh says, feigning sadness, 'I am the lost generation. Never to serve. Born too late.'

Tchancov talks about the treacherous Chechens and Staffe watches Jom bite his tongue, knowing what he does of how Vassily Tchancov made his money – using his cousin's business to create false bearer certificates. He made a fortune, but it became impossible for him to be allowed to stay. Even in Russia, it seems, slates have to be wiped. Between the lines, Vassily is exiled permanently, war hero or not, and with debts to honour.

Jombaugh stands, makes to leave. Tchancov offers his hand and Jombaugh takes it, saying something their fathers and uncles would have understood.

Once Jombaugh is gone, Tchancov says, 'Nice fellow. Pity about the uniform.'

'We're a necessary evil,' says Staffe, sitting down. 'Shame on those who make us necessary.'

'Send them to Stalin,' laughs Tchancov. 'Now, when are we going to see this body? I have businesses to run.'

'We'll go across soon.' Staffe's phone vibrates and he reads the text, from Josie, says, 'I have to leave you for a few minutes. Is there anything you want?'

'Some more cheesecake, perhaps?' Tchancov presents his words as if he hasn't a care in the world, but Staffe sees in the flit of his eyes that all is not well. Vassily cannot afford for his London life to bubble over into a wider domain, to appear on radars in Moscow.

Staffe makes his way to the observation room, a glorified cubby-hole with a television monitor and a desk. He leans forward, watches Vassily Tchancov. A hiss of white noise comes through the speaker.

The door opens and Josie squeezes in next to Staffe. She says, 'Markary's being taken in.'

Vassily Tchancov recrosses his legs, picks at his fingernails. Jombaugh comes into the holding room, followed by another man, immaculately dressed with a Crombie draped on his shoulders. Jombaugh sweeps an arm in the direction of the unoccupied seat. As Markary sits down, Tchancov double-takes. Markary clocks his cohabitant and his mouth drops open. Jombaugh leaves them to it.

The two men regard each other, say nothing.

'Christ, it's like, who's the first to blink,' says Josie.

Tchancov leans back in his chair and Markary wrings his hands, eventually says, 'You here about the girl?'

'Not my girl,' says Tchancov.

'Are you something to do with this, Tchancov?'

He shakes his head. 'Why would I be?'

'You should pray you're not.'

'That's not so friendly, my friend.'

Markary stands up and as he advances, Tchancov uncrosses his legs and glances up into the camera, makes the faintest smile. Markary grabs him by the lapels and shouts, 'I find out this is anything to do with you, you Russian prick, God help me.' Tchancov spreads his arms wide, as if to advertise the fact that he is being sinned against. Markary obscures the Russian, appears to whisper something in his ear.

Then Markary doubles down, letting go of Tchancov and reaching for his nethers. A strangled curse emerges from the speaker and Tchancov stands, still holding Markary by the balls and whispering something back into the Turk's ear, Markary's Crombie unfurling to the ground.

The Russian walks to the door and pounds it twice. When Jombaugh opens it, Tchancov goes into a blindspot from the camera and says to the sergeant, 'I think this was not wise. This man', he jabs towards Markary, pausing for effect, 'can identify his tart.' He steps back out and looks up into camera. 'You have no measure of me, Inspector.'

With Markary slumped back in his chair, gulping for air, Staffe steps quickly out of the observation room and hurries along the corridor, intercepts Tchancov as he reaches Jombaugh's desk in reception.

'I didn't know you and Taki had an association.'

Tchancov narrows his Gulag eyes and brushes his suit smooth. 'Be careful not to judge appearances.'

'Where is Elena from?'

'I don't know,' says Tchancov.

'She worked for you when she first came over. With Bobo?'

'Elena isn't what you think. She isn't what I think.' He laughs.

'And what do you think?'

'I think she's a very clever girl.'

Staffe says, 'Her mother should be told. Don't you think?'

'Families can be strange. It is a shame.'

'It's a shame when families drive each other away, when people are forced out of their country.'

Tchancov frowns, but before he can reply, a door opens heavily down the corridor and a uniformed sergeant leads out Bobo Bogdanovich.

'Surely, Bobo knows where Elena is from,' says Staffe. 'But for some reason, he won't say. Why do you think that is, *Mister* Tchancov?'

'Are you charging him?'

'Would it be your business if we were?' Staffe turns to Bobo, eyes bloodshot as beetroot.

The sergeant ushers Staffe and whispers, 'Not a sausage.'

Staffe approaches Bobo, smells the pungent breath of sorrow from his mucous mouth, and whispers, 'Elena's mother should be told. This is just a case of being a decent human being.'

Bobo looks towards Tchancov and shakes his head, slow. You can practically hear his heart sigh.

Staffe snaps, 'I will need to know where each of you was between four and six o'clock on the seventh of December. Sergeant, take the statements, get them typed up and hold them until they're both signed.'

Tchancov reaches into his jacket and produces a receipt for lunch at the Fat Duck. It is timed at 5.15 p.m. 'As you will know, Inspector, this is an hour from the City – minimum. I have three companions plus the staff. And we shared a *digestif* with the proprietor afterwards.'

Almost too good to be true, thinks Staffe, returning to the holding room, where Markary stares into infinity.

'I really don't know where to start, Taki. I had no idea you and Vassily were so intimate.' He picks up Markary's Crombie from the floor, dusts down the shoulders. He sees a hair on the lapel, holds it between the pads of forefinger and thumb. He drapes the coat across Markary's lap and takes a piece of paper from his pocket. Folds it over and again, with Taki Markary's hair trapped inside it.

Markary runs a finger along the perfect stitching of his coat, says, most deliberately, 'I wouldn't distract yourself by reading any significance into what you saw. Are you going to upset everybody Elena knew, rather than get down to the business of finding her killer?'

Staffe pulls up a chair, sits right up to Markary. 'You set her up in that fancy pad of yours and, believe me, Markary, if you don't tell me why you called Elena Danya on the seventh of December, I'll drive straight round to your wife and ask her.'

'You enter my home without a warrant and I'll have you suspended.'

Staffe considers the nature of this threat. To be calmly told that you will be suspended from duty sends a chill to the bone. He wants to ask Markary who he knows so far up the police food chain. But he schools himself that it is better to say nothing. 'You sent her to the Thamesbank, didn't you?' He leans forward. 'She was leaving you, wasn't she.'

'You're in the dark.'

'I know about her plans.'

Markary's eyes widen and he looks away, wrings his hands. 'I had nothing to do with this terrible thing.'

'You had everything to do with it, Taki. Your mask is slipping, sir.'

Markary laughs. 'You're an unusual man, Inspector. I hear you don't need *this* work. You should opt for an easier life.'

'She said she couldn't do it any more. Do what, precisely?'

'You tell me.'

'Carry your baby? Sell herself? Or is there something we don't know?'

'Charge me, or release me, Inspector. You have nothing.'

Staffe shows Markary out, watches the Turk reinstate the Crombie to his shoulders; his back straight, his head tall.

94

Jombaugh shakes his head, says 'Christ, that's one nasty piece of work.'

'Tchancov?' says Staffe.

'He was an officer in the first Chechen war, running things the *Russian way*. He actually said "the Russian way", as if I'd respect him for it.'

'You didn't disillusion him?'

Jombaugh's voice goes down a pitch, quieter too. He shifts forward in his seat and Staffe notices that his fists have clenched. 'He didn't tell me exactly what the scam was, but he was running something.'

'Like what?'

'Extorting wages from his soldiers. Maybe worse. You hear things that would make your blood freeze.' Jombaugh squares right up to Staffe. 'He could kill that Danya girl. Like treading on an ant.'

Staffe takes out the folded paper from his pocket, writes on it, 'TM hair re Thamesbank'. 'Get this to Janine, will you, Jom.'

Ten

The sun is low to the horizon and the morning mist lies above the fields, which are dusted with snow.

'There's something odd about this, sir,' says Pulford, reading through the list of the contents of Elena Danya's case. He reads it out, under his breath. 'Jeans, lumber shirt, jumper, hat, a Jane Austen novel and a notebook. Underwear and a toothbrush. No make-up or hairdryer. No perfume or hair straighteners. You don't think she was doing a runner, do you, sir?'

Staffe watches England go by. When you are in the city, it is easy to forget that this is all on your doorstep, just an hour or so away. He thinks about Markary and his buried emotions. Perhaps he truly loved the real Elena that she packed away for her trip to the sea.

The train slows and the tendrils of a Suffolk village come into view. Red-bricked Georgian and Victorian houses, a small grid of Edwardian semis laid out like a picnic blanket of tree-lined streets. A lodge with a steep sloping roof, and far away, tall silver birch trees poke at the endless, cream sky, cloudless all the way to the Baltic, it seems.

'They're building some stuff here, sir.'

Staffe looks out of the other window. A different scene altogether. As far as you can see, scaffolding and mini-towers of Portakabins. Blockwork skeletons of houses are scattered to the horizon. A twenty-metre advertising hoarding welcomes you to *Aldesworth Country Town. A New Model Market Town for Modern Living.*

As they pull into the station, the old High Street is only two lines of buildings with a spire church and pastel-painted Tudor shops, an old court house and a half-timbered *Spar* minimarket, all higgle-piggled together, then the fields start again, all the way to the sea.

'This is us,' says Staffe, standing. 'Taxi or bus?'

'What would she have done?' says Pulford.

'Taxi,' says Staffe, pleased his sergeant sees the point of following Elena's footprints to the sand.

All the way, the taxi driver chit-chats about the new model market town. *Gerald Holt*, says the signage on his dash. 'We all thought, that's going to be a shot in the arm for us, what with all the jobs it'll create. Good for the youngsters learning a trade. But the place fills up with jam rolls doing all the labouring and now we find out they're putting up a bloody Waitrose. Progress? I don't know what to think.'

Pulford says, 'Communities need to evolve slowly. It takes history.'

The taxi driver slows down, turns to look at Pulford and says, peering over his glasses, 'You might be right, son. The Signet. That's a lovely place. You been before?'

'No. We're meeting a friend,' says Staffe. 'His friend,' says Staffe, jabbing a thumb in the direction of Pulford. 'She's called Elena. You might have given her a lift, some time. She's beautiful. You'd remember her.'

'A local girl?'

'She's Russian.'

'Aaah. They're pretty them Eastern girls, that's for sure. I do give one of them a run every now and then. Lovely girl. She stays at the Signet, funny enough.'

'Maybe it is Elena?' says Pulford.

'I hope not,' says the cabbie.

'Why's that?'

The cabbie cocks his head, fixes Pulford in his rear view and weighs him up. 'Not sure I should say.'

'She with another fella?' laughs Staffe.

Gerald Holt keeps quiet.

They pull up outside the Signet and Staffe nudges Pulford to get the bags. Once he is out of earshot, Staffe leans forward, proffers a twenty and holds on to it as Gerald Holt tries to take it from him. 'He knows, about the older fella. It is an older fella, isn't it. Foreign?'

The cabbie nods, says, 'Bloody loaded he is. Always gives me thirty.'

Staffe takes another ten from his wallet, hands it to the driver. 'Is she always with him? The fellow in the Crombie.'

'Not lately. She's up here once a month, maybe.' Gerald rubs his chin. 'Crombie. You're right.'

'And how long has she been coming here?'

'You going to freshen him up?'

Staffe shakes his head. 'It's all been sorted. It's not exactly what you'd think.'

'Well over a year, to my knowledge. Not seen him for a while.'

'Have you got a card?'

'Sure,' says the cabbie. 'And ask for room fourteen. Trust me.'

They are checked in by an old boy in a waistoat and stiff, buttoned collar; black tie. He has got the heating turned up so high against the winter cold that he sweats with every movement and, despite Staffe's protestations, he carries both their overnight bags up the stairs. They drop off at Pulford's room first, then go to 14. Fourteen, the number of her apartment in Livery Buildings and – according to the old boy when he trousered a tenner – the finest room in the hotel. 'You don't get given it unless you ask. And you got to be in the know to ask.' He put a finger to his lips when he had said it.

Staffe puts the big old key to the lock. The oak door is thick and heavy, creaking as Staffe stoops under the low lintel. Once inside, it is everything you would ever want.

The floor gives out theatre croaks as Staffe treads gingerly across the threadbare Persian rug to one of two leaded picture windows. Outside, the beach is empty, the sea and sky a seamless pale, metallic blue; milk wisps here and there. The seagulls swoop and rise like Lowrys. He closes his eyes to the surf and squawk; smells the wood and cloth and ozone. He imagines opening his eyes to see Elena Danya on the window seat in her lumber shirt and her hair in a careless clasp; pale eyes unfocused on the vague horizon and knees drawn up to her chin; book downturned and open, a new chapter but not wanting her story to end.

He sits on the three-seater William IV settee at the bottom of the squat bed that is swamped in eiderdown, looks around the room and is swept back through centuries. He pictures a Jane Austen novel unravelling in Elena's head as she drifts to another world, somewhere unreal between the one she left and the one she came to, and he tries to imagine precisely how she came to visit here with Taki Markary, eventually coming of her own accord.

Staffe calls room service, orders broth and a ham sandwich and sets his field recorder to *Rec* then *Pause*. He heads straight downstairs, knowing the old boy will be in the kitchen. It's the kind of meal he'll rustle himself but to be on the safe side, Staffe waits around the corner from the reception desk in the musty lounge, head tilted to a copy of *Suffolk Life*, waiting for the old boy to head upstairs with his order. He'll have four minutes, maximum, to go through the register.

As he waits, he skims through the *Life*, not really reading it properly until he lands on an article about the Aldesworth Country Town new model market town. Gerald Holt smiles into camera with a comment below applauding the development. On the opposite page, the mayor, in full chain of office and holding a silver shovel, shakes the hand of a fellow called Leonard Howerd in a chalk-striped suit. Howerd, according to the caption, is a prominent Catholic and well in with the Duke of Suffolk. His local family seat, The Ridings, has been in the family for centuries. Staffe recalls, dusting off some distant titbit, that the Dukes – the Audley Howards – descend from Mary Tudor.

As he checks the date of the magazine, which is

last June, the old boy totters past reception holding a silver tray out in front of him and Staffe strolls casually behind reception.

He flicks through the register, skimming the left-hand column and looking for room 14, whispering the date of each of Danya's visits into his recorder. Markary appears in June this year and from then, back to the previous Christmas, he came each month. Staffe hears the squeak of the door at the bottom of the stairs swinging open and shut, but still he quickly leafs back. He thinks he sees a name he recognises, but realises it is simply the banker from the *Life* article. Howerd. Room 14, also. He must be in the know. He scrolls down again, sees Markary on the same date but in a different room. 'Twenty-three,' he whispers into the recorder. 'Fifteenth of March 2008. One night.'

'What are you doing?'

Staffe's heart stops for a beat, two beats, then races to catch up. He formulates an excuse, but when he raises his head, it is Pulford. With a scold of the eyes, he closes the register and scoots around the desk.

Rebeccah looks down at Frank, through her hair that has come loose. His eyes are almost closed, eyeballs rolling up. He bites the corner of his lip.

'Did you hear that?'

'I want to go into you, Becca,' says Frank.

'We've got all afternoon.' She leans down, to kiss him on the mouth. She knows that she has him – any time she wants. But this is the game. This is why he comes to her. She can cusp him for an hour, make him feel like a man. Rebeccah cranes her head, looks out of the car, all around, into the spruce trees that surround them. They could be adorned with tinsel, strung lights whispering from their ferns. A memory from long ago pinches her cheek. A good fairy, or a bad uncle?

'There's someone watching,' she says.

This would be no surprise, were they here four or five hours hence. But the dogging lovers don't come until it is well and truly dark. 'We're alone,' says Frank. He puts the palm of his hand on the underside of her breast, lifts it, as if for weight, and sucks at her.

Rebeccah continues to look out the window, scanning the perimeter of the clearing in the wood. She tries not to appear perturbed, but thinks Mitch might suspect she is up to something. He is quite capable of telling Tchancov about her 'foreigners'. Her debt to Tchancov is down to four grand but whatever she earns lately seems swallowed whole by the interest.

Something moves in the undergrowth: crouched and fast. She shudders.

'You like that?' says Frank.

'I feel it *inside*.' She looks down at him, suddenly not wanting to be here one little bit.

Sometimes Frank can look quite dishy, but in this light, his skin is grey with wide pores and a fag-tar, greasy sheen. Meat on his breath.

'You hot and bothered?' Rebeccah reaches round with her hand and, through his boxers, puts her fingers between his cheeks. His eyes close and his smile goes serious, she feels him stiffen. She cranes her neck again and sees a man, in the second length of grass where the trees get thicker. He's not playing with himself – just watching.

'Put me in. Put me in!' pleads Frank, losing it.

Rebeccah takes her hand away from his bottom and slides down into the footwell in the back of Frank's Bentley. She rests her chin on his rubbery dick. His piece is clean and she can barely smell him, just the rich leather of the old Bentley's heated seats. Outside, a dog yaps. Rebeccah looks up at Frank. 'Imagine, when we go away. It'll be soon, won't it?'

'When I can sell the business.'

'It's been a long time. You last the longest time, hey babes?' She runs her tongue down and up, along the shaft of his dick.

He grunts.

'I love you, Frank.'

'You just say that, Becca,' he gasps. His eyes are out of control.

'You're the only one gets me like this, like I want it to go forever. Be forever.'

'Don't talk about them.'

'Who?'

'The others.'

'I didn't say nothing about no others.'

Frank sits up, earnest. 'It's the *implication*. You should stop.'

'I will, Frank. When we go away.'

'Stop! Then we'll go away.'

She looks down, sees he has shrunk and she puts her fingers on him, looks him dead in the eye as she takes her mouth to him, wrapping her lips around her teeth.

'You're behaving like a whore.'

Suddenly, she doesn't know what to say. Should she say she wants him inside her? Or all to herself? Or to just give her all his money and fuck off. Or . . . 'I just want you, Frank. Just you.'

'Stop those *implications*. I told you once!' He pushes her away with the ball of his foot and she rocks back against the Bentley's door. Frank sits forward, head in his hands. 'Get out.'

'We're going for dinner. We always go for dinner.'

'Not any more.'

'Let me have you, Frank.' She reaches out, delves for his dick but he slaps her hand away.

'This was the last time and even that's gone tits up.'

'The last time?' she says.

He looks as if he might equally laugh or cry. 'You know, I really did love you, Becca. What kind of a prick does that make me?' He suddenly seems calm, as if a fog has lifted, a clue is fathomed.

'What about . . .' She begins to sob, realising he is serious. She gathers her clothes together, not daring to look him in the eye. 'What about . . .?'

'I'm not paying today. Now get out of my car!'

Rebeccah has been in the game long enough to trust her instincts, so she stifles her tears and gathers her clothes. Outside, the cold is fit to freeze. The ground is rough. She scurries to the trees as best she can, like trying to run on burning hot sand. At the trees, she quickly steps into her pants. Frank's car hasn't fired up yet. Perhaps he is changing his mind.

She pulls on her top. Frank bought it for her. It is cashmere, lemon, and as it comes over her head, it reminds her of summer – that yellow light when you close your eyes, tight, to the sun. She feels it now and doesn't want this life any more. A hand is on her.

Rebeccah screams, but it seems to be lost in the

cashmere and now a hand is over her mouth and her scream ruptures inside.

Then she hears it.

Before she feels anything – and through the sound of her own breathing and his grunting and the rustle of her top against her hair – she hears the wet, impossibly loud and flesh-metal slurp coming from her own body. It is her side, she thinks, then the pain snipes, long and thin. Then the sound again, this time in her back, she thinks. And a wider pain, less sharp. Spreading.

And the sound. Again. Again. She falls to the ground, away from herself and the lemon sun slips and the forest is white. The ground is sharp on her face. Far away, a dog yaps.

And there is nothing.

Eleven

The sun disappears to Staffe's right, behind the sands, tufted with dunes. Staffe's lungs begin to burn. He is close to the sea, where the sand is wet and firm, but it still makes his leg muscles weep. He has come a mile or so south, towards Warblingsea and in the distance he can see the masts sticking up from the harbour. Beyond, the lights twinkle in the Lord Nelson, on the other side of the reeded estuary.

It will be completely dark soon and the clouds have come in, obscuring the moon. It is not yet five but he turns himself round and begins the run back. As he does, he thinks he sees somebody dive to ground at the top of the beach where the dunes run out.

He stops, squints into the gloam. The final strip of purple sky burns to nothing and he walks up the beach to check if his eyes were deceiving him.

Nobody is up in the dunes. Staffe has the beach to himself and even the seagulls have stopped squawking. He is cold now and begins to run again but the dry sand drags him down and he runs back to the sea, checking over his shoulder as he gains speed. The sea air saps him and hunger advances.

* * *

There is a thin smattering of diners in the Signet's restaurant, which is white linen and silver service; a sweet trolley and a Jacobean sideboard for the cutlery. The floorboards groan and the china chinks whenever the waitress passes by.

A couple in their thirties are awkward around each other. The male tries to order for both of them, but he is uncertain, failing to catch the waitress's eye. A salesman studiously avoids contact of any kind, squirrelling an off-piste treat for himself. A lean man comes into the room, sits on his own, as far away from the others as he can. He looks fit. His face is ruddy, as though he has been exposed to the elements. He seems sure of himself.

Laying the napkin on his lap, Pulford sips from his water, says, 'All those bookings, for her and Markary. It gives you the sense of a real relationship. Markary couldn't have killed her. Surely.'

Staffe downs the last of his pint of Adnams Broadside.

'We didn't come here to eliminate Markary, though, did we sir? You've got it in for him, haven't you.'

'I'm going to have oysters. How about you?'

'The prawn cocktail. Then the grilled prawns. I love prawns.'

Staffe raises his eyebrows. 'The oysters are natives.' Pulford shudders at the thought and Staffe pours them each a glass of the Mercurey. 'I think we should give the ball a kick tonight, Sergeant. This is my treat.'

The service is slow and they drink the first bottle before the starters arrive. Staffe orders another, which they drink before pudding. When he suggests a half-bottle of Sauternes, Pulford grimaces on the first sip, says it's sickly sweet, which makes Staffe laugh. He says, 'And you're the one supposed to have the education.'

'Where exactly do you think I am from, sir?'

'Just missed a first in history and politics from Durham. You captained the first XV at your public school. God knows why you wanted to join the police.'

'There was no silver spoon.' Pulford looks serious. His eyes are glassy, his mouth slack.

'You should make more of an effort to get on with people.'

'Like you?'

'You'll have a glittering career if you play the game right. You want to play the game, don't you?'

'I'll be true to myself, if that's all right, sir.'

Staffe leans back, puts the fork and spoon across the remains of his lemon tart. 'There's better careers, surely.'

Pulford sips at the pudding wine and says, 'When I was eleven, I was happy, just me and my mum.

My dad had run off with her sister. My mother poured her whole life into me. She fought and fought for me to take this entrance examination and I walked it. That's how I got into that school. My uncle took us, the first term, and I had all my stuff in an Adidas bag and a rucksack. The other boys had trunks with their initials on.

'When she had to leave me, my mum cried buckets and my uncle took me to one side and clipped me, said, "You dare show her you're upset."' Pulford swallows, takes a moment. 'She wasn't crying because she was upset and she'd be going back to an empty house and have no one at all in the whole fucking world . . . She was proud.'

Staffe says, 'I can be a prick sometimes.'

'That night, I had her lipstick on my cheek. I shared with three other boys and that night, they got me. Took a limb each and stretched me out, then an older boy came in. He had rugby boots on. He made a right mess of me. They had to call an ambulance.

'A policeman came to the hospital; I can remember him now. DS Cropper, he was called, and he held my hand like my dad never had and he said I could press charges if I liked but these boys had a story and would probably get off and I'd have to do my time at the school or leave. Then he leaned right up to me. His voice was so soft. He said, "You can get these bastards if you're clever." And one by one, I waited for them to step out of line. I grew big, fast. I made my own friends, the hard way.'

He finishes his glass of pudding wine down in one and fills himself back up. A smile implies itself.

'What happened to the boys?'

'DS Cropper said to me, "People do you wrong, you sit on the bank of the river; wait for the bodies to come floating by." So I did, and they did. One of the bastards got into class B drugs; one used to get drink and sell it to the other boys. The older boy who kicked the hell out of me was demanding money with menaces.'

'And you let Cropper know?' Staffe wonders how he could work with someone and not know these things.

'Wednesday afternoons we went into town. It was Cropper's jurisdiction.'

'You got them all?'

'Three out of four.'

'Expelled?'

Pulford nods.

'And the fourth?'

'He's my best mate, still. He was there the other day, when you caught me, playing poker. And that's the beauty of it. Things are never what they seem. There's no simple justice. My mate, they used to beat him up every night – 'til I arrived.'

'You never know,' says Staffe, looking away, catching the lean man with the ruddy face watching them.

Graham Blears reaches for his dog's lead. It is on the bow-fronted cabinet his mother bequeathed him. The moment he raises his hand to reach for the lead, Useless begins to yap, jumping up and down on her hind legs. It is only three hours since they were last out and little does Useless know that Graham gets so much more out of these excursions than she does. For her, it is merely exercise. Important, that he takes full advantage of this day off work.

He checks his watch and pulls open the bureau, takes a Durex from the secret drawer and pops it in his pocket. Graham looks in the mirror and ruffles his sandy hair up. For work, he dampens it down, defines the parting the way a mother would.

It beggars belief how he can ghost through life, so unnoticed. A weaker man might think himself unappreciated, but on balance, the view the world takes of him suits Graham Blears just fine. He knows how to make his marks. He's man enough, for sure.

As he walks to the front door, he feels a weakness in his knees, pockets of air in his lower stomach. Oh, the anticipation!

Outside, the snow is clearing. It will be the longest night soon and the hippies will come to the forest with their cheap cider and their fires and their makeshift Druid priests. But not tonight. Tonight is for normal people.

Graham's pulse quickens as he and Useless leave the High Street behind them. Within ten minutes they are through the kissing gate and into the Forest. The slow rumble of cars deepens the further he goes along the track, their lights are dimmed and the remnants of snow give off a yellow fluorescence. He stops to clip the latex muzzle on Useless. She yaps, doesn't like it, but she is trained not to stray.

'Stay here, Yooce,' whispers Graham. He has picked out the Mondeo on the edge of a group of four cars. The rear courtesy light is on and he sees the busy outline of a familiar woman. He stiffens, feels so, so weak in the knees as the blood rushes to his heart, all around his body. Even in this cold, his fingers tremble. If he was to say anything – which he never has – his voice would quake.

Useless goes into the trees, scratches at the leaf mulch in the patches where the snow has faded completely.

As he reaches the cars, Graham Blears can hear the muffled coaxing and moaning of people going about their business. On the far side, a man stands outside a Renault Mégane, by an opened window, busying himself, arching down to see inside. The Mondeo's rear window glides down and the middle-aged woman recognises him. 'Same?' she says, softly.

Graham nods.

'You all right?' she says to the man alongside her.

Graham watches as the man puts his large, rough hands inside her blouse. She leans on the open window, her head half in the car, half out and she shifts herself so her backside juts at her ready companion who is now up on his knees. Graham peers around her head, to get a proper look as the kneeling man pushes up her skirt, works himself in.

'He likes it rough,' says the woman, looking up at Graham, 'don't you, love.' She opens her mouth, half closes her eyes, and Graham unzips himself, puts on his Durex, lest he catch something off this dirty, dirty whore who looks up at him the whole time that he goes in and out of her mouth.

When he is finished, he slopes back to the trees where Useless is still scratching around.

'Yooce,' he says in a low voice. 'Here, girl.' He feels flat, just wants to be home now, hating himself for doing the things he does. That will wane; resurrect.

The scratching continues and Useless whines.

'Yooce!' he hisses. 'Come here. Now, girl!'

She responds with a whimper and Graham thinks something must be wrong. If anything happened to her, he doesn't know quite what he would do.

He feels his way into the trees, ducking his head down low, fearful that a branch or twig might have his eye out. The hum of a new car emerges into the clearing and a slow sweep of sidelights follows, illuminating the shape of Useless, just a few feet away.

Graham stops dead.

Useless has unearthed a girl, but she looks unrecognisable – as a human, the life all gone from her: just flesh, slitted in her side and stomach. In her face, she seems so afraid.

When he had got home, Blears put Useless into his room, upstairs at the front of the house, and began his deliberations. These soon became preparations. He had kept his cool, earlier, maintained a silence and carefully scraped the leaves and mulch back over the body. This was his body. But what to do with it?

This evening, Blears has bathed and combed his hair flat. His parting is perfectly defined and he is dressed in his best suit. He makes tea in the Prince Albert service and pours the milk into the jug. He brings out the sugar tongs, even though it is only him. He should have gone to the Castle tonight. But this will make up for that.

Indeed, these will prove to be momentous days. He once heard that everybody gets a single chance in life. Graham realises that the same world which can turn a shoulder to him – which can look past him on the High Street or at the checkout or on his ocasional sorties to the Cross Daggers – has today finally beckoned.

This is a time to do. He makes a small clap and rubs his hands together. As he gives the tea a final stir and applies the milk and the sugar, he realises he is trembling. He says, aloud, 'Why not,' going across to the bow-fronted cabinet. He takes a quarter-bottle of brandy, pours himself a half-schooner of the Three Barrels and shifts his chair to look down the garden. He is overlooked at the back, and now they will read about him. He will have to explain why he was in the Forest in the first place, but he has a plan for that. And if they don't play it his way, he simply won't tell them where the woman's body is.

He sips the brandy and shudders, takes a full swallow of the tea and looks up at his mother's porcelain Our Lady. Standing, he feels invigorated as he goes to the glazed kitchen door. His knees are rock solid now. His heart is even. He looks out at his neighbours' windows. 'Let's do it,' he says.

Waiting for the phone to be answered, he regards

his watermark reflection – first, one three-quarter profile; then, the other. He settles on the latter.

The phone is answered by a woman; not what he had expected. 'I'd like to . . .'

'Ambulance, Fire –'

'Police! Yes, please. I must speak to the police. I have discovered a murder and my name is . . . My name is . . .' Blears looks at the phone and his head thickens. The woman on the telephone sounds ever so distant. She echoes. He will abort, his nerve suddenly seeping all the way out of him.

'Mr Blears?'

'I didn't say that.'

'It's here on my read-out. You know, it's a criminal offence to make bogus calls to emergency services.'

'It's a murder, damn you,' says Blears, reaching for the chair, dragging it across the linoleum and sitting heavily upon it.

'I hope so,' says the woman. 'For your sake.'

The oddness of the remark escapes Blears who foggily prepares how he is going to present himself to the world.

Twelve

Staffe pounds his way along the sea's edge to the southernmost jut of the beach, the sun low above the North Sea horizon. He considers what he has learned of Elena Danya: that she was certainly more than a passing fancy of Taki Markary's; that she developed her own affection for this place, separate from Markary's, who seems to have an affiliation with the man called Howerd.

By the time he gets to Warblingsea Harbour, his shins begin to splint and the sweat drips, saltily, into his eyes. Breathless, he stops, hands on knees, gulping for air and enjoying the burn to his lungs. He stands up, stretches, and lets the wind chill the sweat. When he gets back, he will soak in a hot bath, then stand for a minute under the coldest shower, then have porridge with honey; kippers with a poached egg. He licks his lips, tastes the salt, sees someone in the dunes.

He blinks, sweat in his eyes. It is a man, watching him. It is the lean, ruddy-faced man from dinner last night. He is sure. He rubs his eyes and looks again, but nobody is there.

When Staffe returns to the hotel, he settles his bill

with cash, is told that Pulford has already paid for his room, and for half the cost of dinner. 'Has the ruddy-faced man left yet?' asks Staffe.

'I don't know who you mean,' says the receptionist.

Staffe thinks she might have enquired as to whether he had a name for the ruddy-faced man, or a further clue to describe his appearance more fully. 'He is a slender man. He had dinner last night.'

The receptionist smiles wearily at Staffe, as if it is more than her job could be worth to divulge such a thing.

Josie takes the ACL printout to the morning meeting. Today, she has ringed only one item on the Area Crime Log – the list of offences committed outside the limits of the City Police. It is the death of a young woman aged twenty to twenty-six, five feet four, mouse-coloured hair that had been dyed blonde. She had been killed within the past twenty-four hours and buried in a shallow grave in the southern reaches of Epping Forest on the fringe of a clearing which is known to the police as the Kennel. The body was discovered by a Graham Blears, a single, forty-one-year-old actuary who works for Re-Zurich in the City. He has not a single blemish on record and was walking his dog.

The woman had been stabbed six times.

Josie bides her time and when she gets an opportunity to bring up the Kennel murder, the usual gallows humour percolates – fast as morning coffee.

'Mixing business with pleasure, hey Chancellor,' quips one DS.

'You should check it out,' retorts Josie. 'Everyone should try straight sex at least once.' This draws a bigger laugh, followed by a bellow from Pennington, who looks across at Rimmer as if to say, 'You should be controlling this lot.'

'There'll be none of this,' shouts Rimmer. He goes red in the face and leans back against the desk at the front of the room, steadies himself. 'Now, Chancellor, what are you saying? That this poor girl might be connected to the Elena Danya murder?' He looks at Pennington who gives him the mildest encouragement in the form of a rueful nod.

Josie says, 'The body is fresh and according to the coroner there's plenty of dental and medical history – two gold teeth, appendix scar and a metal plate in her left leg. We should get an ID later today. There's no harm checking her out and West Essex CID have said they'd be happy to share.'

'But is she a prostitute?' says Rimmer.

'It's unusual for prostitutes to frequent the Kennel. But she might have been there out of hours and she had miniscule traces of semen in her mouth. Nothing in the stomach. No signs of recent vaginal penetration, but there is junkie scarring to the arms and thighs. Janine hasn't seen her yet but the local pathologist says if we pushed him on it, he'd hazard she was on the game.'

With another look towards Pennington, which receives nothing more than a flat smile, Rimmer says, 'Follow it up, then. But don't get sucked in.' A tempered trickle of testosterone seeps.

'That's enough!' snaps Pennington, standing, signifying the meeting is over and as the room empties, he catches Josie. 'You make sure Rimmer goes with you to interview Blears. This fella's probably going to be a sex pest, you know, if he's been going down the Kennel.'

'Of course, sir.'

'Where's Staffe? I take it he's taken Pulford with him.'

'He's following a lead, is all I know, sir.'

Pennington takes a half step towards her. 'You know, Chancellor, this could be a chance for you.' He looks up at her, smiles his thin smile. 'You're doing well.' He touches her elbow with his fingers.

Graham Blears wishes he had never told the police about the dead slut from the Forest. Now they are coming to his house. How could that be normal procedure? Surely the one visit up to Ilford Police Station – to give his statement, receive his recognition – was sufficient. They were ever so impressed with him up in Ilford and thanked him profusely. His head was spinning so much he can't remember if they commended him for his citizenship. They said something akin to that. But why are they coming down from the City? What the hell did it have to do with them?

He can't be too careful, so he has disconnected his computer and put it in the bottom of the wardrobe, covered in blankets. 'It's a good job we're one step ahead,' he says to Useless as he passes the door to the dog's room. He looks back into his bedroom, double-checks that the wardrobe doesn't draw attention to itself. His suit is laid out, alongside his brushes and comb. All these years, he has kept his head down, gone about his business, tended his secrets, unseen. It doesn't pay to involve yourself with the law.

Rimmer fidgets all the way from Leadengate out to Snaresbrook, scribbling in his notebook and checking the notes from West Essex CID.

'You spoke to Profiling?' she says.

'Yes. I don't see why we have to come all the way out here. We should have got him into the station.'

'Staffe always interviews *in situ*. It gives a fuller picture.'

'And where the hell is he, if this is so crucial?'

'What did Profiling say?'

'That killers often try to involve themselves in an investigation. As many as one in four.'

'But the killer wouldn't report the body, surely?'

Rimmer looks at her as if she can't quite be trusted. 'Have you met Tara Fleet? Very impressive.' Rimmer looks into the middle distance, dreamily. 'Very impressive indeed.'

Josie knows Tara Fleet – a criminal psychologist who knows exactly how to play senior police officers. Especially the male of the species. Rimmer would be a suitable stepping stone for enhancing her own profile.

'Did she say anything about the cases being linked?'

'We need to know more about the victims. But a swanky hotel and a dogging site? Ten miles apart. It's a difficult one.'

Josie goes quiet, slows the car a tad and as they turn into Marigold Gardens – a cul de sac of inter-war semis on the south side of the High Street – she calms herself. All day, since she found the Kennel killing on the ACL, she has been buzzing. Of course it would be better if the cases were not linked; that would mean there wasn't a maniac out there; not a third or fourth woman going about her business with some pervert preying, biding.

* * *

Blears can't believe they have sent a woman.

He returns the net curtain in his front room and regards himself in the art deco mirror, damping down his parting and tightening his tie, makes his way to the front door, waits for the second knock, so as not to appear unduly anxious, and smiles as he welcomes Leadengate CID into his house.

Over tea, he recounts to Inspector Rimmer his precise movements yesterday evening; how he broke from his routine and had never been to that place before. The inspector seems to be a man after his own heart, but the girl, she seems a different kettle of fish. She drinks her tea in one, gulping it down, scribbling away constantly, giving him only the occasional, sidelong glance.

After quarter of an hour, in which Graham has totally confirmed every last detail of the statement he gave at Ilford, the inspector closes his notebook and thanks him for his co-operation.

'Just one more thing, Mr Blears,' says the girl, looking up at him, her pen hovering. 'You will appreciate how keen we are to eliminate you from our inquiries.'

'Eliminate?' His heart skips, sinks down to his stomach and his head blurs.

'It's how we work back to the truth. Sometimes we have to prove innocence in order to expose guilt.' She stares at him as she says, 'Where exactly were you between sixteen hundred and eighteen hundred hours on the seventh of December?'

'How can I be expected to know that?' He looks down into his teacup. 'I work in the City. You know that. I would have been at work, or on my way home.'

'Can anyone vouch for when you got home?'

'I live alone.'

'Anything you can come up with will help us.' She smiles at him, a thick smear of condescension in the corners of her mouth. 'And help you, too. Of course.'

'I don't like what you are saying,' he says, looking at the inspector, but the inspector is opening his notebook back up, appears to bestow a look of encouragement upon the stupid girl.

'And anybody who can verify your evening habits. You know, to prove this visit to *that place* was a one-off.'

'An aberration,' says the inspector.

The girl looks at her superior, nodding earnestly. She flicks through some notes she has brought, says, 'Why did you wait two hours before you called? And why cover the body up again? She was covered with leaves when the local force got to the scene.'

Graham feels his kitchen floor warp. He looks up at Our Lady but the walls seem to shift inwards on him and he feels dizzy. He reaches out to grip the

table, thinks he might be sick. He hears Prince
Albert shattering on the floor. Then the crackle of a
radio. When he looks up, the girl is talking into her
handset.

Yooce curls up in her basket. She lets out a long,
low whine.

Thirteen

The pastel villages of thatched Suffolk soon give way to the suburbs and as they pass through into larger conurbations, Pulford says, 'The Aldesworth Country Town. That's an odd one, isn't it?'

'How do you mean?'

'I was talking to the night porter. He says the whole thing's gone sour. None of the locals have been involved in the construction. It struck me . . .' He passes Staffe some brochures for the new model market town. '. . . as kind of similar to Elena Danya's game. I wonder how much of the cash gets down as far as the girls? Five hundred houses. What does that look like?'

'A whole pile of paper,' says Staffe.

'Money?'

'That too.' Staffe goes into his pocket, hands Pulford a cheque, to cover his room and share of dinner.

The sergeant looks hurt.

'Take it. I insist,' says Staffe.

Pulford shakes his head, says, 'It's only money.'

* * *

Josie Chancellor watches the Scene of Crime team emerge from Blears' house in Marigold Close with bag after bag of numbered evidence. His computer is to be fast-tracked at Data Discernment. Graham Blears was taken in to Leadengate Station for questioning over an hour ago.

As she gets into the car with Rimmer, the police dog team are parking up. They have come to take Useless into care. When Rimmer told Blears this would happen, Blears had burst into tears.

'That was quite a morning's work, Chancellor. You can come along with me any time,' says Rimmer. He slaps her on the thigh and removes his hand quickly. They look at each other awkwardly.

'Thank you, sir.'

Josie feels peculiar, today; not entirely a part of her own body. She has emerged from a shadow. But the sight of Graham Blears, looking for all the world a guilty man, had given her no pleasure. The processing of the evidence and the rigour of all the lawyers and the judge and jury will determine whether they have got their man, but she feels a heavy hand of consequence upon her.

Josie doesn't know whether to laugh or cry. Instead, she calls in Data Pooling and asks them to merge all the cells from this case with that of Elena Danya.

As soon as she clicks off, *Forensics* flashes up as

an incoming call. The second dead woman is, according to her dental records and the prints from three soliciting charges and an arrest for possession of heroin, a twenty-two-year-old known prostitute called Rebeccah Stone, of 21D Arlington Road, Hackney. She was murdered by six stab wounds. A more savage end than Elena Danya suffered; the same Elena Danya whom a Rebeccah had called, talking, in fact, of 'tender petting'. Josie realises she was one of the last people ever to talk to Rebeccah Stone.

How might Blears connect with Elena Danya?

Or – as Staffe will probably see it – how does Rebeccah Stone connect with Taki Markary?

They call this Little Chelsea and it's the part of Barnes the Victorians built for their railway workers. Staffe watches the accountants who live opposite Sylvie. They are putting up their Christmas tree. It should resemble something from Frank Capra, but she throws her arms about, red-faced; he stands, head bowed.

He turns the key, feels awkward using it this first time. The front door gives straight into the lounge and, as usual, she has clothes drying on hangers, drooping from the curtain poles. Books are scattered on the sofa and floor. He picks one up. *Holmes's Intermediate Guide to the Anatomy of the*

Mind. She had told him she had given up on her MA. He could swear she had. He sniffs the air. Lacquer is thick, as if one lit cigarette would send the whole place up in flames.

'Who's that?' She calls from upstairs, sounding concerned. 'Is anybody there?'

At the bottom of the stairs she has a photograph of her mother, taken long ago and since they last saw each other. Mont Ventoux is in the background and the woman seems without a care in all the world. Staffe doesn't understand why Sylvie has this photograph.

'It's me!' he calls.

'Don't look at the mess!'

He imagines what it would be like if they were married. She would improve. He would relax.

He takes the steps two at a time, and goes up again, into the studio she's had done in the loft. He ducks his head as he rounds the top of the stairs, certain now that he will not do what he came for. He will have to concoct an excuse for dropping by. What has possessed him?

Sylvie is on all fours and moaning, low and deep. Her hair is up and held by a quarter-inch paintbrush. Shavings litter the Bokhara rug he bought her. She applies the final stroke to a thin sample of wood and sits up, cross-legged, swivelling to face him.

131

'What do you think?' She looks at the strips of stained wood.

'Who's it for?'

'Some spoiled brat at St Paul's. Father's a Syrian.'

'The walnut one,' he says, pointing.

'You think?' She looks up at him, quizzically, then back at the sample, squinting. 'Hmm. You're right.'

Staffe sits on the beanbag under the hip window. He watches her tidy up. She keeps the studio immaculate. A place for everything. Hands on hips, she looks down at the violin carcass, the components that will govern her next days.

'I didn't know you'd gone back to the MA,' he says.

'I'm sure I told you. I spend my life talking to wood. People are sometimes more interesting. You should know that.'

'Give up work, then,' says Staffe, taking himself by surprise with this sudden tack.

'What?'

'Let me look after you.' He slips his hand in his pocket, fingers the old velvet of the ring's box.

'I've only just got business steady, Will. I'm getting a few referrals now.' It is less than a year since she set up on her own.

'But you want to study psychology.'

'Everybody does, sooner or later. It's very probably a phase.'

'Displacement,' says Staffe.

'Very good. Have you been reading my books?'

'You could study and we could live off my wage. It will be no hardship.' He takes out the velvet box and looks at it. He daren't look at her. Suddenly, he feels sick. The muscles in his arm can barely extend as he reaches out, hearing himself mutter, 'I thought you'd like it.'

Sylvie slides the box from his fingers, says, 'Oh, my,' and goes to a tallboy that stands all the way up to the beam in the gable. She places the unopened box on the cabinet and pours them each a glass of Bushmills. She hands him his and goes back to the tallboy, picks up her gift.

She looks at Staffe, then at the box, as if she is on a game show and considering whether she might be better off leaving it unopened. Now, for Staffe, it feels as if life will never be the same again. She licks her lips, slowly lifts the lid.

When she sees the Urals ring, her smile spreads all the way to her temples and she purrs, 'Inspector, they can say what they like about you, but you've got impeccable taste.'

And with that, she slides the ring onto the third finger of her hand and reaches out, fingers splayed up, considering her jewel. 'Do you mind, Will, if we think about it.'

'*Think about it?*' Staffe realises the ring is on the right hand. The wrong hand.

'I don't want things to change. It's often for the worse, isn't it?' She looks like a child when she says it – not quite understanding her own words.

On his way downstairs, he turns on his phone, sees *Josie Josie Josie* scroll up on his missed calls list. He picks up the last message first and listens as she tells him he has twenty minutes to get back to her or else she'll have to take Rimmer with her to the home of the second dead. He checks his watch and makes the call, with a minute to spare, wondering what kind of omen that is.

The man who lets Staffe and Josie into 21D Arlington Road has said he is called Mitch and that he has no papers at this gaff to prove it. He sits, cocksure and strangely removed as Josie tells him his girlfriend has been stabbed to death.

Staffe considers what Josie has told him about how Rebeccah Stone was murdered, and he appraises her supposed boyfriend with the harshest eye. 'What are you coming down from, Mitch?' he says.

''t you talkin' about.' He pronounces it *abaarht*, which gets right up Staffe's nose. This reconstructed, trendy, dealer cum pimp talks half wannabe black, half mockney. Staffe wants to knock his with-drawals right into next week. He might do.

Staffe looks at Josie, says, 'The girl was stabbed six times. Correct?'

'That's right, sir.'

'And this *prick* is a suspect, right? If we find something here to charge him with, he has to be held on remand because he's likely to abscond.'

'They're waiting between two and four months for trial at Pentonville.'

Staffe hitches his chair right up to within inches of Mitch.

Mitch leans away from Staffe, not looking him in the eye.

'Or,' says Staffe, reaching out and removing Mitch's porkpie hat, 'we could be done in an hour. We wouldn't even charge you for what we found in this place. And I wouldn't let it slip to the guys up the food chain that you've been a blabbermouth. That means *grass*, where you're going.' He pronounces it *graahs*. 'You get me?' Staffe whispers in Josie's ear, 'You sure Pulford's on his way with that warrant?'

She nods.

'You OK on your own with this one for five minutes?'

She nods.

'I need the loo.' Staffe plonks the hat back on Mitch's head, so it comes down over his eyes.

He double-locks the front door and shunts all the bolts across the door. In the bathroom, he looks down out of the window, susses that this truly is the pad of a mid-level drug dealer: the bolts, the escape via the bathroom; the first floor, low enough to risk jumping, high enough for a pursuer not to follow suit.

Staffe lifts off the cistern lid and sees the outline of tape marks, but nothing there now. He sees the way the linoleum curls at the skirting boards and kicks away the stained, damp rug, pulls up the lino. Sure enough, one of the floorboards is screwed down, not nailed. He pulls out his keyring and uses the tiny penknife to unscrew. The board rises. Pinned up to the underside of the next board is a plastic bag full of wraps – each housing a fat corner of powder, amounting to forty, fifty grammes. Minimum. Staffe smiles. In different circumstances he would have kissed the big bag.

As he rolls the lino back, on his hands and knees, he sees that the plastic sealant around the bath is loose and the panel isn't secure. He pulls the panel away and peers in. Nothing there, it would seem, but he reaches right in, smells the damp and dirt of the floorboards. He bangs his head on the shell of the bath and reaches as far as he can, feels plastic against the tips of his fingers. A nerve in his shoulder pinches and he bangs his head again, curses, and snags the plastic between his fingers, wrenches it.

Staffe sits back, cross-legged, and looks at the bag. Not what he expected. He can see there's a Post Office savings book, and a notebook, some doodlings, and an envelope with *PRIVAT* written in a long, elegant hand.

There's a rap at the front door and Staffe stands up, trousers the drugs and tucks the plastic bag full of Rebeccah's secret world down the back of his trousers. He unlocks the bathroom door and rushes into the hallway, sees Josie letting in Pulford.

'You got the warrant?'

Pulford hands it across and Staffe tosses the stash bag onto the floor between Mitch's feet. 'Sing, birdie.'

Mitch furrows his brow. 'You what?'

'Elena worked for Taki Markary. You know that.'

Mitch makes a bad job of trying to look blank.

'Who did Rebeccah work for?' Staffe prods Mitch's bag of goodies with the toe of his Chelsea boot.

Josie says into the radio, 'Sergeant? It's Chancellor. We need a car up at Arlington Road, Hackney. It's number 21. Possession and Dealing.'

'All right!' says Mitch. 'All right.' He sparks up a cigarette. 'He's a Russian.'

Staffe takes the radio off Josie. 'I said, "Sing."'

'I want my lawyer.'

'Six times, she was stabbed. Once for every year you'll do for this,' says Staffe, picking up the bag of wraps, tipping them on the floor. He picks up a clutch of wraps and walks over to the recumbent Mitch, pressing his knee into the dealer's chest and grabbing his nose. When Mitch opens his mouth, Staffe shoves in the wraps and grabs Mitch's face, clamps his mouth shut.

'Sir!' calls Josie.

'Six fucking times, and left to die where dogs go to piss and perverts jack off. Now you tell me what you know or you'll swallow this bastard lot and it'll be just another junkie dying. See who mourns you! You . . .'

'Sir!' Pulford takes a hold of Staffe's shoulder.

Mitch's eyes are bulging and he is gurgling, trying to spit.

'Sir, he's going to play ball. Look!'

Staffe takes his hand away and Mitch spits out the wraps. One of them has burst and he foams, is sick down the side of his armchair. 'I don't know anything,' he sobs and coughs and clutches his guts, spitting out again and guzzling from a can of lager by the fire. 'Without me, she'd have been dead years ago. On the game since she was fucking thirteen so don't blame me for her life. You think I like what she does?'

'It didn't stop you skimming off her.'

138

'She needs me to fix her up. She can't ever give it up. You think I didn't try?'

'What about Elena?'

'Becx was always going on about how beautiful she was and how fucking smart. Just like Arra.'

'Arra?'

'Thick as thieves.'

'Was she one of Markary's girls, this Arra?'

'I never heard of him.' Mitch puts his head in his hands, talking to the floor. 'Arra's just some posh bird playing street.' He is trying to work out if the rock is more harmful than the hard place. Eventually, he says, 'Becx worked Tchancov's patch. Parlours and suff.'

When he gets to Leadengate, Staffe re-rigs the incident room chart. Josie and Pulford input and sort Rebeccah Stone's data.

The murders of Elena Danya and Rebeccah Stone featured different methods. You might say they don't connect – unless it is tit for tat. Markary's girl is killed. Tchancov's girl is killed.

Pulford says, 'I don't see how they have to be linked.'

'Rebeccah called Elena hours before she strolled to her death in the Thamesbank.'

'But why would Tchancov kill Elena Danya?'

'Why would Rebeccah Stone have been in the

Kennel on her own? See if Janine has got anything off Stone's body.'

'We've got traces of semen, sir, from the mouth. She wasn't penetrated.'

'Neither was Elena,' says Staffe.

'That's consistent with a frustrated sexual attacker,' says Josie.

Staffe turns round, frowning. He sees Rimmer coming into the room.

'We've got him. We've bloody got him!' pronounces Rimmer, coming into the room, pinning a typed document to the evidence board.

'What's that?'

'Blears has been identified as being at the Thamesbank Hotel at ten to four on the seventh. Ten minutes before Danya was killed. Ten bloody minutes.'

'Who by?'

'The bellboy, a young man called Mulplant. Gary Mulplant.' Rimmer taps the document with his finger. 'It's all there. Graham Blears is our man. Maybe you should go off on your wild-goose jaunts more often, Staffe.' Rimmer pats Josie on the back and says to Staffe, 'Just so long as you leave me this one – hey, Josie!'

Staffe leaves the rest of them to celebrate getting their man and, once in his office, locks the door, lays out the contents of the plastic bag from

Rebeccah's bath. He is beginning to regret not submitting it with the rest of the evidence. It tells the story of a girl on the brink of getting away, on the back of 'foreigners', paid in to her Post Office account once a week. From the jottings and calculations on the papers inside the savings book, it seems her debt with Tchancov was dragging her down.

He places the brown envelope on the desk. It is marked *PRIVAT* in a long, elegant hand. Staffe looks closely, to see if the envelope has ever been tampered with, but it is quite plain that Rebeccah has been a loyal custodian.

Staffe takes his bone-handled letter opener, inscribed to his father for loyal service. He inserts the blade and pulls it back, quickly. Inside are four sheets, elaborately decorated and each undertaking to pay the bearer £25,000.

'Elena,' whispers Staffe. As he says it – even though he is in his locked office – he looks around, to check he is unheard.

Fourteen

Sylvie has brought crab cakes and green and red curries from the Thai Garden. When Staffe sees the thin segment of her in the opening door, he feels young.

They eat on their laps, watching the ten o'clock news and swapping curries halfway through as they always have done. Pulford pops his head in after a night in copper's corner down the Butcher's Hook and says he will leave them to it.

'Don't be silly, David,' says Sylvie. 'Get a plate. I'm off for an early night, anyway.' She takes the bottle of Crianza with her and tips Staffe the wink, to follow soon. On the hearth, he sees her mermaid mug – from the weekend they had in Copenhagen, the first time they were together. It is her favourite mug and he wonders when she brought it over here, and how significant that might be.

He follows five minutes later, and she seems like a stranger, more demure and faltering in one phase; more brazen and direct in the next. She undresses him, keeping her own clothes on, pushing him back on the bed, gliding over him, using her mouth and nails, not letting him touch her.

She holds herself above him, barely touching him, and Staffe wonders where she knows this from and he wants to ask, but can see how that might harm him. Eventually, she hitches down her pants and sits astride him. She moves slowly, him inside her, and she comes quickly, falling equally quickly to sleep, still wearing her blouse and skirt, and through her soft, mumbling shudders, Staffe contemplates whether the proposal might have changed things. He wonders if, by employing such variety, she was trying to fix something she thought might be broken.

Staffe tries to find sleep but Elena, and now Rebeccah, repeat on him. Everything of tangible significance seems to be dropping into Rimmer's lap, and all because he went on that stupid jaunt up to Suffolk. He should learn to control his intuition. And he should have declared the evidence Rebeccah had hidden. Tomorrow, he will tell Pennington.

Sylvie turns, emerging briefly from her sleep. She wraps her arm around him and says, 'Can we do something tomorrow? Maybe go to Vicenti's.'

'I told Marie I'd take Harry out – in the day. If you fancy it, we could take him to the park.' Staffe takes a hold of her hand, feels the emerald. 'Try and get a kite up.'

As she falls back into sleep, he listens to merry-makers being chucked out of the restaurant in the square, beyond his short back garden. Their good cheer is made soft by the falling snow. White triangles and rhombus shapes of roofs against the black sky look like cubism. It might be a metaphor, he thinks, but as he slides back between the sheets, spooning Sylvie, he isn't sure that makes sense.

The *Telegraph* sport section is spread out on Pennington's desk, next to a cafetière of coffee. He pours Staffe a cup and reaches down, produces Garibaldi biscuits from his drawer. The two men keep their coats on, the central heating playing catch-up.

'The Danya case seems to be progressing well.' Pennington lifts his coffee cup to his lips, sips. 'I must say, I'm pretty impressed with Rimmer.' He laughs and a plume of his breath makes a dying cloud. 'Between you and me, I thought the boat with those words on had sailed. And Chancellor, too, Will. You've done a sterling job, bringing her on.'

'The case has a long way to go. We haven't even got a weapon.'

'Rimmer and Chancellor are there now,' says Pennington, putting down his cup.

'Where?'

'Blears' home. Stripping it bare. This ID from the Thamesbank changes everything.'

'Blears couldn't have done it.'

Pennington looks at Staffe as though he is about to confide, but decides against. 'Sometimes, we just set off on the wrong course. The further you go, the further from the truth you get.'

'What connects Blears to the two girls? What's his motive?'

'They're prostitutes and he's a pornographer. Some of the material he had is criminal. What more do you want?'

'Danya and Stone were friends.'

'That's exactly what Rimmer's saying. Blears found something on the first to lead him to the second.'

'And what took him to the Thamesbank Hotel in the first place?'

'He's an actuary for Re-Zurich on Cannon Street. They had their Christmas do at the Thamesbank last year. He knows the place. You know how easy it is to get a girl to a room. It's just a matter of money.' Pennington fills up Staffe's cup. 'You're the best copper I've got, Will. But I think we have to let Rimmer bring this one in.'

'I understand.' Staffe knows he can't remind Pennington what his DCI really thinks of Rimmer, realises also that this is no time to come clean about Rebeccah's plastic bag.

'Take some time for yourself. Wind down.'

'I was going to see my nephew this afternoon. We were going to fly a kite.'

'You should do that, Will.' Pennington smiles, benignly. An odd look. 'Parliament Hill?'

'Yes, sir.'

Like Pulford said, there are times when it's best to sit on the banks, wait for the bodies to come floating by. He thinks of Elena's cold white corpse. He feels an anger breaching, so incants a mantra. 'Pacify yourself. Pass-if-eye-your-self,' he repeats, thinking, 'As long as nobody else pays the price.'

Gary Mulplant's shift at the Thamesbank starts at noon. Staffe waits in the bar, looking out over the cold, wily river and browsing the Suffolk Gazettes from the dates when Markary stayed at the Signet. He also has the data matches from the two murdered girls.

Staffe looks down the computer distillation of all the information on Elena Danya and Rebeccah Stone. The matches are: profession; city of residence; absent electoral register; absent NI contributions. Criminal records do not match: Elena is clean as a whistle in that respect. Neither of the girls is licensed to drive a car and neither has a history of sexually transmitted disease, nor serious illness, though Rebeccah, it seems, has been knocked about and is prone to overdosing. In terms of their phone records, the murdered girls shared five common numbers: Arra (T-Mobile, pay as you go); Bobo Bogdanovich (Vodafone, pay as you go); Darius A'Court (O2, pay as you go); Rosa Henderson (Orange, contract); Vassily Tchancov (Vodafone, pay as you go, and one of six different numbers registered to the owner).

Something disturbs Staffe about this information, but he can't pin it down. His trains of thought uncouple, and his mind flits to Pennington being happy to see him in the back seat, and to the changes in Sylvie; changes in *them*. His eyes flop back on the *Suffolk Gazette*s and he flips through the first one, from 15 March 2008. 'The Ides of March,' says Staffe, aloud. It was the trip when Markary hadn't stayed in room 14. Sure enough, the visit coincided with the announcement of plans for the Aldesworth Country Town.

So, Markary must have somehow been getting fat off that bit of land, he thinks to himself, turning his partially focused gaze back on the list of data matches. He is bogged down, needs the rough and tumble of an afternoon with his nephew Harry, up on the hill.

And then it hits him – like a rabbit punch, to the back of the head.

'Mr Wagstaffe?'

Staffe looks up at the bellboy. He has a badge that says 'Gary'.

'Rosa,' says Staffe – to himself.

'What?' says the bellboy.

'Rosa Henderson,' thinks Staffe. 'Sit down, Gary.' Is that her surname? How could he not know? But he checks her number in his own mobile handset, mouthing the sequence aloud and following it with his finger on the printout. Figure perfect. 'Damn!' he says.

'Shall I go?' says the bellboy.

'No. Sit down. Please.' Staffe directs his attention to the young man, who has the most piercing, light eyes. Almost white. 'Who's been talking to you?'

'Talking to me?'

Staffe takes out the photograph of Graham Blears. 'You say this man came here last Friday.' He weighs up Mulplant, who is self-assured, shows no fear being interviewed by police. 'How long have you worked here?'

'He did come here last Friday.'

'Is this your idea of what you want with your life?'

Gary laughs.

'You ever been in a prison?'

'What!'

'That poor man could spend the rest of his life inside.'

'He killed the woman.'

Staffe stands. 'Who told you that?'

Gary looks at his hands, fingers knotting themselves. 'I told them everything I know.'

'How tall is he?'

'Five nine.'

'Hair?'

'Kind of ginger. It needs a cut; styling, you know.' Gary tries to laugh but it fails.

'Shoes?'

'Plastic. Black.'

'You got a good look at him, hey, Gary?'

'What else do I do all day?'

'You don't want to arouse me. My curiosity, I mean.'

'You're harassing me.'

'This decision you've made – it won't rest easy.' He slips Mulplant his card. 'Shame, to have such a thing on your shoulders. Let's hope it works out for you. You start feeling bad about this, just call me.'

Mulplant looks down at the river.

Staffe thinks about bodies floating by. When Mulplant stops looking, the detective is gone and he is all alone.

From the kitchen in Marigold Gardens, Josie watches the Forensics team clear up in Blears' snowy garden. They have practically disassembled the shed and put it back together.

'Seems a shame,' says Rimmer.

'What's that?'

'These taters. Aren't they lovely? All knobbled and clods of earth on them. You don't get them like that in the shops.' Rimmer holds the spud under the tap, rubs the soil from the skin, and holds it up. 'See?'

Josie takes the potato from Rimmer, watches Forensics put the last deckchair back in the shed and close up. The garden is thirty feet of lawn, bordered by dwarf evergreens and flowering Alpines. 'Home grown, wouldn't you say?'

Rimmer looks out at the frosted garden. 'Where does he grow them?'

'An allotment,' says Josie. 'I'll get on to the council.' Her blood runs fast and her fingers tingle.

Graham Blears' allotment is as orderly as his house; as is his potting shed, which Josie and Rimmer are systematically turning inside out, watched by two Forensics officers who have just bagged three box files of no-limits pornography, including *US Snuff*.

Josie pulls the rocking chair from the corner and rolls back the rug but nothing is there, no signs the floor is loose. She taps her heels on the boards. No variations in tone. She notices that the floor is just like the ceiling, tongued and grooved, but this feels wrong – this flatness of the ceiling.

Josie goes outside to check she is right: the roof of the potting shed is pitched. 'He's made it like home,' she says, going back in, standing on a box, pressing up on the varnished pine with her nails. Rimmer follows suit and they check the ceiling from each end, working to the middle, but they don't meet because Josie presses one length of pine that lifts. Then the next. She calls the Forensics team, to investigate every last inch of the void.

Fifteen

Charged with the murder of Rebeccah Stone, Graham Blears is being held at Pentonville nick. Yesterday, Josie and Rimmer had corroborated the bellboy's identification of Blears at the Thamesbank, and his fingering of the proven pervert at the line-up was immediate and unwavering. Mulplant has no criminal record and is in the first year of a sandwich degree in tourism at the University of South London. Josie and Rimmer feel he will stand up to any cross-examination Blears' defence may concoct, but for the moment they are confining Blears' charges to the Stone murder.

And as for Blears' defence, he has no alibi for either murder. There are no witnesses from the Kennel yet, but Josie is hopeful that will change after the raid tonight, and this quest is aided by the fact that, so far, they have managed to keep both murders out of the papers. The hardcore doggers – those most likely to identify Blears – will be at the trough again tonight.

'I can't bear this,' Blears says, hands pressed to his drawn, grey face, repeatedly lamenting the separation from his beloved Useless.

Tara Fleet is with Rimmer and Josie: a criminal psychologist specialising in sex-crime profiling, and a little older than Josie. Tara asks Blears if he prefers animals to people. He replies in the affirmative. 'Especially women, Graham?' Tara says.

Blears is clearly distracted and looks at Rimmer, studiously avoiding both Tara Fleet and Josie Chancellor. His eyes look fit to bleed. He says, 'Oh, yes.'

Tara Fleet is like a dog with a bone. She is dressed in a Prince of Wales check suit, tailored to the shoulders and waist. Her golden hair is down in long curls. She forces a smile upon her stern face and waits for Blears to dare look at her, says, 'Women put you here, didn't they, Graham.' She leans back, slowly, crossing her legs. His mouth has opened. 'You're well shot of them.'

He nods, repeats her words in a breathy, penitent's moan. 'Well shot.' Blears looks at Josie, as if he has only just realised she is there. She smiles at him, wetting her lips. 'This will be done soon, won't it? I'll know, soon, won't I?' he says.

'Just as soon as you have told us everything.'

'I want to see a priest.'

'It's that bad, is it, Graham?' says Josie.

Blears blinks rapidly, looks at Rimmer, as if he is waking from a moment's sleep. 'Who are these women? I don't have to speak to them. Get them out!'

'Of course, Graham,' says Rimmer, standing, walking across to him, crouching and whispering low, under the murmur of the tape machine, 'You can have whatever you want. We can tell each other everything. And it will all be over. Then we can bring the priest.'

'Can you have dogs in prison?' Blears asked, his eyes ponding with tears.

Rimmer smiles and nods as Josie reaches down beneath her chair, producing six sealed plastic bags. In five of them are single pairs of knickers: some lacy, some plain; one, a thong. All of them, according to Forensics, are worn. In the sixth bag is a knife.

'You know where we got these, don't you, Graham?'

He nods, looking confused, and then he gasps as Josie puts *US Snuff* on the table.

'The knife, I have to say, Graham, is a perfect match for the wounds on Rebeccah's body.'

'It's not mine,' he says, uncertainly. Graham squints. He is breathless. 'I'm sure.'

Sylvie has a first violinist from the LSO going round at twelve and it could be a lucrative new commission. Good for her reputation, too, so Staffe makes his way, alone, to his Kilburn house. It's not so long since he lived there – before he moved out to provide his sister with a base; immunity from her bad boyfriends and some solidity in life for her and Harry.

He is here for an afternoon with his nephew, but he can't shift Rosa from his thoughts. What on earth is she doing in the phones of the two murdered women? Of course, that's her game, too.

The sun has come out today, quickly melting the snow. He remembers last summer, shudders when he recalls that first time, with Rosa. He hasn't seen her since. Now, he knows for sure, that must change.

As he walks up Shoot Up Hill, Staffe hears footsteps behind him, just out of kilter but at the same clip as his own. He slows. They slow. He speeds up and the echo disappears. He makes to cross the road, unnecessarily, and checks behind him. Nothing. The street is empty. 'Bloody fool,' he says aloud, to himself. 'Relax, why don't you.' It makes him smile.

Now on the wrong side of his old street, he can see right into his house. Harry is sitting in the window of his mother's bedroom, rocking slightly and mouthing words. It cracks Staffe up and in the crisp winter chill, he hears himself laugh out loud, plumes of happy gas coming from his mouth. Harry has his Apple buds in and Staffe tries to imagine what he might be listening to: his father's bad rock or his mother's tortured singer-songwriters? Staffe gave him some Chet Baker the other week and plans to have him into Coleman Hawkins by next Christmas. The boy will be amazing, already is, and as Staffe pictures him growing up, his nephew sees him, jumps up and down and bangs the window. The glass warps and steams up in the brilliant December sun.

In the taxi up to Parliament Hill, Harry chit-chats away, updating Staffe on his new school and his football and his music. It softens Staffe's heart to even contemplate that the young boy might be too bright for his own good. The driver chips in and Harry scoots across to the tipper seat. He talks briskly through the paying hole, telling the cabbie all about his favourite team and players and how the footballers are all paid too much and his team is Orient because they're a proper team. The driver challenges him to go through the team. Harry scrunches up his face and slowly, surely, reels them off, from goalie to strikers.

'I did it, Will! I did it!' Harry spins round and is beaming, holding aloft the pound coin that he has won from the driver.

'You got trouble on your hands there, governor,' says the cabbie, smiling all over his face. They get out of the cab and Staffe watches Harry run off into the park, trailing the kite behind. He wonders at the power of innocents to bring joy into the city.

Then, hands come from nowhere. Cold on his face. Over his eyes.

His heart stops as he recalls the steps behind him on Shoot Up Hill and he spins round, the heart quickly catching up, double time. A familiar voice spears words towards him. 'Guess who!'

Sylvie is beaming, bright-eyed. She says, 'No need to worry, Will. *I* won't harm you.' Then she crouches, opens her arms and lets Harry come bowling back down the hill into her, dragging his kite behind him along the ground.

Two men, each with the collar to his overcoat turned up, stand on a knoll, looking across at Staffe, Sylvie and Harry. London towers glint in the low sun as if they might be silvery confections for a Christmas or wedding cake. DI Wagstaffe sprints away, holding the string to the kite aloft, and the young boy jumps and waves his arms, urging the kite to fly. After fifty yards, the kite loops and catches a gust and sweeps into the air. The young boy cheers and runs to the inspector, who tugs and tugs at the kite to get it high. He ties the string to the belt of the youngster's jeans then holds his hands aloft in triumph, turning to the pretty woman. She claps her gloved hands and opens her arms, invites him to run to her, which he does.

She wraps her arms around his neck and turns to make sure the boy is not looking, then kisses him, full. Their heads move slowly, like clouds.

'That's him?' says the elder of the two men, tall, barrel-chested and erect. He has a perfectly bald pate and a pencil moustache.

'He doesn't look like a detective inspector,' says the lean, ruddy-faced, younger one – hints of soft Scouse in his voice. He adjusts his tie, turns his head towards the low sun and regards the scene around him.

'They say he's unorthodox,' says the Elder.

The Younger says, 'We'll use that, to fuck him over.'

The silver Gherkin glints bright in the east, like a fat candle, alight. You can see it from the inspector's office. But things look different from up here. You can see the whole picture.

In Pentonville, Rimmer and Tara Fleet watch Josie on a monitor. She is opposite Blears, alongside his solicitor. In observance of the ground rules for admissible evidence, it is more than six hours since Blears' last intake of temazepam, as prescribed under expert medical advice. They are ready to roll.

Josie adjusts her skirt, an inch or three shorter

than she would normally wear for work. Her tights are sheer. Minutes earlier, under prescription from Tara Fleet, she had applied lipstick, which she hardly ever wears.

Blears says, 'Where is he?'

'You do not have to say anything,' says his solicitor.

'I want Rimmer,' says Blears.

'You can have what you want, Graham. DI Rimmer is on his way. He just asked me to get things started.' She slides a photograph across the table. 'We took it this morning. DI Rimmer went over specially, to make sure she's all right. Useless is with the police dogs up in Hendon. The best a dog can get,' she beams, keeping her painted talon finger on the corner of the photograph of Blears' dog. He touches it, too. He looks up at her and smiles: involuntary, lascivious.

'It's bad in here,' he says. 'They're all evil.'

'It's better where Useless is,' says Josie. 'She'll be fine, Graham. No matter what you tell us.'

'This is irrelevant,' says the solicitor.

Josie leans back in her chair, looks at Blears, who is staring at her legs. 'How did you get on last night, with the priest?'

'They talked sense,' he says.

'They?'

'Said they believed in me. Said they understood.'

He looks up at Josie, eyes glazed and leaning slightly forward, almost as if he is about to collapse, his neck unable to support the weight above.

'We all want to understand everything, Graham. That's all.'

'This is bullshit,' says the solicitor.

'That's what *he* said,' says Blears.

'The priest?' Josie uncrosses her legs, leans forward. 'The priest said "bullshit"?'

'No. The other one. He said that I had to believe in myself. He said the truth is the truth and I don't have to make things up to make things better.' Blears blinks, looks around the room.

'The other one?'

Blears looks at Josie, then immediately down at his shoes. 'He said, "It won't end until we get the right man." He said to believe in that. He asked me if I was him.'

'The right man?' says his solicitor.

'Are you the right man, Graham?' says Josie.

'You don't have to answer this question, Mr Blears,' says his solicitor.

'I don't know,' says Blears. He looks up, for the briefest glimpse, at Josie. Head down, he says, 'That's your job.'

The door opens and Rimmer comes in with Tara Fleet, says, 'Sorry I'm late. Have I missed anything?' It's the sign for Josie to leave.

Which she does, taking an escort back to reception, running the gamut of wolf-whistles and cat-calls, the whole C-to-F of obscene invitations to copulate and fellate. Sodom puts his head above, too.

At the gate, she checks the visitors' book and runs a finger down the list of entries from last night. At 19.00, Father O'Dwyer had signed in, and there, just below, she sees that, at 19.30, a DI Staffe had signed his name.

Staffe tries not to breathe in the low-rise air of the Atlee tenements. The smell of dogs and garbage cloys in his mouth and nose. There is no need to live like this, he thinks. Then reminds himself how little he knows.

Last night, he had called on Graham Blears who seemed sedated, who seemed to want to believe that he, Staffe, had been sent from God.

'You're here to save me?' Blears had said, hollow-eyed as he sat in the plastic chair on the other side of the metal table, screwed to the concrete floor. 'I have done some terrible things and my hour is come.'

'You must save yourself, Graham,' Staffe had said. 'Tell me what you did. Forget the bullshit.'

'I didn't have the knife.'

'How did you kill them, Graham?'

He shook his head. 'I took Yooce for a walk is how.'

'What about the hotel?'

'They said I was there for a party.'

'You must tell the truth. Lies won't end this for you. They seem the easy way, but it is never so.' Staffe pressed a palm to each of Blears' shoulders. 'I can save you. With the truth.'

'My priest has come. He will save me.' He had smiled at Staffe and his eyes lit up, briefly. For a second, his wits seemed to have recovered, then his eyes grew heavy and his frail smile faded quickly, to the nothing of his mouth's narrow slit. 'I am tired,' he said. 'You should go.'

As the PO led Staffe away, he said, 'He do it?'

'What do you think?'

The PO shook his head, said, 'Comes a point you can't tell. Sometimes *they* can't tell.'

Now, at the Atlee, Staffe steps away from the door he has just knocked on and waits for the mother of murdered Rebeccah to welcome him into her down-at-heel home.

He is surprised Nicola Stone is so young, but when he looks, again, the hair is split beyond repair and the make-up is thick. From within, the smell of fried meat and burnt-out chip fat loops and curls.

'You'll have to come back.' Nicola squints at him, tilts her head to one side and makes a thin smile as she clocks that he is respectable. Handsome, even. She is drunk, even though it is day. 'Who *are* you?'

'Police.'

'I'm not doin' nothin'. He's a friend. Int'ya.' She steps aside and a sixty-year-old man smoking a fag and watching telly from the sofa with his trousers round his ankles waves at Staffe.

'It's about Rebeccah.'

'I ain't got nothin' to do with that bitch. No fuckin' way.'

'I have some bad news. Could I come in, please?'

Nicola steps back and for a frozen glimmer of time she looks as if the life has just gushed away from her. Then she adjusts her footing and plants herself, hands on hips, says, 'What is it?'

Before Staffe can answer, she turns to her gentleman friend and says, 'You fuck off.'

'What about my tenner?'

'Come back later.' As Nicola turns around, her housecoat falls open, shows her lifeless breasts and the apron of skin that folds down over her mouse-grey pubis. She doesn't adjust because she is too busy summoning life into her heavy eyes, looking deep at Staffe.

'She nicked my fella, you know. Four years ago.' Her lip quivers. 'She's not dead.' Nicola takes a step towards him. 'Tell me she's not dead.' She carries on coming, faster, falling into Staffe's arms and sobbing, saying over and over again, 'Not my baby. Not my baby.'

The old boy squeezes past and Staffe kicks the door shut. He holds Nicola, tight. She smells of drink and cigarettes and something else, something warm and like tea-dunked biscuits and from long ago.

Eventually, Nicola releases and tells Staffe everything. In terms of the case, it is nothing; Nicola doesn't know anything about Rebeccah's Russian paymaster or her friend called Elena, or, saddest of all, her dream of tending pets in the sun.

'Did she have pets as a child, Mrs Stone?'

'A gerbil. She killed it, though.'

'You mean it died?'

'Maybe.'

Staffe thinks it odd that Nicola doesn't ask how Rebeccah was killed or if she suffered. All her make-up cried away, all the dirty love rubbed raw, it is clear she knows how to protect herself – that some things are better not known.

Sixteen

Nick Absolom blows out his gaunt cheeks then sucks hard on his plastic cigarette, looking at the SOC photographs of Elena Danya and Rebeccah Stone. The photographs and potted biographies of the girls were delivered by a man in a motorcycle helmet. According to the receptionist, the courier had a Scouse accent.

Absolom has discovered that the Russian girl and Rebeccah Stone were both known by Vassily Tchancov, and when he had gone upstairs, the editor and proprietor had both got hard-ons for the Russian angle. 'We should know all about fucking Russians taking over,' they said. Absolom had heard the rumours about *The News* becoming the organ, the plaything of an oligarch, but he kept his mouth shut, his options open.

Now, he compares his two possible front pages. Absolom runs his nicotine-stained fingers through his fop's hair and stares at the screen.

VLAD THE RIPPER
Twin Sex Murders Point East
Brutal murders within London's sex industry

hint at gang unrest in the capital's sordid fleshpots.

He presses send, leaves it to the legal department to see what they make of it but is certain that this version will be good to go. Tchancov is not named directly and there is nothing actionable in his vague, scaremongering copy. Nevertheless, he ponders what kind of reaction it will elicit from the Russian. Absolom always has an eye for the bigger picture. It is what will make him great – one of these days – and it doesn't escape him that Tchancov's uncle Ludo is up for governor back in Russia. He also knows, in this climate, that times are tough for the Russians. They're all being called upon to make payments, to mend the gaping holes in those billion-dollar blankets.

He picks up his coat and goes down to the cold streets for a smoke. In the atrium, thinking he is watched, he spins round, sees nothing untoward – save a flashlight image of himself in the plate window, looking like a man who has missed something. One package. One call. Too easy by half.

Staffe has not seen Rosa for months, yet here he is at her door in a tight December frost, the last summer coming back in a hot flush that sends a shiver. It reprises the touch of her flesh on his fingers; the taste of her in his breath. That one and only time.

His heart bumps. She looks brand new, her hair cut smart in flyaway layers, her eyes bright. Her mouth drops open when she sees him and she takes a step, so he can't come in. 'Will?'

Like an idiot, he says, 'I'm here on business,' as if that could endear.

'Charming. You can see me any time, you know. We're supposed to be friends.'

'You look . . .'

'Yes?'

'Beautiful.'

She stands aside, nods into the lounge he knows so well. Now, there is a photograph of a man on top of the television. He is tanned and raising a champagne glass; behind him, a tumbling Italianate village and an indigo sea. 'I'd like to talk about a couple of your friends.'

'Girls?' she says, with weight.

He nods, sitting at the opposite end of the sofa to Rosa. 'Elena Danya.'

'You're right. She is a friend.' Rosa's eyebrows pinch together.

A lump establishes itself in Staffe's throat; an equal and opposite pocket of nerves in the top of his gut. 'And Rebeccah Stone.' He tries to look her in the eye, but he wavers. She makes a choking

167

sound. Then it is quiet. He looks up and her eyes are watery. He scoots along the sofa and wraps her in his arms.

Eventually, drawing back, the palm of her hand splayed on his chest, his shirt moist with her tears and smudged with her mascara, she says, 'What happened to them?'

He shakes his head, slowly. 'That's what I have to find out.'

She laughs. A nervous gush.

'What?'

'You said "have to".' She falls into his arms again, says, 'That's what I love about you, Will.'

She is soft, warm, and his chest reverberates with the undulations of her voice. 'I knew Elena, from a parlour I worked every now and then. I liked her straight away.'

'Which parlour?'

'One of Tchancov's joints, out Ilford way.'

'Ahaa. Tchancov.'

'Within a month or so she was hooked into some heavy hitter over in Mayfair.'

'Taki Markary?'

'She was with him later, but I didn't know this guy she left Ilford for.'

'But she was still . . .?'

'On the game? Elena didn't want to be dependent on any man. It was money she loved.'

'What about Rebeccah?'

Rosa smiles, as if she forgets for a moment that Rebeccah is dead. 'There was a time she'd follow me round everywhere, but as soon as she met Elena . . . we were never so close again. Elena took a shine to her, as if Becx was a baby sister or something. I never could work it out, but Elena loved that girl.' Rosa pulls away. 'You know, I introduced the two of them. And now they're both dead. If I hadn't . . .' A sob bursts and she swallows it back.

'That's nonsense,' says Staffe.

Rosa wipes her eyes on the back of her hand and inspects, saying, 'How about you, Will? You got a girl?'

Staffe nods at the photograph on the television and says, 'Who's the fella?'

'I asked first.'

'Sylvie,' he says.

'Aaaah.' Rosa stands up, strokes her skirt down and plays with the zip at the back. She walks slowly towards the door, head bowed, opens it.

'How did Elena end up with Markary?'

'That was all tits up.'

'How d'you mean?'

'She met him through the trick. You should meet the trick through the pimp. "Tits up".'

'You wouldn't describe Markary as a pimp, would you?' says Staffe.

'Not really. He's got the Executive, though.'

'Did Elena work for him at the Executive?'

'I wouldn't say Elena worked for anybody – not after that first month or so – once she got to know the ropes. She was her own boss.'

'How's that happen?'

'She's beautiful and young and strong, and I suppose she got the right connections. It's every girl's dream.' Rosa checks her watch. 'She cottoned on to the bankers. Those pinstripe boys love Elena like a bad wife.' She kisses Staffe on the cheek, holds for a second. 'You'd have liked her. The real her.'

As he goes, Staffe feels as if he has betrayed somebody; which is nonsense, surely.

Here and there, Christmas lights twinkle in the windows of the Barbican's mid-rise flats. Some people are still at work, but most have spilled onto buses, down into the Tube. Many have made a way west for late-night shopping.

He pulls up his collar and raises the clip of his stride to keep warm and he is soon passing the Port Authority building at the back of Livery Buildings, the station not far away, but he steers a course away from Leadengate and follows the snaking red tails of the traffic all the way back to the Square Mile. Between the steel and glass gulleys that run to the Thames, he glimpses the burnished copper domes of the Thamesbank Hotel.

The Colonial Bankers' Club looks nothing from the outside – a slim, mullioned column of a building. Once you are in, it reeks of old England, as if it is decorated with white fivers.

Staffe shows his warrant card, which makes the doorman stiffen, and the steward, witnessing this, smiles with all his restrained might.

'How might I help you, sir?'

'I would like to see the visitors' book.'

'Do you have somebody to sign you in, sir?'

'Not exactly,' says Staffe.

'Then I am afraid . . .'

Staffe whispers, 'There's no need to be afraid. Not unless I ticket all those cars on the double-yellows outside.' Staffe makes a point of examining his watch. 'I'll be back with a warrant anyway. It could be very disruptive – for the lack of a little co-operation, Mr . . .?'

'My name is Dickinson, sir.'

'I'll be five minutes, no more. And discreet. I *can* be discreet when I want.'

Dickinson looks across the lobby. The gentle clatter of pudding and wine, of cheese and port being served rings through from the echoing dining hall. Six gentlemen, three from the Far East, emerge laughing, plotting a naughty night, no doubt.

Staffe says, in a raised voice that makes the group

stop and look, 'Mr Dickinson!' He lowers his voice. 'If you please?'

'Go through into the back,' says Dickinson, referring Staffe to a cubby-hole behind the desk, as if he were showing him trifle from a trolley.

Within five minutes, Staffe has what he wants. He doesn't quite know why he wants it, but there are three occasions on which Taki Markary has been signed in during the past year. The first time he was introduced by a Leonard Howerd and the second time by Lord Audley. Last week, true to his alibi, he was signed in again by Leonard Howerd, only an hour or so before Elena Danya and her unborn child were killed just a quarter of a mile away.

Staffe hands back the visitors' book, apologising for being so uncouth. He actually uses the word 'uncouth'. 'Is Mr Howerd in today, Mr Dickinson?'

'I'm afraid not, sir.'

'Never mind. I'll catch up with him.' He treats himself to a smile as he goes out into a thickening mist. The streetlights are a soupy orange. He will treat himself to a couple of pints of ale in the Jampot before travelling home, to meet Sylvie. Tomorrow, he will lift the crust of this case. Good and proper; bib and tucker.

Rimmer sucks in the cold night, breathes out long trails of hot air and transfers his weight from one foot to the other, looking behind. He has three unmarked cars as back-up and suddenly wonders if he is underequipped. His heart beats fast as he holds his arm aloft, waving the cars in to the forest clearing. He says, to Josie, 'Let's see what we can catch.'

'As long as we don't catch what they've got,' says Josie as they follow the cars into the Kennel.

The uniformed officers tap on the windows and step back from the six parked cars. Curses spill into the forest as doors are opened. They soon turn to pleas as many states of dress are hurriedly repaired. The officers herd the doggers into a line and Rimmer is amazed to see that he would be one of the younger participants. He steps forward and something like a frisson judders through his body as he directs his first question to the first exhibit: male and approximately fifty, wearing a suit and saying, rubbing his hands on the sides of his thighs, 'I have a wife; she can't find out. Anything but that. My wife, she can't find out . . .'

'Your name and address. Answer the questions and you will be free to go.'

The line of people falls quiet and these doggers, who only minutes ago were thrusting and groping and moaning with animal intimacy, have fallen coy. The smell of sex, over-ripe, curdles with fear. It is too heady a mix for Rimmer, who doesn't know quite how to treat these people.

He takes out his notebook and, in turn, asks each person to verify who they are and whether they have ever seen the people in the three photographs: Elena Danya, Rebeccah Stone and Graham Blears. The inquiries are deliberately undertaken here in the field, where it is cold. Josie holds the torch, capturing their reactions in high relief.

Twenty minutes after they started, Rimmer and Josie swap. She squares up to a woman in her early fifties who gives the name of Margaret Shinwell. This is verified by her driving licence. She came alone and she is married, has been for twenty-eight years. She is crying, and Josie assures her everything will be fine, but does she really know what risks she is taking by coming here? The woman nods, vociferous, and Josie shows her the photographs in quick succession: Elena, Blears and Rebeccah, in that order.

'Do you recognise any of these people?' says Josie.

'I never seen him.'

Josie shoots Rimmer a quick glance, says, 'Say that again.'

'I never seen him.'

'There are three pictures here, Mrs Shinwell. Two of them are of women. Why say you haven't seen *him*?'

As Margaret Shinwell struggles to find an answer, Josie notices she has stopped crying.

'You know him, don't you?' says Josie, holding the photograph of Graham Blears right up to her face.

The woman is trembling now, shaking her head, saying, 'No, no, no.'

'Don't you!' shouts Josie.

'Your husband won't find out,' says Rimmer.

Margaret Shinwell looks at Rimmer as if he is the doctor most likely to tell her what she has is benign.

'I promise,' says Rimmer, putting a hand on her shoulder.

'He'll bloody well find out if you don't tell us,' says Josie. 'We can drive you home right now and take your full statement there.'

'I seen him a couple times, is all.'

'How many times? And when?'

'I can't remember,' says Margaret, looking anxiously at Rimmer.

'It was two nights ago, wasn't it,' says Rimmer.

Margaret nods, says, 'What has he done?'

'We can't say he has done anything for sure. But these two girls,' says Josie, stabbing the photographs of Elena and Rebeccah with her finger, and lowering her voice to a poisonous hiss, 'these poor girls are dead. And one of them died here. Now, I don't care how you get your kicks, but you will tell me everything you know about this man.'

Talking to the ground, Margaret tells Josie how

she took Graham Blears into her mouth while being gratified by another man. This, within two hours of the latest possible time of death for Rebeccah Stone.

Although Rimmer is her immediate superior, Josie wants to put Staffe in the picture. She's still fuming that he had been to see Blears the previous night without telling her but she has kept Staffe's visit to herself, a part of her aware that he might know best and fearful that if she is wrong there might be more to come.

Margaret Shinwell is put into a squad car, for Leadengate. As the last of the doggers drives away, one of the uniformed officers comes across, tapping a rolled-up *News* against his thigh. He holds it up. 'Last edition,' he says. 'Squad driver picked it up, said you should see it.'

By torch, Rimmer and Josie read, together.

'Are these photographs taken from the morgue or the scenes?'

'They've been clever, cropping like that.'

The two photographs of the murdered girls show only the ghostly pale faces of Elena and Rebeccah, down to the chest plate. Their eyes are closed, like Rossetti lovers being sent off to watery graves.

'I see this is Absolom,' she says, tapping the front page. 'A nasty piece of work. Shouldn't we tell the press about Blears now?'

Rimmer looks weary, but he reaches out to her

and pats her on the shoulder, says, 'You did a bloody marvellous job tonight, but I've a horrible feeling Pennington will take the case away from us. He's never liked me.'

Sylvie's hair is wet and she is wearing one of his shirts.

'Where's Pulford?' says Staffe.

'Out.' She leads him into the Queen's Terrace lounge by his lapels, pushing him onto the sofa, sitting on his lap. Suddenly, she looks just the same as their first night, when he was tempted into a club so trendy that he didn't know a single person who had even heard of it.

Her fringe hangs down in wet thongs and her eyes are clean as a whistle – like a country girl. Not like that first night when, back at one of his flats up in Maida Vale, she had pulled out of a long, deep embrace and smacked his hand away, saying, 'Manners! I had you down for a gentleman.' She had smoothed down her tiny dress and knelt at his Cobb coffee table, tipping out the powdery contents of an intricately carved teak pillbox. 'You having a line?'

Staffe had shrugged.

She said, 'You'll treat me right. I can tell you know not to hurt a girl.' He later learned that Sylvie had discovered, earlier that week, her mother was pregnant by her French boyfriend – the latest in a constant line. She would never meet that sister.

Now, Staffe pulls her towards him. He kisses her and she opens her mouth. He holds her away, looks into her eyes and says, 'Remember our first meal?'

'I remember the drive home.'

'I spent a fortune on you.'

'And I . . .' She stands up, unbuttoning the shirt and letting it slide to the floor. 'Was worth every penny. You said so.'

'I love you,' he says, glancing towards the door.

'How much?'

'Every inch of you.'

Sylvie raises a leg and plants her foot on the sofa. 'You haven't even noticed what I'm wearing.'

Staffe looks her up and down, smiling. She twinkles her left hand and his eyes go wide and bright. The Urals ring catches the light and he gasps. 'You're saying yes?'

She pushes him back, kissing him, saying, 'You'll treat me right, won't you, Will? Not hurt me.'

Pennington strides into the incident room, dressed in black tie from his interrupted dinner at the Salters' Hall. He was mad as hell on the telephone, but by the time he arrives, he is calm.

The four of them sit around a table: Rimmer with his notes in front of him; Josie twirling a pencil like a majorette, her adrenalin surging, still; Pennington, composed as an undertaker; and Tara Fleet, who has come straight from the gym, her hair and make-up immaculate and low-riding velour track-suit seemingly fresh from its wrapping.

Tara reads the transcript of the interview with Margaret Shinwell. 'Of course what I say can only steer you. It will be dismissed in court as specula-tion,' says Tara. 'You can call me or somebody else as an expert witness, and as far as I can see, this is textbook stuff. His behaviour, as far as we know it – the prison interviews and the computer drives, then the snuff magazine and the underwear – and now *this*, all represent a repressed but irrepressible need to impose, born from a ritualised programme of sexual passivity and social exclusion.

'In the Kennel, Blears makes do with being fellated whilst another man brings the woman to orgasm, but he has his payback. Leaving Danya naked, the repetitive stabbings of Stone. These look like two different murders, by two different people, but they are both precisely the types of behaviour you could rationalise to a type such as Graham Blears. Especially when one led to the other.'

'Then the need to be seen – by coming to us,' says Rimmer.

'Exactly.' Tara Fleet tosses the transcript down and looks at Pennington, pleased with her analysis.

'Recognition. A temporary, but essential inversion of the exclusion.'

'A type?' says Josie.

Tara looks at her as if the young DC is holding her fork and knife the wrong way round.

'He's our man, then?' says Pennington.

'It's totally plausible.'

Pennington picks up the copy of *The News*.

'We've got Absolom downstairs, sir,' says Rimmer. 'We think maybe we should tell him we've got Blears.'

'Of course you should. But be careful. We win this prosecution in court, not on the front page. Give Absolom as little as it takes to turn his story round.'

'Will you see him, sir?' says Rimmer.

'Naturally,' says Pennington, as if something lovely has just dropped in his lap. 'I can't wait to wipe the smile off that little scrote's face.'

Seventeen

Staffe has barely slept, and as the wagons on the Brompton Road begin to rumble, he makes a cafetière of coffee, lets it brew and returns to his books. *Who's Who* lies open at H and he re-reads the entry for Howerd, Leonard Patrick Mark. Born 1955, educated at Ampleforth and St John's College, Oxford. Howerd married Imogen, nee Audley. He has two children, Roderick and Arabella, and is Deputy Chairman and Head of Corporate Finance at Laing's Bank. He is a fellow of the Royal Geographical Society, the Royal Horticultural Society and the Royal Yacht Club. His wife died in 2005. Blood doesn't get much bluer than this, yet what interests Staffe most is the unknown, stark relief to the published history: his daughter, domiciled in the telememories of two dead whores.

The day emerges, pale and misty, and he mooches into the kitchen, puts a dash of vinegar to the pan of water, delicately breaks two eggs into a rolling boil so they form, and hold, teardrop shapes. He toasts two rounds of pain rustique, pours the coffee, butters the toast and scoops the eggs. As he takes the breakfasts up on a tray, he catches himself humming *Pavane for a Dead Princess*.

After breakfast, Staffe climbs into a pair of gunmetal-grey chinos. Sylvie comes up behind him, laughing. She slaps his backside and says, 'Mornings aren't exactly a minefield for you, are they, Will?'

'How do you mean?'

She points into his wardrobe. 'Four pairs of chinos and four pairs of jeans. Two leather jackets and one suede one. Four blue shirts and two white. Two pairs of Chelsea boots and two pairs of loafers. That's it!'

'Don't you like the way I dress?'

'Don't worry, I'm not going to try to tailor you. I'm taking you off the peg.'

A loud rap from the front door is followed by two rings on the bell. Staffe pulls on a blue shirt and rushes to the door, says, 'What's up?'

Josie walks past him and into the lounge, tossing last night's *News* onto the coffee table. She puts her hands on hips like a little missy. 'This! And your visit to Blears – for starters. You could have told me you were going to see him.'

'Nothing came of it.'

Josie taps the copy of *The News*. 'Where did Absolom get his front page, sir?'

'You think it was me?'

Josie looks past Staffe. Sylvie is leaning against

the frame of the door and the two women smile at each other, cool and polite. 'I'll see you down the station, sir,' says Josie.

'I'll come with you. Just give me a minute.'

In the kitchen, Sylvie is putting coffee into the cafetière – enough for three people. 'Don't worry. I know,' she says.

'Know what?'

She puts her arms around him. 'You have other people's lives to slide into and out of. That's what turns you on about your job, and it's part of what I love about you.'

'You love me?' he says.

She punches him in the chest and holds up her ring finger. 'Don't be an idiot.'

'Will you go public on Blears' arrest now?' says Staffe to Josie as they walk down from Farringdon tube. The night snow is grainy and hard and people walk gingerly, sometimes slipping and laughing.

'Pennington's spoken to Absolom already.'

They are outside the Port Authority building and Staffe taps Josie on the shoulder, points towards the Barbican. 'I'm going this way.'

'We've got all the witness statements from the Kennel and the evidence from Marigold Close is all bagged and indexed. You should have a look.'

'I will.'

'We got an ID on Blears from the kennel. And Tara Fleet's preparing an expert witness report.'

'Tara Fleet! Was she Rimmer's idea?'

'What did you say to Blears?' asks Josie.

'I wanted to look him in the eye. I wanted to hear him tell me he didn't do it.'

'And did he?'

'Get Tara Fleet to ask him.'

'Did he deny it, sir?'

'Not exactly.'

He watches Josie go, thinks back to what she was like just eighteen months ago, when she first joined the team. His team.

As he crosses the Barbican piazza on his way to Rosa's place, walking against the grain of people walking to their financial jobs, he wonders if there will be some kind of law of diminishing returns that applies to Rosa and her profession.

The last time, she told him to phone ahead, so he takes out his phone, seeks her out and presses green.

'Will?' she says down the phone. 'It's not like you to call.'

'Can I see you?'

'Of course you can. But I have to go out soon.'

He makes the knock on the door.

She says, 'Hang on. Don't go away.'

He smiles, at the prospect of his surprise playing itself out, but he immediately questions how inappropriate it might be, to want to see her light up for a moment.

The door opens and her face does light up. She says, 'Will!' Steps forward, hugs him, then moves back, holding onto his hips.

His arms hang by his sides.

'Why the long face?' says Rosa, inviting him in.

She makes tea, constantly lamenting the fate which befell Elena and Rebeccah.

'There are some names in their phones,' he says.

She sits alongside him on the sofa and he shows her the list, distilled from the dead girls' data matches.

'We know Bobo and Tchancov. And you, of course,' says Staffe. 'What about the others?'

Rosa says, 'Kimberley was one of the girls but she moved away, back up to Manchester – a year or so ago.'

Which figures, thinks Staffe. The last call is over six months old.

'But this one, this Arra, she was friends with Elena and Rebeccah. They were thick as thieves.' Rosa shakes her head. 'She's not my cup of tea. Not by a long chalk.'

'One of the girls?' says Staffe, knowing Mitch had said not.

Rosa shakes her head again. 'No way. But not so you'd know – unless you knew.'

'What do you mean?'

'She's a rich little girl gone wrong. Her boyfriend . . .' Rosa taps the paper with a French manicured nail. 'This bloody Darius. He deals – to Becx. And to Elena, for her clients. Elena can take or leave the stuff, but not Rebeccah.' She is talking about the dead girls as if they might be meeting up later to shop out west or kill a couple of bottles of dry white. 'Rebeccah can't help herself.' She glazes over, talks low, as if to herself. 'Life's hard enough without making it so. Arabella had choices, but you know, if Rebeccah or Elena had those choices, they'd be here now.' Rosa's voice begins to crack.

'Arabella. Her surname is Howerd?'

Rosa nods. 'You didn't just come for a chat.'

'Do you have to go out? We could talk, if you wanted.'

'The Metropole. It's a good number.'

'You shouldn't go to hotels.'

'Don't judge me, Will.'

He wraps an arm around her and she flinches. He holds her tighter and puts his other arm around her waist, pulls her close and her body goes slack. They stay like that – her head tucked between his chin and chest. Eventually, she taps him on the leg and he unravels his hold of her.

Staffe nods at the photograph of the man with

the Italianate village behind him. 'You never said who the fella is.'

'He would never hurt me.'

'Is it serious?'

She smiles, sadly, and walks to the door. 'I have to get ready.'

He says, 'It's strange how you're in the middle of this.'

'Mine's a tiny world, Will. You'd be amazed how few real pervs there are in this city.'

The sugar dusting of snow is brittle with frost, like brûlée. Yesterday, London's snow turned to slush almost as soon as it fell, but the temperatures are so low today that it has retained its crust on the pavement. There is a chirp in the air, a fairytale Christmas just around the corner. Staffe goes through the stained-glass portal to the Laing's empire, and its deputy chairman, Leonard Howerd.

'There is nothing in the diary for Mr Leonard,' says the erect butler, hands behind his back and a feint of a smile delicately sculpted into his earnest face. He is wearing tails and a stiff collar and has a look of the Guardsman about him. He looks Staffe up and down as if he has no place in this parish.

'He wouldn't be expecting me,' says Staffe, putting a plum to his voice, placing his warrant card discreetly upon the high-countered, teak-panelled desk.

'But I can't imagine he wouldn't make time to see me for a few moments. It is a matter of the utmost gravity.'

The butler looks over the rims of his pince-nez glasses and says, 'I shall see what we can do. But Mr Leonard *is* a very busy man.'

'As am I,' says Staffe.

They wait for 'Mr Leonard' to pick up and Staffe leans forward, says almost under his breath, 'Whether Mr Howerd can see me or not, he will see me. I can always return with some uniformed officers. It's simply a question of what he would prefer.'

Leonard Howerd looks as though professional attention from Elena Danya would crack him like a Ming vase. He slowly passes an upturned palm in front of him, towards an empty chair on the opposition's side of the satinwood partners' desk – like a peasant casting seeds into ready ground. His thin-lipped mouth is tight.

'Taki Markary is a friend of yours,' says Staffe.

'I know many people. You do in this line, Mr . . .?'

'Inspector. Detective Inspector Wagstaffe. Was it he who introduced you to Elena Danya?' As he says this, Staffe scrutinises Howerd's reaction. And, right enough, he stops blinking and his eyes widen.

His thin mouth opens and he stares into his lap for a moment.

'Is Mr Markary in some kind of trouble?'

'I'm afraid that I ask the questions, Mr Howerd. And I would like to know exactly where and when, and in what circumstances, you met Elena Danya.'

'Is this all you have come for?'

'This, and to find out where your daughter might be.'

'Ah. I see. What has she done?' He smiles. 'Aah. Another question from me. Not allowed.' Howerd interlocks his fingers, seems to consider what information he should impart. After a long silence, and as if reading from text, he says, 'Taki and I have a business arrangement, near my home in Suffolk. It is something for which I have dispensation from my directors here, and from the Bank of England. In the course of these arrangements, I had cause to meet Miss Danya,' he pauses, 'on a number of occasions.'

'And she was a friend of your daughter's?'

'I would not attempt to choose Arabella's friends.' He stops, frowns, and says, 'Was? You said Miss Danya *was* a friend.'

'Oh. I'm sorry. Elena Danya has been murdered, Mr Howerd. But you know that, don't you. Now, where can I get hold of your daughter?'

'I don't understand what business . . .'

'*I* don't understand! You are in cahoots with Markary, and his murdered mistress bought her drugs from your daughter.'

'I am not in cahoots.' Howerd checks his watch, is clearly fuming.

'You hosted Markary at the Colonial Bankers' Club last week?'

Howerd nods.

'Why did Elena Danya call the club while you were there?'

'I haven't a clue. Is it so?'

'It was one of the last calls she ever made.' Staffe stares Howerd down. 'Silence isn't one of your privileges, Mr Howerd.'

'I am perfectly prepared to be interviewed under the appropriate conditions.' He reaches into a drawer and hands Staffe the business card of 'Sir Ralph Waikman, Essex Court'. 'If you call my barrister's chambers, I'm sure they can arrange for your questions to be answered.'

Staffe says, 'You are too kind,' thinks that this isn't the time for that. In fact, he has a short cut he can take – just around the corner.

Finbar Hare is not quite in Howerd's league but he has been in and around the City all his working life. Many years ago, he and Staffe partied, hard. Now they struggle to see each other once a year. This is the first time Staffe has visited Finbar at these new glass-and-steel offices. As he enters the marbled atrium through five-yard-high revolving doors, Staffe's phone vibrates and Finbar's name fades to Janine. He answers.

'You asked about the dead foetus, Staffe? Well, Taki Markary is definitely the father. No mistake. It's a match from the hair you gave us.'

'Lucky for Taki we seem to have the man who killed his unborn . . .?'

'Daughter. Josie came to pick up the reports. They're within a whisker of a confession, she said.'

'It wouldn't surprise me one bit,' says Staffe. 'He might be a pervert, but he strikes me as an honour-able man.'

'Blears?' says Janine.

'I'll let Markary know,' says Staffe, hanging up and getting into the lift.

All the way up to the trading floor, London spreads wider and wider, like a magical city in a pop-up book. The snow-white fields of Essex and Herts and the Chiltern Hills crumple beneath the clear sky. As he rises, Staffe sees that Markary, with his impeccably bred wife and his power-mongering friends and associates, would be better served if the bastard daughter to his whore mistress was prevented from entering this world.

Finbar Hare meets him at the lift. Staffe's friend

of twenty years, with whom he played rugby and drank furiously, has changed further in the year or so since they last hooked up: his stomach hangs over a belt that won't stay and his hair has thinned; his face is puffy and pale. Staffe tries desperately not to say, 'Bloody hell, man. What's happened to you?' But Finbar slaps his belly and laughs, motions for Staffe to go into his office. He says, in a slow and soft-earth voice that always made women swoon and men unable to dislike him, 'Couldn't this have waited a couple of hours? We might have had a drink. Or are you still off it?'

Staffe shrugs. 'Off and on.'

'You should come round to the house. Flick would love to see you.' Staffe must express surprise because Finbar says, 'Oh yes. We're back together. Again. Miracles happen. But this isn't a social call.'

'Leonard Howerd, Fin. He works for . . .'

'Laing's. I know. Christ, what's the poor bastard done to have you delving into his life. He's a chosen one, you know, Staffe. Tread softly, my man.'

'I can be subtle, you know.'

'Ah, so some things do change.' He looks at his watch and makes a grumpy face. 'A quick snifter?'

'Don't let me stop you.'

'You know, word is that old Leonard might be up for the nod in the New Year's list.'

'What's he done to deserve that?'

'As if we'd ever find out.' Finbar laughs, pouring himself a nip of whisky and holding the bottle up to Staffe, who shakes his head, wishes he could find time to meet his friends more. 'Arise Sir Leonard. For services to the world of money and your third-world yomping and all that dead game you litter East Anglia with. And God, of course.'

Staffe says, 'He's related to *those* Howards?'

'All the way back to Mary bloody Tudor – except Leonard's lot let it slip – out of line. But his wife got them back on track.'

'She's an Audley.'

'And deader than a dodo. Poor Lenny. I only met him a couple of times. We hosted him at Twickers once and had him over for a directors' lunch.' Finbar leads the most irreverently charmed life. He got capped for England, just the once, and that disastrous debut is possibly the only bad luck he ever suffered. In fact, it made people like him the more, and smoothed his way into what he does now. 'Talk about establishment. You know his second cousin thrice removed – or whatever – has organised three state funerals and two coronations. Earl Marshal malarkey. Still, when his wife popped it – a few years ago, it knocked him for six. Loved her to bits, apparently.'

'What about the children?'

'Bloody disaster, is what I heard. Son's a gay boy

and the daughter's a junkie. End of the line!' Fin laughs.

Staffe looks at his watch.

'Flying visit?' says Finbar. 'Honestly,' he walks around his desk, punches Staffe in the shoulder. 'Give us a ring and come round for dinner. You got a girl?'

'Sylvie.'

'Christ, man.' Finbar clicks his fingers and whistles. 'Still batting above your average, then? Bollocks! If you're still with Sylvie, you've *got* to come round.'

'We will,' says Staffe, opening the door.

'What's he done, then, our friend Sir Leonard?'

'I'm not sure he's done anything at all.' He smiles at Finbar and shrugs, sorry that his profession is now standing between them. 'Did he . . . did he like his ladies? Ladies of the night.'

'Don't they all? Dirty bastards,' says Finbar, 'judging by the time we showed him at Twickers. But you know that.'

'What?'

'The higher they are, the lower they get.'

'Anything dodgy?'

Finbar shrugs. This time it is his profession that stands between them, all Jermyn Street and Royal Enclosured.

* * *

Graham Blears, grey, drawn and haunted, is led into the interview room by two prison officers who don't give a toss whether he is a twoccer or a serial killer. One of them takes a copy of *The News* from his back pocket, unaware that his con is the man fallaciously described as Vlad the Ripper. Later today, Absolom will U-turn and the front page will feature Blears.

His solicitor whispers in his ear and Blears nods, somehow resigned, but summoning the strength to ask of Josie the wellbeing of his dog, Useless.

'She's just fine, Graham. Once we have put this to bed I'll find a proper home for her. I promise, she'll be loved.'

'You remember what we agreed?' says the solicitor.

Blears nods and says to Josie, as if Rimmer was not even in the room, 'I know what I have to do.' Through a high window, he sees the brick tenement wing of the jail, running away, like the façade of a Victorian mill.

'Why don't you start at the beginning?'

He shakes his head. 'You have your evidence, so I'm told. And I have been an evil man. I must make my peace.'

'It's important, Graham, that you tell me if there are any other girls. We've spoken to Margaret and she has told us what you like.'

'Margaret?'

'Your friend from the Forest.'

'She knows me?' A smile suggests itself.

'Did you harm any other girls?'

Blears shakes his head and his solicitor produces a sheet of typewritten paper from his briefcase, says, 'This is what we agreed. I have to know, before we sign and witness this, that nothing has changed.'

'The tariff is a matter for the judge, as you know, but we have the CPS on side,' says Rimmer. 'Our expert witness has already documented what she thinks. Grafton would be appropriate.'

At this, the solicitor nods, approvingly. Grafton is the most progressive high-security prison in the country. What the Tory tabloids would describe as a holiday camp.

'I don't care where I go,' says Blears, no qualms about serving his time. Grafton would claim to give Graham Blears his best shot at making a fully functioning and safe contribution to society, some time down the line. But Graham is unconcerned. He takes the pen from his solicitor.

'Did you know the girls were friends?' asks Josie.

'Of course they are. They're all just the same.'

'*How* did you know?'

Blears smiles, as if he has something to be proud of, as if he is governed by a higher deity. He holds the pen as if it were something holy and turns his attention to the document. As he reads it, his face briefly changes.

Sylvie has a plate on her tummy, littered with parkin crumbs. Staffe had made it for Bonfire Night and she had said it wasn't 'the kind of thing to blow my hair back'. It makes him smile now, seeing her in her low jeans and short smock top, with the parkin all eaten up.

Pulford evidently doesn't know quite how to take her. He is sitting up with one leg draped over the other, hands clasped in his lap. His hair is unwaxed and floppy.

Staffe asks Pulford what he has done with his day.

'I was pulled back onto the trafficking case. They had a whole boatload coming in to work on a shopping mall out in Essex. The licences traced to somewhere in Mile End, but the place was shut up when we got there. Not a whiff.'

'Seems like we both missed out on the murder cases,' says Staffe.

'Josie says they got an ID on Blears from some middle-aged woman; says she gave him a – you know,' he looks towards Sylvie, then at the floor.

'A blow job?' says Sylvie.

'A couple of hours after he did for Rebeccah Stone. Bloody pervert. I can't get my head round it.'

'Is Josie the pretty one?' says Sylvie.

Both men nod and mumble, 'Yes. I suppose so. Kind of.' As if it hadn't occurred to them.

'Rimmer and Josie reckon Blears wants to confess. They're talking to the Crown.'

'Tidy,' says Staffe.

'You know, sir, sometimes cases can come together. Surely. You told me that crimes have to be caught hot. And for Blears it was just too much of a burden, that realisation – of what he had done.'

'I'm glad we got our man,' says Staffe.

'I'm off to bed,' says Sylvie, holding a cup of cocoa. 'Don't be too long.' She bends down, kisses Staffe, and as she does it, she takes a hold of his flesh and pinches him just above the nipple. It smarts. When she has gone, he rubs it, looks down, sees that his shirt is smudged with leaked mascara – exactly where his fiancé had pinched him. 'Oh shit,' he says, aloud.

'What?' says Pulford.

'How are you getting on with Rimmer?'

'He seems to have taken a shine to Josie. It's like he's skipped over me.'

'You want me to have a word with Rimmer about the case?'

'Let Josie have her day in the sun. As long as we've got the bastard, that's the main thing, hey, sir,' he says, checking the time on his watch, leaving.

Staffe takes off his shirt, stained with black tears, and puts it in the linen basket, walks quietly on padding feet to his bathroom. He showers vigorously, taking it as hot as he can bear – then a notch higher for the count of twenty, then immediately onto full cold full blast for as long as it takes him to count down from sixty. He walks naked and wet to the bedroom. As he eases the door shut, Sylvie stirs.

He tries to slide into bed without waking her but she backs into him and takes hold of his hand. She says, soft, 'You showered.'

'It's been a long day.'

'I don't know you. Do I, Will? Not really.'

As soon as Staffe is certain that Sylvie is asleep, he eases his way out of bed and creeps down the corridor, walking on his toes until he gets to the lounge. He takes his phone from his jacket pocket and seeks out Rosa, checking his watch and deciding this cannot wait until morning. He thinks of her in the Metropole Hotel with a stranger; thinks of the two dead girls' numbers she still keeps in her phone. He looks into the night as he calls her. Flecks of snow are falling, slowly in the radial haze of the streetlights.

'Were you awake?' he says. 'Sorry. But you got back OK? I worry about you. You have to be extra careful, Rosa. Promise me you'll be careful. OK. Goodnight. I'll be in touch soon. Me too.'

He clicks off the phone and turns to put the handset back in his jacket pocket. As he does, he sees her.

Sylvie says, 'Who is Rosa, Will?'

Eighteen

Staffe draws back his hand, rattles the lion's-head brass knocker to the four-storey town house in Mayfair. He thinks he should perhaps have been more respectful to Leonard Howerd at the bank. But then he thinks of Elena Danya and Rebeccah Stone. Bugger that. He knocks the brass lion head again, knowing Howerd will have left to go to his bank.

A young man answers: tall and frail, handsome and boyish. He is dressed as if his mother may have laid his clothes out for him, except his mother was taken by Peruvian bandits five years ago. This is Roddy Howerd, a freshman scholar at St John's, Oxford. Latest in the line.

'Is Arabella in?' says Staffe, looking Roddy in the eye, holding it until the boy looks away.

'I'm afraid not.'

'When will she be back?'

'Who are you?'

'I told your father I would be coming round.' Staffe shows Roddy his warrant card and puts a foot into the house. 'I won't be long.'

'She's staying away at the moment.'

'Staying away.' A strange phrase. 'Best not talk in the street, hey?' Staffe thinks it odd that Roddy hasn't asked what trouble Arabella might be in.

Roddy shows Staffe into a beautifully furnished drawing room on the upper ground floor, overlooking Bryanston Square. With his back to Roddy, looking out onto the Square, Staffe says, 'Tell me about your mother, Roddy.'

'I thought you were here about Bella.'

'Her friends call her Arra. Have you met her friends? Two of them are dead, so when I ask you about your mother, when I ask you anything at all, I'd like an answer. Do you understand?'

Roddy nods, looks at his feet.

'What did your father do to lose Arabella?'

'She's not lost. Bella has always done her own thing.'

'Does she take after her mother?'

'I was fourteen when she died.'

'I'm sorry. Did you know Elena?'

He shakes his head.

'Rebeccah Stone?'

Roddy shakes his head again, like a shy one in class.

'If I find out you're lying or haven't told me everything, you can kiss goodbye to your degree – that's for sure. Now! Where is Arabella?'

Roddy replies, quick as lies, 'I don't know.'

'If any harm comes to her, you'll have blood on your hands. Is that what you want? Now, do you have an address for her? A boyfriend?'

Roddy shakes his head. Staffe knows that as soon as Daddy gets home, the shit really will fly.

He turns his attention to an oil painting. 'Where is this?' The painting, of a boat in a sunwashed harbour, is almost Impressionistic, but with a Fauvist palette of lilacs and yellows and blues.

'The Med?' says Roddy.

'Could it be Turkey? You're a Classics scholar, Roddy?'

'Father was. I'm a mathematician.'

'Aah. Like the rest of them.'

'There is something of a tradition.'

'Except your father. It must be difficult, all that to live up to. You really are quite a family.' Staffe knows there is a chink in the line, without which you could trace Roddy all the way back to Mary and the men who set fire to those martyrs outside his Oxford college.

'It seems normal to me.'

In the corner of the room is a Byzantine icon of the Virgin with Child.

'Turkey?' says Staffe. 'Taki Markary's a family friend.'

Roddy shrugs, his hand busy in his pocket.

Staffe has what he wants, for now, and if his

instincts are correct about Roddy, then Leonard will really struggle with that faltering family line – should Arabella not issue forth with progeny. On his way out, Staffe clocks a panoramic group portrait. *Ampleforth Leavers, June MMIX*. Roddy is extreme left, right at the back.

Staffe says, 'Yes, please. I would love tea. Mint, if you have it.'

Sema Markary smiles, says, 'Taki lives by it.' She knows not to be overly familiar, takes a backward step and leaves the room. As she goes, she smiles tightly at her husband and narrows her eyes. Staffe sees that she loves and respects Taki. She will not make the tea herself, of course. The Markarys have people who do that.

'You have a beautiful wife,' says Staffe.

'Why are you here?'

'It's delicate.' Staffe goes across to the Sickert and admires it.

'You've seen it before, Inspector.'

'What do you think our friend Sickert would have made of Vlad the Ripper?'

'It would seem the press have got that one wrong. Unless Graham Blears has Russian ancestry.'

'Aah. You have been following the case.'

'You know damn well I have an involvement. If only through your harassment.'

'This signature?' Staffe has leaned right in to a vivid portrait of a beautiful woman who could be Turkish, or Persian. Staffe thinks the setting is the garden of a villa on the Bosporus. Aghia Sofia's dome and minaret are implied with six deft strokes in the background. 'Imogen Howerd. What do you make of her work?'

'This is at our villa in Istanbul. They are family friends.'

'Why might Leonard Howerd kill his wife, Mr Markary?'

'What?' Markary is appalled.

'They are a troubled family.'

'Only Arabella,' says Markary.

'How did you meet Elena Danya?'

The door opens and Sema Markary directs the maid to set the silver tray down on the ebonised petit table in the window.

Markary stares at Staffe, rigid with fear at what the inspector could say.

Staffe waits for the maid to leave. Sema stays. He says, 'Arabella was a friend of hers. Is that how you first met?'

'Arabella Howerd?' enquires Sema. 'Oh, dear. Has she been up to nonsense again? Always fighting with poor Imogen.' Sema Markary looks at her portrait, the smile gone and her eyes cold, unfaltering. 'Is Arabella tied up with that Russian girl? I'm always telling Taki to be less generous, Inspector.' She turns back to Staffe. 'Not like me. I'm different.'

Sema leaves and Staffe pours tea. The glasses are filigreed with gold and the tea smells of Smyrna. Through the window, he peruses Mayfair. The snow remains on the roofs and railings of the Georgian rows – a scene for pen and ink. 'It was your daughter they killed, Taki,' Staffe says. 'Elena was carrying a daughter and you were the father. We have the proof, if you wish to see it.'

Markary's glass slips through his fingers and smashes. Both men look at the diamond scatter of the crystal and the Turk says, 'You don't know how solid we are, Inspector. I suggest you look elsewhere. Good luck with that.'

'Don't pretend you were born to this life. You're no Leonard Howerd,' says Staffe, standing.

'What do you mean?' Markary looks deeply affronted.

'Before *she* took a shine, Taki, you were running guns to the Arabs. You know how to get blood off your hands. You've had to try harder, haven't you. Not so close to God as some, hey? And in my book – that gives you less to lose.'

Staffe waits for Josie and Rimmer in the far snug of the Hand and Shears and allows himself a pint of

Adnams. The glass's etched crest denotes the brewery. As he waits, in the warm glow of the fire, logs spitting, he wonders how much money there is to be made up in Aldesworth Country Town.

As soon as he sees Josie and Rimmer come through the door, raising their arms aloft and striding towards his table, Staffe can tell Graham Blears must have chucked up his confession.

'Tonight, we drink!' says Josie, her eyes twinkling and Staffe can't help but feel glad in a part of his heart. He raises his glass and wiggles it and she marches off to the bar.

Josie gets stuck into a conversation at the bar with Dick, and Rimmer pulls up a stool. 'She's done well, the girl. A bright cookie.'

Rimmer tells Staffe how the CPS are happy with the corroborating evidence. He jokes about how Blears had obsessed about the welfare of his dog; and then, as the pints are sunk, he confides that he had secretly feared his return to duty and how much he appreciates Staffe letting him take the lead on this investigation. 'Imagine, if you hadn't gone off like that.'

Staffe raises his pint of Suffolk ale. 'To you. Your old man would be proud.'

Rimmer's eyes glaze over and he looks down into his beer, says, 'I'm not half the man. Not half the copper.'

'Go easy on yourself. Those are big boots to fill.'

'You know, he died within a year of retiring. There's more to life than that, surely. I'm up for pension in six years, and between you and me, it can't come soon enough.'

Staffe wonders where this is all coming from and contemplates the power of hubris.

'You're different though, hey Staffe. You couldn't cope without this, could you.'

Staffe tries to picture the long, empty arc from morning to night; can't begin to imagine how the days would fill themselves without this life he has formed for himself. Suddenly, he feels quite weary.

On his way out, he pats Josie on the back. 'I'm proud of you,' he says.

'You can see that Blears did it, sir?'

'Seems you were right. Follow what you believe, Josie. No matter what you hear. You'll be right often enough, and if you're not – there's always the law.'

She laughs and puts a hand on his shoulder. 'You should stick around, sir. It's going to be a big night. We're going down the Butcher's in a while.'

Staffe yields to a tug from the station; kicks back against something else. He kisses Josie on the cheek and leaves, swallowing away everything he might say.

* * *

Pennington sucks on a plastic cigarette and when he sees Staffe in the doorway of his office he smiles, warmly. Pennington seldom smiles warmly. He reaches into the pedestal drawer of his desk and draws out a bottle of Scotch, goes back in for two glasses and holds them up. Staffe nods.

'You look done in, Will.'

'I've been with Rimmer and Chancellor. Seems congratulations are in order.'

'We got that bastard, good and proper.' The DCI hands Staffe his glass and they chink, then slug. Pennington recharges them.

'I'm going to take a break, sir.'

'Nobody barks up a tree quite the way you do, Will. Not just barking, shaking the bloody fruit down before it's ready.'

Staffe laughs. He likes the image. 'You're not always so phlegmatic, sir – about my harvesting.'

Pennington stands. 'Take your leave, Will. And if I might suggest, you could do a little gardening.'

'You don't have any doubts about Blears, sir?'

'There's no doubting the quality of the evidence against him. Go easy, Will.' Pennington shakes Staffe's hand, gripping his shoulder with the other. 'Have a merry Christmas, and plenty prosperity.'

'Prosperity?' thinks Staffe. That's relative. Prosper like Pennington or even himself. Or prosper like Markary and the Howerds?

Staffe goes into his office and reaches right to the back of the drawer of his filing cabinet. Rebeccah's plastic freedom bag is still there, as is the *PRIVAT* envelope, the bearer bonds within. But it is something else that Staffe wants. He replaces Rebeccah's things, pockets Mitch's bag of wraps and makes his way to visit Rebeccah's so-called boyfriend.

Mitch has a fresh cut above his eye and a swollen jaw. ''t you want?' he snarls. 'You lay one finger on me, I'll call my brief.'

'Where does Arabella live?'

He shrugs.

'Her boyfriend, Darius – he's a dealer, right? You'll know where his place is.'

'No way, man.'

'I bet you're still playing catch-up, aren't you, after I had away with your little stash?' Staffe prods Mitch's swollen cheekbone. 'They've been a-visiting, I see.'

'The fuck you want? I don't know where they live.'

'There must have been fifty grammes of decent stuff, I'd say. You hadn't had a chance to let it down.'

Mitch keeps his beady eyes fixed on Staffe's hands, flinching as he goes into his pockets. 'Leave me alone!' he shouts, all street disappearing from his voice.

Staffe shows Mitch what he is carrying. In the palm of each hand, at least a grand's worth of coke. Mitch's coke. 'Supposedly, it helps the memory.'

'You're not going to fuck me over?'

'Lie, and I will. Otherwise . . .'

'Haverstock Hill, just round the back of the Steeles. It's Jarndyce Road. Number seventy-two. The street's full of Polish builders. They're a fucking nightmare.'

Nineteen

Rosa mulls her finances as she runs a bath. The smell of cinnamon and cloves rises and spreads with the steam. She swirls the bath water and curses as the phone rings.

It has been a slow day, at the end of which she treated herself to a dusk stroll through Borough Market. Lunchtime, she saw Max, one of her regulars, which was eighty quid in – not the stuff of nest eggs, which a girl of her age should be incubating.

Rosa doesn't recognise the phone number and her thumb hovers. Red or green? Green or red? She wants an early night but today hasn't really got her anywhere.

She chooses green, recognises the tone of his voice immediately. You would too, if you'd heard what it uttered only the day before, in the Metropole Hotel – looking up at her, saying he loved her and what he would like her to do to him. But it was only words and over soon enough. He didn't even go inside her. She held him afterwards. Two hundred buys you love.

Tonight, he asks for the same thing, the same price, and he asks her to wear white.

Rosa turns off the bath taps, orders a cab. She lays out the clothes to his specification; the nest egg a couple of days closer to hatching. She lets out the water, turns on the shower.

Tchancov downs his vodka and asks Staffe if he would like coffee.

Staffe declines, says, 'What did you make of the article in *The News*?'

'Vlad!' he laughs. 'We get it all the time. People think we are what we are not.'

'There is such a thing as a Russian gangster, though – here in London.'

'I won't play that game, Inspector.' The cocky smile from their earliest meeting has gone and the man who took Markary down all those pegs seems a pale outline of himself.

'Times are hard for everybody, I suppose, Vassily.'

'The world turns, still.'

'Like cogs. We have to keep going at other people's pace, keep finding new ways. I see your uncle Ludo is up for governor again.'

'That's a faraway land.'

Staffe thinks it is, perhaps, closer than Vassily might wish. 'My colleagues keep an eye on things. There seems to be an insatiable desire to work in England.'

'My uncle Ludo is like a father.' For the first time,

since Staffe met him, Tchancov shows sadness, regret. Something unrequited, or unforgiven, is written on his gaunt face.

'There has never been a Mrs Tchancov?'

'You should be going.'

'Not before I have told you our news. We have a man for the murder of your girl. And Elena. He has confessed. In a way, I suppose he's one of yours.'

Tchancov pours himself another vodka, downs it immediately. Pours another. 'A Russian?'

'No. He likes his sex. He's a consumer, Vassily. A right pest, so they say.'

As if by magic, the Mongolian with the scimitar sideburns appears in the doorway of Tchancov's lounge. 'Hardly one of mine,' he says. 'If you have a confession, why are you here?'

'A matter of courtesy. That's all.'

'Would it be discourteous of me to tell you to leave?'

'I could write, next time. Get some nice paper. Some lilac paper, like Elena used when she wrote to you.'

'You should learn to accept things for what they are.'

'Show me her letters, Vassily. I'll accept them for what they are. You have nothing to hide.'

'There are no letters.'

'Which answers your question.'

'What?'

'As to why I am here. You choose to lie to me – even though we have our man. Time well spent, wouldn't you say?'

Rosa strolls confidently past the concierge of the Metropole, gets into the lift with a businessman. He says, 'Good evening,' in a soft, low voice that suggests he thinks he is in with a chance. He is northern European, probably Danish, and she nods, angles herself away from him, pressing 4. He reaches across and presses 6, his eyes up and down and all over her. The floors come slowly.

It pings 4. He says, 'Have a good evening.'

Although she has done this several hundred times, tonight she wishes she was home, drifting to sleep with a book slipping from her fingers. Tonight, curiously, she fears she may be in the game two or three years too many.

She goes left, down a long corridor, and left again, around the service shaft. Rosa breathes deep and runs her fingers through her hair, pulling it forward so it frames her face. Then, through her dress, she pulls up her pants at the sides and fixes them just so, hitching her stockings up. She stands erect and closes her eyes, transports herself to a place from which she can push herself all the way out. She knocks, twice. As always, her heart beats faster, harder. The door opens away from her, shows her into somebody else's world.

He is lean and seems younger tonight – and kind, as if he couldn't do harm. Her instincts are good.

As soon as the door is shut he puts a hand on the slope of her shoulder and neck and kisses her, mouth slightly open, on the lips. His mouth is wet and tastes of vodka, his other hand around the back already, to where her buttocks meet her thighs. He squeezes gently and she cannot help but utter a low gasp.

He asks if she wants a drink. She declines, fathoming that he is from Liverpool. Maybe from Ireland in the past or the other way round. He asks if she minds if he does and she shakes her head, watches him pour a neat Smirnoff from the minibar and go to the easy chair by the window. It is one of many hundred windows in this hotel. This one looks into the top of a department store on Oxford Street. Nobody sees in.

Rosa says, 'You want to watch me?'

'Undress,' he says in his soft voice that seems to need love.

She reaches behind, to unzip her dress, and he says, 'No. Pull up the dress. I want to see your legs. Be slow.' He seems uncertain, almost as though he can't believe what he is saying.

Rosa bends, crosses her hands and takes the left

hem of her dress with the right and vice versa. Far away, she hears a car horn. Otherwise, in the hard and secret heart of the city, it is silent; slowly, she pulls up her dress, a translucent white chiffon, over her head. Through it, she sees only a warm amber glow from the bedside light.

'Stop!' he says. 'Please. Stop.'

She can hear him stand. She smells vodka coming off him. She realises he is behind her. Again, he puts one hand on the slope of her shoulder and neck and he kisses the lobe of her ear through the dress. He brings his teeth together on her. Again, she cannot help but gasp and she feels the slow descent of his other hand, first on the plump of her hip above her pants, then on the underside of her tummy.

'What do you want?' she says.

'Stay just the way you are.'

Suddenly, Rosa is afraid, is unsure whether a door has opened, perhaps the en-suite. Is there another man here? 'Let me take the dress off,' she says.

'Your friends,' he says, the tenderness seeping away and his hand tighter on her neck. 'You know the things you know. You know the people you know. It's no good for us and it's no good for you.'

'Please!' she pleads. 'I don't know anything.'

'But you do. Tell me what you know about the other two.'

217

She can barely hear what he is saying. Her blood drums deep and fast in her ears.

Rosa's voice warbles as she makes her reply. All she wants to do is to scream, then sob and collapse and let this all be over. 'Elena?' she says, thinking that as long as she is talking he won't kill her. He killed the others, though. 'Elena never said anything to me, just about clothes and the books she liked to read. That's all.'

'And her boyfriend? The one who stuck it up her?'

'She never said she was pregnant.'

He says, 'I never said she was pregnant. You been talking to your policeman friend? He needs to let it all lie, wouldn't you say?'

Rosa's hands are still above her head. She says, 'You said "stuck it up her". What's that supposed to mean if . . .' She coughs, '. . . it doesn't mean . . .' She coughs again, spluttering now and feels his grip on her throat release and she brings her hand down, as if to go to her mouth to abate the coughing, but it doesn't. She leans forward to cough again, but within the convulsion she brings her head back. Fast! As hard as she can, smashing into his mouth. She hears the crunch of bone on flesh and teeth, and in the very same instant, he cries out into the room as she takes a hold of his balls with one hand, as hard as she can – as tight as she can muster and tugging, tugging, feeling her nails splinter as she does it and twisting round to face him, seeing his bloody face and reaching up, punching him in the throat, watching his eyes bulge and then grabbing his hair, hard as she can and dragging his head down, down towards the carpet. In a single, frozen moment, she sees the detail of the carpet, burgundy with small gold diamonds. She sees his head on the floor and can't hear his curses any more – just his head on the carpet, turning to look up at her, his whole body flexing.

'You stupid, stupid . . .'

But he doesn't finish. She lifts up her stiletto foot, and she stamps down on his head with all her might, the heel's pointed tip skidding off the curvature of his skull, but raking down across his face, making him clasp his head with both hands.

Rosa turns, runs for the door and opens it, kicking off her shoes and tearing off down the corridor, turning right past the service shaft and down along the corridor, then right again, hearing his curses rise and diminish as she gets to the lift, punching at the Down buttons but seeing both lifts are up at 9 and 11. She pushes the fire door, takes the steps two at a time, half flight by half flight, not knowing who might be waiting when she gets to the lobby.

She bursts through the doors and barges into a

group of Far Eastern tourists, checking in. She runs behind the desk, throwing herself into the arms of the concierge, screaming, 'Save me! Save me! Call the police, I've been attacked. Call the police, I've been attacked!'

The concierge tries to usher her away into the office behind reception but she won't have it, insists on remaining where she can be seen until they call a man called Inspector Wagstaffe at City CID. She screams blue murder until that happens, until every last one of the Japanese tourists has checked in and two security guards have sat her down, until she can be sure that the man in room 411 is gone.

When she is calm, they tell her room 411 is empty tonight. They have been in and the room is untouched.

Staffe is spooning up to Sylvie to keep warm. She has kicked off the sheets in a fretful sleep. He dreams that he is awakened by a ringing telephone, then is awakened by an elbow from the woman he loves. As he turns over, trying to regain sleep, Sylvie says, 'It's yours, Will. Your phone's ringing.'

He fumbles for his mobile, knowing this will hardly be good news. The man on the other end speaks calmly, telling him that a friend of his has been attacked and that she was quite insistent that they call him. The man tells him he is from the

Metropole Hotel and that the woman is called Rosa.

'Is she . . . is she alive?'

As Staffe wakes fully, he discerns that the man thinks this a strange question. For a sliver of a moment, as he dresses hurriedly, Staffe wishes for another life, far away from this. Then he hears somebody behind him and the rustle of clothes.

Sylvie, blinking, rubbing her face, has a silk robe around her and is padding towards the kitchen, saying, 'I'll make you some coffee.'

'I have to go straight away.'

'Will, you need to tell me about her.'

'When I get back.'

'I need to know if anything is going on. I won't let that happen to me. I've seen what it does.'

He wants to convince her that he is nothing like her mother, that after all these years he has finally realised she is the one. But now is not the time.

'She's a friend.'

'Strange kind of friend. I catch you calling her in the middle of the night and then next thing you're off on some rescue mission.'

Outside the Metropole, Staffe tells the cabbie it'll be a while before they know where they're going but to put his meter on and turn off the intercom.

Sliding the window shut, he says to Rosa, 'I can't help you if you don't tell me everything.'

'I keep telling you, I'm not hiding anything, Will. Why would I?' Her mascara has run and her bare shoulders tremble. She has refused his jacket, insists she is 'boiling up', but she is ice cold to the touch.

'Tell me again what he said to you.' He scoots right up to her.

'He said, "You know the people you know." He said, "It's no good for us and it's no good for you." He asked me to tell him everything I knew about them. "The other two," he called them.'

'And what did you tell him? What do you know?' She tenses up and he can feel it.

'I don't know anything!' Rosa's eyes are wide and red. 'He asked about the one who stuck it up her.'

'Oh, Jesus,' says Staffe. 'He knows she was pregnant.' He slides open the glass screen, tells the cabbie to take them to West Smithfield, to the City police morgue.

'I'm not going there,' says Rosa, leaning away.

'You want to get out?'

'Why are you being like this, Will? You're supposed to be my friend.'

Staffe pulls her close, watches the city lights over her shoulder, thinking who might have known Elena was pregnant.

Twenty

'I'm not going in,' says Rosa. Staffe has sent the taxi away and they are round the back of the Royal London, on Rook's Way, outside the City police morgue. From behind, the grand Victorian pile looms, brooding and sinister; like Bedlam.

Through the meshed safety glass, Staffe sees the outline of Janine coming towards them.

'What's to be gained?' says Rosa.

'You could pay your respects.'

Rosa clutches her own torso with wraparound arms. Her eyes are wild now, and dark. The tears have run dry, the fear is all played out.

'It might jog your memory,' he says.

'Where can I go, Will?'

'You will come to mine,' says Staffe.

'If I play ball?'

'Regardless.' He takes her hand and leads her past Janine. Curiously, it is warmer in the morgue than outside – until they get to a metal door. All their clicking shoes come to a halt and Janine lets them in with a coded punch of the entry pad.

Inside, the light is harsh, but the perimeter of the room is black as night. Staffe shows Rosa a seat at the edge of the room and hands her a blanket. She wraps it around her and watches as Staffe follows Janine into the far dark. Slowly, into the brilliant light, they each wheel a trollied bench. Staffe has Elena and Janine Rebeccah.

Rosa tries to look only at their hair and their faces. But her eyes trail down to the cross-stitched scars of their autopsied bodies and she grabs her mouth. The dead girls are the colour of the moon.

'You know what I'm going to say,' says Staffe.

'This could have been me.'

'It could be somebody else, too. If there's anybody else who knows what you know, Rosa.'

Rosa shakes her head. 'I don't know what I know.' She walks to the dead girls and reaches out, laying her palms flat on the faces of the two girls. Rosa closes her eyes, stays like that for a minute, then two. Five.

Eventually, she lifts her hands, opens her eyes, and she turns to Staffe. 'Whatever I know, once I've told you, that's it. That's all I can do. I don't have any more cards to play.'

'You have to tell me.'

Janine turns off the operating lights and leaves Staffe and Rosa in the soft light from the washroom at the back of the morgue theatre. Staffe raises a hand to bid her farewell then turns to Rosa, taking her hands in his. 'You must believe that anything you tell me won't harm you. I won't allow it.'

'For Elena and Rebeccah and me . . . It's us against the world – it has to be. You let so much in, you give so much of yourself . . .' Rosa talks into her lap, running her thumb along Staffe's knuckles. '. . . You have to keep something for yourself, for each other. We trust each other.'

'That has to change now,' says Staffe.

Rosa sighs, choosing her words, with the greatest of care. 'Elena started behaving differently, the last couple of months or so. She kept saying I should find a way out. I always thought she was happy in the game. It was a while before I understood.' Rosa looks at Staffe, shakes her head and looks back into her lap.

'Understood?'

'That she was getting out.'

'They didn't kill her because she was getting out, surely? She was having a baby. Markary's baby, for Christ's sake.'

'I don't think it was anything to do with the baby. No, Elena knew something.'

'Did Rebeccah know it, too?'

'Becx had her own plans. They wouldn't have worked out if Tchancov had got wind of them. She has a little girl, you know. Her mother looks after her.'

'Her mother!'

'Her mother loves her, Will. As best she can.'

'Maybe she and Elena have been blackmailing Markary.'

Rosa shakes her head and Staffe can't tell whether she is still holding back.

'Did Bobo know it wasn't his baby?'

'*His* baby!' Rosa looks up at Staffe.

'Jealous lovers lose their minds.'

'You don't know? That was all an act. Elena was Bobo's sister.'

'What!'

'He followed her over here. That's how he got his job with Tchancov. He's nothing to do with any of this.'

Staffe lets go of her hands and sighs. 'There's nothing more?'

Rosa says nothing.

'What is it?' he says.

'Becx was complaining that she wasn't in the club.'

'Not pregnant?'

'No, not that. Elena would talk with Arabella. They had secrets.'

'Arabella Howerd,' says Staffe, as much to himself as Rosa.

'Elena had a thing for Darius.'

'Arabella's boyfriend?' says Staffe. 'It seems like everybody had a piece of Elena.'

226

'Elena had a piece of everybody, is how it was. But if you ask me, it was the real thing for Elena.'

'With Darius? More than Markary?'

'She's a young woman, Will. And they all seem to go for Darius. I don't get it myself, but he's got something, that boy.'

They get back into the cab, and as they go into the dark night – towards Jombaugh, who will tend her until Staffe is all done – Rosa whispers into his chest that the man who lured her knows she has a 'policeman friend'. 'You have to let it all lie, Will.'

Staffe has impressed on Rosa that he will return to the station for her in an hour or so and that she will stay with him. Now, in the dead of the London night, Jarndyce Road slumbers, tranquil. The skips and builders' vans are bathed in mist like a natural part of a timeless landscape.

It is clear that only one floor of the house is occupied and Staffe lobs up a handful of gravel, smattering the main window. There is no response, so he lobs up another. And another, until a light comes on and an angry young man opens a window, shouts, 'Fuck off!' holding a breeze block. Fair to say, he is used to trouble.

'A'Court!' calls Staffe.

'I said fuck off!'

'Police. Watch your language and let me in.' As he waits, Staffe sees that despite the commotion, the street sleeps on. It would appear that most of the houses are either under, or awaiting, redevelopment.

'What do you want?' says Darius A'Court, opening the front door, seemingly coming down from something.

Staffe pushes past him and up the stairs, following the sweet smell of weed. 'Is Arra in?'

'Leave her alone.'

'It's a bit late for that.' When Staffe gets to the top of the stairs, he stops dead.

Arabella's long, thick blonde hair is tangled and her skin is dry, but with her long, fine features and her powder-blue eyes, the young Howerd looks as if she is Elena Danya, back to life. 'I'm here about Elena,' says Staffe.

'Is it a mistake? Is she all right?' Arabella speaks slowly and her words drift into each other, like snow on the wind.

Staffe shakes his head.

'Say nothing,' says Darius. He puts an arm round Arabella. It makes her smile.

'You were in her phone. And Rebeccah's.'

'They're my friends.'

Staffe makes his way into the living room. The walls are bare and a hippy throw hangs at the

228

window. The scent of weed is thick and it smells as if they might have rustled some soup. It is damp, cold as outdoors. 'You don't need to live like this.'

'I look after her,' says Darius.

Staffe turns on Darius, stands nose to nose. He can see what women might find in him. His eyes are dark and glassy. He has a faraway, lost look. Staffe whispers, 'I bet you do.'

'What's happening?' says Arabella, sitting on the edge of a threadbare sofa, wrapping a blanket around her. For an instant, as she looks up at Staffe, he can see all her deep beauty. Fleetingly, she appears to be strong, capable. She is beautiful, but soon, she is lost again, reaching her hand out for Darius.

'What happened to you, Arabella?' says Staffe.

She smiles, dazed.

'Don't you fit, with all that history, that old England?'

Arabella's eyes cloud over and Darius sits beside her, hugs her to him.

'Did Elena like the old England?'

Arra looks sidelong at Darius. 'Lots of people like Elena.'

'Who was the father, Arra?' says Staffe. 'You knew she was pregnant.'

Arabella shrugs Darius away. He looks hurt – as if this is the tip of an argument they have had many times. She puts her hands to her face.

Staffe says, 'Darius? Any clues about the father?' He turns to Arra, says, 'I bet the baby would have looked like you. You and Elena are very alike.'

'It was a baby girl?'

'But you and Rebeccah are different, aren't you. Elena knew something, didn't she, Arra? Tell me. I want to know what she knew.'

'They *are* dead, right?' says Arabella, as if history might be rewritten.

Staffe wonders when she last had something to hope for – in her rich and landed, God-blessed existence.

'I guess you miss your mother, don't you, Bella.'

'She called me Bella.' The way she says 'Bella', her name sounds like something fine.

'I'd like to take you to your father. I think he should see you.'

Arabella looks up at Staffe and she has tears in her eyes. Her hands, knotted together, shake. 'You want to use me. But I'm no good to you.'

'You have to tell me what Elena knew.'

Arabella looks away, lets her body slump into Darius's arms. She looks Staffe straight in the eyes and as her lids shut down, she murmurs, 'He loves me. He's the only one.'

Darius smiles, as if he has something to be proud of, as if that is a rare thing.

* * *

230

It is clear to Sylvie that Staffe is desperately trying not to wake her. He slinks into the Queen's Terrace flat and takes the woman straight to the lounge.

From the bedroom, Sylvie hears Pulford say, 'Who's the girl?'

Staffe ignores the question and Sylvie draws her gown over her shoulders, breathes in, long and slow, and holds the air in her lungs. She will not make a scene, but she will get to the bottom of what is going on.

When she opens the door to the lounge, Staffe is kneeling at the woman's feet. She is on the chaise longue, cupping a mug of tea. Sylvie can see that she has been crying. Staffe stands, but her focus is on the woman, following each flit of the eye. She has a certain beauty. Easy to see that men would want her.

'This is . . .' says Staffe.

Sylvie crosses the room, extends her hand and says, 'Rosa, I presume,' sitting beside her. 'Welcome to our home. A bit of a madhouse, I'm afraid. Is there anything we can get you?'

Rosa shakes her head, looks up, past Sylvie, to Staffe.

'Something sweet. Go and get the biscuits, Will.'

'She doesn't want one.'

'Well I do!' Sylvie looks at Rosa as she says it, forcing a smile and the instant Staffe is through the door, she says, 'I'm Sylvie. Will's fiancée.' She searches for a look of surprise on Rosa's face, but none is forthcoming. 'Perhaps you should explain what's going on.'

'Maybe Will should tell you.'

'Maybe he should. But I'm guessing you know him better than that.'

'I'm in trouble.'

'So why not go to the police?'

'Will is the police.'

'It's a rather personal service, isn't it?' Sylvie leans back, crosses her legs and looks Rosa up and down, notices the thick denier at the top of her stockings; thinks, 'Not in this weather.'

'Will is a friend. We've been friends for years and years.'

'We've been lovers – on and off, for years and years. Strange, that he's never talked of you.'

'I'm a prostitute,' says Rosa.

In the scheme of whatever Rosa has been through, thinks Sylvie, this admission must be nothing, but nonetheless it makes Sylvie feel ashamed. 'Have you been more than friends?'

Rosa smiles with weak lips. Her eyes are seven parts dead. 'I know this is your home, but you wouldn't believe what I have been through tonight. You should ask Will about us.' She looks out, into the night. 'Not that there is an "us".'

'Is this to do with the two other girls?'

And now, Rosa does break down. She convulses, trying not to cry. Sobbing, she says, 'They were my friends.'

Sylvie shifts towards her and wraps her arms around Rosa. She is cold and her skin feels hard, perhaps because of the gooseflesh. As she breathes in and out, she realises that Rosa smells of absolutely nothing.

In the dark, a heavy footfall peters to nothing. Another door closes.

Arabella shivers, reaches out with a long, slender arm for flesh, but Darius is gone. She wraps her arms around her own body, runs her hands along her ribs. She tucks her knees up to her chest and nestles deeper into the bed. An engine splutters then dies and her dreams come back as a reprise of the footfall and doors, and in this thin prelude to sleep, Arabella smiles, waits for Darius to come back; his flesh to hers. They will soon find a better place, to conduct this life.

Opening her eyes, she turns over, waits for him to come. The door opens and she gasps at what she sees.

Arabella doesn't recognise him, nor his friend; at first she thinks this could be happening within her sleep, still. They wear masks, so it could be Darry, but why would he? He comes across to her, fast. His hands are rough with her. They're talking in tongues and she lashes out with her long legs, but she hurts when they kick against the men in the masks. She hits out with her arms but soon becomes breathless.

In the end, she surrenders – quite willingly. A darkness comes, like blessed relief, as a shroud drapes itself over and all around her, bringing with it a profound silence. She cannot even hear the wash of her blood or the beat of her heart.

She feels she is gone to another place and hopes Darius knows how much she loves him. She should have told him so. She wishes she had seen her father one last time, prays to all that is sacred that she will somehow feel a final embrace from Imogen. And strangely, she fears for Roddy. Alone with his father, smothered by all that.

Arabella has a memory of him coming to her after Imogen died. He sat on her bed and held her hand – but it was he who was crying. He was four-teen years old and she hears it now, but these thoughts, these feelings already feel like an echo, ebbing, ebbing away until there is nothing but nothing.

Twenty-one

Staffe knocks, waits a beat, then turns the handle. Pennington looks up, as if caught in mischief, but all he's doing is reading the *Telegraph*.

'There's been another attack.' Staffe pulls up a chair.

'Attack?'

'On a prostitute. So, unless Graham Blears broke out in the night, he's not your man.'

'It could be a separate incident. Not everything is connected, Will.'

'If you close this case, how many other girls could be putting themselves at risk. She could have bloody died, for Christ's sake!'

'Who could have died?'

'She is a friend of mine, as it happens.'

'Rosa Henderson?'

'How do you know about her?'

Pennington folds the *Telegraph*, perfectly. 'She was in the phones of Elena Danya and Rebeccah Stone. I made it my business to discover the ins and outs of her. I *am* a detective you know.'

'So you can see she's connected. And last night she was attacked. In a hotel – just like Elena Danya.'

'How come it wasn't reported? It should have been on the area bulletin.'

'She called me.'

Pennington grimaces. 'And you have her?'

'I feel like a bloody duck on the fair.'

'I have a killer, Will. I have a confession. We didn't exactly beat it out of him.'

'I found Arabella Howerd. Her father and Markary are in a deal together, up in Suffolk.'

'That's where you went.'

'Is there a reason I shouldn't go back?'

Pennington shrugs, as if he is indifferent, but Staffe knows him well enough – which Pennington knows. 'Howerd's well connected,' says Pennington, standing up, making it clear this exchange has run its course. And in doing so, punctuating the last thing he said.

Leonard Howerd will not go into the bank until after lunch today. He is in his favourite armchair in his study, which is off a half landing at the back of the house, overlooking his private garden. The branches of the silver birch and the laburnum are white-hatched with frost. He looks down at the *Spectator* which he has been nursing for two hours while he waits.

Better times waft up from the garden, tapping the windows, almost. Even when he was up to his eyes in work, when the bank was on its knees after his father died and the vultures were swooping, he would lay down his papers and listen from here. He would sneak a peek so they wouldn't see him: Imogen and Arabella. That was before everything changed, for the worse. Like her mother, Arabella loves too well. He misses Imogen terribly, if he is truthful, and it takes its toll on Roddy, he knows. But he can do nothing about it.

The telephone rings.

The voice is not unfamiliar and the instruction is within the realms of what he might have expected. He tries to pretend this is progress, but his heart lags behind, like a stubborn child.

Leonard treads gently into his son's room, puts his hand on Roddy's shoulder and squeezes, then ruffles his hair. He thinks about how it was Imogen who always took the shine to Roddy, and as he flutters from sleep, Leonard suffers a ghost stroke from the boy's mother.

He turns, quickly, but of course nothing is there, and when he turns back, Roddy is sitting upright, blinking at his father, saying, 'Is it time?'

Leonard puts his hand on Roddy's head, which makes the son flinch. 'I'll make us some tea and we can go through everything. You're aware of the consequences should we falter.' Leonard talks to his son as if he is addressing his board of directors.

Roddy forces a weak smile and swings his legs out of bed, donning his dressing gown as he makes his way down the stairs, sentried by portraits of many generations of stern-faced Howerds. At the bottom turn is a self-portrait of his mother. Sometimes, it seems as if Imogen – the Saltburgh sea grey and yellow behind her – is secretly smiling in the painting. She had confected her pigments to imply despair, but today, Roddy sees the secret smile and he feels sure that on this of all days, she will look down on him.

As his father brings a pot of tea to the kitchen table, Roddy says, 'This is the only way, isn't it.'

Leonard is attentive to every detail of the milking of the cups and stirring of the pot, the setting of the saucers and the strainer. Imogen used to ask him why he couldn't just make it up in a mug like everybody else. He would reply that soon everybody would be doing that. He doesn't answer his son.

'Are you afraid?' asks Roddy.

Leonard doesn't entirely understand his son's question. When there is only one thing to be done, one thread of honour in this pall that cloaks them, how can there be such a thing as fear?

The morning snow has been walked away on Cambridge Heath Road. The steel and glass, the

238

teak and linen of the City are behind Staffe now as he strides through the market waste of plantains and ladies' fingers, going to a sweet, rotting mush. Even though it is barely lunchtime, the stallholders have had enough, are packing away. He passes the Blind Beggar with its Gladstone livery and its thinly veneered, cheap and bashed modern interior. John the Hat would turn in his grave.

Left, under the viaduct, London becomes suddenly black and his steps echo. The arches are so low he has to stoop as he passes through and the other side is Wilmot Street, where he once owned a flat in the mansard roof, next to the Hague School with its gothic gables and bittersweet playground songs.

Staffe looks back to the dormant cranes, like giant metal spiders warring on the world, and he realises he is on the very limit of his jurisdiction. The sounds here are sharp and sporadic: dogs and smashing glass; squealing cars and a shout here, a scream, there. He turns left onto the High Road and past Pellicci's Café, pausing to check the Chicken Peperonata is still on.

He pops into a newsagent's to make a quick purchase and then heads away from the piste of saris and salwar kameez – some are luscious emerald or burgundy, some putrid lilac or tangerine. Soon, it is grey and bleak in the canyons and courtyards of mid-rise Victorian tenements and sixties deck-access. He looks up at the Atlee, Nicola Stone's block.

There, on the corner and looking like she doesn't belong to these streets, is Rosa. Her eyes glisten and her hair is soft. She raises a hand, pulls her coat around her.

Staffe and Rosa make their way up and are shown into the lounge. Cans pit the coffee table like a chess game gone wrong and Nicola picks one up, takes a swig. She is still in her dressing gown. By the sound and smell of things, a man is in the bedroom.

'Thought they'd got the bastard done for my Rebeccah,' says Nicola.

'Rebeccah knew something she shouldn't have, Mrs Stone. Something her friend Elena told her. It's what got her killed and I need you to think hard about anything she might have said to you.'

'Who's this girl?' says Nicola, nodding suspiciously at Rosa.

'A friend of mine.'

Rosa smiles at Nicola, knowing the gossamer separation of a hard plight from an impossible one. 'And Rebeccah was a friend of mine, Nicola.'

'You trick with her?'

'Did Rebeccah mention she had any plans?' says Staffe.

'She were always daydreaming. Just like her father.' She nods in the direction of the bedroom.

'Would she have spoken to him about it?'

'Don't you go getting him all fired up.'

'Did she ever talk about Elena?'

Nicola Stone shakes her head, drains her can.

'D'you keep a room for her here?'

'It's full of shit.'

'Did she ever stay over?'

'When she was fed up of that prick.'

'Mitch? When was the last time?'

'Couple weeks ago. She'd come now and again to get her post, see the baby. Always used this as home.' She regards Staffe with suspicion, weighing something up.

He reaches into his pocket, pulls out forty Bensons and puts them on the table. 'I'd like to take a look round her room. Do you mind?'

Nicola Stone opens a packet straight off, sparking up.

As he passes the main bedroom, Staffe glimpses Brendan Stone sitting on the edge of the bed. The room is thick with smoke and Brendan has a child in his lap, rocking to and fro. His gaze is so lost he doesn't see Staffe, who slips into the small bedroom at the end of the short corridor.

Pictures of boy bands and soccer players collage an entire wall. There is no linen on the bed and one

241

single wardrobe without a door. Through the window, you can see across the bin bays to the cranes of the City.

A banana carton under her bed is full of summer clothes. Staffe replaces it, careful not to disturb anything. Sitting cross-legged on the floor, he pulls a box from the bottom of the wardrobe. It is full of papers: lottery tickets with the numbers all ticked and crossed in a sparkly gold ink. They are clamped together with a bulldog clip.

Beneath the tickets is a thick wad of bank statements, wrapped in pink ribbon and in perfect sequence. Rebeccah lived her life with nothing to spare. Her living and spending would have been principally cash, but this numerical sketch of her life reveals she did £20 a month on her Oyster card. A further £20 a month went to AfrikaChild, which makes Staffe want to weep. She received £170 a month from the DWP, £95 for child benefit, and made irregular, small withdrawals from ATMs around central London. Except . . .

Staffe hears raised voices from the living room. It sounds as if all hell has broken loose. The child is wailing.

. . . Except, three weeks ago, Rebeccah took out £40 from a machine in Saltburgh. The day before, she paid £23 to Eastern Rail. Staffe scans either side, thinking she might have made a payment to a hotel, but there is nothing. He quickly reties the ribbon, retaining the one bank statement and making sure the room is just as it was.

Brendan Stone is in the living room and nods at Staffe as he comes into the room. He points at an empty chair and Staffe sits down. 'You find what you came for?'

Rosa has the baby in her arms. Staffe guesses it is maybe eighteen months old.

'I don't know what I came for,' says Staffe.

Nicola Stone gets up, leaves the room with a grunt.

'She blames herself, and there's a fuck of a lot to blame herself for, but that don't change fuck all as far as I'm concerned.' Brendan picks up the two packs of Bensons and tosses them back at Staffe. 'I won't tell you what's gone on in this place, all the time Becka was a girl. The shit she's seen and had to get her head round. I'm ashamed for letting it happen and for not being around enough. My life's a fuck-up, I don't mind telling you.'

Brendan leans forward and rolls a cigarette. It is like watching a magician. With his left hand, he picks a small clod of Drum and with his right, he unfurls a paper. He brings the two together and in three slow turns of the wrist, the fag is licked and lit. He leans back, exhaling, says, 'There's not a fucking thing in this shit world that I wouldn't do

243

to catch the cunt that done for my Becka. And I'd like to think you'd have the fucking grace to let me know who he is. Let me get to him an hour before you boys in blue.' Brendan's jaw is set and there is life in his eyes where only a few minutes ago there was none. 'If I help you.'

'How might you help me, Mr Stone?'

'You giving me your word?'

'I can't do that. And anyway, you'll know we have got the man who murdered Rebeccah.'

'You think that, what the fuck you doing here? Go on, then. Fuck off!'

'You know something?'

'You make me that promise.'

Staffe locks his eyes on Brendan Stone. 'This thing that you know, it's about Rebeccah going up to Suffolk, isn't it? And her friend Arabella Howerd.'

Brendan's eyes flicker and he looks away from Staffe. Staffe wants to make the promise, but he plants his hands on his knees, stands up. 'I'm sorry you can't help me, Brendan. Truly, I am. But I'll find him, and if I don't, or if I do but I can't put him away because of something you know but won't tell me – well, that's something that you'll have to get your head round, isn't it.'

'I'm her father, for fuck's sake!' Brendan Stone stands, faces up to Staffe.

It appears, to Staffe, that the world can't hurt Brendan Stone any more. So what chance would he have, should he take a step closer? Staffe's heart beats fast and his surging blood makes his fingers prickle. He forms a fist, says, 'You've left it a bit late to be the doting father, Brendan. You can't use me to make that kind of fucked-up peace with her.'

Stone stares him out, the veins in his temples pulsing thick, fast. He puts his hand up to his mouth, takes a hold of his roll-up and it is all Staffe can do not to flinch. Stone exhales, says, 'If my only peace is fucked up, that'll do. That'd be a fucking blessing.'

Rosa hands the baby back to its grandfather, saying, 'What's her name? She looks just like Rebeccah.'

Brendan smiles kindly on Rosa, says, 'Elena. You knew she had a baby daughter?'

'She never told me her name.'

Twenty-two

Roddy Howerd has been frozen to the spot for twenty minutes outside Leadengate Station, running through his lines, visualising the innards of this dark, gothic home of the Peelers, formerly an inn.

Now, going up to the front desk, seeing the large, happy-go-lucky sergeant smiling at him, he rehearses a final time, waits, says, 'I want to report a missing body.'

'Body?' says Jombaugh, looking up at the tall, immaculately dressed young man. He couldn't be anything but the real thing – born to rule. Of his type, he seems nervous, but he speaks with great clarity.

'It is my sister. The family is most distressed.'

'You said body, sir. Not person.'

'A slip of the tongue.' Roddy looks down. This is exactly what they had agreed upon. Precisely. Word perfect. Roddy knows his father thinks he falls short, but this is where he is at home. This could be a stage, and in this crucible, Roddy finds a small pocket of time in which to contemplate that this might be the one thing his mother passed down to him. 'Since Arabella was taken, the family has feared the worst.'

'Taken?'

'Oh yes. We are quite sure she has been taken.'

'And her name?'

'Arabella Howerd.' Roddy gives the address, an outline of her last known movements, says, 'I don't know how to say this,' looking away, as if ashamed. 'Arabella has always had a wild streak and she is by no means an angel. She used to take drugs, occasionally, I believe. And I should perhaps say, simply to save you time and trouble, and so you can fully understand why we are so agitated, that she was a friend of those two poor girls who were murdered recently. A friend, I must add. Not an associate or colleague or anything like that.'

Jombaugh stops writing and looks at the young man, so clearly distressed about his sister's disappearance. *Howerd.* That name rings a bell. 'Howerd?' he says. 'Is that with an "e"?'

'Precisely. You may have heard of my father.'

Jombaugh nods towards the door to Roddy Howerd's left, says, 'Would you like some tea?'

'Black. No sugar.'

Once the young man has closed the door behind him, Jombaugh puts his head in his hands, thinking as fast as he can. He curses Staffe but calls him anyway, recounting what Roddy Howerd had said.

'He said his sister had been "taken". He referred to her as a "body". I'm about to tell Rimmer, of course. And Pennington.'

'Thanks for the wink, Jom. I appreciate it. How did the young Howerd seem, Jom?'

'Very concerned about his sister, but composed, I'd say.'

'How does he know she was taken and hasn't just got wasted somewhere?'

'They're worried because she was a friend of the two murdered girls.'

'The ones Graham Blears killed,' says Staffe, ending the call, looking up at the steel-and-glass, shameless opulence of the home of Devere Chance, Finbar Hare's firm.

Staffe shows his card and the receptionist responds with disproportionate respect. Perhaps they think he is here on matters fraud. Had they known that it was simply a matter of common murder, he might be given shorter shrift, rather than a personal escort.

'Twice in a week, hey Staffe? To what the honour?' says Finbar.

Staffe splays his hands and raises his shoulders. 'You said you'd ask around, about that development up in Suffolk.'

'Howerd again? Poor bastard, to have your teeth clamped on his arse cheek,' laughs Finbar, opening

248

the door to an oval glass shell of a meeting room with precipitous views all the way down into the jungled atrium. Rooms that look inward.

Staffe looks up through the atrium's glass roof to the milky sky above. 'Have you got anything for me?'

'It's being built on Howerd's family land, that's for sure. He's got plenty left, mind you – enough for a bungalow or two – and half a dozen golf courses.'

'Mary Tudor's corner of England, I'd guess.'

Fin shakes his head. 'Almost. But not quite. Howerd's line ran out a couple hundred years back and they had to get a husband to take the wife's name. But the Duke insisted they change the "a" to an "e".'

'An "L" of a difference.'

Finbar laughs. 'But Lenny's marriage to Imogen Audley got them right back in the tree.'

'Audley? As in the cardinal?' says Staffe.

'You got it, my son. Cardinal Bernard Audley, sending up smoke in Rome.'

'Shame Roddy's the other way inclined.'

'Best hope Arabella comes out of this phase, then,' says Finbar.

'And who's developing this almost royal land?'

'Difficult to say. There are three Jersey companies involved, run by a firm of project managers based in Mayfair. But the ultimate shareholdings of the

development companies are nominees in Liechtenstein. It's not unusual. Loopholes in the tax
regime.'

'Do you have the details?'

Finbar goes into his desk, hands Staffe a piece of
paper. *Bluecoat Holdings*, *Oakvale Developments*
and *Pinfold Housing*. All three companies have
listed as their hundred-per-cent shareholders a firm
based in Liechtenstein called Laissez SA.

'Who is doing the building work itself?'

'Not one of the major housebuilders,' says Finbar,
sitting down. 'Which *is* quite unusual. The project
managers have appointed subcontractors directly.'

'Why do that?'

'To keep the contractor's profit for themselves.
But it's a big risk because most of the subbies will
be itinerant workers. If the build fucks up, you've
no one to sue. They disappear,' he clicks his fingers.
'Like that.'

'Poles?'

'Probably.'

'And who is this project management firm?'

'Again, this is unusual. Not one of the big outfits.
I've never heard of these boys and nor have our
analysts.'

'Eggs in one basket,' muses Staffe, looking back
at the list that Finbar had given to him. 'Is this the
project manager? Mount Street Management.'

'Only incorporated eighteen months ago. They've got a couple of decent people on the notepaper.'

'It's all a bit thin, isn't it? That development has five hundred units going up.'

'And a commercial element. End value is about three hundred million.'

'What!'

'It would have been more, but they had to put some starter units in there – to get through planning.'

'Howerd would have helped with that, presumably.'

'Don't ask no questions . . .' says Finbar. 'Whichever way you look at it, some palms will have been greased.'

'And pockets lined?'

'It's not the cleanest game in the world, as you know.'

'They're taking profits all the way down the line. The land, the planning gain, the development and the construction. A nice deal for Howerd, wouldn't you say?'

Finbar goes quiet, turns and looks out across the City. The glass flanks of the financial world glint in the sun. The Thames shines, like a new coin. 'There is something else, Will.'

'Tell me.'

'You know, where Howerd's concerned, you

should think twice before you go barking up the tree.'

'What is it, Fin?'

Finbar turns around, all jollity evaporated. 'One of my analysts knows all the housebuilders – the sort you'd expect to be throwing up a development like Aldesworth Country Town. It's a hard business. These are hard people.'

'Go on.'

'My man says that one of his clients was within a gnat's chuff of getting the Aldesworth contract. They shaved their profit right down to the bone.'

'But they pulled out.'

Finbar nods. 'My man wouldn't say any more. He swore me to secrecy on this. It's a question of face for these people, but he says if they'd gone ahead, there would have been unforeseen complications.'

'Of a foreign nature?'

Finbar says, grimly, 'You know?'

'Did he mention a man called Tchancov?'

'Don't push this, Will.'

Staffe shakes Finbar's hand. They look each other in the eye, clear to see Finbar Hare fears for his friend.

Bobo Bogdanovich is wearing a singlet top, jogging bottoms and a film of sweat. He fills the doorway.

'You have no business here,' he says, wiping his head with his forearm.

'Tell me about Arabella Howerd, Bobo.'

'I don't know her.'

'A friend of your girlfriend's. She went to Suffolk with her. You remember that, Bobo? Is that where they first met?'

Bobo pulls on his left ear with his right hand, a deep crease running down from his hairline.

'Course you don't.' Staffe takes a step back, deliberately looks left and right, down to the street, as if checking for back-up. 'You don't have a girl-friend, do you, Bobo? You should let me in. We might not have long.'

'What do you mean?'

'Why don't you want me to find the man who killed Elena?'

'You got him.'

'Do they know she was your sister?'

He stares open-mouthed at Staffe and, for a moment, stops tugging at his ear.

'I need to know what got Elena killed. I know you know, Bobo – whether you know it or not.'

The puzzled seam deepens, as if Staffe has set him a calculus problem.

'I don't know what you talk about.'

'Tell me about the building up in Suffolk. Did you help Vassily put the squeeze on up there?'

'I don't build.'

'What do you do, for Vassily? If he asks you to jump, Bobo – do you jump?'

Staffe wants to ask what kind of man would stand by and let his sister get murdered, then protect the people who did it. He waits for Bobo to meet his glare but when he does, Staffe can see no shame; not a flicker of guilt at doing the wrong thing; no hint that Bobo might be putting his own welfare first.

The penny clunks.

Staffe turns and walks away. As he goes, he waves a flimsy hand at Bobo then calls back from the top of the stairs at the end of the concrete deck. 'They got you, hey, Bobo? All the way back home.'

Even in the grey light of the December dusk, Staffe can see Bobo's bottom lip protrude. Elena is his older sister and there's no doubt he loved her, but she is gone and their mother and father are still alive and kicking; other sisters and brothers, too, perhaps. That's Staffe's guess.

Making his way back through the rows of terraced houses, he glimpses mid-rise sixties blocks, flaked to almost nothing. Here, giant crosses of St George block out the light to the windows so the skins can't even see the salwar kameez shops. This is the tinder of England and, outside the Marquis of Cornwallis, a group of Somalis, long-limbed and large-skulled, like Giacomettis, choose to cross the road. The smoking whites and Asians laugh, flick their fag butts at the Africans.

Staffe thinks of Suffolk, of Elena and Rebeccah being there, the Howerds, too; and perhaps Tchancov. What might he gain from the disappearance of Arabella Howerd?

The forensic interpretations have arrived from the expert witness and Josie has entered the findings into the database, sent copies of Discovery to the CPS and to Blears' counsel. As she lifts her collar, Josie feels the papers in the inside pocket of her coat. She pulls her lapels tight, clasps them as she runs, as quickly as she can in these heels, to the Hand and Shears.

She goes into the far snug and asks Dick for a hot toddy. Waiting, images of Graham Blears flicker. She contests what, precisely, has brought her here.

Dick brings the hot toddy across and waves the money away. 'He can pay. Lovely girl like you left drinking on her own.' He winks at her, and as if on cue, Staffe comes in through the narrow saloon doors and orders a pint of Adnams.

He looks weary, but manages a smile and his eyes become bright. He puts a hand on her shoulder and kisses her on the cheek, near her mouth. He never kisses her. His jaw pricks her with its afternoon shadow and he smells of a long day.

'You don't kiss me.'

'Is that an order?' he says, laughing.

'An observation.'

'I'm on leave and you're a friend.'

She places the papers on the table, sips from her hot toddy. The cloves and the spirit remind her of Boxing Day walks. She wonders what she might do this Boxing Day, who she will spend it with. 'What do you want with these, sir?'

'How's Blears getting on?'

'He's on the vulnerable wing.'

'Suicide watch?'

'No. Not that I know of.'

Staffe suddenly looks angry. 'Blears is a danger to himself. He can't die on us!'

'You still don't think he did it?'

'I honestly don't know, Josie.'

'We have a knife from off his premises. We have witnesses at both scenes. We've got his bloody confession for crying out loud!' Josie realises she has raised her voice and sees Dick looking across. She leans forward and hisses at Staffe. 'We've not rustled this up from nothing, you know!'

'How'd he do for Arabella Howerd, then?'

'She's only been gone a day or so. There's no body.'

Staffe puts the papers in his coat pocket. 'Did I ever tell you about my friend Rosa?'

Josie nods. Her eyes go wide, sparkle. She has come a long way in the year or so they have been together, but she is still so young, so green.

'She had a gig in the Metropole the other night; second time with the same fella. He attacked her, said he wanted to know what she knew.'

'Is Rosa all right?'

'All right as she can be. He referred to the other two girls. He knew Elena was pregnant.'

'Where is she now?'

'Staying with me.'

'But you're with Sylvie. Aren't you?'

He nods. 'Of course I am.'

Josie finishes her hot toddy and plonks it on the table, buttons her coat back up.

'Where are you going?'

'I need to see the transcripts of Rosa's statement. I'll have to talk to her. And so will Rimmer.'

Staffe reaches out, holds her arm and whispers, as if he was making a tender confidence. 'But it didn't happen, Josie. Rosa didn't go to the police with this. I'm telling you as a friend.'

'But you're my boss, sir.' She gives him a disgruntled look, as if she is betrayed. 'Except, you're not.'

Staffe watches her go, then hitches his chair closer to the fire. He takes out the papers and reads about Arabella. As much as is publically known.

Arabella Imogen Geraldine Howerd was educated

at St Mary's School, Ascot, but left without A levels, despite the offer of a place at Somerville College, Oxford. She has never been on an electoral roll, nor claimed benefits nor paid National Insurance stamp or PAYE.

She was charged with possession of ecstasy, crack cocaine and MDMA at Bishopsgate Police Station on 1 May 2009. The charges were subsequently dropped as Miss Howerd had not been offered independent legal representation, and that case of misapplication was presented to the CPS by Sir Ralph Waikman of Essex Court.

Arabella has never taken a driving test, is currently registered with neither a GP nor a dentist, but was admitted to A & E in Stratford, East London, in November this year when a stomach pump was administered. She was brought by Darius A'Court and a suicide attempt was posited but not pursued. Less than a month later, her brother, Roderick, notified City of London Police that she was missing.

Staffe throws a stone up at the first floor window of 72 Jarndyce Road. Hippy blankets are still pinned at the windows. Along the street, builders are hard at work under lights. Staffe can tell they are not British, not at this hour. In a street nearby, kids are playing out. Staffe hears the thump of a football, the scurry of young feet. In the corner of an eye, he thinks he sees a twitch of swirling orange and purple fabric.

'He's in,' says one of the builders, approaching. He has a cheery face, a fag in the corner of his mouth, and speaks his English with the long, squeezed vowels from beyond an Iron Curtain. 'We keep our eye on the place.'

'Squatters holding out on you?'

'He's a clever son a bitch.'

'And your boys get their drugs from him?'

'What you mean!'

Staffe turns away, hands the builder a card. 'If your boys buy a bit of stuff off him, just call me. I won't do you for possession. You've got my word. And he'll become the last of the squatters.' Staffe winks at the builder who shakes Staffe by the hand.

'My name Stanislav.'

'Are you Polish, Stan?'

He shakes his head. 'But I have permit. Very clean permit.'

'I don't doubt it,' says Staffe, walking across to the skip, picking up half of a London brick. 'Russian?'

Stanislav shrugs.

'What about the girl?'

Stanislav says, 'I not seen her for days.'

Staffe weighs up number 72, gives himself a run-up, brings his arm back and launches the brick.

The glass shatters.

From inside, Darius shouts, 'What the fuck!' He looks down in anger, undiminished when he sees it is Staffe.

Darius sits in the room's only armchair toking on a roll-up and swigging from a can of supermarket beer.

'What the fuck am I going to do now? It's freezing in here,' he says in his posh, faux-Cockney drawl, nodding at the smashed window – the dark night beyond.

'Call the council.'

'Don't take the piss.'

'Where's Arabella, Darius?'

'I'm not her keeper.'

'But you are, aren't you?'

'The fuck's that supposed to mean?'

'Roddy has been to see us – you know Roddy?'

'No.'

'He reckons she's been gone a couple of days. She must have been taken just after I visited you.'

'What's it to do with me?' Darius seems suddenly lost. 'I try to save her from herself. At least I try – like you said.'

'Why do you play around with this life?'

'What do you know about me? My dad hasn't a pot to piss in. He lost it all when I was fifteen.

We're fucked.' He tries to laugh. 'I'm not what you think.'

'And what do I think, Darius?'

'I'm a poor little rich kid.'

'Who thinks he's a dealer. Maybe you're not what you want to seem.'

'I do my best for her,' says Darius.'

'You're not doing much of a job.'

'You've seen Arra,' says Darius. 'She can be so beautiful and gentle. We need to get out of this life. We were trying.'

'How?'

'Getting clean. It's hard.'

'Resisting temptation is beyond you, though. You had your hand in the honey jar, didn't you. With Elena.' Staffe crouches, so his face is right up against young Darius A'Court.

'You can't intimidate me,' says Darius. 'You heard of Sir Ralph Waikman?'

Staffe shoots out a hand and grabs the cigarette from his mouth. He puts his knee on A'Court's chest and places the burning cigarette right up to his nostril. 'You can call Waikman once I'm done.' He puts the cigarette into A'Court's nostril, careful not to let it touch. He holds it there for the count of three then withdraws it.

'I don't know where she is. I don't fucking know. I haven't seen her since you came here last.'

Staffe puts the cigarette to the other nostril, gives it a count of four, and watches Darius's eyes go wide as foglamps. They begin to water. He waits until it dawns on Darius that this is only going to get worse, then says, 'You tell me everything about Arabella and the last time you saw her and what she did the last few weeks. Then I'll get someone round here with a warrant and we'll run you out to Mr Waikman's house. He's got a fine spread just up the road in Hampstead, you know. He's a family friend of the Howerds. Wonder how keen they'll be when I tell them what you said about Arabella?'

'I haven't said anything about her.'

'Were you and Elena up to something together? Up to something in Suffolk, maybe. And Rebeccah, too?' Staffe holds the cigarette up again, and Darius begins to squeal. As he does, his voice becomes gradually more refined.

'Those girls were tight. Tight as.'

'Would Elena have used Arabella?'

'What!' Darius laughs. 'No way. Nobody uses Arra. Arabella's in her own club, whether she likes it or not.'

'Did she know Vassily Tchancov?'

'She'd met him.'

'And you, Darius?'

'I know my limits, Inspector.' He laughs again. 'I'm not the prick you might think I am. Arra says she loves me.' He shakes his head. 'I think she does. What can I say? You can never be sure.'

'Why did you have a thing with Elena? What exactly did Arabella think about that?'

'That's private.'

'We can take this to the next stage, make it public, if that's what it takes. Now, what do you think of Leonard Howerd, Darius?'

'He's all right. A step up from my old man, that's for sure.'

'What's Arabella's problem with him?'

'Arra's getting better.'

'She's missing. Hardly a parenting endorsement.'

Leaving, Staffe thinks he might have been too hard on the boy. He waves at Stan and wonders how easy it might be for them to get their labour licences. How many of them are in this city? How cold that trail from where they hail.

An illegal pall of cigarette smoke hangs in the corridor and Newsland's finest cokehead seems pleased as punch to see Staffe. It must be a slow evening for revelation. Well, that's about to change.

Absolom goes to the open window, drawing on a cigarette. It is freezing in the room and Absolom is wearing a donkey jacket. 'To what the pleasure, Inspector?'

'I've got you a front page.'

'I bet you say that to all the boys.'

'The Howerds. You know them?'

'Bankers?'

'That's the one. This is about the daughter.'

Absolom flicks his dimp and draws the sash window closed. He scoots his chair up to the desk, starts tapping away at his computer keyboard, engines searching.

'The daughter's a bad girl gone bad,' says Staffe.

Absolom squints at the screen. 'Leonard is a serious dude. If he wasn't a left-footer he'd have been a knight by now,' he laughs.

'He's fancied for the sword in the New Year's list, apparently.'

'So what's the lovely daughter done?' He leans in to the screen. 'She looks like Danya.'

'Gone missing. She was hooked up with a small-time drug dealer. He's not seen her for days. The brother came in to report her gone earlier today.'

'Hardly front page,' says Absolom, clattering the keyboard. 'Mother, Imogen, hearsay suicide out in South America, but blamed on bandits. A troubled family that can't enjoy life despite the riches the world chucks at them. A different world, they'd have been in the palace. Says here the dead mother's uncle is a cardinal. More of a weekend supplement piece.'

'Unless young Arabella was best mates with

Rebeccah Stone. Unless her boyfriend was the dealer of choice for Elena Danya.'

'Don't shit me, Staffe!'

'And now missing.'

'You're saying this girl could be the third whore? She's no prostitute, surely.'

'They are women before they're prostitutes; human beings before that.'

'But you've got your man.'

'Listen, Absolom. I'll say this once and then you're on your own. You can go straight to Pennington for all I care. Arabella Howerd was the last person to speak to Elena Danya, by phone. And she was with Rebeccah Stone the night before Rebeccah was murdered.'

'She's been killed, you reckon?'

Staffe spreads his arms wide, as if he might be appealing to a referee, or renouncing all his sins. 'Get digging.'

'You've got more, surely.'

'The boyfriend gets off on being down and dirty just the same. Deals to the poor and famous but he doesn't quite fit that new world he's in. You'll find him squatting up in West Hampstead. Seventy-two Jarndyce Road, if you're quick.'

'Are you on this case, or what?'

'You leave me out of it.' Staffe gives Absolom dead eye. 'I can have you sacked, chucked out of the NUJ, and fined five grand for smoking in a place of work.'

If Staffe was a betting man, he'd put his houses on a *News* lead on the Howerd disappearance, come the midday edition. Maybe he should tip Pulford a wink.

The inspector leaves the building with his collar turned up against the wind that whistles off the river. The two men are frozen to the bones of their toes. They have been waiting for half an hour and it has become difficult to form shapes with their mouths when talking. Lights glow through the stained windows of St Sepulchre and night warbles with the smooth choral sweep of 'In the Bleak Midwinter', being practised, late.

'Here he comes,' says the Younger, ruddy-faced and grimacing as he talks, scratching his tongue on his broken tooth, the stitches in the cut across his head pinching in the cold. 'The bastard.'

'I've got him,' says the Elder. 'You'd better tell them what might be coming their way.'

'Do we know?'

'He's going through hoops we didn't know were there.' The Elder pats his young accomplice on the back, says, 'And don't get emotional. She turned on you because you let her.'

'I don't see why we can't just fuck him up, proper.'

'He's police, and that's a last resort. This isn't Northern Ireland.' The Elder scurries round the corner to his black London hackney carriage, flicks the switch to the orange light, just in case he drops doubly lucky, but the inspector has waved down another cab, so he throttles back and turns off his 'For Hire', follows at a safe distance. As he goes, he watches his younger apprentice talking into his phone, thinks of all he has taught the whippersnapper, since he had his life saved by the boy. But he knows that what they owe each other counts for nothing in this game.

Twenty-three

Staffe takes off his coat and brushes past Pulford towards the kitchen. The frozen smell of cold night comes off him. He looks all done in.

Pulford says, 'You heard about the Howerd girl? Her brother came into the station, says she's missing.'

'Bad girls like her go missing all the time. That's not my problem.'

'Josie's in a bit of a stew about it all.'

'And Rimmer?'

'He says that her friends have been killed and she's bound to want to get away from it all. But what about Rosa?'

'What about Rosa?' says Staffe. 'Where is she, anyway? I was with her earlier. I told her to come straight here in a cab.'

'If Blears didn't do it, and the reason they want Rosa dead hasn't gone away . . .'

'Where is Rosa? And Sylvie.'

'Gone out.'

'They shouldn't be out! What *exactly* did they say to you?'

'Sylvie was reassuring her. She said she would

come up with something to make it safer. I got the impression it was a private chat they wanted. You know.'

Staffe goes to the bathroom. He sees that Sylvie's toothbrush is still there, but the one they had given to Rosa is gone. He rushes to the bedroom, sees that some clothes have gone from Sylvie's drawer – easy to spot because there's only a skeleton supply here. He looks in her drawer, where favourite underwear remains. But soon, new fears wash up, to replace the old.

Rosa sleeps lightly. Her dreams are troubled. Her mouth is dry and she gets up, tiptoeing down the hallway for a glass of water from the bathroom. She can smell resin and woodshavings and wonders where this is coming from. She looks in the mirror and realises she didn't wash off her make-up, and it slowly dawns on her what she surrendered that evening. She and Sylvie had drunk wine and talked of Staffe and she had let slip the circumstances surrounding that one lapse. Sylvie said it didn't matter, that she had been in a relationship whilst away from Staffe. But, she had added with some poignancy, she had told him all about it.

On the way back to her room, Rosa thinks she hears something at the door. She stands on the landing so she can hear and just about see. Holding her hand over her mouth, her pulse drums fast and loud in her ears.

A key is in the door and a leg steps in. She can tell it is a man, by the size of him, the way he moves. He eases the door closed, and pads into the house, out of sight. She waits. And waits, then hears movement in the kitchen, as if he is going through drawers. She goes into her room and gets her phone, scrolls down through her numbers until she sees *Staffe*. She calls him and scurries as quietly as she can back to the top of the stairs.

She listens, straining, praying to hear a ringtone. And she does. She sinks to the floor, clutching the newel post, wanting to weep with joy. She hears his voice, low and soft, whispering, 'Rosa, Rosa?'

'I'm upstairs.'

'Are you OK? Is Sylvie OK?'

'She's asleep. I'll come down.' As she makes her way, she realises she is only wearing an oversized T-shirt and knickers. She's not showing anything, but she tugs it down to her knees anyway and realizes it's probably his.

In the kitchen, he is putting down a knife, sitting into a chair at the table. He looks as if he is running on vapours.

'Sylvie said it was best to come here, to tell no one. I was worried, Will. So worried they would come for me again.'

He stands, wraps his arms around her, whispers into her ear, 'You should have told me, at least told Pulford, where you were going.'

'We thought it best not to. If you didn't know, they couldn't know.' She leans back and he holds her by the arms. 'You weren't followed here, were you?'

'Hopefully, he knows better than that,' says Sylvie, standing by the door.

Rosa takes a step away and his hands slide down her arms, to his sides. She sees him looking at the empty wine bottles, then at Sylvie; back to Rosa, then at the floor.

Eventually, he looks at Sylvie and says, 'You brought Rosa here, to protect her,' contemplating the lengths you might go to in sheltering somebody. 'Thank you.'

Staffe walks down the Castelnau with a real clip to his stride. It is just before dawn and he has slept for two, maybe three hours. He has the streets to himself, but cuts down to the river path before he reaches Hammersmith Bridge and walks to Putney. The Thames is swathed in a silver mist and the sky is clear, the moon full. Ducks glide by the bank, just the occasional light in the buildings opposite.

He thinks about the Howerds' proud family line, all the way back to the Reformation; the culmination of so many lives of endeavour, of doing the right thing, and suffering that forfeit, that chink in the line of descent five generations ago. How it might suit Howerd to have Arabella disappeared over some horizon, gone the way of her errant mother before shame strikes. But that will all backfire now, if Absolom does his worst – which is what the serpent journo does best.

What will it take to bring young Roddy to preserve the family? All on his narrow shoulders. He checks his watch and slows down, not wanting to arrive too early. He wants Roddy all to himself this morning, so stops off for breakfast at a caff just off the Fulham Road.

The place bustles with truckers who have made their city drops, and builders in high-vis and rigger boots. They belch and joke and rib each other. Some bury their heads in the *Sun*.

An old girl in a tabard brings his sausage sandwich and his mug of tea and one of the builders slaps her backside playfully with a rolled-up newspaper. He gets a clip round the ear, which sets everybody off, and Staffe laughs out loud. He likes its sound, the shape it makes of his face.

The builders and drivers drift away and Staffe leaves his crusts and a healthy tip, returns the smile of the old girl who is clearing tables. Her husband wipes down the counter between slurps from a pint mug of tea and his happy glow flicks off like a light. Her too. You can hoodwink anyone in this city. They do it with global warming and credit crunches. If you wanted to disappear a black sheep, you might do it by disguising it as a serial killing of whores and junkies. How desperate would you have to be?

Staffe works his way up towards the south side of Hyde Park. He cuts up Kensington Church Street and past the palace with its endless Princess tributes. Staffe says aloud, 'Families!' and crunches across the frost-crusted grass, the morning light coming pale, the traffic up on Bayswater roaring and grinding.

And Bobo? Letting people think Elena was his lover when all along he was her brother. Why do that? And does it make him a Danya or her a Bogdanovich? Or neither of them either. And if he ever could trace Elena back, what family secrets might he uncover there? He remembers the savagery of Bobo's grief. Grief, so close to shame.

It is now nearly three days since Arabella went missing. He calls Pulford to get on to T-Mobile to see when Arabella Howerd last used her phone. As he talks, he stops, looks ahead to Hyde Park Corner and rubs his head. He does it with such ferocity that people stop and watch. They think he is one of the nutters. He has walked five miles and round and round in circles.

* * *

'My father is out,' says Roddy Howerd. Even though he is a student, Roddy wears cavalry twills and a double-cuffed shirt. He wouldn't look out of place in White's, or the Lords.

'It's you I came to see.'

'Me?' says Roddy, as if everyone who calls comes for father.

Staffe sidles into the wide hallway with its Victorian tiled floor and an extremely rare uphol-stered Georgian settle. Classical music, presumably Radio 3, is playing at the back of the house and Staffe takes a half flight down to a large kitchen where the scullery, pantry and parlour have all been knocked into one. A large George III breakfast table is at the centre. He can smell roasted coffee beans, says, 'There's nothing finer than the smell of fresh coffee.' Through the French windows he admires the beautifully planted private rear garden.

'I take it you would like a cup.'

Staffe had seen the lever-pull Italian machine and says, 'I'd like it cut, please. A thimbleful.'

Roddy smiles, approvingly, grinds beans afresh.

As he does it, Staffe takes a close look at a framed Onslow print of the Great Eastern Hotel, with diners dwarfed in its pillared and domed dining room. 'I'd hazard you've been through Liverpool Street Station a fair few times, hey Roddy?'

'You could say that.'

'All those trips up to town from The Ridings?'

'What do you know about The Ridings?'

'They're building one of those brand spanking new country towns up there.'

'Do you have news of Arabella?' says Roddy.

'What did you do?' says Staffe, jokingly. 'Sell off a few acres of the estate?'

'Why are you here?'

'I need to know more about Arabella's friends. And I need some photographs, as recent as you've got.'

Roddy hands Staffe his coffee, served in a thick Illy cup, with saucer. 'I wouldn't know about her friends. Not my type of people.'

'She had a boyfriend, Darius.'

Roddy shrugs.

'She used to go back up to The Ridings?'

'Never.' Roddy is quite adamant.

'She must have favourite haunts. Places she went with her mother when she painted, for example.'

'They didn't get on.'

The coffee is thick and hot and bitter. Staffe waits for the rush. Gets it. 'How bad was it, Roddy, between Imogen and Arabella?'

Roddy turns on his heel and says, over his shoulder, 'I'll see if I can find a photograph.'

Staffe follows him into the hall, having noticed Howerd's study at the back of the house. Looking into the drawing room, he says, 'I'm a bit of a collector. Do you mind if I have another look in here?'

'I won't be long,' says Roddy, climbing the stairs.

The moment he has disappeared from view, Staffe takes a half flight up into Howerd's study, goes straight to a slant-lid desk. He thinks it might be Queen Anne and daren't even guess at its value.

In the top drawer is a small leather ring binder with Howerd's current-account statements in it. Coutts. At the last count, he was £220,000 overdrawn. Staffe looks quickly back through the statements, sees that amounts of £25,000 had been withdrawn in cash four times in the past four months. The last, three weeks ago.

He can't believe the Howerds are quite on their uppers, but wonders why Leonard might run a personal overdraft at such levels. He goes through the small drawers on the desktop and takes out a batch of correspondence. Two letters from the Nationwide, approving in principle a mortgage of £750,000, and a letter from Binns Contractors in Ipswich, quoting £320,000 for repairs and renovations to The Ridings, Little Mumplings, nr Aldesworth.

In the bureau's galleys, Leonard keeps old envlopes, to make lists or notes. Seeing a solitary pale lilac envelope, Staffe eases it out, takes it in his fingers, sees Leonard's name and address, drawn in a long, elegant hand.

Staffe hears a fast tread on the stairs and slides the letter back, returns the drawer and positions himself in front of a large framed photograph. A beautiful woman, crinkling at the eyes but tall and with a model's frame, stands beside a man in cardinal red. He has her cheekbones and straight nose. The same as Arra, also.

Roddy appears in the doorway, 'You were going into the drawing room,' says Roddy.

'This is Imogen and Uncle Bernard, I take it,' says Staffe.

Roddy looks out of the window, as if Imogen might rise from a crouched tending of the Michaelmas daisies beyond the arbour and wave up to him.

He holds open the album at a page that has three photographs of a teenage Arabella. Staffe takes a firm grip of the album and pulls it towards him. Roddy keeps a hold, saying, 'Choose the one you want and I'll remove it. My father won't be pleased that the album has been tampered with.'

But Staffe smiles him in the eye and tugs, once, firmly. He sits in a club chair to the left of the window, leafing through the album.

'It's private.'

'The more I know about her, the more chance

we've got.' And then he sees why Roddy was so reluctant.

Two young men are standing by a *taberna* with a turquoise sea beyond. They are laughing and the fair Roddy has his elbow on the other's shoulder. The darker of the two is unmistakably familiar. Darius A'Court.

'Is this how Arabella met Darius?'

'I met him on holiday,' says Roddy, his voice cracking at the edge.

'I asked Darius if he knew you. He said he didn't.'

Roddy shrugs, unable to disguise the fact that he is hurt.

'Why would he do that, I wonder?' says Staffe, leafing back to the photographs of Arabella. He removes one, hands back the album to Roddy. 'And why would you – when I asked you earlier – imply you didn't know him?'

'I have things to do,' says Roddy.

'When was the last time Vassily Tchancov visited here, Roddy?'

'I have never heard of the man.' Roddy speaks without hesitation, is utterly convincing; almost as if somebody else had spoken for him.

'I believe I know where I might find Arabella.'

'What!' Roddy's assuredness collapses. He is neither happy nor relieved that his sister might be found. 'Where might you find her?' He is, no doubt about it, afraid.

The Elder has quite taken to driving his hackney carriage and can't help but smile at the realisation that his plan has panned out so sweetly. He even has his story plotted ahead, should his Knowledge fail him. He looks in the mirror at his quarry, who desires to be driven to Barnes. The inspector, up close, has kind eyes and a soft look to his face, despite the hard lines of his jaw and eye sockets, his two-day stubble. But he seems troubled, the poor man, as if struggling with an impossible crossword clue.

He decides to go through the park, thinks this will show that he is what he purports to be. But halfway in, he takes a left around the Serpentine and immediately realises the error. It is a wrong turn no true cabbie would make.

'I'm afraid we should have gone straight on. Unless you're caught short,' laughs the inspector.

Best tell his best lie, he thinks. And whilst he makes his volte-face, he says, 'To be honest, sir, and I shouldn't be saying this – but you look like a decent kind of fellow – this isn't my cab.'

'Aaah.'

'No, it's my son-in-law's. Had it three years and going gangbusters he was, then they hit rough water, so I said I'd help out – doubling up on the shifts. I do my best, but this Knowledge business, it's no walk in the park.' The Elder laughs out loud. 'I'll tell you what,' he says, eyeing Staffe in the mirror. 'Have this one on me. All this fannying about!'

'Absolutely not!' says the inspector.

When they pull up outside Sylvie's urban cottage, Staffe looks up and down the street for signs of anything unusual. All the way, he has been checking whether they are followed. As he gets out, with the cabbie gushing his thanks, he stops, leans against the hackney carriage and says to the driver, 'How do you fancy a proper fare, and a good run out?'

'How do you mean?'

'I need to go up the coast. It's a couple of hours. Switch off the meter and I'll pay you a ton and a half. Same again tomorrow if you bring us back.'

'You bet!' says the cabbie, giving Staffe a thumbs-up and looking as though he's got six numbers up on the lottery.

'I'll be twenty minutes . . . What's your name?'

'Thomas. Who's going? You and the wife?'

'Not exactly,' smiles Staffe.

Sylvie has to draw back the net curtain with her elbow because she is up to her forearms in resin.

She watches Staffe chit-chatting with the cabbie, looks up and down the street to make sure nobody has driven past or parked up, keeping tabs on him, but the road is quiet as Cotswolds.

She rubs her hands with a spirit rag, then plunges them into a dilution of lavender oil and camomile. She dries on a terry-cotton towel and makes her way down from the loft studio, wringing her hands together with a coating of moisturiser.

As she walks down the floating cedar treads into her open-plan lounge–diner–kitchen, she hears Staffe and Rosa talking in suppressed tones. It seems Rosa is resistant to whatever persuasion he is attempting, and when she clocks Sylvie, she gives him the eyes to say that they have company.

'I need to go away,' says Staffe.

'I'm a burden here,' says Rosa.

Sylvie looks daggers at Staffe. 'Oh no! No way. That's not happening, not after . . .'

'She has to come with me. I have to protect her. You know that.'

'That was before I knew what you chose not to tell me.'

'I don't want to come between you two,' says Rosa.

'I can't leave her,' says Staffe. 'And I won't put you at risk by her staying here.'

'That's chivalrous.'

'This is serious, for crying out loud, I'll be back in a day or so.'

Sylvie ushers Staffe into the kitchen area and hisses, 'There's only so much I will take.'

'Everything will be fine,' he says, pulling her towards him, making to kiss her on the lips, but she turns her head, looks into the garden. It is tiny but when she bought the place, she was going to do all sorts with it. Lately, she has been thinking of not having another summer here.

'We'll see,' she says. 'You do what you have to do, Will. You always do.' She opens the door to the garden and goes out, feels the cold, plays with the Urals ring on her wedding finger.

Later, Staffe comes to her and kisses her on the cheek and says he'll be back and everything will be fine. She has barely moved, staring at the overgrown garden. The front door closes and she feels afraid, doesn't want to go back in. But where else could she go?

Twenty-four

Thomas the taxi driver and Rosa watch Staffe tramp across the building site towards the two-storey Portakabin that is Aldesworth Country Town's site office. 'You married?' says Thomas, drawing his thumb across his pencil moustache.

Rosa draws heavily on her cigarette as she leans against the cab. 'No!' she laughs, 'He's *getting* married. But not to me.' She looks away, to a gaggle of workers dragging speedily on shared cigarettes, kicking their boots. 'I'm not the marrying kind.'

Rosa takes out her Bensons, walks up to the bricklayers who are waiting for a fresh mix. It will be nice to use the bits and bobs of foreign tongues she has picked up down the years.

Clay and gravel cloy to Staffe's shoes and he kicks off the mud against the enormous wheels of a dumper truck. A group of labourers make their way out of the office, keen to get back to work in a hurry; they talk earnestly to each other in what could be Polish or Russian. He watches them go and looks around the site. Everywhere, trucks and men are on the move, delivering materials or taking away waste; laying blockwork or kneeling bolt upright on sloping roofs and throwing tiles. Staffe taps on the door.

'Fuck off!' is the reply.

He pushes the door and steps in. The place is oppressively warm, and fuggy with farts and butane gas. Behind a draughtsman's desk, strewn with charts and plans, sits a fat man.

'Police,' says Staffe, showing his card. 'Who are you?'

'Small,' says the fat man. 'Lawrence Small. It's a piss-take, isn't it?' he laughs. He reaches across the desk with all his might, as if taking a circuitous swimming stroke, picking a business card from a pile and holding it out for Staffe to take. It leaves Lawrence Small breathless.

'You're the project manager?'

Small nods and smiles, seemingly relaxed that CID have sent an inspector to see him. Almost as though he was expected.

Staffe says, 'This is one hell of a site. How many men you got here?'

'Depends. Four hundred at the moment but soon we'll be swamping the place with sparks and chippies.'

'You're lucky. Seems like the roofs are on just in time for winter.'

'That's not luck. It's my job,' says Small as proud

as punch. It is almost as if he had said, 'Look at my beautiful wife.'

'You using local boys for the electrics and woodwork?'

Small looks at Staffe, suspiciously. 'Gas work, we have to. They're all Corgi registered. This is a tight site, inspector, but I can say that I have no problems with my foreign casuals. They're on site at half seven and work through 'til six. Just half an hour for lunch and they work like stink.'

'You get long days out of them.'

'They get all the breaks specified by law. And they're all legal.' Small reaches around his stomach to open a drawer. He slaps a pile of documents onto the desk.

Staffe flicks through the papers. The odd one or two are Polish and some are Ukrainian. Most seem to be Russian, on special ninety-day permits, due to expire in two weeks or so. 'Good thing for you they work like stink. These permits are about to expire.'

'We'll get them extended if we need to. All our men have enough points, don't you worry.'

'I'd have thought it's a pain in the arse, dealing with immigration.'

'Our sponsors are very good. The men are given all the help we can.' And Small stops himself.

'I suppose your directors are pretty well connected,' laughs Staffe.

'Never see them.'

'It's that local fellow, isn't it? What's his name . . .?'

'You haven't said why you are here, Inspector.'

'Leonard somebody.'

'I don't know any Leonard.'

'And that Turkish chap. Markary! That's him. Taki Markary.'

'I've got a meeting to go to,' says Small, pushing himself away from the desk with all his might, the castors on the chair squeaking and groaning.

'You must have good Russian connections – for the permits. You mentioned your sponsors.'

'I mentioned that I have to go,' says Small, gathering papers together, hurriedly, randomly.

'How many units are on site, you say?'

'I didn't.' Small tosses a sales brochure to Staffe. 'Hot off the press.' He pushes past Staffe, but Staffe takes hold of the big man's arm. Small is sweating now, smells of burnt onions.

'What's the build period on a development like this?'

'Sixty weeks.'

'Impressive,' says Staffe, standing, happy to have learned as much from Small's evasions as what the project manager had volunteered, but with a final shot across the bows.

'Do you work for Vassily Tchancov, Lawrence?'

286

Small's eyes flicker and his chin fails him. 'I have to go.'

'Does he get the men for you?'

'They just arrive. If anything goes wrong . . .' Small, quite unnecessarily, looks behind him, 'I can call him. Look, I have a family. You know what it's like in construction right now.'

'I need to know who the workers' sponsors are.'

'I can't tell you that.'

'The site is legal, right?'

Small nods, now sweating violently.

'Then you have nothing to fear, surely.'

'What has he done?'

'What kind of a gun does he have to your head, Lawrence?' Staffe knows he will achieve nothing more here. But he has what he came for.

Lawrence shakes his head, looks as if he is standing at a stake, dry as tinder.

'You'd best forget I was here,' says Staffe, leaving the hot fug, feeling the chill, like a welcome breeze. 'For both our sakes, you had better keep this visit to yourself.'

Back at the car, Rosa tells him the men say they're on two hundred quid a week, for a six-day week, but they get another hundred a week sent straight home. Staffe does the maths, which isn't rocket science.

Given that he'd have to pay local builders at least

a hundred quid a day, Small is saving at least £300 a week per man. For sixty weeks, that's £18,000 a man. Minimum. Four hundred men, that's over seven million quid that the developers are making – over and above. Courtesy of the licences.

'Did you ask them how they get their licences?' he asks.

'I did.'

'And?'

'They clammed up.'

They park up in Saltburgh's Georgian square and in this snow-petalled dark, it looks unchanged from across the centuries. You expect to see ladies in hooped, corsetted dresses and men in frock coats walking into the Signet. The Elder says, 'I might stay the night. What I save on diesel will pay for a B&B and some fish and chips.'

Through the front doors of the hotel, the Christmas lights pulse on and off, winking that Saint Nick is close. Somewhere, beyond, the sea comes and goes, comes and goes, in the dusk. The sweet smell of hops drifts from the brewery.

The detective looks at him: long, as if appraising, says, 'Which regiment were you in, Thomas?'

'What?' The cabbie seems shocked, wary.

'Your shoes. They're so spick and span. You must have been in the army.'

'Aah,' says Thomas, mustering a smile.

'I'll give you a ring in the morning, Thomas, when we're ready to go back.'

The Elder watches the two of them go into the hotel. He thinks that they would make a good couple; that he wouldn't mind being in the inspector's shoes tonight. And he also thinks he will need his wits about him; thinks also about the regiment and the Troubles, how he met the Younger.

He was trapped in his car on his way back to barracks from seeing a girl. That was bad enough, but there was a new road block and he was forced into an unfamiliar part of town, alone in his car. There were four of them: IRA and he didn't even hear see the gun, didn't hear the shot, just the windscreen smashing. His shoulder flicked out of its socket, away from him.

They dragged him out of the car. All he remembers is the silence, the utter silence. No sirens or screams, just the blood spewing down his arm and chest and them raising their guns and the Younger rushing forward, standing over him with his arms out to the other three and shouting, 'No. Leave him. I know him.'

'That means he knows you, you daft fuck,' one of them said.

'I'll take my chances,' the Younger said.

The Elder had nodded at the young man, recognising him from years before, when he had pulled his squaddies off the fifteen-year-old. They were kicking his head in, stamping on his knees.

A year after he was saved, when the Elder could no longer take being passed over for bum-fluffed pansies, and when he went into unseen security, he gave the Younger a call. He was there when the Younger took his first man down, the army way. Off and on, they have been together ever since.

'I don't understand why we had to take this room,' says Rosa, looking for an en-suite, disappointed.

'This is where Markary brought Elena. It's where Howerd stayed,' says Staffe, looking out to sea.

'It's a double bed for God's sake, Will.'

'I'll take the sofa.'

'What will Sylvie think?'

Staffe looks at Rosa with unfettered bewilderment.

'You have a good one there, Will. You keep hold of her.'

'Don't worry, I will.'

'She looks to me like she can't take much more messing about. You've been together before, why d'you split up last time?'

'She was in therapy, and I suppose I didn't fully understand.'

'Therapy?'

'Her mother left her and her dad, went to some hippy commune. She lives in France now.'

'She's over it, though?'

Staffe shakes his head. 'She's convinced she's like her mother. Once, when we split up, she said she was from the same pod.'

'And is she?'

'She's just like her dad, but he's in bits the whole time. I suppose it's her defence mechanism. She really can't stand to end up like him, but she can't say that to herself, can she?'

Rosa looks at Staffe as if she doesn't know what to say. 'Well I like her, and you'd be an idiot to lose her. If the phone rings, you take it – that's all I'm saying.'

And with a trill of fate, the phone immediately rings. They each take an involuntary step back, looking at the phone, then at each other. Staffe sits on the bed, picks up, hears it is Pulford.

'How did you know I was here?'

'Two plus two.' Pulford sounds agitated. 'I take it you haven't seen *The News* today.'

'Let me guess. A piece on how Arabella Howerd has gone missing.'

'Blears' lawyers are demanding he is released. They're saying she could be the third woman and this puts him in the clear.'

'Is Josie getting it in the neck?'

'Not as much as Rimmer.'

'What are they going to do about it?'

'The official line is that her disappearance has nothing to do with Danya and Stone, but Absolom's article blows that out of the water. The girls all knew each other.'

Staffe thinks about the wider web that entangles Rosa with that triumvirate. 'Read it to me.' He leans back on the bed, closes his eyes. He can hear the surf outside.

Pulford says, '"City police have covered up key evidence in the case of the two murdered prostitutes, Elena Danya and Rebeccah Stone."'

'Jesus,' says Staffe. 'He's not exactly holding back.'

'"Arabella Howerd, the bad-girl daughter of top Catholic Leonard Howerd, was reported missing three days ago. Miss Howerd was a friend of both slayed prostitutes and is believed to have been one of the last to speak to each of the deceased. Graham Blears is being held for the murders even though Miss Howerd disappeared after his arrest. City Police were unavailable for comment and banking bigwig Howerd was also tight-lipped. Miss Howerd leaves a trail of drug-related misdemeanours and is believed to have a liking for London's fleshpots. Prostitutes are outraged that the police might be covering up key evidence relating to the killings of Danya and Stone. Belinda Preistley, spokeswoman for Working Girls, is demanding that DCI Pennington reopen the case."'

'Is that it?'

'There's more on the inside pages, but mainly glamour shots and a few quotes from street girls – trying to whip up a Ripper storm.'

Staffe feels a white blast of clarity. But it goes, immediately, the way it came. 'Have you got that data from T-Mobile for Arabella's phone?' he asks.

'She hasn't made a call or texted for four days. What are you doing up there? Do you want me to come up?'

'I need you to get round to Bobo's place and ask him about the immigrant workers up here, find out what you can about where they come from, how they're treated. And ask Bobo why Elena was writing to Howerd and Tchancov.'

'Was she?'

'Oh yes.'

The phone goes quiet and Staffe can tell that Pulford isn't exactly relishing the prospect of facing Bobo alone.

'And chase up some companies for me. Bluecoat Holdings, Oakvale Developments and Pinfold Housing, and a Liechtenstein company called Laissez SA.'

'What am I looking for?'

'Anything with a Russian flavour.'

'Tchancov?'

'Keep an open mind, Pulford.' Staffe hangs up and looks out. The moon is just on the wane. 'It's beautiful here,' he says to Rosa. 'You enjoy it. I'm going out for a few hours. Best have your dinner sent up. And treat yourself to a bottle of wine.'

'I'm coming with you,' says Rosa.

'I'm afraid not.'

Rosa puts on her coat, a plaid jacket that Staffe had bought for Sylvie. 'Do you want to try stopping me?'

The bells drill the prison air – all around, but for Graham Blears, it is muffled. His mouth is dry and his sinuses are full of dust. The weight of the mats on top of him makes it hard to breathe, but he waits, still as a cocked trigger, for the last of the doors to slam, the last of the keys to turn. The echoing of inmate curses and officer jibes drifts away, down the corridors and onto the fire road.

Tomorrow is full lock-down, a consequence of short-staffing over the festive season, and today the men are doubly boisterous – which aids Graham's cause. He was counted off the wing and onto the gym; was then also counted off the gym, but had sneaked into the storeroom, had buried himself here, beneath all the kit. They won't be able to count him back onto the wing, of course. They will check the missing number, and check again. They will try and fail to reconcile with all the other units and with the hospital, and the officers will be supremely pissed off but it will take them twenty minutes, maybe half an hour, before there is a full-scale search. By then, he will be done.

He reaches inside his sweat pants, into his boxers, and with finger and thumb he fishes down, from between his buttocks, the wrapped-up page of *Heat* magazine. Unwrapping, slowly, like pass-the-parcel gone horribly wrong, and nestling in a montage of up-skirt flesh and cleavage and big hair, is his home-made knife. He pushes the mats off him and clambers across the kit, presses open the door from the storeroom to the gymnasium.

All is calm, a rare thing in prison, he has soon realised. To be honest, this little slice of time he has served has not been as horrific as he expected. He could do more, no doubt about it – but he chooses not to. His time has come. It is something he need not bear, and after a life of lonesomeness and stifling misery, he knows a better place awaits; knows, too, that he will find a peace beyond whatever reckoning awaits him. He was not for this life. Useless will be well cared for, he is sure of that, and nobody will mourn him. No misery will ensue.

His breathing is tight and his fingers begin to tremble. He puts one foot in front of the other, walks towards the wall bars. A pale light intrudes through the narrow windows all around the top of the gymnasium and he regards his knife. Graham had dismantled his safety razors, pressing the blades into the plastic head of the toothbrush on the reverse of the bristles, an eighth of an inch apart – wide enough to cut an unstitchable wound. He had then burnt the bristles and the bottom of the plastic until the handle melted away.

Graham tucks the knife into the waistband of his boxers and reaches up for the bars, climbs slowly. He wishes there was a full moon, something of significance for a last night like this. As he gets higher, he takes shorter reaches. Just one bar at a time and when he looks down, he feels a rush. It warms his loins and he climbs faster, wanting it to be over. Just over. For ever.

Not quite at the top, he is happy to stop; satisfied that the height is sufficient – to finish him off. The basketball hoop is way down and the markings of the court are like a hopscotch pavement. He remembers listening, in his boxroom in Marigold Close, to children playing hopscotch. In the summer, Mother sent him to bed when it was still light. He wouldn't sleep, though – not until the last voice faded from the street.

He turns his body round, tucking his heels into the gap between the bars and the wall and reaching down for the blade. He has to hold on with just one hand, leaning out, so high above the gymnasium floor. Graham feels sick. He takes the blade and, the way he had planned, puts it to his neck, feeling with his index knuckle for the jugular. His bowels go completely slack and he feels the warmth. Can smell himself.

This is no way to die.

He wants to close his eyes, but also wants to see the ground meet him. He has thought of nothing else, these last days.

He takes a deep breath, tugs with all his last might from his Adam's apple to his ear. Strangely, he hears the long *phiss* of his flesh, the fine spray of his blood in his eye. It makes him blink and he realises he is holding on when he should be letting go. He looks across at his hand, gripping the bar, sees a wash of blood, vivid red, all across his sweats, and drops the makeshift knife. He hears its light rattle on the gym floor, then a key at the door.

Graham takes a hold of one hand with the other and pulls, feels the world alter on its axis and he loses his footing, hears a cry from below, sees the walls and floor and the corrugated panels of the ceiling tumble in on themselves. Something in his leg cracks and the pain is fierce, worse than the cut to his neck. He waits for the air to be fast all around him, for it to be over in no time at all. But instead of the ground meeting him, he hangs, upside down. He foot is trapped between the bars and the wall. He thrashes around, trying to free himself, but can't and the white-hot, searing pain of what he has done to himself cuts him, long, incessant. The voices grow louder, more desperate, then subside. The life drains from him. Soon, the pain is too much. His eyes close and the last dim light turns black.

The darkness is thick, tight, holds her by the throat, it seems. She has a gag around her mouth and any sounds she can discern are muffled. Her senses are melded into one and she is dizzied from hunger.

For days, Arabella has seen only black, heard little, tasted nothing she can recognise. She thinks she might be swaddled in something like a sleeping bag. They certainly zipped all around her before they carried her, when she seemed to float from indoors to out. Then, after the vibrations of what could have been a car journey, she thought she could smell ozone.

Now, they have left her again. No more muffled noises, just the lull and return of an imperfect stillness. She remembers feeling this way asleep on the *Imogen* and though it is the last thing she needs, she is visited by memories of her mother and father and how they were once deeply in love. Nobody saw into the darkness of that love, once the doors were closed; only her, and Roddy.

She begins to cry and the tears are warm on her cheeks. She feels them soak into the fabric of whatever blinds and hoods her. She is afraid, for what might happen; at everything she has done and what she thinks she might know. What she would do, to be held tight; for a toke, or a line.

Twenty-five

Pulford twitches each time a car rounds the corner and drives towards the niche he has found for himself, opposite Bobo's deck-access tenement.

Bobo's flank of the block has only one stairwell, and Pulford can see all comers from here. A car roars past, picking up speed and squealing as it rounds a corner, going deeper into the warren and further from Bethnal Green's main drag.

Pulford takes the deepest of breaths and rubs his hands, ready to go up, but wary of the response he might get. As he takes his first step, a long-base Mitsubishi pick-up glides to a silent halt outside the stairwell to Bobo's place and the doors open and close quickly: pum-pum, pum-pum, like four silenced shots.

The four men are built like boulders and wear tracksuits. Two of them disappear into the stairwell and the others wait by the trucks, looking up and down the street.

Pulford waits for Bobo to let them in, for the door to open. A glow of light emerges from within. He winds down his window and holds his breath, trying to discern the sounds in the night. He thinks he hears a strangled human cry.

The two men on the street talk into their chests and Pulford is torn. Should he intervene, or call for back-up? He's not officially here, though.

His phone vibrates against his chest. It is Josie.

'You need to come in, David,' she says, clearly upset.

'I can't. I'm on surveillance.'

'You have to,' she says.

'What's wrong?'

'Blears has killed himself. Come now. *Please*.'

Staffe walks towards the minicab outside the Signet and Rosa says, 'We're not calling Thomas? He'd take us.'

'Let's leave our friend to his own devices. See what he gets up to.'

'What do you mean?' says Rosa, wrapping a pashmina around her neck. It is aquamarine and flows like water.

Staffe ushers her towards the minicab, says, 'This is Gerald.'

Gerald Holt makes a fuss of opening the door for the lady, saying to Staffe, 'The Ridings, you say?' He is clearly impressed.

'You'll have seen some comings and goings up there, these last few days,' says Staffe. 'Roddy and Arabella are back up for Christmas, I take it.'

'I don't think anybody's home,' says Gerald.

'How can you be sure?' says Staffe.

'I usually see them, when they're here.'

'Nobody's supposed to know she's home. I hope I can count on you for your discretion,' says Staffe, patting Holt on the shoulder.

Gerald clearly thinks it odd, as they approach The Ridings on this bitter eastern night, that Staffe wants to be dropped at the end of the driveway, but Rosa comes in on cue, complaining she feels sick, needs some air. Staffe tells him to call by in, say, an hour. But to stay on the main road.

The drive is a hundred yards long and halfway up Staffe stops, listens to the sound of Gerald's taxi peter absolutely to nothing. Soon, another sound replaces it and Staffe smiles to himself, glad to have got something right, belatedly. But he wonders just how sinister it might be – the percolating diesel of Thomas's London hackney carriage in the Suffolk night.

It is plain to see that nobody is home. No cars parked, just a couple of outside lights on and the two-storey stairwell and landing lit up, presumably on a timer. Poor Howerd. Could it be that money got so tight the domestics have been laid off? Or simply not required in these interesting times.

He immediately goes round the back of the house, looking for signs of alarms. There are none. The garden is formal but overgrown, and the bay-lined square around the fountain is thatched with weeds. The lawn, giving onto a ha-ha and the fields beyond, is half a foot high. In the full moon, the house seems gothic: a modest Jacobean seat with a Victorian addition jutting perpendicular, but somehow time-less, the sum of all the ages.

Staffe can see there are blind cellars beneath the main house and he tries the door to a conservatory, which itself has a door into the main house. It doesn't budge, so he pulls the sleeve of his jacket down over his hand, punches a pane out and reaches in, unlocks the door.

Glass crunches as he works his way round, picking up pots and urging Rosa to be careful. The house key is under a dead tomato plant.

The house smells of centuries. He tries all the doors off the main hallway, soon coming across the entrance to the cellar. Before they get halfway down the worn stone steps, they smell life.

'Someone's been down here,' says Rosa. 'A woman. I can smell her.' There are three low-ceilinged, vaulted cellars, one with a few bottles of wine and lines of empty racks, one with bicycle skeletons, wooden skis and hickory golf clubs. The third has a padlock hanging like chunky jewellery from its handle. On its floor, a blanket, sack and vestiges of food.

'She was here all right,' says Staffe.

They make their way through the ground floor by the stair lights and, once they find Howerd's study, which has double-aspect shuttered windows to the front and side of the house, Staffe looks around, picturing what a wonderful place this would be – to escape. Staffe hands Rosa a torch. 'I'll take the bureau, you go through the desk.'

'What am I looking for?'

'Anything financial, or letters. Just make a pile of whatever seems interesting.'

In the large middle drawer of the Dutch walnut bureau, Staffe finds a postcard. It feels rough and the edges are uneven. He holds it up to the torch and sees it is a watercolour of a shore, as if painted from the sea. From the palette employed, he immediately recognises the artist. He squints, studying the image of lilacs and pale blues and yellows, and can see a minaret rising from a village in the mountains beyond the shore. 'Imogen,' he whispers.

'What?' says Rosa.

Staffe turns the hand-painted postcard over. All it says is: 'My darling R. Be safe. Be extraordinary'. The unceasing tide of a mother's love.

'This is Imogen, too,' says Rosa, approaching Staffe. She hands him an invoice from the Warblingsea Chandlery. It is a bill for £9,700 – a second reminder for unpaid repairs to the mast and bilge for a vessel named *Imogen II*.

On top of the pile of papers Rosa has made is a small ream of travel documents from the last ten years or so. He can see why Leonard keeps them. It is quite a log and relates the travels of a man for whom the world is not large enough: Nairobi, Auckland, Lima, Vancouver, Buenos Aires, Rangoon, Phnom Penh, Lima again – the last time – and Istanbul. Istanbul once, twice, thrice, all within a year. The year before Imogen died. The year before Taki Markary moved to England.

'Stay here, I'm going to look around,' says Staffe. He makes his way from room to room, the boards creaking, the doors squeaking. It is a house only used for weeks in the summer, he suspects. As he rises from landing to landing, up into the heights of the house, a sliver of moon is seen, here and there. On the second floor, he looks towards Aldesworth, can see the outline of a crane, which makes him sad.

The house is as old as the Howerds, older than the town house in Mayfair, and Laing's, and the Colonial Bankers' Club. Yet you can see the new money from here. He can't imagine Leonard not being ashamed and can't comprehend what you might do to preserve this, against a tide that comes and comes and comes.

He hears a creak on the stairs, turns off his torch and leans flat to the wall. The moon catches a photograph. *Ampleforth Leavers, 1974*. Somewhere, there will be Leonard – in this same life, unrecognisable.

Another creak, closer this time. He wants to call out for Rosa but knows he can't give himself away. He holds his breath, hears another stealthy tread, another board betraying its age. He clenches his fist, looking at all those boys, in subfusc, so long before their time.

Staffe breathes out, slow, feels his pulse release as he steps out, raising his hands above his head, smelling – in the musty curtain and rug and dusty wood – the scent of Rosa. Her eyes are wide and he looks beyond her. Sees only dark.

'Are you alone?' he says, afraid.

'There's no one here, is there?' she says. 'I was frightened. And I found this. It doesn't seem to fit.'

She hands Staffe a photograph of an infant boy with a straight nose and dark skin. He is naked and has a serious look on his face, holding a bucket and spade up to whomever is holding the camera. Staffe takes it from Rosa, puts it in his pocket and holds Rosa's hand, leads her down through the house.

Outside, her eyes are large, watery in the bold, silvery light from the moon. 'Do you think they killed Arabella?' she says.

Staffe shakes his head. 'Quite the opposite.'

Twenty-six

Leonard Howerd puts down his mobile telephone. He doesn't say 'thank you' to Gerald Holt, nor even goodbye. He blows out his cheeks and sighs.

'Is he at the house, Father?' says Roddy, carrying charts from the aft berth, nimble and alert at the prospect of setting sail, instinctively stooping so as not to bang his head on the ceiling of the boat's galley. He appears to be completely at home.

'Holt dropped him off half an hour ago.'

'Do you think he'll come?'

Leonard ignores his son's question and sits opposite a third man. Younger, lean and dressed head to toe in black, he has a ruddy face with a stitched cut across his head. 'I want to see her,' says Leonard.

'You agreed not to,' says the Younger. 'We're not fucking about here.'

'Do you have children?'

'That's no business of yours. You don't need to know anything about me – except I'm on your side.'

Leonard says, 'I don't suppose you can stop me, if I insist on seeing her.'

The Younger shakes his head. 'I know my place.' His face assumes an extra furrow of sadness.

'She is blindfolded.'

'That's not the point.'

'You should wait, Father,' says Roddy.

Howerd gives him a scolding look, as if he has talked out of turn, in company. He says, to the Younger, 'Give me your aftershave, whatever you wear.'

'Watch yourself. This could still go wrong, and then we'd all be in the shit,' says the Younger, handing him a bottle.

Howerd holds it to his nose. 'This stinks.'

'It's everyman. That's what they say.'

Howerd dabs the scent on his wrists and onto his index finger, applying it to his temples and behind his ears. Its aroma is abrasive, makes him splutter.

'What's to be gained?' says the Younger.

'I am tired of losing people.'

The Younger pulls across a curtain to reveal a sheet of plywood cut to fit the cross-section of the hull. Within the plywood, a door has been made and this is padlocked, top and bottom. Once this door is opened, another door, the original, leads to the bow berths.

Howerd takes a deep breath. The smell claws his throat. His daughter has been here just a few hours, but the ingrained stench of days weeps, thick.

He knows why it has to be this way, knows that

undue tenderness will scupper the deception. But even so . . .

A brace of tears break and he is taken aback. For a brief snatch of time, he feels liberated; likes himself a little more. He didn't weep when Imogen went; told Arabella not to cry when he said, 'Your mother is dead.'

Leonard crouches down and his bones creak. He could reach out and touch her. He wants to pull away the scarf that is wrapped around her head, binding the rags that keep the sounds of this small world from her. He wants to pull away the blindfold and see what her eyes reply when he tells her that he is sorry, for everything. He wishes it had been possible simply to love his daughter at all costs and to protect her – nothing more.

'Who's there?' she says, her voice muffled and hoarse and mostly lost in the gag. She sniffs like an animal and tries to reach out but her arms are bound and she falls off balance.

Instinctively, Howerd reaches for her and catches her. He holds her for the longest second and pushes her upright again.

'Who is it?' she says, muffled.

He sits back on his haunches, weighing up the pros and cons if he held her.

'Daddy?' she says.

And he knows that one lapse has been sufficient.

He should have known better, after all his years of doing the right thing. Too late, now. Slowly, uncertainly, he pulls himself together, reaches out, pulls off the hood and sees, in the gloom, the unadulterated relief that flickers when she sees him. Then goes off, like a concussion.

Gerald Holt is back at the bottom of The Ridings' driveway. He has drunk his flask of tea and figures the inspector will want the lift back to town on a night like this. In his position, Gerald must do what is asked of him.

The heater is on high, but icy white hexagon flowers have formed on the wing mirrors. He will be glad when his favours are all evened out but to console himself, he pulls out the brochure from the glove compartment and treats himself to a peek at the artist's impression, the floor plans of his promised land.

A tap on the window makes his heart thud and he throws the Aldesworth Country Town brochure to the floor.

Wagstaffe's face is at the window. Where the hell did he come from? He is smiling and Gerald feels known. He fixes a smile and flicks the door locks off. But the inspector has gone. Gerald looks around but cannot see him, nor the woman. 'Hello!' he calls, winding down the window. He checks in the rearview but can see nothing. The wing mirrors are useless because of the frost. He turns on his headlights, but all they reveal is two beams of falling snowflakes.

He starts the engine, thinking this will bring them running. Gerald puts his foot to the accelerator, pulsing the revs. He wants to drive away but knows he has to honour this side of a bargain.

The passenger door opens violently. The night howls in with a black sweep. It is Wagstaffe, sitting heavily alongside; the back door opens, too. The inspector smiles at him, reaches down at his feet and picks up the brochure.

'No,' says Gerald. 'That's . . .' The words trap in his throat and he feels a softness wrap itself around his neck, pulled tight from behind. He raises his hands to ease the pashmina that strangles him. He can't breathe, but as he raises his hands, a terrible pain shoots down his legs and up into his belly. He looks down, sees the inspector has him by the balls. The inspector's hand is large and hard. Gerald wants to weep, wants to close his eyes and this be over.

'I need to know', says the inspector, 'where Arabella is. You have seen her.' The scarf cuts into him, the pain in his gut gets deeper, sharper, and Gerald raises his hands to his neck, tries to ease the pressure, but he is too weak. 'The truth cannot hurt you, Gerald. But the law can.' A false light appears alongside, in the inspector's lap. He has Gerald's phone. He tries to say 'Don't' but he can utter it only in his head, which is screaming. He would say anything now, but it is too late. Life is slipping away. He prays. He sees his grandson first, and then his daughter. Finally, he sees his wife and in the last morsel of his prayer he begs forgiveness.

Everything goes slack, and Gerald feels his head, too heavy to support itself, snap away from him.

'Will you tell me everything, Gerald?' says the inspector, releasing him from that grip.

'Yes.' The syllable burns in his throat, but Gerald thinks there is a God. His prayers are answered.

Pulford unclasps from Josie and her tears tack to his cheek and neck. She doesn't look him in the eye as they release. He could tell her not to blame herself or feel ashamed, but such advice merely suggests the opposite.

'Go,' she says. 'And thank you for coming.'

'Where's Rimmer?'

'With Tara Fleet. Concocting a new theory, I suppose.'

'You had the evidence, Josie. He confessed. Maybe it was a matter of honour for him.'

'Honour?'

Something Staffe had said.

'Do you need a drink?' he asks.

Josie shakes her head. 'I might go and see him.'

'Blears? Don't do that!' Pulford has heard the gory details from Jombaugh, of how Blears had stuck himself, like a pig; had contrived to kill himself, that his meat not be poisonous for anyone wanting his body in his afterlife.

Nobody had ever heard of anything like it, according to the Governor of Inmate Activities.

Staffe and Rosa rise above the Alde river in Gerald Holt's cab, then sweep down into the low-lying folds that crumple along the south side of the estuary, to Warblingsea. In the distance, the water tower signals Saltburgh. Staffe sees masts and he winds down the window, slows the car. 'Don't you love that sound?'

Rosa leans across, supporting herself by putting her hand on his thigh. The clinking masts are like chimes, distant, on a cusp. 'What is it?'

Staffe is sad that, for her, it is a new sound. 'It's not just a sound,' he says. 'Just like the ozone', he sniffs the sea air, 'isn't just a smell.'

'I don't understand you, Will.' She looks down at her hand, takes it away. 'Are we here?'

'I don't think so. Not yet.' He raises a finger to his lips, slows further, for what he knows must come. The engine is low and, looking behind, he sees the black cab come into view then back off, keeping its distance.

Staffe waits for a blind bend and accelerates, stretching the gap to the cab behind. The road swoops down and round, seemingly below the close sea, as if reeds can hold back an ocean. Staffe drops Holt's car from fourth to second and puts his foot to the floor. Gerald shivers in the passenger seat, quite unsure, still, what fate might befall him, and the consequences for his daughter.

The revs spool into the red. The engine screams blue murder and Staffe kills the lights, steers violently left, down a rutted track, and waits for the sound of the London taxi. It comes louder and louder, roaring past the track, its suspension squealing. Once it is gone, Staffe tells Holt to get out. 'I'd leave town, quick if I was you, Gerald. Give it 'til the new year.'

Staffe reverses back up the track, puts the lights on, illuminating the frozen Gerald, not wanting to move, not wanting his future to come get him.

Following the red tail lights of Thomas's cab, they catch him, quarter of a mile from the harbour. Staffe sees the chandlery up on the left and a line of shacks that sell fish, so he puts the car into neutral, kills the lights again and they glide, soundless, with nothing but dark in the rear view. He steers the minicab behind an old Nicholson on a stand, pulls Rosa's head down, out of sight.

'Where are we going now?' she says.

'I'm staying here. You drive the car back to town. Stay at the Bull, though. Don't go near the Signet. Here,' he hands her a wafer of twenties.

'Are these the people who killed Elena and Rebeccah?'

'Leave the car by the Magnet Café, on the edge of town. And use a false name.'

'I can do that,' she laughs, nervous.

They look at each other, locked in a distant moment.

A cloud drifts across the moon and Thomas's lights smudge the night with red, then die. It is silent, save the coming and going of the sea, the masts chiming.

He runs across the boatyard, slowing so he can hear beyond his steps and the rush of his own blood. The driver of the taxi, clearly Thomas, makes his way past the jetty which serves the ferry to Saltburgh. Staffe curses Thomas's betrayal, but in the same breath gives thanks that his plan has worked. Staffe knew that if they believed or even feared his lie to Roddy, about knowing where Arabella was, they would have to follow his every move. All he had to do then was turn the tables on the lie that revealed the truth.

Thomas hooks a leg over the chains that bar access to the boats. He steps straight on deck, the second boat from the harbour wall, looking back before he disappears below.

The livery of the boat, and the lettering, *Imogen II*, is just as Gerald Holt had described. Now he is here, Staffe's choices go to vapour in the sea fret, as rock and the hard sea come together.

Pulford gets a daggers look from the curator of the IT suite who then looks contemptuously at his watch. The sergeant goes back to his screen, scrolling through the Companies House database, cross-checking the Aldesworth development companies: Bluecoat, Oakvale and Pinfold. Vassily Tchancov isn't listed as director or shareholder. He does the same for Laissez SA and the story is the same. He leans back, rubs his eyes, thinks he should have taken Josie home, stayed with her until she found some kind of peace.

'Bloody documents,' he says, chucking his pen across the room.

The curator scuttles across and tells him to 'shushh', even though Pulford is the only reader in the room.

He stretches, fetches the pen, wishes he was with Staffe, at the sharp end, rather than tracing the Howerds' title – all wrapped up in land for centuries and them more bankers than farmers. Which makes him think – maybe it could be about the land and not the companies.

Pulford asks the curator to get him into the Land Charges Registry for Saltburgh and Aldesworth; receives a snarl for an answer. 'Otherwise, we could be here all night,' he says, getting the desired response.

He soon sees that the consideration for the sale transfer from Leonard Howerd to Aldesworth Developments was relatively modest: a mere £750,000. In the Companies Register, he sees that Landesbank of Hanover have registered a debenture against the assets, including the land, but an interest is also registered in the name of Magellan Holdings, relating to a profit share agreement. The interest was registered only six weeks ago.

'Magellan,' says Pulford. He checks the company's details, flicks back through his notebook. Magellan Holdings' registered address is Cobalt Street, St Helier; its company secretary, a Henry Desai. Unremarkable, save that they are exactly the same address and secretary as he had noted for Vodblu.

At last, Vassily Tchancov puts his head above the parapet.

Twenty-seven

Staffe steps gingerly onto the *Imogen II*, peers through the narrow windows that look down below decks. He can hear raised whispers but is unable to discern what is being said. He continues along the rails to the bow. Here, he can see the combed and oiled hair of a suited man who seems to be on his knees. His head is bowed, but Staffe knows him. 'Howerd,' he whispers to himself.

Unable to see the object of Howerd's attentions, he crawls around to starboard, peers down. From this angle, he sees that the gentleman banker's face is pinched with suffering. His hands are turned down, as if in prayer.

When he presses his face to the glass, Staffe sees the object of Howerd's penitence. Wrapped in blankets and bound at the feet, the body is dead still.

'Come on,' says a voice within and Staffe recognises the kindly tones of Thomas. 'Don't ruin all we have done.' From above, Thomas looks as if he would be unable to bring himself to harm a fly: a big man with round shoulders and bald pate, a pencil moustache and twinkling eyes.

'This is my time, with her,' says Howerd.

Thomas retires as Howerd says, over and again, 'I'm sorry, Bella, I'm sorry, Bella. We'll be fine, now. We'll be fine, now,' as if he is trying to convince himself, or some higher order, that this ordinary and beautiful act – of a father loving a daughter – could be true.

Staffe, distracted by the scene below, hears too late that somebody has come above decks. The engine expectorates and he turns round. In the fullness of the moon, he and Roddy, stooping by the fenders, scrutinise each other.

'Are we going somewhere?' says Staffe. He thinks it might be a trick of the moonlight and the dappling sea, but Roddy Howerd appears to smile.

'Bella is safe,' says the young heir. 'We have always loved night sailing.'

'She is safe from whom?' says Staffe.

'You don't know?'

Roddy makes his way below, leaving the fenders out, and calling, 'Father! He has come.'

Staffe follows him down. Leonard Howerd is now sitting at the round table in the *Imogen II*'s galley. He stares at his hands, locked in a slowly twisting, constantly ravelling knot.

'You have Arabella,' says Staffe.

Howerd raises his head and summons vigour to his eyes. They are bloodshot. 'She is safe.'

'I must talk to her.'

'You are a guest here, Inspector.'

'I'm not here as your guest, Mr Howerd, or your lackey. I have come to find out who killed Elena Danya and Rebeccah Stone.'

'You're barking up the wrong tree,' says the Elder, looking not so kindly now.

'And I'm expected to believe you, Thomas? If that's your name. I guess not.'

Behind the Elder, a younger man studies a chart. He is lean and has a ruddy face, a stitched wound across his forehead. Staffe's head floods and he steps towards the Younger. 'Where did you get that cut?'

He doesn't look up, simply says, 'Fuck you.'

Staffe continues, 'Do you like hotels? Do you have something against prostitutes?'

The Younger doesn't look up, still. In his soft, Scouse accent, he says, 'You put her in harm's way.'

'Who the hell *are* you?'

'You wouldn't understand,' says the Elder.

Staffe considers something of what he doesn't understand: the decades of the rosary, England's shadowy lineage, the privacy of clubs. He says, to Howerd, 'Why did Elena Danya visit the Colonial Bankers' Club? An unusual place for your whore, if you don't mind me saying.'

'She wasn't my whore.' Howerd regards Staffe

with an unblemished superiority he simply can't help.

The Elder says, in low, measured tones, 'Mr Howerd had nothing to do with any of that. There is irrefutable proof.'

'He signed her in,' says Staffe. 'A week before she was murdered.'

'We have new information. This will ensure Mr Howerd's situation is not misunderstood.'

Staffe turns back to Howerd. 'How does a man like you end up in cahoots with someone like Markary? Your father must turn in his grave.'

'You have no business with my family, Inspector.'

'You keep strange company. Brothel keepers, immigrant workers. You had a thing for Elena.'

'Shut up!' shouts Roddy.

Staffe feels a tight grip on his arm. He flexes, but the grip tightens. It is the Younger and Staffe twists to face him but feels himself sag to his knees, unable to resist.

Leonard smiles down at Staffe, thin-lipped, life returned to his eyes. 'Roddy will tell you, I'm not much of a father.'

'Why are you so keen that I don't speak to your daughter, Leonard?'

'As you can see, she is secure.'

'She was taken against her will. That's a crime,' says Staffe, on his knees, looking up.

The Younger stoops, hisses at Staffe, 'You know fuck all.'

'Surely your own daughter wasn't blackmailing you?'

Howerd nods to the Younger. 'Let him go. He needs to understand.' He looks directly at Staffe as he is unhanded. 'Do you believe in Right?'

'I believe in evidence. I have just visited your site, Leonard. You have quite a source of cheap labour there, and I'm guessing Vassily Tchancov is sorting you out.'

'Guessing? I thought you believed in evidence.'

'I'll get the evidence. But I know, by his admission, that he knew Elena. Was he putting the squeeze on you, Leonard?'

'It's not a term I would use. But I have had cause to undertake some research into Mr Tchancov.' He holds out his hand. 'You might call it an investigation.' The Elder passes him a buff folder, marked *VT*, top right.

The Elder invites Staffe to sit down, which he does – opposite Howerd. 'You will have asked yourself why exactly Rebeccah Stone's employer would want Elena Danya dead.'

'Tchancov?'

'Believe me, Inspector, had we not removed Arabella when we did and how we did, she would have been in the gravest danger.'

'And Rosa?' Staffe regards the Younger, with contempt.

'She was never at risk.'

'What would Tchancov have to gain?' says Staffe.

Thomas nods towards the buff dossier and Staffe opens it, reads quickly, his thoughts colliding, bleeding sense as he absorbs the press cuttings and military discharges, charge sheets and witness statements.

'This is for flavour, Inspector,' says the Elder. 'There is more.'

One charge sheet is dated four months before Vassily Tchancov's discharge document from the Russian army. It is translated, as are the rest of the papers.

The charge was for the rape of a girl, Ludmilla Shostavic. The girl was fourteen years old and her mother ran a farm on her own in the Urals, near the camp where Tchancov's company had been based.

The Elder says, 'Wherever he went, Tchancov would coerce farmers to take his men on as labourers. The wages were paid straight to him, but Mother Shostavic worked the land herself and had no money for wages. It didn't take Tchancov long to find a means of exchange. Ludmilla was thirteen when it began. Ludmilla took it for a year, then hanged herself, from the hay winch in the barn.' He pulls from his pocket a photograph of a young girl hugging a boy. Whilst the girl is quite indistinctive, the boy is not. He is, indisputably, Bobo Bogdanovich. 'This is Ludmilla, with her brother, Bobo. He changed his name.'

'Ludmilla was Elena's sister? Elena knew about this?' Staffe takes the photograph from the Elder. 'She's not in the photograph.'

'You really don't want to dwell on where she might have been when this was taken. What she was . . .'

'Tchancov would have remembered her.'

'She was young and there were many. Believe me, Inspector.'

'I don't think I can go down this road. This isn't evidence.'

'He's a powerful man, and really quite wealthy – though we have cause to believe he has been called upon to stretch himself, of late. Elena knows how to get the last drop from such men.'

'She was blackmailing him?' Staffe recalls the *PRIVAT* envelope from Rebeccah's trove, the lilac correspondence in Tchancov's house. 'How did you get this information?'

'We knew Miss Danya might bring you to Mr Howerd's door. We had to prepare the truth.'

'This isn't exactly my idea of proof,' says Staffe. 'I don't subscribe to hearsay.'

'Perhaps you should start,' says Howerd. 'That man is a bastard, of the lowest order.'

'Hearsay, Mr Howerd? How about you and Taki Markary – I'd never put the two of you together and I dare say you wouldn't either. But I can see Imogen with a foot in each of your worlds. And I know that in your world, under your God, you could never divorce each other, no matter how much you loved or hated each other. I guess Taki and Sema were a real comfort.'

In the doorway, Arabella appears. Her blankets shed, she stands tall, frail, holding onto the frame of the door. Her fair hair is lank and her eye sockets are dark, hollow. Her pale skin is mottled with dry, red blotches, her lips the colour of milk.

'It is time you went,' says Howerd.

'Not until I have spoken to Arabella. I can see that if my curiosity was at all aroused by your relationship with Elena, then Arabella's disappearance would throw me off that scent.'

Arabella squints, trying to recall who Staffe is. The Elder stands by her, whispers into her ear, wary in the extreme as to what she might say. 'Have you brought Darius?' She says it to nobody in particular. 'I want Darry.'

'I would like you to come with me, Arabella,' says Staffe.

She shakes her head, says, 'I am happy here,' as if reading from a cue card.

And Staffe knows he has missed that boat. He buttons his jacket all the way. It will be cold up top. He feels the photograph that the Elder gave him, of Bobo and Elena's sister. He says, to the Elder, 'You were in the army, weren't you? I'll check.'

'Don't waste your time. I don't exist any more.'

'Is that where you met your scummy friend?' Staffe looks at the Younger.

'I wouldn't rile him,' says the Elder. 'I've trained him, but he's different from us.'

'Thank God for small mercies.'

'I take it you won't be needing that lift in the morning.'

'I'll manage on my own.'

On deck, Staffe looks around. The slap of sea on dock in the dark punches through the wind. The long beach he ran along just a few days ago trails away north, like a knife smear of oil paint.

He will call on Tchancov, try to get to the bottom of what Arabella might have known but was prevented from saying.

As he steps over the harbour chains, Staffe looks back. The Younger watches him, with cool, dead eyes. This is the man from the dunes. Staffe senses that he moves to an alternate beat.

* * *

Taki Markary sits at a table by the window and wipes his eyes, looks out to sea. 'Elena,' he says, under his breath. He brought her here, occasionally, to the Nelson, down the coast from Saltburgh and the other side of Warblingsea estuary. She liked the lobster but would never finish it. She always took some away in doggy foil. The staff would swarm around her.

Afterwards, they would take coffee in the lounge and he would watch her read her book. Always with her book; mouth open, entranced, her eyebrows pinched by the puppetry of story. She loved it here, and she loved Taki, too – so he believed.

Still, at night, when Sema puts her hand on his stomach and hooks her thigh over his and breathes heavy, Taki can see Elena. In dreams, they are sometimes here.

The last time they came, she ate all her lobster and afterwards they drove straight back up the coast to the Signet. Elena didn't read that night. Instead, they talked.

She asked him why he had never had children. She seemed angry, accused him of having a cold heart. Taki told Elena that she had no business asking such questions and he and his wife wanted children but Sema couldn't carry them. It was because of a fall from a horse when she was younger. 'So don't talk to me about a cold heart when my wife cries at night for children she cannot bear. Imagine her tears if she knew I was talking about such things with a whore in a hotel.'

Waiting, now, for another woman to come to 'their' place, he feels the full weight of his history.

His chest becomes tight. He thinks he misses a beat, two, and on the perimeter of his vision, he feels her. He shoots his cuffs, chin up, turns slowly – a gentleman.

Crow's feet pinch the corners of her eyes, but her cheeks are high and wide, her nose straight, and she is absolutely alive. Too much life. Here and there, men subtly turn.

She sits beside him, takes his breath clean away. For an instant, an old love issues new.

'Hello, Marky,' says Imogen, breathily. Despite the years, she is every inch the woman she ever was.

'You don't change,' he says.

'Then you know nothing. How is Arabella?'

'Safe, I hear. Do they know you have arrived?'

'It's been five years. I think we can all wait another day. I need to be ready for it.' She takes a lusty swallow of Markary's wine. 'And how is Roddy?'

'The same. He's a quiet one.'

'I miss him so,' she says, wanting to say more, but deciding against.

Markary calls the waiter over and, as if it is a proclamation, Imogen requests a glass and another bottle, orders lemon sole. 'I know it's not on the menu, but could you ask Chef to do me a tiny side bowl of black butter, and a few capers. Thank you.'

The waiter nods, anxiously, 'Of course. Of course, madam,' he says, as if nothing could possibly be too much trouble for this lady.

Her hair is shorter and she has a Mediterranean look to her, but still Markary is afraid she will draw attention to herself, may be recognised.

'Don't worry, Marky. I didn't ever come to this place. It's where Leonard would bring people – if you know what I mean. And even if they thought I was me, they'd be wrong, wouldn't they?'

'You really haven't changed.'

'Some things can't change, but thank God I'm not one of them. Poor Leonard, he's stuck with his lot.'

'I thought that's what you wanted.'

'It's for the *best*, but it's not necessarily what you would choose.'

'Have any of us got what we would choose?' says Markary.

'It's a bloody mess, but as messes go, it's quite a fine one.' She laughs and her eyes sparkle. In the candlelight, all the years he has known her roll away.

The waiter comes with his starter and Markary eats his whitebait, one by one. Every four fish, he takes a delicate bite of the buttered brown bread. He eats with his fingers, the way you should and the way you are prohibited from in places such as the Colonial Bankers' Club.

'You still enjoy life,' she says.

Looking at her, that long and fateful afternoon reprises – on the sun deck by the Bosphorus, drinking wine whilst Leonard and Sema were away, sailing. Of all the women he had ever had, she could never be sated. Like the sea, she came and she came.

He holds up a small fish. 'Nothing like the real thing. The catches we landed in Turkey, fresh from the sea.'

Imogen says, 'It's still the same – over there.'

'Nothing is the same.' Taki finishes his whitebait. 'What good can come from this?'

'We have to think about the greater things,' says Imogen. 'Do you think they will get the Russian before I go back?'

'I don't understand how you can fight so hard for this and then return to the shadows.'

'It is what's right. It's what we strove for and not as if we have a choice. There is no free will, here, Taki.'

This saddens him. If anybody's spirit was born to be free, it is Imogen's. He thinks about accidents of birth, raises his glass. 'To the Howerds,' he says.

Imogen says, 'To what is right.'

'And if there is a slip, between the stirrup and the ground, as you say?'

'I will confess.'

'To your priest?'

She laughs. 'That will happen, come what may.'

The waiter brings Imogen's sole and Markary's calamari. He lifts a forkful to his mouth, tastes the sea. The flesh is tender, perfect and melting. He closes his eyes and sees the Black Sea, the sun dipping to a more eastern west. 'How is Mark?' he asks.

Imogen reaches down, picks up a small, hand-sewn clutch bag, produces a six-by-four photograph and shows it to Taki. The young boy with the dark skin and the mop of jet-black hair and the straight nose smiles into the camera.

Taki takes it but Imogen grabs it back, returns it to the bag. 'I'm afraid you can't have it,' she says.

'But I'm his father.'

'Exactly.'

'You don't know what it's like, Imogen.'

'Oh, I do. But you shouldn't worry. I love him enough for the both of us.'

'Too much can be as bad as too little, don't you think?'

'We need to love, Marky, but we have to take it when and where we find it.'

Twenty-eight

Staffe swivels in his chair, turns his back on Pulford and stares loosely into the windblown snow above Cloth Fair. The words garble. The truth beyond them rings untrue.

Blears is dead. He took his own life as if he were both pig and slayer.

'There's better news, though, sir,' says Pulford.

'Better? Is that an appropriate term?'

'For the case, yes. We can hook Tchancov up to the development in Suffolk. The registered address and company secretary of Vodblu match to a Magellan Holdings. Magellan has registered a charge against the land up there. It relates to a profit-share agreement. Do you think he was extorting Howerd? Shall I bring him in?'

'I'll pay him a visit.'

'Why would you do that?' says Pennington, coming into the room, twirling a pen between his fingers. He stands next to Staffe, planting a palm on his DI's shoulder.

Staffe explains what he knows to Pennington, shows him the photograph of young Ludmilla and the charge sheets for the Shostavic rape.

'I think that maybe Elena was blackmailing Howerd, on Tchancov's behalf, to get him a fatter share of the profits in Aldesworth Country Town. He's supplying all the immigrant labour up there, making millions. He scared off the big UK contractors to get the job.'

'They'd never testify to that,' says Pennington.

'Elena came to avenge her sister.' Staffe taps the photograph of Ludmilla Shostavic, and closes his eyes, recalls the first time he saw Elena Danya: pale and naked; beautiful and dead. 'She came with her brother, Bobo. She was trying to turn the tables on Tchancov.' Staffe picks up the charge sheets and slams them back down on his desk.

'You have nothing to prove that she was blackmailing Tchancov or Howerd.'

Staffe has been in a quandary all the way from Saltburgh, and now, with heavy blood, he goes to his filing cabinet, reaches deep, puts his hand on the envelope marked *PRIVAT* in Elena Danya's hand. But in the moment, he thinks better, lets go of the envelope.

Pennington says, 'You're just making all this up.'

'The truth is, sir, I can't prove Danya was blackmailing anybody. I need to speak to Bobo. He's the only one who can prove it was Tchancov behind everything.'

Pennington stands, picks up the photograph and Vassily Tchancov's rape charges and discharge from the army; gives them a final once-over. 'I've made some enquiries of my own. You're right about Tchancov – he is under pressure. His cousin is coming to live in London.'

'Uncle Ludo's son?'

Pennington nods. 'Nikolai. Quite the bastard, by all accounts; he could buy and sell Vassily with his small change.' He pats his DI on the shoulder. The contact is soft, implies with great force that Pennington wouldn't want to be Staffe.

As Staffe passes through reception, Jombaugh says, 'Somebody to see you, Staffe,' pointing, as if to say, 'rather you . . .'

Brendan Stone sits, still as death. When he sees Staffe, his eyelids flutter.

'You've heard?' says Brendan, looking at the floor. 'About the bastard killed my Rebeccah.'

'He topped himself, Brendan.'

'You sure about that?' Stone looks up, his eyes are wet, his lips pursed to nothing.

'I've seen the coroner's report.'

Brendan taps a rolled-up copy of *The News*'s morning edition against his thigh. 'I was thinking why he'd kill my Rebeccah. I been making my own enquiries.' His eyes are dark and hollow; they blink,

fast, and he bites his lip. He doesn't want to cry.
Not here, of all places.

'I only know what's in front of me, Brendan.
Have you got something for me?'

'I've got more friends in Pentonville than you've
got in this world, you bastard,' says Brendan. 'What
have you got for me?' His voice is cracking. His fists
are clenched.

'I said before, the law has to run its course.'

'I want the one that done my Rebeccah, the one
that . . .' His head drops and his shoulders shake.

Staffe wraps his arms around Brendan Stone. The
man is hard as war but he weeps like a Latin widow,
incanting beneath his breath, within his sobs, over
and over, 'six times . . . six times . . .'

His nose and cheeks and mouth are wet with
tears, his voice like porridge, thick with the mucus
of grief. Stone interlocks his fingers on the back of
Staffe's neck and pulls until their foreheads rub.
Staffe tries to pull away, but he can't.

Brendan Stone's words are warm.

Ten minutes later, walking down Cheapside and
calling Janine, what Brendan said is stuck like silt in
Staffe's mind. 'Give him me. He stuck my Rebeccah
and he's out there. I *know*. I *know*!'

Pulford is with Staffe in the niche he was in just
twenty-four hours ago – before Blears had committed

suicide; before they knew why Bobo Bogdanovich and Elena had come to England.

They go up to Bobo's floor. It is dusk and this is dead time on the junkie streets. Everyone is done for the day and only animals can be heard, the occasional clatter or curse from within the domestic as they pass along the deck.

'I don't see how Bobo could work for Tchancov, not if he raped Bobo's sister,' says Pulford.

'They were working to a plan.'

'How do we know it's him?' says Pulford.

'He's in the photograph. It's clearly him.'

Pulford says, 'But how do we know the girl is Ludmilla Shostavic? There's nothing to say the photograph and the charges have anything to do with each other.'

They reach Bobo's door. Staffe pats Pulford on the shoulder. 'Good point, sergeant.' He knocks and there is no reply. 'You have the warrant?'

Pulford shows him the document.

They knock and there is no reply, so Staffe brings out his ring of keys. On the third attempt, the lock yields and Staffe stands to one side, lets Pulford lead.

This time there is no smell of furniture polish. No such luck. Even in the hallway, the smell of drains is thick and sweet and ripe and Pulford pulls up the neck of his sweater, over his nose.

Staffe says, 'Shit. We're too late.'

'Bobo,' calls Pulford, opening the bathroom door, sees nothing is inside. Not the source of the smell. He advances slowly towards the bedroom door and lingers.

'You want me to go in?' says Staffe.

Pulford shakes his head and turns the handle, breathing deep as he does, looking at the floor, breaking himself in, gently.

He sees Bobo's shoes, first, just inches from the ground. They sway, the slightest degree, by the draught from the door.

The smell is tight as a headlock.

Pulford takes a step forwards and Staffe says, 'Come away. Leave this to Forensics. Just check for a note. Go through the drawers. Here.' He hands Pulford a pair of plastic mitts.

'I should have called the station, got someone round here last night.'

'You were with Josie. They'd have killed him come what may, David. Thank God you didn't get caught in the middle of it.'

Together, they go through all Bobo's effects. It doesn't take long. Everything is gone, save a note – in Russian, signed *Bogdanovich*. When Pulford hands it to him, Staffe says, softly, 'Bastards.'

They step outside and close the door.

'Stay here and wait for the SOCOs.'

'Where are you going?' asks Pulford.

Staffe puts heavy hands on each of Pulford's shoulders and crinkles his eyes. 'Don't beat yourself up about this. We'll get these bastards.'

'Please tell me, sir. Where are you going?'

'Shoving my head where it doesn't belong.'

Sylvie doesn't take the usual pleasure as she applies the last stroke of varnish to the violin carcass. It is walnut, as Staffe had suggested, and it looks just fine. She has some good wine in the fridge for such occasions: the culmination of design, cutting and gluing, sanding and varnishing, the fretting and the acoustics. 'You leave a little of yourself in there,' Shivorski, her maestro, once told her. It feels truer than ever tonight.

She turns off the light and makes her way downstairs. She will drink the wine and flop in front of the telly. She may wake late and find him in the house. When he poaches her eggs, soft-yolked and teardrop-shaped, she feels certain that he loves her – despite any evidence to the contrary.

On the sofa, she curls her legs under her bottom and takes a sip of wine. The phone rings, which startles her.

It is her father.

'I'm engaged, Dad,' she says.

'Who to?' says her dad, deadpan.

'Don't be silly.'

'You pregnant?'

'Dad!'

'You want babies, though. I'm not getting any younger. Your mother – she . . .'

'Oh, Dad, don't. Are you pleased for me?'

'You'll be your own boss, won't you, love? You were always your own boss.'

'I still am.'

'That's my girl. Now tell me what you want for Christmas.'

'It's OK, Dad.' She knows he has precious little put by.

'Don't worry about me. This is a big day. My girl.'

'I'll come see you, Christmas dinner – don't forget. We'll both come.'

When they are done, she feels sad. She should call her father more, she knows – but she always feels low, after, feels – if she is honest with herself – that it is only a matter of time before she turns into her mother. It is not his fault, but if she doesn't see or speak to him, that possibility seems more remote.

Tchancov is sleekly dressed in a pale grey suit. The light picks out the pocks in his face and his colourless eyes flit left and right as if there is plenty to be wary of.

Violins hack at the perfumed air. A final movement.

He leads Staffe into a sumptuous drawing room, fit for tsars, and they sit opposite each other across an Empire coffee table.

'Stravinsky,' says Staffe, looking at Tchancov's wedding hand. The intaglio ring shines. He has big hands, for such a small man.

'He's a countryman of mine,' says Tchancov. 'Not always popular.'

'He had to make his life in foreign fields. Your intaglio must remind you of home.'

'I think your intelligence is the wrong kind, Mr Wagstaffe – at least for the purpose at hand.'

'These must be difficult times for you, Mr Tchancov – having to prove yourself all over again, in these hard times. And now your cousin is coming.'

Tchancov is taken aback and for a moment it is possible to imagine him as a child, left all alone by cruel friends. 'You should mind your own business.'

'My business is to find the killer of Elena Danya. I was hoping Bobo might cast some light.'

Tchancov doesn't flinch or even blink. 'Then why are you here?'

Staffe takes out the photograph of Ludmilla Shostavic and shows it to Tchancov. He is unmoved.

'You recognise the girl?'

He shakes his head.

'Elena's sister, Ludmilla Shostavic.'

Tchancov blinks, rapid, the glint from his eyes all gone.

Staffe hands him a copy of the charge sheet and his mouth opens like a coin slot. His pale face loses its final semblance of colour. When he speaks, it is quiet. His voice trembles. 'Is there nothing these bastards won't do to bring shame on me?' He pours himself a glass of vodka from a cut-glass decanter and drinks it in one, standing with his back to Staffe. When he turns back, his face is set rigid, the eyes totally dead. 'The whole truth cannot hurt me, Inspector.'

'You were using Elena to blackmail Howerd.'

Tchancov raises his eyebrows, curls his bottom lip, as if considering an offer. 'And *why* would I blackmail him?'

'To get a share of the action up at Aldesworth. But Elena knew all about you, and turned the tables. That's why you would have her killed.'

'You have a vivid imagination.'

'And you have a charge registered against Howerd's development company, to protect your contract with him. Were you getting greedy, Vassily? Is there pressure from above – from your paymasters?'

'You should be speaking with my accountant. I do as I am told.'

'Bobo is dead, too.'

'No! I would know.' Tchancov curses in Russian and goes to his telephone. He speaks rapidly for the best part of a minute, then slams down the handset. 'My solicitor is coming.'

Staffe taps the photograph of Ludmilla and her brother, says, 'Recognise him?'

Tchancov peers at the image. 'You surely don't think I killed Bobo.'

Staffe shakes his head, takes back the photograph and the charge sheet. 'At the moment, I can't prove you killed anybody. Not recently, not directly.'

As he waits for his solicitor, Vassily drinks vodka, becomes maudlin.

'Tell me about the letters Elena wrote you,' says Staffe.

'She didn't.'

'I saw the lilac envelopes. If you didn't kill her, the letters can only help you.'

'They can't prove I killed her.'

'Elena?'

'The Shostavic girl. She killed herself. You don't know what it was like in that war. You need to be born to it. I wasn't. I was left alone in the world. You have to find ways to survive.' Tchancov looks at Staffe as he pours himself another vodka. 'You know that.'

'You should tell me the truth, Vassily. It is an

opportunity to preserve your honour. Your only chance.'

'I know what is best for me.'

'Someone killed Bobo.'

'I can assure you, Inspector, it was done to damage me.' He laughs. 'Was he really her brother? To think – he knew enough to save me.' Vassily stares into his glass, realising how badly he has miscalculated the will of his enemies, and Staffe decides he has done enough, for now. As he goes, the man with the scimitar sideburns looks daggers at him. He walks away down the Bishops Avenue, every currency represented in sprawling neo-Georgian and mock-Tudor splendour. England through the ages. Getting into his car, Staffe gets the wink from the onlooking, hidden Pulford.

The Elder watches the iron gates glide open. Not for a moment does he envy Vassily Tchancov's wealth or power. In the back of his Bentley Mulsanne, the Russian cuts a sad figure. 'That's him,' says the Elder, pointing from the driver's seat of his hackney carriage. His finger follows for a moment then sweeps across the road to the sergeant's unmarked Mondeo. 'But you won't have long. That's the lackey, about to follow him,' he says, pointing out Pulford who pulls away, follows the Bentley at a safe distance.

'Aren't we following them?' says the Elder's passenger.

'We don't need to. I have a device.'

'And you're sure it's him?'

'You've seen the proof. I've told you what your daughter knew, and why Elena was involved with him. It's up to you what you do with it, so long as you don't mention a word about us. Don't mess with us, Brendan. If you do, you'll be in mourning again.' The Elder starts the engine. Into the rear-view mirror, he says, 'But I know it won't come to that. This is a case of honour. Yes?'

In the back, Brendan Stone looks into the haunted eyes of Ludmilla Shostavic, feels his heart tugged. His blood flows cold as he anticipates the moment he will stop this bastard in his tracks.

He thinks of nothing more, all the way to Bow.

When Pulford had arrived at the Castle, he called Staffe, who said he would be straight round. Pulford explained there was an enormous brute on the back door and the main door to the pub was closed. It seemed derelict, from the outside. 'How will we get in, sir?' he had asked.

'I'll work something out,' Staffe had said. 'You make yourself scarce, sergeant. I don't want to scare the horses by going in mob-handed.'

344

Now, Staffe parks up. Parts of Bow have been taken over by artists and media artisans, but Shiel Road seems beyond the wit of man. Its grim Victorian houses are boarded up: metal plates riveted to window frames and doorways, the easier for crack homes to stay unseen.

Officially, the Castle is still a going concern as a pub. It has a sign hanging and a flunky's name above the door. Staffe knows how these places work. They buy in half a dozen kegs of Carling a week that go straight out the back, off to some other establishment.

Like Pulford said, the front door is locked and Staffe goes round the side, knocks, twice, checking behind him. His heart bumps and his fingers tingle. He knocks again, preparing his carrot and his stick: two fifties and no ride down the station; the further information that this place will be closed down soon and he'll be out of work anyway.

He knocks again, as hard as he can, and when he tries the handle, is amazed when it yields.

Pulford was right about the brute. He has an oversized head, the same circumference as his neck, sloping straight to his shoulders. He wears training sweats with the arms cut off. His shoulders are like hams, the colour of fat. But most importantly, he is horizontal. Flat out, at the top of the stairs down into the cellar, his legs are splayed and his arms

345

crossed over his chest. The big man's face is split in two, his nose butterflied.

Staffe strides over the man, goes down into the bowels of the pub. The steps to the cellar are steep and the smell of stale beer blends with sweat and bleach. A narrow corridor runs between the basement rooms and he gently presses open a door, peeks in; then another. The rooms must be sound-proofed so that in the corridor you can hear nothing of the Gomorrah within.

In the third room, a man is at the rubber-envied mercy of a masked woman, who stands on an upturned crate, wearing only a strapped-on, flesh-coloured, make-believe cock.

Staffe closes the door, unseen, and makes his way down the corridor. He is about to open a fourth door when he hears a high-pitched wailing from the end of the passage. A door is ajar and he advances, slowly, feeling each step, wanting to retrace, to leave this stone unturned, but knowing he can't. Too much suffering at the hands of this Russian, with hidden truths to bury.

He reaches the door, pushes it open, tentatively. Inside, it is dark and the wailing louder, relentless. On the floor, in the centre of the room, is a young woman, barely more than a girl. She is naked, save for white ankle socks with a pink trim. Her blonde eyes look up at him, beseechingly, and she says,

'Look. Look what they have done to him. What do I do now? Where do I go now?' She speaks in a faltering accent from beyond an Iron Curtain.

Above her, Vassily Tchancov is lashed to iron rings, attached to the ceiling beam. He hangs, loose, as if Hieronymus Bosch has depicted St Sebastian. He is cut from ear to ear, from nipple to nipple, from his navel to his pubis and down along his thighs. A pond of blood is thick as soup beneath him.

Staffe takes off his jacket, drapes it on the back of a chair and moves, slowly, towards the body.

'Too fucking late, Inspector.' The voice comes from behind and when Staffe turns, he sees a column of light, an outline figure.

A shadow falls fast across the downlit room and Staffe smells metal, tastes blood in his mouth, sees the painted concrete floor rise slowly. A dull, deep pain washes all through him and he waits for the ground to stun him, but he is out before he lands, just the snapshot, crystal-clear image of Brendan Stone's face: sharp-boned, dead-eyed. The reprise of his pleading words, 'Give him me. *I know. I know*,' in the bright black.

Twenty-nine

Pain skewers Staffe's head from his jaw to the crown of his skull. It sears from temple to temple. Lights flash behind his eyes, like Roman candles, but he senses the flesh of a soft voice. His eyes flutter and the light becomes white, then dulls. A shape forms: a pale face and cherub ruby lips. He knows the voice, watches the mouth make its shapes.

'Staffe? Sir?' She is crying, this angel.

'Move away,' says a gruff voice, from Grimm tales.

Staffe's arms feel weak and his face stings, his mouth tender. He pushes himself up off the floor, doesn't believe what he sees – even though he has seen it before.

'Lie back,' says Josie.

Pennington says, 'Stay where you are, Staffe. This is ours to take care of.'

'How many?' mutters Staffe, counting the long, deep cuts carved into Tchancov. 'Seven,' he says, seeing that they have left the knife in. One more than Rebeccah Stone.

Staffe eases himself to his feet and totters. Josie and Janine support him, lead him to a bar stool. At his feet is a steel shovel, the handle cut down. It is what Brendan Stone smote him with.

'Leave us be,' says Pennington. 'Everybody out.' When they are alone, he stands over Staffe, says, 'Is this what you wanted?'

'Where's Brendan Stone?'

Pennington looks quizzical. 'Rebeccah Stone's father?'

'He must have followed Tchancov. Or Pulford.' Staffe has a belated notion that he should say nothing.

'If you weren't meddling, he couldn't have found Tchancov.' Pennington rubs his face with both palms, as if he is working on a persistent stain. 'What the hell are we going to do? This bloody case won't lie in peace.' Pennington crouches, settles on his haunches. 'You bloody well told me about Tchancov. You came with the evidence – and now the bastard's murdered. It was tidy. It's going to be that way again, Will. We'll have to think hard about what we can do with Stone. But it's not your decision. You're going to let this one lie.'

Staffe runs a finger gingerly along his cheekbone, feels his mouth, rubs a broken tooth.

'Get yourself off to hospital. You've got concussion. Bloody lucky not to have a broken jaw.' Pennington's phone rings and he responds to the caller with nods and monosyllables, then says, 'Rebeccah Stone's father, apparently.'

Staffe stands up, nursing his ribs, turning his battered mind to what he can possibly do about Brendan Stone, but he realises he hasn't got his jacket. He looks around the room, sees it on a chair by the pool of blood, a photograph jutting from the inside pocket.

He goes across, stoops beneath the cross, Tchancov above him, like religion gone horribly wrong. In this instance – as he plucks the image of the young child with the dark hair and the straight nose, and standing in the pool of Tchancov's blood, cardinal red – he sees the light.

Pennington clicks his phone off, says, 'You had that evidence linking Elena and Tchancov. That will stick, be the end of it. A just end, wouldn't you say? So cut yourself this bit of slack, Will. It's the right thing, trust me.'

'The right thing for who?'

'It's from on high.'

Staffe takes a hold of the handle, opens the door. High-wattage scene lights blast a flat white light along the dark corridors in the Castle's cellars. Officers in translucent, synthetic suits dust the doors and bag discarded belongings.

At the top of the stairs, the brute who had been on the door is being heaved onto a stretcher by three ambulancemen. Outside, the bitter cold has taken the day early. Staffe shivers, knows he should go to hospital but he has a grave decision to make. If he delays, these lives and deaths will be swept away for their own devices.

He watches Pennington climb into his car and beckons Josie across.

'I'll drive you to hospital,' she says.

He shakes his head. Each word hurts and he speaks low, so close to her ear he can smell the conditioner of her hair.

'What the hell have they done to you!' Sylvie stands back, stabs her fingers into her hair, aghast. 'I thought you wouldn't be back. I had a feeling. By the look of things, I was nearly right. You should see a doctor.'

'I can sort it out,' he says, wincing as he talks.

'Come with me.' She leads him to the bathroom, dabs his broken face with lint dipped in iodine, saying nothing to comfort him when he grimaces.

'My dad called. I told him about us.'

'What did he say?' mumbles Staffe.

'He was pleased for me. I said we'd go over, on Christmas Day. We can do that, can't we?'

Staffe stares into the mirror, sees the back of her, forces his mind to another place, beyond the pain. He will bring Brendan Stone to justice: this criminal who abandoned his daughter to her whore mother's charge while he was in and out of every jail in London with his drink and his drugs, his violent robberies. Yet now he divines that he can screw up the law once and for all and play God with a knife.

Or, is the love of a father a mystical thing, as beautiful in measure as the horror of surviving your own children. And is the world a better place, for the passing of a rapist, a war criminal?

'Are you listening to me?' says Sylvie, tossing the bloodied and indigo swabs into the basin.

Unmarked pursuit vehicles are parked up at each of the three exits to the Atlee estate. Any con worth his salt wouldn't touch this scene with the sharpened end of a bogbrush – and that goes for Brendan Stone.

Staffe slopes away from the invisibly sieged building and tries every shebeen and lock-in he knows from Bethnal Green to Bow and all the way back up to Hackney, but nobody – apparently – has seen Brendan Stone. It would seem everyone has heard about his good deed, but the monkeys in these parts don't speak no evil.

He makes his way back into the City, down the back streets from Shoreditch. As he walks across Finsbury Circus, the City workers mill in small numbers and Staffe thinks he might be having a brainwave, but his matter is so fried, he can't judge.

The City is unnaturally quiet. He stops a man in a suit and an open collar. The man has a jaunt to his step and a smile on his face. 'What's wrong?' says Staffe.

'Wrong? Nothing's wrong.'

'Where has everybody gone?'

The man scrutinises Staffe's cuts and bruises, then laughs, patting Staffe on the shoulder. 'Tomorrow's Christmas Eve. They've all got better places to be. Except you and me.'

Beyond the man, the sun licks the Barbican Tower. It is like a sign, like a wand upon his matter.

Staffe says, 'Merry Christmas,' to the man's back and as he does, he laments Brendan's orphan grand-daughter, left all alone in the world when her mother was murdered. He says the name of that daughter of slain Rebeccah, 'Elena,' and thinks about the opportunities she will never have; the slim chance she won't go the way of her mother, and her mother's mother.

'You can't just turn up here. Call first.' Rosa looks at her wrist, even though she wears no watch.

He can smell stale Chinese food, and cigarettes. 'I wanted to see if you're all right.'

353

She blocks the doorway by leaning against the frame with an outstretched arm.

'You want me to go?'

She nods.

This contravenes the nature of their relationship. They are frank, direct. He waits for a truth to betray itself in her eyes. She looks past him, dead still, waiting for him to go, but a cry emerges from within and he finally hears what he came for.

A baby cries.

A baby cries and Staffe hears the unadulterated, pure love of a father imploring the infant to be well. 'Ssshh, Elena. It's all right. It's all right.'

'He couldn't leave her,' says Rosa. 'He has nobody to take her. You've seen Nicola, she couldn't tend a baby, not on her own. Just let him be, Will. I beg you.'

'No,' says a voice from inside.

Rosa turns around. Behind her, Brendan Stone, granddaughter in arms, stands in a half-light.

In these moments, Staffe knows what must be done. He doesn't despair at the thousand repercussions to the decisions he has to make today. In this moment, in the company of the whore and the murderer, he is filled with wonder at all the different love there is in this city.

Brendan raises the child to his face and he kisses her cheek. Elena gurgles, smiles at her granddad. As he hands her to Rosa, Elena reaches out for him with her tiny, pudgy hand.

Staffe takes a hold of Brendan by the soft flesh under his arm.

'I'm sorry I hurt you,' says Brendan, to Staffe, looking back at the infant child.

Rosa says, 'You can't take him away from her, Will.'

'I can't not,' says Staffe.

Brendan says, 'It's the only place I can be.' He looks up at Staffe. 'Isn't it.'

Staffe thinks of what consequences will flow, in the wake of Tchancov's death. 'You need to look out for yourself, Brendan,' says Staffe, shuddering to think that a jailbird like Brendan regards prison as the safest place for a villain.

'The damage was done a long time ago,' says Brendan. 'You know, I thought it was the right thing, truly I did. I believed it all.'

'Believed what?'

'That a wrong would be righted, that I'd find a kind of peace, at least some satisfaction.' Brendan Stone looks at Staffe, pleadingly. 'He did kill her, didn't he? That Russian bastard.'

'Who told you that?'

'For the love of God,' says Brendan, led away by Staffe, before the infant Elena sees her grandad fall completely to pieces.

All the way to Leadengate, Staffe thinks what it must be like, to be the father of a daughter, unable to protect. And for the mother of a son, also. He reconsiders what he knows of Imogen and Roddy; how little he knows of Darius and his mother.

Christmas Eve

Christmas Eve, babe, in the drunk tank. The Butcher's Hook is half market workers, half coppers from the night shift. It's barely lunchtime, but you'd think it was midnight. The pub has been hosting the craic since before dawn.

'Is it true?' says Josie. Her eyes are moist and heavy-lidded, half-moon and waning. 'Christ, sir. You should get some stitches.' She touches his nose and puts a finger on the corner of his mouth.

'Is what true?' says Staffe, nursing his pint. Josie could be asking him if it is true that there's an almighty stink brewing since he brought Brendan Stone in yesterday.

'About you and Sylvie getting married.' They are partially obscured from the throng by a gaming machine. She takes a step closer, all Coco and ethanol. Her lips are plump and her make-up all wiped away.

'How do you know?'

She looks over her shoulder towards Pulford who is necking with a WPC from Community Liaison. She turns back, places a hand on Staffe's chest, the in of her thigh pressed to his knee. 'A little birdie.'

Staffe puts his hands on Josie's shoulders and she looks up at him, goes tippy-toed with her eyes closing and he kisses her, on the cheek, whispering in her ear, 'Merry Christmas, Josie.' He takes a step in and wraps his arms around her and they sway away with toothless Shane and when the song is done, Staffe says, 'I'm through.' He releases her and she totters a step back, holds the gaming machine.

'Through?' She scrunches her eyes at him.

'You did a great job, Josie.'

'You were right. We were *all* right – about Blears and Tchancov and . . .' She looks puzzled.

'I have to go,' says Staffe.

'Stay.'

Pulford comes across, holding two bottles of Beck's between the fingers of one hand. 'Dance with this young lady, would you, Sergeant?'

'Bugger off,' says Josie, pushing between them both, heading for the bar.

Over Pulford's shoulder, he sees Jombaugh come in. He stays by the door, beckons Staffe.

He says to Pulford, 'Be at Howerd's house, first thing in the morning, like we said.'

Pulford gives him a resigned look.

Staffe pushes his way towards the door, past Josie, staring into her drink. In a crowd of people, she looks all alone.

'You've got it?' says Staffe, to Jombaugh.

'There aren't that many A'Courts. His charge sheets helped – he even got done at that school.'

'Ampleforth?'

'Expelled for insolence, apparently. He moved back home with his mother in 2003. She has the same address, still, but now it's a flat. He's shown a heap of different addresses ever since 2005.' Jom hands Staffe an A4 envelope. 'Are you going to tell me what you're up to?'

'I really appreciate this,' says Staffe. 'Merry Christmas, Jom. Give my love to Katherine.'

'I could come with you.'

'It's Christmas, Jom. You have a good one.'

Outside, he takes shelter from the whistling cold in the high Victorian splendour of the meat market. Staffe leans against an iron pillar. It soars above him, all the way up to the intricately worked, many-gabled roof. He opens the envelope.

Cardinal Bernard Audley stares up at him, into the camera. The Pope smiles and Bernard does not. Bernard wears his crimson cassock which, according to the caption beneath, 'recalls the heroism of the martyrs. It is a symbol of a love for Jesus and his church that knows no bounds.'

The article pre-dates poor Imogen's South American death by three weeks and – as far as Staffe can calculate – she was already in that far-flung Christian continent.

Further down the account of the Consistory for the creation of Bernard, the Pope referred to Mark's gospel, said, '. . . to serve, and to give his life as a ransom for many.'

He returns the research to its envelope, looks at the archive of pictures the case has issued him: Ludmilla Shostavic, staring forlorn beside brother Bobo; Roddy Howerd with his arm draped around his sister's suitor; the dark-haired child of the east with the straight nose; Uncle Bernard and his holiness.

Gary Mulplant looks Staffe dead in the eye as he saunters up to the detective inspector in the bar of the Thamesbank Hotel. He is in his civvies, carries a suit hanger over his shoulder, says, looking at Staffe's face. 'What happened to you?'

'You're finished,' says Staffe.

'What!' Mulplant loses his composure. His shoulders slump and he holds his suit hanger in front of him, like a shield.

'For Christmas. You've finished working for now?'

Mulplant smiles, unconvincingly.

'Did you hear that the man you ID'd has killed himself?'

Mulplant nods.

'You should be bloody ashamed of yourself.'

'I saw him!'

'You enjoy your Christmas, Gary. I've got too much to do right now, but in the New Year, I'm coming back. I've got new evidence and I'm having you. You'll never work in this or any other industry again. You're going inside, young man.'

'I'm not. They . . .'

'They?'

'Nothing.'

'There's no one left who knows the truth about that day. Only you. I'm going to leave you alone for a week. You'll have a worse fate – in their hands.'

'You can't talk to me like this. I have the name of a lawyer.'

'Is it Sir Ralph Waikman?'

'What?' Mulplant switches his weight from foot to foot.

'He's going to be too busy to represent a nobody like you.' Staffe stands down from his bar stool, tells the bartender to make himself scarce, which he does without saying a word. 'Describe Elena for me – what she did that afternoon when she came here.'

'She was beautiful. I mean *really* beautiful.'

'How?'

'Fair and tall. Everybody stopped. She turned all our heads.'

'All?'

'There was me and Victor, the concierge, and a guest. An Arab man.'

'How did she move?'

'Like she didn't touch the floor. She was in a fur. She had a phone call; went to the windows, I think.' Gary narrows his eyes, seems happy to drift back, to see her again. 'The large windows overlooking the river and she had her back to me and . . .'

'And what, Gary?'

'And I wanted to touch her. Anybody would.'

'What did she say?'

'I wasn't listening.'

'They hadn't come to you yet?'

'No.' Mulplant looks up, eyes wide. 'Who? Who do you mean?'

Staffe takes a hold of Mulplant, presses his thumbs to the sweet spots behind his ears. 'I'm going to show you a photograph. If you saw this person on the afternoon that girl was murdered here, you nod. If you didn't, you stay perfectly still. You understand?'

Mulplant nods.

Staffe releases him, takes the photograph from his jacket, shows it to the bellboy.

Mulplant nods.

Up at Jarndyce Road, it had been impossible to tell whether Darius A'Court had flown his coop. The place looked no different, but on his way out, Staffe had seen Stanislav, the builder, loading up his pick-up. He had told Staffe that he and his workers were driving for the port. They had a Dover crossing and said that, with a bit of luck, they would be in Minsk for Christmas dinner. Their wives and mothers and brothers and children would all be there. And he told him, too, that Darius A'Court had scarpered, first thing. Stan reckoned he wouldn't be back any time soon.

Darius's mother, Geraldine A'Court, according to Jombaugh's investigations, lives in the attic of a grand house on Warwick Way, overlooking the canal at Little Venice. 'I used to own the whole building,' she told Staffe, with more pride than sadness in her face as she showed him into her home.

When they separated, her husband got nothing from the divorce and she kept this house, garnering sufficient rent from having split it into flats to live quite nicely. The bastard husband now lives with a younger version of herself, she tells Staffe without malice. 'He will pay for his transgressions,' she says, with absolute confidence.

'And what about Darius?'

Geraldine's face melts at the mere mention of his name. 'Has he been messing around again? You can't imagine how hard it hit him; all that upset. He was such a wonderful, kind child. He's still that same person, you know. I'm so proud of all the things he has done.'

'Do you still see him?'

'Not since he moved to Greece. He's so busy, with his music and his art. And so many friends. He was always such a popular boy. He took such a knock, you know, when we had to bring him from Ampleforth. You do know he went to Ampleforth?'

Staffe can't bring himself to tell Geraldine that he knows Darius was expelled. He wonders if Darius might have got himself expelled to avert the shame of their sudden lack of funds. Did he fall on a sword at such an age, all those years ago, to preserve a reputation? Has he misjudged the young man?

'Is there something wrong, Inspector?'

Staffe also can't bring himself to tell Geraldine A'Court that her darling Darius is not in Greece, so he says, 'One of his bad influences, I'm afraid. A young man called Roddy Howerd.'

Mrs A'Court nods, sagely, and takes a shoebox from the drawer of a Queen Anne secretaire. She is a quite striking woman, with a narrow, pale, porcelain face and bobbed golden hair, but dressed ten years beyond her age in a knitted twinset. She issues not an ounce of allure and seems, to Staffe, perfectly pious. 'Roddy Howerd,' she says. 'Such a very good family. He and Darius were ever so close, a couple of years ago, when Darry first went to Greece.' She proffers a photograph, of the same hue as the one Staffe had seen in Roddy's album. 'He knew the Howerd boy at school. He was in the year above and I think there was something.'

'Something?'

'Darry was quite obsessed, for a while. I'm told it's normal. I spoke with my bastard husband about it and he said it was all part of growing up and being English. He laughed about it. Roddy even came here one half-term, when we had the whole house. There was such a hoo-hah about it before-hand. Darry wanted it to be just so.'

'Didn't Darius go out with Roddy's sister?'

'Arabella? I know about her. We have friends in common – from Ampleforth. Darius has a fickle heart. A good heart.'

'He was comfortable in those circles?' asks Staffe.

'He is *of* those circles, Inspector. A chance circumstance, one bad business decision, does not undermine everything.'

'Darius gets his breeding from you, I suspect,' says Staffe.

Geraldine cannot help herself. She smiles from ear to ear. 'A'Court is not his father's name, you know. My father had no sons. I was an only child.' Geraldine looks ashamed. 'My father allowed Peter

– my bastard husband – to take my hand, on the condition that he also took my name.'

'Peter is your ex-husband, surely.'

'The A'Courts don't divorce, Inspector.'

'Ahaa,' says Staffe. 'Like the Howerds.'

'Exactly. A wonderful family, in so many respects, but that daughter. My word!'

'Not everybody can be blessed with good children. We take that for granted, I suppose.'

'I take it you are a father, Inspector?'

'I'm afraid I can't discuss my personal situation whilst on business.'

'Of course. And your business? Have I been of any help?'

'I think so, Mrs A'Court.'

'Can I ask what Roddy has done?'

Staffe shakes his head. He imagines Darius A'Court under his mother's spell, his grandfather's, too: all that history on his bony shoulders and probably an entirely different strain from his bastard father's blood, and all tits up – until he met Roddy Howerd, at school, and followed him to Greece. Then Roddy's sister – with the same thing to offer, but more, perhaps. A few lean years and a grand plan unfurls; a promise from the highest deity.

'I'm sure Darius will tell you all about Roddy next time you see him, Mrs A'Court. Does he have any plans to return home?'

'I'll be the last to know,' says Geraldine. 'How youth is wasted on the young.' She flutters her lashes and for an instant, he sees the maiden her, with all the world ahead.

Staffe promises to pass on her regards to the Howerds and as he leaves her to a steeped, confected peace, he thinks of Brendan and Rebeccah Stone. Fathers and daughters and mothers and sons. He closes the door on Geraldine A'Court, tries not to imagine her all alone on Christmas morning.

Gone twilight, and the City is dead, just the odd gaggle of smokers and thin trails of people in suits and Santa hats, making their ways down into the tube. A wisping mist comes off the Thames. The buses are like something from greetings cards.

Staffe looks up at the slice of olde England. The Colonial Bankers' Club is tall and slim, built from red brick and dressed with stone, a Jacobean tower squashed in by a Victorian branch of Glyn's and an eighties infill of glass and steel, TO LET.

He rehearses what he will say but his words smudge. He pushes open the door, holds up a hand to the steward, his collar stiff and his mouth agape at the unpretty picture of Staffe's battered face. 'Don't worry, Dickinson, I'll find my own way,' and he strides towards the dining hall, opens the double doors, looking around the room.

Here and there, diners look up, wonder what such a specimen is doing here. In the far corner, at a small table under a portrait of Thomas Coutts, Staffe sees what he wants.

When Howerd and Markary see Staffe coming, his face cut and swollen, they look at each other, frowning.

'Merry Christmas, gentlemen,' he says, pulling up a chair, sitting between them. 'I come bearing gifts.'

Howerd's smile remains tight, resolute.

'Your children miss their mother most, I imagine, this time of year, Mr Howerd? Especially Roddy.'

Markary intervenes. 'You have no idea.' He folds his napkin, his cheese only half eaten. He dabs at his mouth and a petal of port stains the linen.

'I don't understand what you have to gain, Taki.'

Markary shrugs.

Staffe turns back to Howerd. 'And Uncle Bernard? Does he ever get in touch – after what happened?'

'What did happen, Inspector?'

'His First Consistory. You missed it. You were in Peru.'

Howerd says, 'This is becoming tiresome, Mr Wagstaffe.' He raises a hand, beckons a waiter.

The waiter arrives at the table and Howerd says, 'This man is leaving, Samuel. Please show him out.'

Staffe turns to the waiter, hisses, 'If you want me off the premises, tell Dickinson to call the police.'

'Why exactly have you come?' says Howerd.

Staffe addresses Markary. 'In your case, new blood comes and new blood goes, but for others, life goes on, the way it has for centuries. The Howerds have been solid so long, it shouldn't surprise us.'

'Surprise?' says Howerd.

'That you emerge unscathed from the death of Elena.'

'What is the point of this?'

'I said I have a gift. Tchancov's arse is in a sling for you.'

'There was a time when you thought I was responsible,' says Markary. 'It pays to keep faith.'

'Faith,' says Staffe. 'Faith in what is right.'

'How long will he serve?'

'Forever. As you know.' Staffe stands. 'But he left a few crumbs.'

'Crumbs?' says Howerd, colour draining from his face.

'Like Hansel and Gretel, but easier to read. I've been reading about your family, the original line, before you ran out of genes. John Howard – that's with the "a", of course – helped kill the princes in the Tower, so they say.'

'That's conjecture. And a long time ago,' says Howerd, unflustered by what he sees as Staffe's little joke.

'It would mean murder was in the family. Those poor young Princes, paying such a price. Merry Christmas,' says Staffe, turning his back. From the door, he looks back, at Thomas Coutts looking down on one of his own. Howerd is signing his account, making hasty arrangements.

Staffe cannot remember when London was ever like this – such empty streets.

The door to Sanderson's jingles behind him and the old boy behind the counter, in his moleskin apron, peers over his pince-nez. He puts the perused gems back in the safe and prepares to close the oldest jewellers in the Square Mile.

Staffe feels the velvet box, wonders if this booty will be enough to save his skin tomorrow. He swings his arms as he crosses Cornhill, the Bank of England to his right. He is pleased with what he has done, and watches a big red bus sail into the river fret. He picks up *The News* from a vendor who is finishing up and pops into the Jampot, otherwise known as the Jamaica Inn. He used to come here with Jessop after an offal lunch in the George and Vulture for a pint and some old times' sake.

It is easy to see why the men come here, mainly

in their ones and leaning on the wooden bars in the tiny wooden snugs with their beer and their newspapers; the sawdust beneath their feet and the dim lights above their heads. But there is no escaping, for Staffe, the fact that it is Christmas Eve. He can't bear the thought of home, and having to tell Sylvie he can't be with her, tomorrow, so, to kill the Eve, he opens the paper and drinks his pint.

In *The News*, Nick Absolom is trying to make sense of the slaying of Vassily Tchancov – intimating that his murder, at the hands of Brendan Stone, might be the collateral damage of oligarchical muscle-flexing. Staffe drinks lustily from his pint and mulls Absolom's words, considering an even bigger picture. Suddenly, he feels unsuitable for what awaits him tomorrow.

Christmas Day

Staffe wakes, groggy. He can hear children playing, so knows he has slept deeply. Sylvie is asleep, still. He doesn't want to wake her, and knowing what he must do – today of all days – he chooses to leave her sleeping.

As a child, Will had always awakened in the dead of night, Christmas Day. He would lie in bed, rigid with stifled anticipation at what Santa might have brought him. Eventually, his father would come in and he would pretend to be asleep, allow himself to be jostled awake.

His mother and father would sit cross-legged in their pyjamas on the living-room floor, amongst the nest of wrapping paper, playing with him and Marie – making up the numbers for Cluedo and Kerplunk.

He showers warily, so as not to disturb Sylvie nor reopen his cuts or alarm his bruises. Dressed, he chomps a muesli bar and swigs a coffee on the hoof, looking for his phone and eventually finding it in the lounge. On his way out of the room, he clocks a golden parcel in the fireplace. Where Santa would have left it.

'Open it,' says Sylvie, rubbing her eyes, arms wrapped around herself in the doorway.

'When I come back.'

'Come on, Will.'

'We'll have more time – let's not rush it.'

'I have a bad feeling, Will. Where are you going? It's Christmas Day. We should be together.'

'It's just some work I have to do.'

'We're supposed to be going to my dad's. I told you.'

He walks to her, puts his arms around her, but she pushes him away, says, 'I'll think of something to say to him, shall I?'

'I've got you something special.'

'I have a bad feeling.'

'Don't be silly. I'll be fine.'

'I'm talking about me,' she says. 'At least open your present.'

He opens the golden parcel, feels a slow wash of melancholia as the kindness is revealed: a full set of Sabatier knives. On the canteen, Sylvie has written, *I took a quid from your pocket, so this is not a gift. Cook for me.* He sits in the spoonback, recalculates. He might not need to go until after lunch.

His phone rings. It is the code for Saltburgh and he immediately knows it is a mariner's call.

The man says, 'I'd say they'll be on their way soon. Once the tides are right.'

'When's that?'

'A couple of hours. They're all provisioned for a trip, from what I've seen.'

Staffe imagines the harbourmaster peering out into the marina through binoculars. He hangs up, puts the knives down, remembering how Vassily Tchancov died, slashed until his flesh hung in tatters from his bones.

Sylvie says, 'Give me my present before you go. At least stay until I have opened it.'

'Let's wait, until we have time – together. I have to go now.'

'You haven't got me anything.'

'Is that what you think of me?' he says.

'I know you.'

'You bloody don't,' he thinks, gathering his keys and wallet and phone together, brushing past her.

'You leave me then, you bastard. On Christmas Day.'

He puts the wallet and phone in his jacket pocket, feels the velvet box; the emerald pendant safely secreted, within.

The Younger watches the inspector drive away. He recognises that look in the eye, has seen it often in the faces of supposed enforcers of law. He had told the Elder what the inspector would do, and they had discussed the need to grasp the horns. The finer details are his own.

He has the measure of the inspector, knows he can shake him free of this case once and for all. He has prepped her place, knows it inside out; knows exactly how she would most likely, accidentally, come to grief.

As Staffe drives the empty roads north and east to Suffolk, he looks again at the image of the murderer as finally and reluctantly verified by poor, ambitious, fucked-up Gary Mulplant.

The phone rings. It is Pulford, telling him that Leonard Howerd and Roddy and Arabella have just climbed into Leonard's Bentley. He enquires as to whether he should follow.

'No, I'll be waiting for them. The roads are too clear today. They'll notice you,' says Staffe, looking in his rear-view mirror. The silver Mondeo drops back again. It has been with him all the way.

'What should I do?'

'Give them a head start, then make your way to Warblingsea Harbour. Keep your phone on, and your head down.'

'I've got the records from A'Court's phone, sir. You were right. He got a call from the Colonial Bankers' Club – an hour before Danya was murdered.'

Staffe hangs up. As he drives, he pictures the movements of Darius A'Court that day – sees it in sepia.

* * *

Sylvie puts the Sabatier canteen back in its gift box, makes a space for it in the cupboards at the bottom of his dresser and boils the kettle to make herself an instant coffee.

She sits at the table in the kitchen and wraps her hands around the mug. It is the oversized souvenir from Copenhagen, a mermaid's tail swirled around the handle. She bought it for herself on the long weekend she and Staffe took – the first time they were together. She only brought it over here, to his place, a week ago. He hadn't noticed.

Sylvie hears the front door go and her heart bumps. It isn't him. She is sure of it. He has his own, practically silent way of coming into a house. Even so, she calls, 'Will!'

Silence.

Sylvie grips the mug tighter and the heat within makes the pads of her fingers tingle. She stares at the door, wants to call out to Staffe again, but something – between her heart and her throat – stops her.

She hears a tread in the hallway, the whine of a door being opened, then closed. Sylvie wants to leap up and grab her phone and call the police but this feels ridiculous.

Could it be Pulford? Or did she leave the radio on?

A heavy creak in the hallway, the creak of a

person. He appears in the kitchen doorway, making not such a large shape and forcing a thin smile. His face is ruddy and he has a scar down his forehead. It is fresh, pink.

'I won't harm you,' he says. 'Not unless I have to.'

Sylvie knows she should scream.

The mug is beginning to burn her now, and her hands yearn to tremble so she grips tighter and she feels sick. Her stomach, shrunken, gives up on her and she turns her head so she cannot see this man.

'It is Christmas,' she says. 'I have to visit my dad.'

'Not today,' says the man, coming towards her. 'You're going to do everything I say, when I say it, and if you don't get to see your dad – ever – don't blame me. It's that fucking boyfriend of yours. You get me?'

Staffe considers everything that has been done to maintain this secret, how much suffering has bled into so many lives. In this context, he should fear for himself. But today, all he can think of is the plight of Brendan Stone, and the lonely, lonely death of Graham Blears.

This is a day to right the wrongs. He steps down, into *Imogen II*, goes below decks.

He is not surprised to see Darius A'Court, but has never before seen the woman sitting at the table in the saloon, sipping from a cup. She is sun-dried and skinny, has her hair cut short and side-parted. She wears an offshore sailing coat and salopettes – dressed to go.

'Imogen?' he says.

'Inspector,' says Imogen Howerd. 'I am right and you are wrong. I have papers to prove who I am.'

'Whoever you claim to be, I see you're planning to harbour criminals.'

'You should be careful what you say, Inspector,' says the Elder, emerging from the aft cabin. 'I see you didn't get the chance to take Tchancov in.'

'It seems that in this world you can bury the truth,' says Staffe.

'Surely, this case is laid to rest.'

'You'd be amazed.'

'And so would you, Inspector. Throughout this investigation – from the moment you began to mudsling – we have made it our business to keep abreast of developments. You have nothing to hold against us.'

'It would have been edifying to talk some more with Bobo Bogdanovich; and Vassily Tchancov, for that matter.'

'We should all celebrate the death of such a man,' says the Elder.

'Brendan Stone will serve life because of you – as

if losing his daughter wasn't enough.' Staffe looks around the cabin. 'Where's that shitty little mercenary of yours? The one who likes to beat up women. I'd like him to know I'm not done with him.'

'Why are you here, Inspector?' says Imogen.

'I have come to see Darius. I need to talk to him.' Staffe looks at Darius, who seems somehow diminished. 'I'd like to know what your plans are now; now that Arabella is returned. Will you help her all the way back into that fold? I would have thought there would be rewards, for a saviour like you.'

'We look after people we love. It's not a crime,' says Darius.

The Elder's phone rings. He answers, listens, and his face sags into a frown. It is an expression Staffe has not seen on him before.

After protestations, the Elder holds out the phone to Staffe, says, 'This will have to play out. You'd better speak to him.'

'Who?'

'The Younger.'

A lazy voice at the other end says, wearily, 'Hello? Who's that?'

Staffe recognises the voice. 'Sylvie! Are you all right? Where are you?'

'Is that you, Will?'

'Where are you?'

'I'm tired. So tired.'

'No point trying to do anything, Inspector. Just do what you're told,' says the Younger. His voice is soft and he seems calm, assured. 'I won't be fucked about. This is going to end. Today, you understand?'

'Don't touch her!'

'I won't need to. She's a clumsy thing. An accident waiting to happen.'

'I can trace this call.'

'Not to me, you can't. Now hand me back to the Elder.'

'I'll find you!' Staffe hands the phone back and sits heavily at the chart table, wanting to grab the Elder, to rattle him until he gives the word for Sylvie to be released, until he bleats out the truth – all of it, and nothing but.

However, he knows he is a step behind, and that the Elder is beyond his reach. He turns to Imogen Howerd, says to her, 'You can go. I'm not here to stop you.'

'What about Darry?' Imogen says.

'You'd be a fool to take him with you.'

'I need crew. Darry's a dab hand.'

'You've got family can help you out with that.'

'You'd let me go, just like that?' says Imogen.

'The power of love,' says the Elder, putting his phone into his pocket. 'Our friend, the Younger, seems to have everything in hand.'

Staffe tries to block out what could be happening to Sylvie, is unable. 'There's nothing as powerful as love, like you say, Darius,' he says.

'I'm not falling for your games,' says Darius.

'It's not a game. They called you, from their club, just an hour before she was killed.'

'That's a lie.'

'It's an alibi, for them. A noose, for you.'

'I should be careful, if I was you, Inspector,' says the Elder.

'I spoke to the bellboy. He never saw Blears.'

'That's bullshit,' says Darius. He looks at the Elder, desperation oozing from his pores in the cabin chill.

'You're not really a dealer, Darius. You haven't got that in you, have you? But you had enough coming in to look after yourself and Arra. You lived in that shithole squat but you always had the readies to get wasted or high, and to eat and go out partying. Leonard was bankrolling you, wasn't he?'

'Why would he?'

'You couldn't know it would escalate the way it did, or that Elena would push things too far. But to be a Howerd, Darius, that would mend everything that ever went wrong with your life.'

Staffe weighs Geraldine A'Court's love for this son, considers the hand the poor boy was dealt by his parents: 'I know why you did it, Darius. Honestly,

I do. I have visited your mother and I understand. I know what is at stake for you and her. You were trying to secure a future, preserve your past.'

'This is bullshit,' says Darius.

'Let him finish,' says the Elder, his eyes flitting, fast as thoughts.

'I know it wasn't your idea. How would you ever come up with such a thing? And why would you?' Staffe looks at Imogen. 'You probably didn't even know that Elena had found out about Imogen not being dead; that Leonard had concocted a way to bury the shame.'

Staffe takes out the photograph of the dark young boy with the straight nose. 'Your son,' he says to Imogen. 'Too bad, to bear a Turk's bastard, on the strike of Uncle Bernard's finest hour.'

'What?' says Darius, a step or two behind.

'I adopted this boy,' says Imogen. 'I have the papers. And you forget, I have no Uncle Bernard. I'm not her. We buried her.'

'That your uncle could become cardinal. How proud the family must have been.' Staffe says, to Darius, 'When they said Elena was a problem and she had to go, did they promise – if you could do that thing for them and if you could deliver Arabella back into the fold, which was your game all along – you would be welcomed into the family with open arms?'

Darius turns to the Elder, who looks away.

'. . . Of course they did. And of course, you couldn't resist. You knew that if you hadn't killed Elena, someone else would have. You knew what a conniving bitch she was. She tried to split you and Arra up, didn't she?'

'Shut up!' shouts Darius. He looks at Imogen, now, imploring help. 'Tell him!'

'Is this what you're proposing, Inspector?' says Imogen.

'I'm proposing the truth. It's all I know, I'm afraid.'

'And your fiancée?' says the Elder. 'The truth can be exchanged for her?'

'The world will see that Darius was the one who dragged Arabella down. Your daughter can return to her family and all will be well. I have no vendetta, provided nothing – and I mean nothing! – happens to Sylvie. I just want the murderer.'

'And Leonard and I?' says Imogen.

'As you said, I can't disprove that you are someone else. And it's not my business anyway. All that matters to me is you had nothing to do with the murders. Leonard may have to wait for his knighthood, I guess, but your name will be saved.' He turns to the Elder. 'But Sylvie will have to be brought to somewhere safe, to someone I can trust.'

'But it's not true!' says Darius.

'Isn't it?' says the Elder. 'We'd look after you. You know that.'

'He could just let it lie,' says Darius. 'You've got his fucking girlfriend, for Christ's sake.'

'I need to talk to you,' says Imogen, to the Elder. 'Just for a minute.' She walks into the bespoke airlock in the bow of the boat and he follows her. Their voices are low, muffled, impassioned.

Staffe hisses, to Darius. 'Listen, and listen well. I have the proof. You hear me! The bellboy told me he saw you that day. I'm afraid your fate is nailed to the mast.'

Darius looks at Staffe, open-eyed, like the adolescent in the photograph again – as if he would quite happily lose himself in his mother's skirts. As if in a trance, he says, 'I can't trust anybody.'

'They're cashing you in, Darius. It's not a question of trust. The truth has come to take you.'

The doors to the airlock open and close. Imogen's face is set. She says, low and even, 'There is only one way this can work. When the family arrives, Roddy sails with me.'

'You'll be crossing Biscay,' says Staffe. 'Just the two of you?'

'We have Lord Admirals to our name, Inspector. I think we can tackle Biscay,' says Imogen – as if the elements cannot touch her.

The Elder says, 'Arabella can enter a programme

of rehabilitation and Leonard will issue a statement explaining his disappointment and his hope for a recovery. The Crown will look kindly upon Darius. He will be represented by Sir Ralph Waikman. You will process him and you will lay this case to rest. If you can agree, I'll speak to the Younger. Otherwise . . . You have other people you care for – a nephew, I believe.'

'You bastards!'

'You can't judge us,' says the Elder.

Staffe tries to work out where Sylvie might be, tries not to picture the state she is in – drugged or otherwise sedated, by the sound of her. He knows what is right, what he should do, but this is no time to bring Rebeccah's killer to book.

He says to the Elder, 'You'll bring Sylvie to Leadengate. Once I've seen her, I will process the charges. And once that happens, the harbourmaster will give you the all-clear.'

'I need to see Arabella,' says Darius. His voice is frail, warbling; his face the grey of bad truths dawning.

The Elder takes Staffe's hand and they shake. Staffe wants to ask if it was his bastard accomplice, the Younger, who ran Rebeccah through with the knife because of what she learned from Elena on that trip to the seaside; the Younger, who has Sylvie's life in his hands. Staffe's pulse quickens.

'Is there any unfinished business?' asks the Elder.

'What we know and what we can prove are often different. Sometimes, we have to wait for a missing element. I have nothing whatsoever on you or your friend. I don't even know your names. But be assured, if I ever come across him again . . .'

'This will not happen.'

Staffe wants to whip this cold, calculating man into shape, wishes he had brought one of his new knives with him. His hands have formed fists and his face must betray him because the Elder takes a step back, reaches into his jacket and with the imperceptible curl of a wrist he unleashes the full extent of a telescopic steel cosh. In the same instant, a car parks up outside. There are three slams of the doors.

The Elder says, 'Are we on the same hymn sheet?'

Staffe nods.

The Elder pushes the cosh back into itself and they each watch as the Howerd family come below decks. First Roddy, then Leonard and finally, weak on her feet and leaden with medication, Arabella.

When she sees her daughter, Imogen emits a low, strangulated wail, like something from another culture.

Huddled between father and brother at the bottom of the steps, Arabella is bewildered. Leonard ushers her towards her mother, and the truth dawns. No apparition; this is a resurrection. Arabella cannot believe what she sees. 'It's all lies,' she says.

Darius goes to her, puts an arm around her and guides Arabella towards Imogen, whispering that he loves her, that he is going away. 'For our love,' he tells her. 'I'm going away for our love.' But Arabella doesn't understand. She lets herself be wrapped in her mother's arms. The two women stand there, like that, until the Elder and Howerd prise them apart.

'I have to go,' sobs Imogen. She turns to Roddy. 'Are we ready?'

Roddy comes to her, whispers something which makes her smile, approvingly.

'I will see you again?' says Arabella, now in her father's arms.

'Before you know it. I love you, Bella.'

'Whenever people say that, they leave me.' Arabella shrugs off her father and reaches for Darius, who looks at Staffe.

Each wishes for a better solution.

The Elder leads the way above decks and Imogen says to Leonard, 'There is a greater good. Isn't there?'

'Of course, my love.' To see his jaw weak, you might think he doubts the wisdom he inherited.

* * *

The Younger looks in his rear-view mirror, sees the shape of the inspector's fiancée in the back of the ambulance. She lies still, now. He had to calm her down, whilst the pills worked their magic. He can't abide people who hit women and he feels ashamed at what is sometimes necessary on this path that chose him.

When this is all done, he will go to Ireland, spend a week in retreat before he visits his mother. She has a lovely new place now, a long way from the Falls Road. Same country, different world. Her garden runs all the way to the Shannon banks. He will fish and she will call him for dinner and then he will walk into the village, have a pint or two in this place where nobody knows him. The Elder has assured him that, after this, there will be no calls for a good while. This job requires that the dust settles, good and proper. It is always difficult when the police get involved.

The bastard's girlfriend moans, in her half-sleep, murmuring into the muzzle he has put on her. He has planned, quite meticulously, how he will tend her. He has everything that is required in the glove compartment and it will be administered in her house. Her attic is stacked to the gunnels with varnish and lacquer and other flammables. She will have spilled some on her clothes and been careless with a candle, then fallen asleep. He is confident that further measures will not be necessary.

If all goes well, he will be on a ferry from Fishguard by first light tomorrow. It will be Boxing Day and his brothers will have gone back to Liverpool by then. No loss. Ignorant bastards. In the mirror, he watches as he presses the salmon-pink, soft new flesh of his scar. If he presses hard, it pains him – in a sweet way.

Putting the key to the ignition, he prays his mother will not concern herself with what has happened to him.

As he drives away, along a mews-lined, cobbled street, he makes a small detour, pauses at the gated entrance to a private garden square. Where the garden meets the street, the church nestles back. This is where the Elder first brought him, at the beginning of this job. It is St Philip Neri and he has confessed here. Now, he looks at Our Lady, hands clasped in stone prayer, above the arched entrance, looking to the ground as if all our sins are upon her shoulders. He feels his heart slow and he understands, absolutely, quite how we must all suffer.

The waters are grey, the horses high and white out at sea. It is choppy beyond the bar, but Roddy is keen with the ropes and cleats. He is lithe, his movements precise.

Nearby, church bells peel and the gulls flap their wings, squawk off, circling high. On the far side of the harbour's hardstanding, Staffe sees Pulford skulking in a doorway. He says to the Elder, 'I need the toilet.'

'I'll come with you.'

The toilet block smells the way you'd expect it to and Staffe goes into a half-door trap, drops his trousers, hoping he can summon what is necessary, all the time scrolling through his phone, creating white noise as he punches in his message to Pulford . . . *They have sylvie. Follow man with me til he meets the one with the scar – he killed reb stone.*

He manages to ablute and turns off his phone. When he emerges, he jokes about giving it a few minutes. The Elder doesn't laugh, just says, 'You are a man of your word?'

'It's all I have,' says Staffe.

'So you'll bring the charges against A'Court – and only him.'

'Oh yes.'

'And Leonard and Imogen?'

'I have given you my word.'

Staffe leads the way back to London, Howerd driving Darius and Arabella in his Bentley, the Elder turning off when they get to the bottom of the A11, disappearing back into his secret world.

As they drive the empty roads, Staffe works out how he will accomplish a final summoning to justice of the man who killed Rebeccah. He laments what the Howerds have writ for poor Darius, how quickly he became dispensable, and didn't even know, fully, why he was called upon to take Elena's life. His bile rises.

But they hadn't counted on Rebeccah. Hence, the Elder and the Younger – whatever circle they form a part of – digging up what Vassily Tchancov had left in his bloody wake. And when Graham Blears turned up . . . Manna from heaven.

By the time they get to Leadengate, Staffe has arranged for medics to be on the scene, fearing the worst for Sylvie. He leads Darius into the holding room, suggests that Arabella stay with him. 'Love is a precious thing,' he says to Leonard. 'Regardless of who it is wasted on.'

Leonard manages a thin-lipped smile. He looks exhausted, as if he might agree to anything.

'I need a few minutes with Darius,' says Staffe.

'How can I trust you?' says Howerd.

'Imogen and Roddy will be on their way now. You should call Waikman, get him down.'

Staffe closes the door on him, praying that this is the right thing, and calls Jombaugh. 'Call me the moment Sir Ralph Waikman gets here.'

He turns his attention to Darius, who is holding Arabella. They touch each other like lovesick teenagers. Sad, that they got in so far above their heads.

'You know, I wasn't going to do it. I had thought I could, kidded myself I could, but when I got there . . .'

'Do what, Darry?' says Arabella.

'. . . She fell. She fell against that fucking radiator. She was cut. What could I do?'

'You could have helped her; not suffocated her. And you could have saved Graham Blears. Can you imagine his agonies? You did a terrible thing, Darius.'

Staffe watches the truth dawn on Arabella, who says, 'Sir Ralph will make it all right, won't he?'

Howerd comes in, goes to Darius and whispers in his ear.

Darius nods, forlorn, broken, says, 'All I can hope is that I can somehow make amends, and that Arabella and her family don't suffer unduly.'

'What are you saying, Darry?' says Arabella.

Darius looks at Howerd, who shakes his head. He says nothing more.

The Younger has Sylvie in the attic, had to carry her up, fireman style. At one point, he thought he might have to show her the back of his hand again, but she went quiet, must have seen the intent in his eyes. She is curled in a ball, under the hip window. The white spirit is poured on her jeans and the sleeves of her jumper, on the floor all around her for good measure. He takes out the matches, sniffs in, hard. It clears his sinuses, gives him a rush.

Looking at her, he can see the second dose of pills have taken effect. She will be dead to the world in a minute. Her eyes lid down, heavy, and he regrets that he has to do this. Equally, he knows that an unenforced threat is its own death sentence. It cannot ever be allowed. These are the terms of engagement.

His leg vibrates. He plunges his hand into his pocket, looks at the phone. Seeing it is the Elder, his heart gladdens, briefly. Perhaps the ether is bringing tidings that there is another way. He hasn't killed often in his life. The first was a bomb-making Unionist in the North; tit for tat and twenty years ago, when he wasn't even a man, and just a week before he first met the Elder. His heart beats fast.

'Are you in the ambulance, still?' says the Elder.

'No. I've switched her. We're ready to go.'

'You mustn't. We have what we want.'

'What we want?'

'Bring her to the station, to Leadengate.'

'What has changed?' Something inside the Younger subsides. A fast lifeform dies and he feels a vial of disappointment burst in his belly. He is ashamed of his own reaction, knows he will have to answer for it. 'What has he said to you?'

'The family is safe. He has what he wants.'

'What is it that he wants?' The Younger's head feels foggy. 'What have you given him?'

'The murderer. It's all that concerns him.'

The Younger thinks, 'Which murderer?' and suddenly feels as if a hand is upon his shoulder, a bead trained on the back of his head. It is as though time has turned and he is, once more, estranged on the Shankill Road – the day the Elder gifted him this life.

The Elder says, 'Put her back in the ambulance and drive it to Leadengate Station. Clean yourself from it and go.'

'Go where?'

'I don't need to know,' says the Elder.

The phone clicks dead.

The Younger knows there is an opposite reaction to everything you do.

The Elder makes his way back to his car and promises himself that next Christmas, he will look in on his family. His daughter has a newborn baby he has only seen twice. He sighs as he points the key at his car. It jingles and he opens the door, clocking, as he gets in, the young sergeant in the car across the road. He spotted him as they came onto the Old Street roundabout. He reconciles himself. He will have to do what he must, whether the sergeant sees him or not. This will mean another spell away.

* * *

Sir Ralph Waikman pulls up his chair to talk to Darius A'Court. Howerd stands against the wall, arms crossed, looking on intently. He scrutinises Darius's every move, seems impressed with the young man. If Staffe didn't know Howerd, he might think there is an element of pride in Howerd's expression.

Staffe says, 'He has been read his rights. Do you want to hear it again?'

'You have new evidence, I hear,' says Sir Ralph. 'I will need to see full disclosure, by the close of day.'

'The bellboy identified Mr A'Court at the scene.'

'Anything my client might have said will have to be reconsidered, I am afraid.' Waikman leans forward, lowers his voice, says to Darius, 'There will be no more duress.' An ember of hope seems to glow in the young man's eyes.

Howerd goes to Waikman, whispers in his ear.

'Aaah. I see.' The beknighted brief turns to Staffe and says, knowingly, 'Do we have an understanding?'

'I have spoken to the CPS. There is a will to bring this case to a speedy conclusion.'

Howerd nods, and when Sir Ralph looks back to his client, the hope seems all gone from Darius's eyes.

Staffe says, to Waikman, 'We have almost reached the end of this line.'

'*This* line?'

Staffe realises he has to rekindle a threat. God knows where Sylvie is. He considers the strength – and the weaknesses – of his hand. 'I don't know how far to pursue this case, Sir Ralph. I have some interesting theories about your client's motives.'

Howerd says, 'And what about our agreement?'

Waikman says, 'Interesting?'

'I would like a few minutes with Mr Howerd.'

'You have a proposal?' says Waikman.

'Oh, yes. I think you should be there, too.'

Staffe leads Howerd outside. 'The fresh air will do you no harm,' he says. 'Imagine being on that boat – all the way to Biscay, and beyond. It would be nice if Imogen made it back to the Black Sea.'

'You gave your word.'

'I said I'd bring charges. And I said Imogen would be free to go.'

'You have conditions?' says Waikman.

'You deceived me,' says Howerd.

'May I burn in hell for all eternity – such heinous bloody sins,' says Staffe, his voice trembling. 'I would happily send Roddy down for being an accessory, and you might quite easily die in prison if we ever uncovered all the conspiracy evidence.' He takes a deep breath. 'Just like Graham Blears.'

'Not quite the same,' says Waikman, who is cool, aloof. 'Such evidence is thin.'

'But as you say, I gave my word,' says Staffe. 'And you gave me yours. Now where the bloody hell is my fiancée!' he hisses, taking care none of the milling uniforms gets wind. 'And while we're here, I'll remind you that I won't rest until I have whoever killed Rebeccah Stone.'

In this instant, the doors to the station are battered open and a pair of community officers, decked out in bicycle helmets and high-vis vests, force their way into reception. 'We need some medics,' they say.

Between them, Sylvie is slumped, her legs dead, feet dragging on the parquet floor.

'We found her outside – in an unmanned ambulance, would you believe? She's out of it.'

Jombaugh steps in, taking a hold of Staffe, whispering in his ear, 'You stay out of this. This is too close to home to make a scene.'

Staffe shrugs Jombaugh off and walks to Sylvie, wraps his arms around her, holds her tight, says, 'You're safe.' He presses his face to her head, whispers, 'It's over.' He can smell petrol, says, 'What the hell have they done to you?'

Her hair is dank with sweat. She groans. 'You lied.' Her breath is sticky and he can smell her insides as she sighs, 'Stay away from me.'

The medics come into reception from the First Aid room and Jombaugh takes a tight hold of Staffe. 'The last thing she needs is more upset. Bide your time, Will. Do you want this all out in the open?'

Staffe jabs a finger at Leonard Howerd. 'You know who killed Rebeccah, God damn you. I want a statement to prove it.'

'If, hypothetically, my client were to do such a thing, the Crown might conceivably pursue Mr Howerd's involvement,' says Waikman.

'Unless the perpetrator confessed. The confession would be enough for us,' says Staffe. 'There were times when men would fall on their swords. Now, we are more civilised, but you could imagine such a thing, Leonard,' says Staffe, wrestling with how honourable he has been – when you look at what he allowed to happen to Sylvie and Brendan Stone. 'This way you are tarnished with a single black sheep. Every family has one. Think about the secrets you can preserve.'

Sir Ralph whispers to Howerd and approaches Staffe, putting an arm around his shoulder, leading him back inside. As they go, Staffe turns to Howerd, says, 'And there is one final thing I have to ask. A small matter – a private affair.'

As he tells them, he looks over their shoulders, to the holding room, where Sylvie was. But she is gone.

* * *

The Elder places the note on the mantel of his young accomplice's fireplace. The handwriting is a perfect copy and will stick in court. He has been at this juncture once before, but was granted a pardon. This time, it is simply too grave. When you mess with police, there's a price to pay. Otherwise, the files never close, and this is a file that has to close.

He looks out at the young sergeant's parked Mondeo, three doors down. He checks the action of his Ruger revolver, a 101, chosen for its double action. You can't be too careful when taking down a pro. Especially one of your own. Split seconds might stop the reflexes from killing them, and he blocks out how fond he is of this victim. Still nothing more than a terrace hooligan when they second met, when the young hoodlum saved this soldier's life.

Since, he has fashioned that boy into what he is today. He has much to answer for. He checks the chamber for its .357 Magnums. With a heavy heart, he returns the cylinder and switches on the TV. The front sitting room flickers. Its glow should deceive the surveilling sergeant for a minute or so. It's all he needs.

He slips out the back of John Parnell's rented ground-floor apartment and across the gardens, knowing where its tenant, the Younger, will be: a final prayer before he fully disappears – if the Elder knows his man. Which he does.

Jombaugh blocks Staffe's path to the First Aid room, says, 'She's adamant.' Through the grilled window, Staffe can see Sylvie, drowned in thick red blankets, a male nurse on one knee in front of her, administering an injection. She looks up, catches Staffe's eye and at first it seems she doesn't recognise him. Her hair is greasy, combed back. Her eyes Balkan hollow and grey-black.

He is appalled with himself, knows he needs to hold her, to tell her he loves her and that he will never allow such a thing to happen again. He pushes past Jombaugh, who says, 'Be careful what you say to her, Will.'

Staffe pulls open the door, not quite understanding why Jom said what he did. He takes the velvet box from his pocket, removes the emerald pendant and holds it out.

Sylvie shakes her head and, soft as a distant dove, she says, 'It doesn't matter what you say, Will.'

Suddenly, he understands what his sergeant meant. 'I'm sorry.'

'I'm better on my own. I suppose I should thank you for that.' She removes the intaglio ring. It seems to take every last drop she has and the nurses look on as if Staffe is some ogre from fables.

He says, 'You keep it,' holds out the pendant. 'I wasn't lying.'

'We could be at Dad's and thinking everything was going to be just fine,' she says. 'But you couldn't. I know that.' She smiles at him. 'Someone has saved me, Will. And it's you.'

Boxing Day

Staffe runs the Castelnau as far as the track to the river, then down stream along the right bank to Putney Bridge. There are no ducks on the Thames. Perhaps it is a family day, on land.

Working his way through the Harbour development, he thinks of all the profit being made, up in Aldesworth, and what that can and can't buy. He touches the paper he is carrying, tucked down the back of his tracksuit bottoms, damp from sweat, still worth the same, though.

On the Embankment, Parliament behind him now, he sees St Paul's and the smaller domes of the Thamesbank Hotel. Gary Mulplant will be far, far away, his young wings clipped. Staffe hopes the other young man, Darius A'Court, might have been visited by his mother. He hopes she will never be made to understand her part in his downfall.

He focuses on the Thamesbank's burnished domes, like something you would see across the Bosphorus, and he sees that beautiful and young woman, pale as death, on the moonlit floor of that hotel room. He never spoke to her, can never understand the depths of her ambition, her realised desires. Elena and Bobo will be flown home. Arabella will be getting lines on her fair face by the time Darius emerges from his sentence.

In the City, he puts in a hundred-stride sprint along Cheapside, collapses through Leadengate's doors and into Jombaugh's reception. Panting, he asks for Pennington. Jombaugh nods and Staffe climbs the stairs.

Pennington is looking out on a part of his domain, says, 'You finally put it to bed, Staffe.'

'Just the one loose end, sir,' he says, sitting down, rubbing his quadriceps.

Pennington spins on his chair, raises his eyebrows at Staffe's sporting attire.

'What loose end?'

'The bastard who killed Rebeccah. We will have to see if that confession materialises. You know how these people can go to ground.'

'These people?' says Pennington. 'I guess there are things we will never understand. Do you ever think that there are other worlds, running alongside us? We don't see them or hear them. We can't touch them.'

'We can smell them, sir.'

Pennington opens the drawer to his desk and takes out an envelope, lobs it to Staffe. 'Pulford brought it in. I read it. Felt I had to, in the circumstances. But I'm showing it you now.'

The envelope is addressed to *DI Wagstaffe, Leadengate Police Station*. Inside, the letter is short and written in an ugly, thin hand.

> *I, John Parnell, acting of my own volition and being of utterly sound mind, confess the lives of Rebeccah Stone and myself. She was executed for violations against society and I undertook to kill her independently. My reasons go to my grave. Both killings are absolutely a matter of honour, in ways neither you nor the legal system can understand. May God forgive me, and you, and all of us.*
> *John Parnell*
> *25 December 2009*

'You say Pulford brought the letter.'

'It was in Parnell's flat. Pulford followed the other one there, but lost him. The body was found in the garden of St Philip Neri, just before midday.'

'Ironic,' says Staffe. 'Suicide is a sin.'

'He was shot in the head. There were no prints at all on the gun. He wasn't wearing gloves.'

'An execution?' says Staffe.

'Can this be the end of it?'

'Not quite,' says Staffe, standing. 'But don't worry. Just one final, private matter, sir.'

'I heard about Sylvie. I'm sorry, Will. You said you might take a holiday. Where might you go?'

Staffe remembers Stanislav, driving for the port and the vast continent beyond. Sometimes, his world seems so small.

'Another country,' he says, leaving.

'You never call,' says Rosa, standing aside, welcoming Staffe in.

In the lounge, baby Elena bangs her toy pram into furniture. She spits bubbles and her chubby cheeks are impossibly rosy. On his knees, wiggling a doll at her and making her chortle, is the man from the photograph with the Italianate village behind him.

'This is Mike,' says Rosa.

Staffe looks for Mike's wedding finger, sees it is bare. He gives the man the benefit of the doubt and a handshake, his warmest smile.

'You look terrible, Will,' says Rosa.

And, true enough, he feels terribly weak, utterly eroded by this case. He puts his hand out behind him, sits back heavily on the sofa. Rosa hands him a glass of water and he sips from it, hears the infant Elena gibbering nonsense.

He pushed too hard, for a woman he didn't even know, and now he is bereft.

Staffe forces down the water, hands the glass

back to Rosa. 'I can't stop. I'm going away, but I've got something for you. For Elena, really.'

He hands her the envelope marked *PRIVAT*, watches Rosa's mouth drop open as she sees the bonds.

'She needs someone to look after her, to be with her, all the time – at least until she goes to school.'

'This is . . .'

'It belongs to whoever holds it. It was Rebeccah's and now it's yours. Hold it for Elena. It's a matter of honour.'

Exclusive extract from the new D. I. Staffe novel
Pain of Death
Publishing May 2011

One

Staffe sinks to his knees, the floor surprisingly warm, here beneath the City. He feels the ground-water leech into his trousers and he leans close to the face of the dying woman. In this false light, her skin is the palest blue, almost neon, and her broken lips are strangely bright, like burst plums. He searches for a glimmer of life but there seems to be none. Then she moans. He could swear she does, so he puts his ear to her mouth. There is nothing, just his own drumming of life, within.

Water drips, seeping all around them. It is cold and the old stone vaults echo the constant murmur of the small generator. A camera clicks, punctuating the buzz of the crime-scene lights.

A paramedic asks Staffe to move away and another stands over the woman, drapes a blanket over her; red. It covers her body, not the face.

'No,' says the photographer. 'I need her the way she was.'

Beneath the blanket, the woman is as she was: naked from the waist down, a cotton dress hoisted up around her breasts. No underwear.

A scene of crime officer in plastic overalls removes

the blanket and looks away as the photographer tries to lock the scene, in time.

'We have to move her,' says the doctor. She wears red, patent chunky heels and her hair is done up in a swirling twist. Her plastic suit rustles in the subterranean melée and she sounds unsure as to whether she is doing the right thing by moving the woman. The night she had dressed for was in a different, brighter world.

'You must take her,' says Staffe, snatching the blanket from the SOCO. As he replaces the blanket, he sees the smears and clusters of blood, some dried, some fresh. It is all over the down curve of her tummy, and her legs, and between. He averts his eyes, too late, ushers the paramedics.

'We need more time,' says the photographer.

Staffe grabs the photographer's camera, says to the doctor, 'I'm sorry. Please take her away.'

The paramedics lift her onto a stretcher, as if she were a Faberge egg. Written on all their faces is the doomed concentration of people who wish to save lives, who often as not tend the new dead.

The doctor places a hand on Staffe's elbow, grips it lightly, saying softly, 'She might be all right. She really might.'

They smile at each other, weak as baby birds.

He watches everybody leave, taking their kit with them: the SOCOs and medics in separate groups. The photographer gives Staffe his dirtiest look.

The Inspector remains in this tunnel the Victorians designed to house the machines to build a line that never was, beneath the Thames. His chest tightens.

Far away, at the bottom of the spiral shaft that delivered them here, the iron door slams shut. It takes the last light and for a moment all Staffe can hear is his own heart. From the dark, distant, a light flickers. It slowly grows larger and as the man comes closer and closer, Staffe thinks he looks like something from Hammer, his eyes intent and narrowed. His bearded jaw juts and his thin lips are dark; a crescent of blood across one cheek. Blood on his hands and his shirt front, too.

This is Asquith, Secretary of the Underground Victorians. Staffe knows he will have to question him, will have to search for a link between Asquith and the dying woman, but this is a Historian. He found the poor, captive and dying woman and called the police. Killers don't call, and even if they do, they don't stick around.

'Strange,' says Asquith. 'All my days, I have peered into the past, but this is now, isn't it? They will come here, to the scene of this murder.'

'She's not dead. And how would you know it's murder?'

'This will be history.' Asquith looks as if he can't

quite fathom a common truth, or his father's name; certainly can't grasp that he will be a part of somebody else's visitations.

'Go,' says Staffe. He watches Asquith disappear down the tunnel, towards the streets and libraries, the hospitals and homes. Water drips, and the rats constantly scuttle and scratch. They say you are never more than twelve feet from a rat on the London streets. Beneath, you're amongst them. He tries to imagine what it would have been like for the woman down here.

How long had she been below ground? Who had brought her and why had they done what they did: the blow to the head, the scratch marks on her arms, and all the blood – down *there,* caked on the tops of her thighs and smeared on her stomach. Her lip was lacerated, too. The doctor reckoned the woman had probably bitten through it herself.

He shivers, pulls his jacket tight around him and the tunnel becomes coffin black once again as the light from Asquith's torch fades completely. The iron door slams shut again. It feels final.

Staffe turns on his torch, its batteries weak, or a failed contact. The weak beam stutters as he casts around the scene, flickering on the dark stain of blood on the ground, where her legs had made their confluence. 'Damn,' he says, aloud, hearing his own echo, praying she survives; that whoever did this can be caught.

He makes his way, piecing together a critical path he will follow, but he catches his boot on a discarded tool box and falls, into the harsh dark, landing on an elbow, grazing his hand on the wet stone floor.

As he reaches the iron door, his torch fails and he reaches, feels for the latch in the black, grazing his fingers and knuckles. He remembers a promise he had made for today, finds the latch, heaves the door. Daylight falls through the shaft, like weak water and for a moment, it blinds him.

Above ground, it is a fine, spring day, a pleasant surprise for the city folk who are out, shirt-sleeved, bare-legged. Staffe carries his jacket slung over a shoulder, and walks past the entrance to Leadengate and past the *Hand and Shears*, stolen away in the shadow of Saint Bartholomew's flint Church. He is sorely tempted, but instead makes his way up to the hospital of the same name. Pushing open the swing doors, he rubs his elbow, grimaces.

'What are her chances?' says Staffe, looking past his Detective Sergeant to the woman in bed. In the hospital light, blue-white, her skin like wax, and against the brilliant white starch of ward linen, the dying woman seems in a far worse state – as if you could hear the sub-audio screams of her bruises and cuts in this harsh and clean environment, where there is no thing such as chance. Back in the tunnel, it had seemed as if she might be saved by apothecary, faith, or some alien dimension.

'Touch and go. More go than touch.'

'Has she said anything?'

Pulford shakes his head. Both men angle towards the woman, neither wanting to get too close. 'We have had the ID confirmed, sir – from her prints.'

'She's got a record?'

'Strange, isn't it, sir? When they're naked and beaten up and put between those sheets and fed on a drip, their history counts for nothing. Could be hooked on the crack pipe or pulling in a million a year in the City.'

'What kind of record does she have?'

'Benefit fraud. And ABH.'

'ABH?'

'Against the dad.'

'The dad? There's kids?'

'Oh yes. But the kids are in care. And the doctors reckon there's another one, a baby. They reckon she's had a baby, just.'

'What!' Staffe looks at her, remembers the smeared blood and what he thought were wounds. 'She had a baby down in the tunnel?'

'Forensics have been in, but there's no signs of a placenta or . . .'

'Christ! We've got to speak to this poor woman.'

'She tried to get a termination, sir. She was on the books here, as it happens, but they sent her away. She was too late.'

'When was this?'

'Months ago.'

'This could be a back street job gone wrong.'

'The doctors can't say.'

'What's she called?'

'Kerry. Kerry Degg.'

Staffe sits beside the woman, takes her hand in his, careful not to disturb the drips that tunnel their way into her veins. Life dripping into her, dripping away. 'What kind of animal would take her down there?'

'Perhaps she went in herself. Forensics say she could have been down there a couple of days. But no more. There's no, you know . . .'

'Excrement,' Staffe sighs. 'And when did the baby happen? Can they say?'

'She's haemorrhaged pretty badly, sir. They say they need to keep her stable. They can't go into that. Not yet. Not until she's better; or . . .'

Staffe tries to imagine what might make a woman go to such a place to have a baby. 'And the husband?'

'Sean. They've been married six years, since she was seventeen. He's thirty six and clean as a whistle.'

'We'll see about that.' Staffe reaches out, squeezes her hand, as firmly as he dare, to see if her eyes will flicker or her pulse change. But she is dead to his attentions, for now.

He studies her, clinging onto life, having issued life; having had cause to attack Sean Degg, her husband of six years; having been deemed unfit to hold onto her own children. And as he gazes at her, stripped of all make-up and her jet black hair combed flat, lank, something inside him stirs. He thinks he might know her.

Staffe turns to his young sergeant. 'It makes you wonder whether what we do is for the best.'

ff

Faber and Faber – a home for writers

Faber and Faber is one of the great independent publishing houses in London. We were established in 1929 by Geoffrey Faber and our first editor was T. S. Eliot. We are proud to publish prize-winning fiction and non-fiction, as well as an unrivalled list of modern poets and playwrights. Among our list of writers we have five Booker Prize winners and eleven Nobel Laureates, and we continue to seek out the most exciting and innovative writers at work today.

www.faber.co.uk – a home for readers

The Faber website is a place where you will find all the latest news on our writers and events. You can listen to podcasts, preview new books, read specially commissioned articles and access reading guides, as well as entering competitions and enjoying a whole range of offers and exclusives. You can also browse the list of Faber Finds, an exciting new project where reader recommendations are helping to bring a wealth of lost classics back into print using the latest on-demand technology.